HER OWN REVOLUTION

Château de Verzat Series
Book Two

DEBRA BORCHERT

LE VIN
PRESS

Cover design by Lynn Andreozzi
Book designed and typeset by Bookery

Map: A map of Paris in 1789 from William R Shepherd's *Historical Atlas*, Henry Holt and Company 1921. *Wikimedia Commons*, public domain in the United States of America. [https://en.wikipedia.org/w/index.php?title=File:Map_of_Paris_in_1789_by_William_R_Shepherd_%28died_1834%29.jpg]

Published by Le Vin Press
Year of Publication 2023
ISBN: 978-0-9894545-6-8 (Ebook)
ISBN: 978-0-9894545-7-5 (Trade paperback)

First Edition

 OR BERRY

MY CHEVALIER

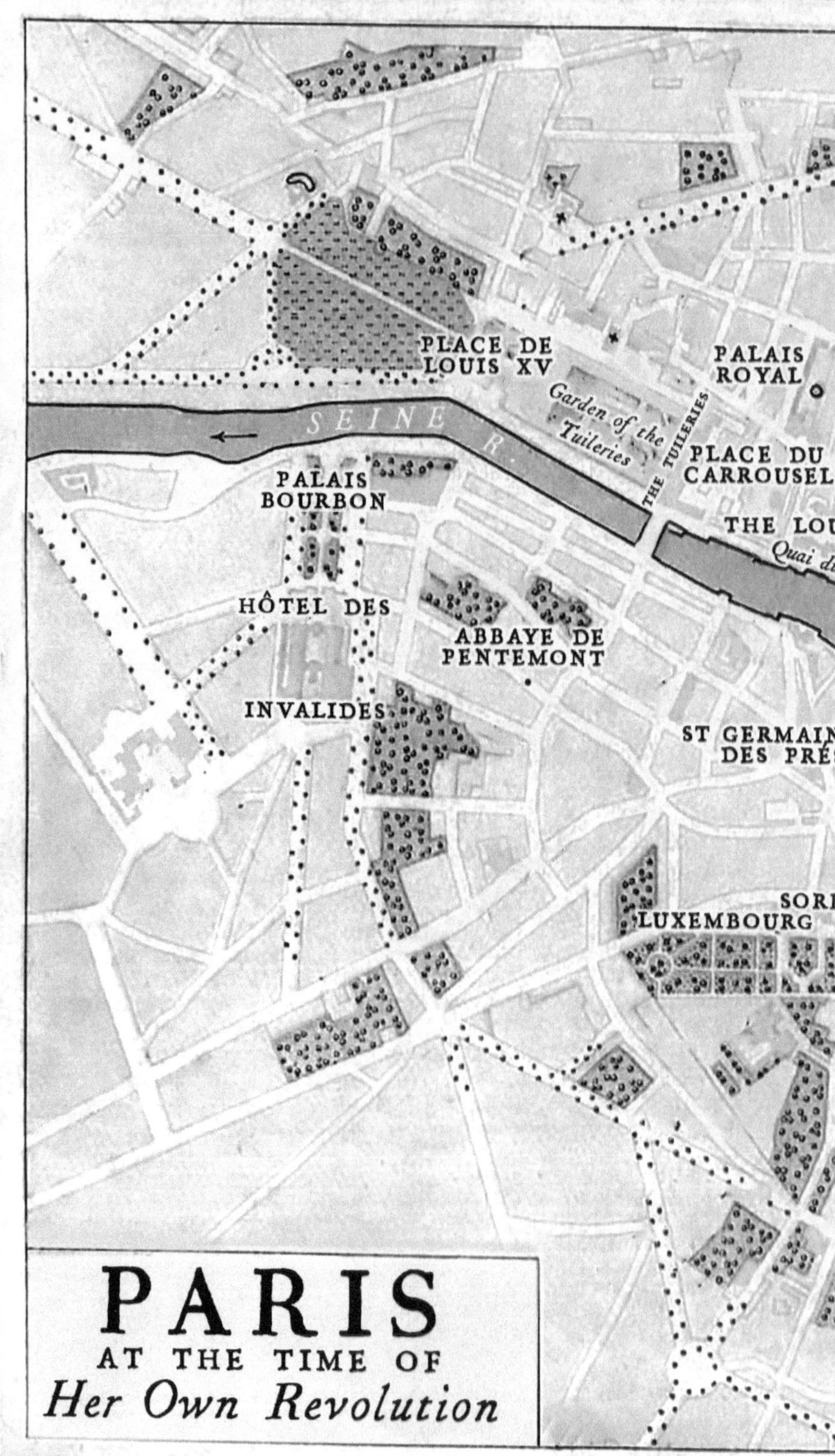

PARIS
AT THE TIME OF
Her Own Revolution

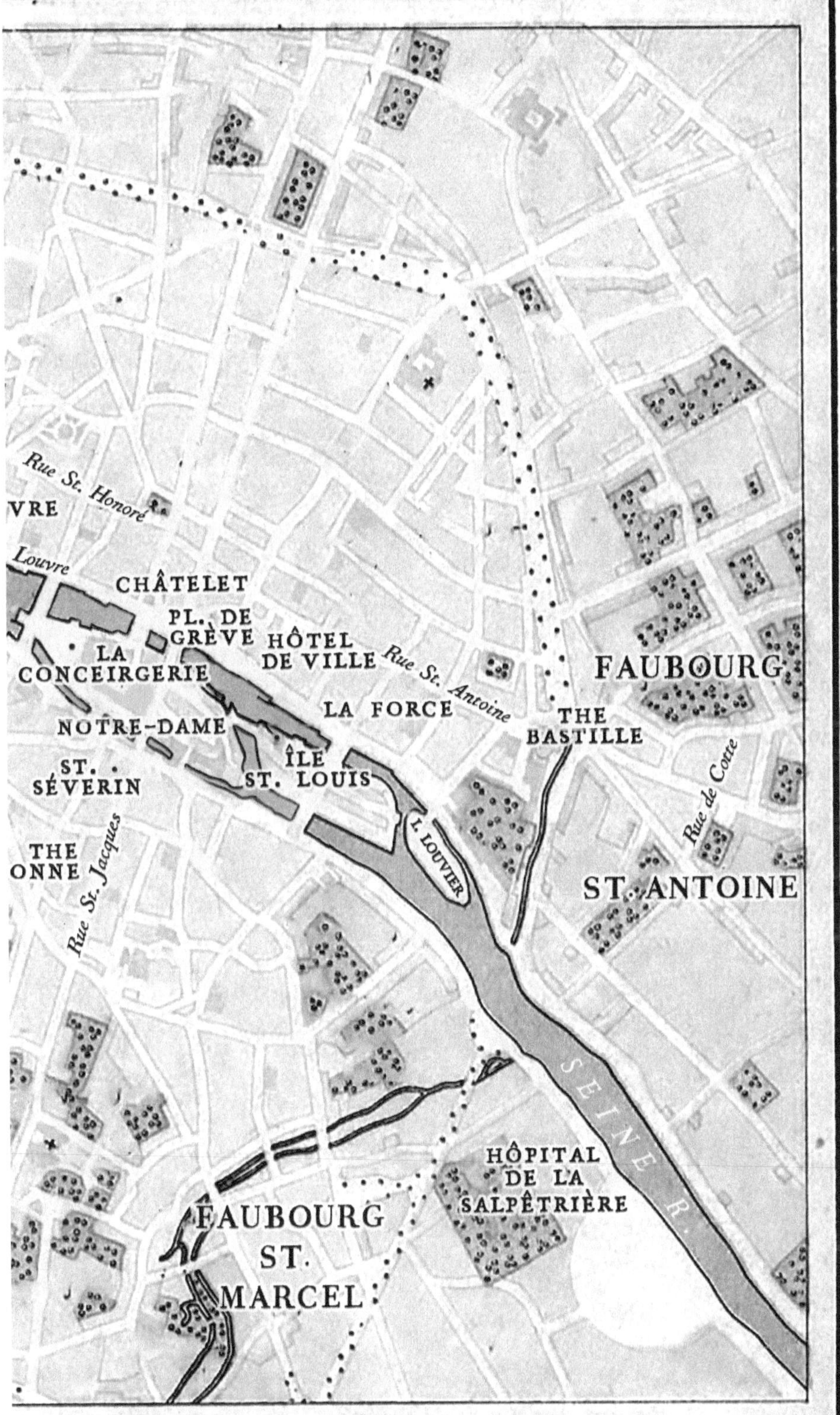

Rue St. Honoré
VRE
Louvre
CHÂTELET
PL. DE GRÈVE
HÔTEL DE VILLE
Rue St. Antoine
FAUBOURG
LA CONCEIRGERIE
LA FORCE
THE BASTILLE
NOTRE-DAME
Rue de Corre
ST. SÉVERIN
ÎLE ST. LOUIS
THE ONNE
Rue St. Jacques
L. LOUVIER
ST. ANTOINE
SEINE R.
HÔPITAL DE LA SALPÊTRIÈRE
FAUBOURG ST. MARCEL

AUTHOR'S NOTE

ALL WRITERS OF historical fiction strive for authenticity, but sometimes we may find conflicting facts in our research. Other times, we are faced with using a term a modern reader might not recognize.

Confusing for readers is the evolving names of streets, buildings, people, and locations. Place Louis XV became known as Place de la Révolution, the home of the guillotine at the time of Louis XVI's execution. The Directory named it Place de la Concorde, but after the Restoration of the Monarchy, Louis's brother wanted to name it Place Louis XVI to honor the beheaded king, but Charles X returned the square to its original name. After France's second Revolution the name was returned to Place de la Concorde, and as of this writing, it remains so. Still with me? The guillotine also moved around a bit, starting at Place de Grève, moving to Place du Carrousel, and on to Place de la Révolution.

While incorporating historical fact within the creations of characters and story I sometimes make concessions. Antoine Fouquier-Tinville was the public prosecutor during the Reign of Terror. He had a daughter, Geneviève, however, I made her a few years older to give her more agency. All of Geneviève's escapades are fictionalized.

For the proceedings of Fouquier-Tinville's trial, I consulted a digitized version of: *The Public Prosecutor of the Terror, Antoine Quentin Fouquier-Tinville*. Translated from the French of Alphonse Dunoyer by A.W. Evans | Herbert Jenkins Limited, Arundel Place, Haymarket, London | 1914.

Eagle-eyed readers may find blunders or anachronisms, for which I take responsibility. If so, please let me know through my website (www.DebraBorchert.com). In appreciation, I'll send you a short story leading up to the French Revolution and thank you in my next book in the series. Merci beaucoup.

HER
OWN
REVOLUTION

I

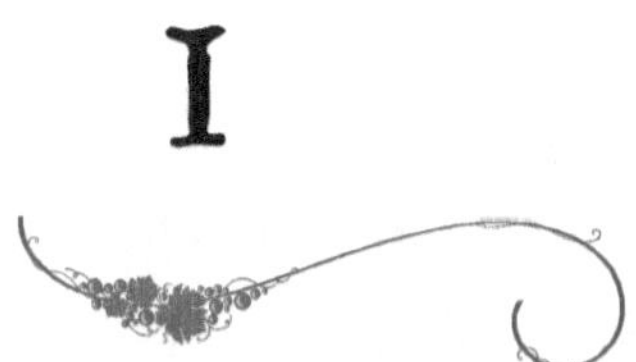

Paris
August 3, 1793

IF I HAD the same rights as a man, I would not have to dress as one.

After waiting for Cook to leave for the market, I raced through the kitchen, down the servants' stairs, and into the cellar. The pungent odors of ripe apples, stale wine, and fusty onions thickened the air. I pulled out my bundle from behind the vinegar cask and unbuttoned my gown.

The irony of having to masquerade as a man to have equal rights made me want to spit in Robespierre's face. I wrapped a strip of cloth tightly around my breasts. All the talk of Liberté, Egalité, Fraternité. I pulled on my brother's tunic.

Liberty? All women were free to do was starve. I stepped into my brother's breeches and knotted a ribbon at my waist.

Equality? Pah! Our latest government passed a law enabling all men to vote. I tied my neckcloth.

Brotherhood? What about sisterhood? I shoved my arms into the waistcoat. After four years of governmental discussion, girls were finally guaranteed an elementary education. But universities were still closed to women.

Voices from the kitchen stilled me. If my stepmother caught me, she'd send me to a nunnery. My fingers grew numb from grasping the frock coat lapels. Her heavy footsteps headed for the dining room. I shook out my stiff hands.

We had won the right to divorce, but how were all the divorced women supposed to support their children? The memory of Lisette, my former neighbor, standing amongst the prostitutes gathered at the banks of the Seine, calling and taunting sailors, chilled me.

I stomped my feet into the too-big boots. An unmarried woman's signature was still worthless. But not in America—there women could own businesses and property. I should have gone to America with Henri. I should not have been so stubborn. I had been his mistress for a year, why had I refused to accompany him as one? I adjusted the breeches, trying to ignore my own nagging voice: He never said, I love you.

Coiling my hair into a bun, I pushed my brother's tricorne down over my curls, opened the cellar door, and peeked out into the late afternoon. A steady rain beat upon the cobbles, washing chamber-pot slops into the gutter at the street's center. The heels of my brother's boots were higher than my usual shoes, and I concentrated on keeping my balance as I straddled the gutter.

Staying on narrow back streets, I adjusted my gait, trying

to appear confident. As was my habit, I began to pick up my skirts but clutched the frock coat instead and looked around for anyone who might have seen me.

If caught impersonating a man, any other woman would appear before the Public Prosecutor—my father—who would order her head shaved and sentence her to an insane asylum. But if I were arrested, I would disappoint my father, who would feel obligated to make an example of me. As he had recently sentenced Charlotte Corday, the first woman to be guillotined, I feared being dragged before him far more than eight-months in a madhouse.

I splashed through puddles. If I didn't sail for America soon, my stepmother would have me married to an old goat I didn't love. But if I had identity papers proving I was a man, I could get a job that paid enough money for passage. Henri had urged me to visit his printer friend, Pierre. How would I convince Pierre to make false papers—a traitorous crime, for him and me? What if Pierre refused, or worse, told my father? I'd make Pierre agree. Today.

Dark gray clouds hung over the river and twisted up the turrets of la Conciergerie, the new home to Marie Antoinette. Even if Henri couldn't marry me, I was going to join him in America, no matter what crimes I had to commit. Surely he'd tell me he loved me when he saw me again.

Rain slid down the back of my neck, making me shiver. I pulled up my collar. The only right women earned that was equal to a man's was the privilege of facing Madame Guillotine.

2

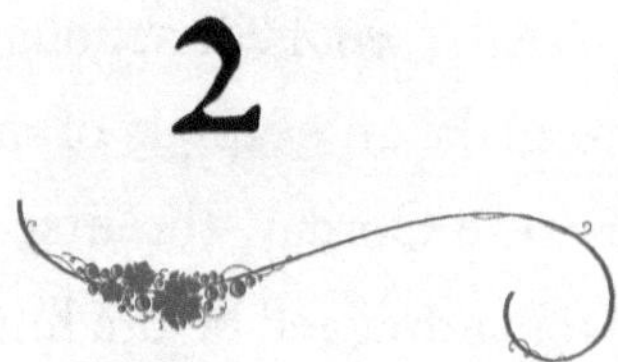

Paris
August 3, 1793

THE RAIN LET up as I crossed the Seine. A herd of sour-smelling sheep wound around me as I entered Henri's old neighborhood, one of the poorest in Paris, Faubourg Saint-Marcel. Walking amongst men, wearing frayed blue tunics and pushing carts, I realized Henri had been one of them before he learned that, although illegitimate, he was a noble. And as the new government despised nobles, had Henri stayed in Paris, he would face my father and the guillotine. At least Henri was alive, even if an ocean away. The empty spot Henri had left in my heart ached.

I shook the rain from my frock coat, inhaled deeply, and entered the printshop. A young man pounded the pad of an inkball onto a tray of type, and I tasted a bitter stickiness in the air. Behind him, two men pulled a creaking wooden arm that screwed a press down onto paper.

The clacking of a dozen men's fingers rapidly shoving metal letters into trays vibrated in the room. If women were taught to read, they could have jobs like these men instead of selling their bodies to feed their children. My heartbeat matched the clicking. "Is Pierre here?" I shouted.

A tall, angular man with wisps of gray hair tied in a brown ribbon at the back of his neck looked up, wiped his hands on his ink-stained leather apron, and pointed to himself.

"Henri Detré sent me."

He jerked his head toward a tiny office in the rear of the shop. I followed, and he closed the door, muffling the racket.

"Haven't seen Detré around." He leaned against a shelf filled with pamphlets.

I kept my voice low. "He left Paris."

"For his father's château?"

"America." Henri trusted Pierre, so I could be generous with information. "He and his sister emigrated to save the château and the winery."

His graying brows hooded his eyes.

"Before he left, he told me to see you."

He crossed his arms over his chest. "Why?"

My courage drained, making my legs shake. I wiped the sweat on my upper lip. "An identity card."

"Anyone can get one at city hall."

"I have one." Fingers trembling, I pulled my card from my waistcoat and offered it.

He looked at it, looked to me, and back at the card. "This is for a woman, Geneviève."

"That's me." I removed my hat, unleashing my hair. His eyebrows jumped, and I tucked my hair back under the tricorne. I willed my voice lower. "But I need one for the man who stands before you."

Pierre shook his head. "Your father is Public Prosecutor."

I stepped back. As I had feared, he'd recognized my father's name. "He doesn't know."

"And should he find out?"

A hot metallic odor seeped into the room, reminding me of the heated iron pokers Sanson used to make prisoners confess in the dungeon below my father's office. Would Papa allow Sanson to torture me into saying Pierre's name should my false papers be confiscated? "He won't."

Pierre wrapped his hand around the back of his neck. "You wish me to commit suicide?"

"You're not a criminal or a Royalist." That was true. But if he made false papers for me, he'd be a traitor, and we'd both be executed for treason.

"You could turn me in for helping Henri, a noble."

"Henri is my friend…and…"

Skepticism etched his face.

I hoped Henri would be my husband one day, but I didn't say so. "I would never betray Henri, Monsieur."

He rubbed his neck. "And Henri knows you as a man or a woman?"

I had to act confident. I pressed my hands on the desk and leaned forward. "He assured me I could trust you."

"Did Henri assure the man or woman?" He tossed my identity card on the desk.

I retrieved it and stood tall. "Both."

"If I had a daughter, I wouldn't like her dressing as a man." He scratched dried ink from his palm. "Could be dangerous."

"I'm safer dressed as a man—if I have an identity card to prove I'm a man." I shoved the card into my waistcoat and tugged it down, further flattening my breasts.

"And what if they conscript young men?" He hitched his thumb on his leather belt. "What if they pick you up, thinking you're a man? You want to go to war? Would Henri want you to go to battle?"

The thought of fighting brought a wave of nausea, and I swallowed against it. Self-righteous indignation came easily for men. "I will go back to being Geneviève—wearing gowns, needing a chaperone, being useless."

I pressed my hands together. "Please, Monsieur. I met Henri at University, which I attended dressed as a man. Henri believes women are his equal and deserve an education and the right to work." Tears were gathering, and I blinked furiously. "I need a well-paying job so I can earn enough money to join Henri in America."

A sad smile came over him. "Each day, before Henri climbed the stairs for his lessons with his tutor, he greeted everyone in my shop, often bringing bread when none could be found. He wanted to help commoners. None of us knew he was a noble until his father was murdered. It's good he went to America."

"It's safer for him there, for now." My voice wavered. "Please, Monsieur. Henri sent me because he trusts you'll help me."

"What will you use the papers for?"

"You would agree it is safer for a man to travel aboard a ship than an unaccompanied woman?"

He cocked his head, staring at me. Sweat trickled down the binding around my breasts, but I stood tall.

He wiped his hands down the front of his leather apron. "What name?"

"Jean."

He let out a puff of air. "Family name?"

I would honor Henri's peasant name. "Detré."

Pierre looked like he'd eaten a sour cherry. "Date of birth?"

"I'm twenty-one." I clipped my words to appear confident.

He shook his head.

My voice wavered. "Twenty?"

"Are you eighteen?"

I nodded. It wasn't such a bad lie. I would be in a few months.

He sighed. "Thirty livres—and your promise—"

"Thirty? To buy a pig or sheep costs thirty livres."

"If not for Henri, it would be double." He put his hand on the doorknob. "We could both be sent to prison for this."

A chill shot down the back of my neck. And it would be my father who sent us there. "I will return with the money."

He kept his hand on the door. "You must promise to never ask this favor again."

That was an easy promise to keep. I knew no one else who needed false papers. "Of course."

He grunted and opened the door, allowing me to leave before him.

A fluttering grew below my ribcage, and I pressed my clasped hands against it. I had to appear confident, even if I trembled with fear, for, if I stopped to think about being caught, I'd never leave the house. And that would be the worst kind of prison.

I walked through the shop, the clacking sounds fading as my own voice nagged in my mind. Even if I dressed as a man and got a good paying job, it would take months to earn enough money to pay Pierre. I wanted to sail for America now.

I headed home, walking along the Seine. The whores were already taunting the sailors. How much did they earn? What did they do to prevent becoming with child? The Châtelet, where Papa kept his office, stood brooding like an angry rooster, on the other side of the river.

I had clerked in Papa's office once; I might be able to convince him to hire me again. I could delay paying Pierre until I earned money for both the papers and passage. No matter what, I needed false papers for the ship. I'd be much safer dressed as a man crossing an ocean.

3

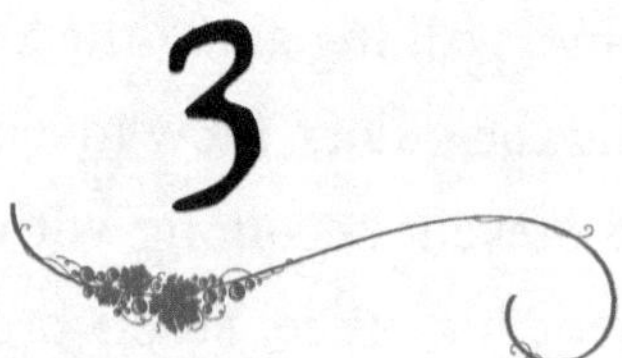

Paris
August 3, 1793

I LAUNCHED MY SCHEME at dinner. A pristine white linen cloth covered the table. Two Sèvres porcelain candlesticks flanked the matching tureen, sitting at the table's center. A violent decoration for a dining room, with two red foxes climbing the taper holders and hunting exotic birds around the bowl of the tureen.

My stepmother sat, like a hen on a nest, next to my father. Her gold-colored gown cast a waxy yellow hue to her skin, accenting the wrinkles that crisscrossed her neck and bulging bosom. At her shoulder, an ornate brooch sparked in the candlelight.

Forcing myself to speak before my throat closed, I rushed my words. "Papa, I learned much about laws while I clerked for you last year." I did not say I needed to understand the idiotic laws if I was going to violate them. I sipped my wine. "Now that the Committee of Public Safety is in control, and the sans-culottes have not rioted in months, I wish to resume my duties to learn of our new government."

My stepmother clinked her spoon against her bowl. "My dear, it is dangerous for a woman to leave her home. You worry your dear papa. Antoine, you should never have allowed her to clerk." She pat, pat, patted Papa's elbow, making him smile.

I nodded like I agreed—but I wanted to shout, women deserve the right to have an education and jobs other than doing laundry or selling fish. Just as Henri had spoken at the National Assembly. If there were such a law, I would not have had to impersonate my brother to attend University, and I could become an attorney, like Henri.

Papa inhaled the steam rising from his soupe d'aspèrges, looked up, and blinked. His curving hairline and whiskers made his face a heart shape, and his narrow nose and round eyes gave him the appearance of a confused, loveable bird. I wanted to hug him. But ever since Maman died, he seemed distant.

"Geneviève, you're nearly eighteen. You've not much time to find a husband." My stepmother's lips formed a tight little bow.

Eighteen, not eighty. I chewed a chunk of bread. If I'd left with Henri, at least I'd be a mistress. "I've no need of a husband. I wish to support myself."

"My dear, your behavior is unattractive to men. If you do not marry you will have no one to support or protect you."

A scream crawled up my chest, and I inhaled so deeply to stop it, my stays dug into my ribs. If I ever did get to change laws, I'd banish corsets.

She smiled lovingly. "Where would I be without your dear papa?"

I wanted to say, in a nunnery, but that wouldn't convince my father. "Women are equal to men and can perform jobs just as capably."

"That is not very romantic." She held Papa's hand, smiling adoringly.

What an old coquette. But a coquette nonetheless, and the reason Papa was attracted to her. Would I be able to bend and twist myself to get the man I wanted? Was any man worth that? Henri loves me, and he knows I dress as a man. "You have a bit of soup on your cheek."

Her hand flew to wipe the nonexistent drop.

"It may not be romantic, but I wish to be of service to the République."

"The best way to be of service to the République is to marry and have children."

"Yes, but if I do marry, my husband could die, and I'd have to work or starve. Isn't that correct, Papa?" He squinted at me. Was he listening?

My stepmother fanned herself. "How unladylike."

"Starving is unladylike. But women who work to support their families are most honorable ladies." I smoothed my serviette over my lap, calming my voice. "And what other opportunity would I have to support myself and children besides doing laundry or whoring, like our former neighbor, Lisette?"

Her eyes widened with alarm.

I'd meant to shock her, but I didn't stop to gloat. It was my father I had to convince, for no other man would hire a woman. "With experience as a clerk, I would be able to support myself and family—including you and your son—should something happen to Papa."

She fingered her brooch. "I am certain your father has provided for me in that event. As your husband would provide for you. Is that not correct, Antoine?"

Papa took a swig of wine.

"Perhaps. But I don't want to do other people's laundry, would you?" I asked.

"Geneviève, do not frighten your maman." Papa poured more wine. "I would like some more of your delicious soup, Etty."

My father's pet name for Henriette made me cringe. I'd never allow anyone to call me Genny. Calling women by children's names subtly diminished them. But that did not occur to Etty; she considered her pet name a sign of love and affection.

She plucked up the ladle. "Have I told you, Geneviève, that my mother received this Sèvres porcelain as a wedding gift and gave it to your father and me for our wedding?" She lifted the lid, ladled more soup, and replaced the lid with reverence. So proud that Papa loved her family recipe, she placed the bowl before him like it was a crown.

She'd told me that story every time we had soup—every day.

She rested the ladle on a porcelain dish. "Perhaps we shall give it to you and your husband on *your* wedding day."

I pressed the locket my real maman had given me against my heart. My mother had been nothing like Etty. Maman was warm and kind and listened to me. Etty's pride in things rather than people made me miss Maman as if she had died the day before, not fourteen years earlier.

Etty patted her serviette at the corners of her mouth, like a satisfied cat licking cream from its whiskers. "You have little time to find your true love," she stroked Papa's arm, "as I have." She shook her serviette and settled it upon her lap. "I know you do not wish to be a vieille fille or a burden to your family."

"Being a spinster is not against the law." I'd never possess her élan or subtle cruelty. "And I will never be a burden to you or anyone else—if I have a job as a clerk." I bit a crust of bread, shattering crumbs across my bodice, and chomped. "You praised my penmanship in the past, Papa. And you know I'm faster than all the male clerks in your office. I would make you proud."

Papa's eyebrows lifted and a trace of a smile crossed his lips. "You may accompany me tomorrow, Geneviève." He caressed Etty's hand. "On one condition."

I gulped wine; its heat rushed through me. Whatever he wanted had to do with marriage. "And what is that?"

"That you marry whomever Etty chooses as an appropriate husband for you."

The wine soured my stomach. I inhaled, imagining all the ways I could shock most any man my stepmother could find and drive him away.

She sat beaming, waving her fan before her face like a flag. "You have already rejected far too many suitors, my dear. I shall be lucky to find another who will take a woman of your age." She tapped the fan. "But I do know of a gentleman I think you will like!"

I wondered if an open fan could be used like a guillotine blade.

"Do you agree?" he asked.

"If I can clerk until a suitable husband is found, Papa." I smiled my sweetest smile while biting my tongue.

He patted Etty's hand. "Do not fret, ma petite souris."

My little mouse. She was more of a rat.

"I will send her home to you in my carriage before dark." Papa returned to his soup.

Etty waved the fan so hard she fluttered her curls.

"Merci!" I nearly choked on the bread. Tomorrow I'd start earning money to pay for my identity card and then passage to America—if I wasn't arrested for impersonating a man first.

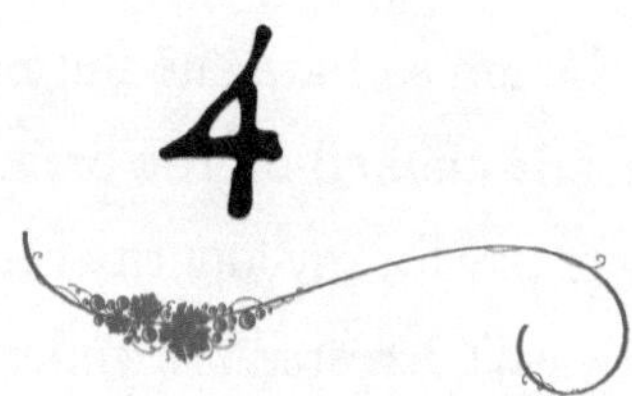

Paris
August 4, 1793

HENRI TOLD ME the guillotine represented equality, even in death. Before I began my clerking duties, I wanted to see where Charlotte Corday had lost her life. I asked Papa for the use of his carriage so I could deliver some old clothing for Lisette's children. A ruse that Etty heartily approved.

Despite the rain, Martin stood smiling, next to Papa's carriage. He wore a frock coat and breeches of a dead-leaf color, but his waistcoat was a saffron-and-white-striped silk, which I suspected he bought from the secondhand seller in the market. His buttons were too bright, his tricolor cockade too large, and his jabot too fine for a groom.

He tried hard to get my notice, but his fawning actions and clothes made me want to abandon my trip. "Drive past the Place de la Révolution, please."

He opened the door and bent at the waist, flinging out his arm. "Anything you wish, Mademoiselle."

"Your bow is that of a servant of the Ancien Régime. Do you wish to sentence us both to death?"

His shoulder tilted, like he was preparing to run.

"Do not call me Mademoiselle. We are both citizens."

His face reddened. "Yes, Ma—Citizeness."

I got in, pulled the door closed, and peered out at the darkening streets. Martin climbed up onto the bench, and the horses jolted. We sped through the rain.

Pounding my umbrella handle on the ceiling of the carriage, I signaled him to stop. I pulled the leather straps to lower the window and peered across the empty square at the wooden platform: the stage for the machine of death. At the center stood a narrow wooden structure with two beams looming so high they swayed in the buffeting wind. At the top, suspended between the beams, a metal blade sliced the gloom. Raindrops slid down the edge. Rivulets of bloody water streamed around cobbles on their way toward the Seine. Hours had passed since the last execution.

A bitter taste burned my throat. How many died to produce so much blood? When would it stop? When spectators stood ankle-deep in it? Even if they dug gutters to the Seine to carry the blood away, Revolutionaries wouldn't stop.

Although people dodged puddles in the streets, Place de la Révolution was empty. I wasn't surprised. Spectators needed bright light to witness an execution's full horror. At first, only royal and noble blood was shed here. Now, in a frenzy of democracy, anyone's head could be chopped off, blacksmiths, chandlers, and laundresses alike.

Waterlogged pamphlets littered the cobbles, reminding me of my reason for being there. The headline blazed in my mind. *Prosecutor Sends Woman to Guillotine.* I closed my eyes, seeing Papa's lovable owl-like face, hearing his gentle voice calling me Gen. Did he remember my face when he sentenced her? I did not doubt the article, but I could not reconcile the Purveyor to the Guillotine with the man I knew as Papa.

I sat back and stared at the blade. Being my father's daughter was no guarantee against facing the machine of death.

5

Paris
August 4, 1793

Papa SAT ACROSS from me in his carriage as we rumbled over the cobbles, past porters carrying crates of vegetables to les Halles. "Geneviève, please be kind to Etty."

"Of course, Papa." I patted the dagger in my reticule. "She is most kind."

"She has your best interests at heart."

"I know. I am grateful for her ensuring I learned to embroider and sing," I laughed, "however off-key."

He smiled. "You have a lovely voice."

A presence was all Etty had ever been to me, never a warm, loving mother. The Abbey Sisters had been more nurturing. "And she is right. I do not wish to be a burden."

He leaned toward me. "That, you will never be."

The carriage reached the towering stone fortress of the Châtelet, where people haggled over chickens and vegetables in market stalls lining the square. A fine mist brightened the violets, like the ones Maman and I had often picked at the river's edge. I breathed in the sharp odors of briny fish, earthy spices, and ripe cheeses—all the fragrances Maman loved. For a moment, her spirit lingered.

Papa guided me across the square as rain spattered the cobbles. We walked to the arched entryway and hurried up the steps into his office, where clerks scribbled in the weak gray light. The few I had worked with the previous year mouthed their greetings as I passed.

Nearest Papa's office, the head clerk, Imberton, twisted a blotting cloth in his left hand and scratched a quill across a paper with his right. Smudges of black ink stained his cuffs, camouflaging the fraying fabric. He had never liked me, I suspected because he thought women had no place in the Prosecutor's office, and from his dour look, I didn't think his attitude had changed. We stopped at his tall, slant-top desk.

"My daughter will be copying my files for distribution, Citizen Imberton." Papa told him. "Bring the papers from my office."

Imberton sprinkled a fine sand over his work to set the ink, shook the paper, and looked up. "Certainly, Citizen Prosecutor."

Imberton followed Papa. I read the paper he'd been copying. I stopped halfway down the list of names: Comte Louis de LaGarde.

I'd not seen nor heard that name since I attended University. I brushed away the sand, the day vivid in my mind.

No one had known I was a woman at University, and I had succeeded at my masquerade for a year. But one day, Henri and I were laughing over my success at embarrassing the pompous LaGarde in class. LaGarde, thinking I was a man, meant to exact revenge and humiliate me. He drew his rapier from its jeweled scabbard, rested its tip at my neckcloth, and with one deliberate swipe, sliced through my waistcoat, tunic, and binding—revealing my breasts.

The sight of my bosom had shocked him, but he'd recovered quickly, calling me a whore and accusing me of attending University illegally, which I was. Although Henri had drawn his pistol to defend me, I delivered the coup de grâce, invoking my father's name and title. Henri had assured me that men were so terrified of my father, none would further expose my masquerade.

LaGarde never returned to University, but his action of revealing me as a woman had changed everything for Henri. I closed my eyes, feeling Henri's warm chest against my cheek, inhaling his fresh clean scent. He was the only person who knew I dressed as a man, the only man who believed me his equal. I hoped I hadn't missed my chance with the only man I'd ever loved.

Imberton returned and handed me a stack of papers. "You will work next to me." He pointed.

"What are you copying?" I asked.

"The list of prisoners to be called for the guillotine."

My stays poked my ribs. "What are their crimes?"

"Royalist sympathies—traitors."

The papers rustled in my hands. LaGarde was a bully. I despised his arrogance. Another woman might be glad of his fate. But he did not deserve to die just for being born a noble. If Henri were here, his name would be on this list.

Imberton held out a bottle of ink and a quill.

"Merci." I took the bottle, but the quill slipped. As I grasped for it, I knocked his open bottle of ink, spilling black liquid down the length of the document. I gasped. "I am sorry!" I dabbed my handkerchief at the paper.

His mouth dropped open, but he quickly closed it.

"I will copy it for you. Please forgive me, Monsieur, I mean Citizen. I will stay late to finish my work after I've copied this for you."

With his fingernails, he picked up the paper and held it out, ink dripping onto the floorboards, and dropped it into a metal bin. "Three copies. Every letter must be correct."

"I will finish them in no time, Citizen." I placed the original on the desk next to his, took a clean sheet of paper from the shelf underneath, and opened my bottle of ink.

The list was numbered but not alphabetized. I read each birthdate and name of men, women…a child of four years. I envisioned five-year-old Auguste's round blue eyes and felt his chubby fingers grip my hand. A child, like my brother, sentenced to the guillotine? Had my father sentenced him? If not for Papa's talents, many prisoners would go free. Did he fear the Committee for Public Safety would try him for conspiracy if he didn't condemn the people they sent?

My gaze landed again on Comte Louis de LaGarde—a man I thought I hated. But had he not exposed me as a woman, Henri and I might not have fallen in love. And now LaGarde was condemned to death for the same crime Henri committed: being born a noble.

If I replaced his name...but what name? I forced myself to be honest: I spilled the ink on purpose to buy myself the opportunity to change the list. But if LaGarde was not sent to the guillotine, would rotting in prison be any better fate?

Should anyone discover my replacement, I, too, would be tried as a conspirator—by my father. I could not claim my action was accidental, for the Committee of Public Safety needed neither evidence nor proof. What if the Tribunal condemned Papa for my crime? He'd never lift my chin with his knuckle, forcing me to look at him and tell the truth, again.

Rain lashed the window. I closed my eyes and stared into a blood-soaked basket awaiting my head, hearing the jeers of the crowd, smelling my own fear as the wooden oubliette clamped around my neck. I saw my blood join the unending stream of gore to the Seine.

I rubbed my eyes. I'd never see Auguste grow up. He was my stepmother's son, but it was my skirts he tugged when he wanted to be picked up, my hand he pulled to visit the fishpond, my voice he begged to sing. I'd never fold paper boats for him again, never have children of my own. I'd never see Henri again.

I shivered and watched the clerks standing at their desks copying court documents. My crime would condemn them, too. The tallest, Armand, was saving for passage to America, which he'd never see. The funny one, Denis, smiled all the time, ever since his twins were born. He'd leave them fatherless and his wife a widow. Imberton hid his frayed cuffs with his frock coat sleeves. He pinched every sou for his daughter's wedding, and he'd never dance at it. A chill draft swept the back of my neck.

If I were responsible for sending these innocents to their deaths, was I any less guilty than the Tribunal? Yet could I live with myself knowing I could have saved LaGarde's life?

I dipped the quill. If I wrote, instead of LaGarde, the name of one already dead, the number of names on the list would be the same total. But what would the guards do—after calling out that name, searching the cells, not finding the owner? The guards would never confess they had lost a prisoner. Would they take another in his place? No, for when that prisoner's name was called, they would have the same problem. I could replace a name, maybe two, on every list.

Imberton cleared his throat.

I brought the quill down. Guards would begin doubting themselves, go crazy thinking they had misplaced prisoners or, worse, the prisoners had escaped. The guards would accuse one another. Insurrection would mount. My writing names of the dead would undermine the whole system. Maybe I *could* save lives as a woman.

A knocking caused me to look up.

Imberton stood before me, his eyebrows raised. "Do you need assistance?"

"No." I tapped excess ink from the quill and scrawled: Jacques Manuel. My hand quivered. To save one life, I'd be risking many. Wiping perspiration from my forehead, I dipped the quill again.

My hand trembled, spattering ink. If I allowed an innocent man to go to his death, what did that say about me—my character? Did I want to be that person? Even if I despised that woman, did I have the courage to change the names?

I ran my fingers over the rough, dry paper. If I made four

copies and destroyed the original, would Imberton notice? I would have to copy the style of the original writing and make the three others different. I copied the date exactly, then stroked an elaborate G. Guillaume Pricaud. The name of one already dead.

I didn't know if I had enough courage to do this, but I did know I had to make certain I wouldn't be caught.

MORNING MIST CURLED along the Seine as I crossed over the Pont Neuf. The shadows cast upon the river by la Conciergerie were as ominous as its pointed-roofed towers, Gothic arches, and barred windows. The Convention decreed the medieval former palace be converted into an impenetrable prison for convenience—it already had a dungeon and torture chamber. If anyone discovered I was a woman, I'd be an immediate guest here.

I pushed my weight into my boots, pulled my tricorne lower to shadow my face, and walked past the iron gate to the guard-house.

The damp stone walls of la Conciergerie glistened in the flickering torchlight. With a scuff of my too-big boots on the uneven stone floor, I forced myself to pick up my feet. Tallow candles sputtered, filling the guard's room with a fatty smoke stinking of mutton. Tucking the bottle of wine under my arm, I dug out Auguste's identity card from my waistcoat and handed it to the guard, hoping the shadows were too dark for him to read accurately. Using my little brother's card had occurred to me when I had taken him for a walk the previous week. If Etty asked, I would claim I forgot to return it.

I tilted my tricorne down to shadow my face and lowered my voice. "I'm here to see Louis LaGarde."

The yellow-eyed guard glanced at the card and back at me. "You're older than five years." He poked a corner of the card between his teeth.

My fingernails dug into my palms. Did he know my older brother—whom I was impersonating? If this guard exposed me, I was risking not only my life but my father's reputation. "The number is faded, Citizen, I am twenty-five. Do you think the son of Antoine Fouquier-Tinville would present false papers?"

His tongue sucked at the hole where a tooth had been. He pushed the card toward me and stared at the wine.

"This is for LaGarde."

He glanced at his list. "Not here."

"He'd better be—my father put him in here!" I snatched up my card and placed the bottle on the desk, hoping the bribe would keep him from telling others about me.

He reached for it.

I plucked it up. "LaGarde won't mind sharing. Do you have a cup?"

He pulled a wooden one from a drawer and set it before him.

Grateful I'd thought to lightly cork the bottle earlier, I wiggled it out and poured.

The guard tapped his finger against the cup. I poured another measure and recorked the bottle. "LaGarde, Citizen."

He gulped down the wine, belched, and jangled a brass ring of keys. A young guard came from the corridor. "LaGarde," the yellow-eyed man growled.

The younger nodded, took the keys, and bade me follow him.

Would these guards be sentenced to death if they couldn't find the prisoners whose names I had substituted with those of the dead? I wouldn't care too much about the yellow-eyed one, but this one probably had a sweetheart, siblings, parents. I'd have to learn the guards' names to ensure they didn't go to the guillotine for my crime. I pressed my hand against my chest, checking the binding was tight.

The stench of vomit, sweat, and weeping sores intensified with every step we took farther into the bowels of the prison. I swallowed against the urge to gag. We passed large, cramped cells filled with people of all ages. A mother picked fleas from her daughter's scalp. Women, dressed in ripped and dirty finery, sat in a circle sewing and whispering prayers. An old man rolled a stone to a blond boy of about three.

How could a boy be guilty of treason? My father would condemn him for his noble blood. I saw Auguste, his laughter bubbling and free, his chubby fingers grasping my thumb, his arms gripping my leg when he was frightened. Did Papa not think of his own son when judging this boy?

I stumbled, righted myself against a slimy wall, and wiped my hand on my breeches.

The guard stopped and opened a wooden door. "Ten minutes." He stuck out his hand for a bribe.

"The other guard drank your share."

He shrugged. "As usual."

"Ten minutes. Merci." I took a deep breath and stepped into the dark. Straw cracked beneath my boots. The door slammed shut. I jolted. The key grinded in the lock. The sour stink of an unemptied slop bucket made me want to cover my nose. LaGarde stood in the corner, his shoulders hunched, his blond hair hanging in greasy strands. The sound of the guard's footsteps faded.

My legs trembled. I could be thrown into such a cell. "Do you remember me?" My voice was as weak as the light.

He peered at me and then a grin slowly emerged. "Who could forget *your* charms?"

My face warmed as the memory of his exposing my breasts rushed me.

"So, my execution has been delayed so you—Monsieur Fouquier—could gloat."

I shook my head and held out the wine. He didn't move, so I placed the bottle near his feet. "It's not what you're accustomed to, but the guard enjoyed some of it." I pulled out bread, sausage, and cheese.

He rubbed his forehead. "Ah, a last meal."

I ripped off a piece of bread and offered it. He snatched it and gnawed, catching the crumbs with his hand, and licking them from his palm.

I detested the pity I felt. I couldn't be the only one who cared about him. "Has your family been to visit?" Withdrawing my dagger, I cut a hunk of sausage and tossed it to him.

He caught it and waved his fingers at the cheese, which I also tossed. "What family? My brother? Killed defending the King at the Tuileries. My parents? Murdered in the September Massacres."

"I'm sorry." His losses seemed not to affect his appetite in the least, but still, I would have to break down his defenses to save him. "Any friends visit?"

He bit into the cheese and closed his eyes as he chewed. "I have no friends."

That, I believed.

He chomped at the bread. But as he turned his head away and stopped chewing, I knew it was not from lack of hunger. He was missing someone. "A lady?" I asked.

"Yeah." He snorted. "My whore." His low voice rumbled against the stone walls. "What about you, Fouquier? Got a whore of your own?"

"Wish I did."

He laughed.

Had there been more time I'd have laughed, too. "Has your mistress been to see you?"

"Like I, she is a guest of Bicêtre prison." He tilted his head back as if praying for patience.

"For prostitution?"

"For Royalist sympathies!" He swatted at a fly on his neck. "She despised the Queen." He laughed. "Even a whore has more courage to be honest than I have."

It was only a matter of time before her name would appear on another list. The binding around my chest tightened as sympathy filled me. "I can get a message to her."

"Why would you give her a message from me? To taunt her?" He kicked a clump of straw. "Torture us both?"

"To let her know you're alive." The muscles in his face flinched. He resembled a beggar, a depth to which, I imagined, he had never dreamed of falling. "What should I tell her?"

"What else can a dead man say?" He cried a laugh. "Adieu!" He slid down against the wall until he sat in the straw with his legs stretched out.

I crouched down and whispered, "Did you tell anyone you've been sentenced?"

He shook his head.

"Guards? Prisoners?"

"No."

"You must not tell anyone of your sentence. No one. Do you promise?"

He cocked his head and, for a moment, he was the old arrogant LaGarde. "Why?"

"Hush." I listened for footsteps. "So long as they do not call your name, you live. Understand?"

"They will call. I have been condemned."

"Your name will *not* be called. You will *not* go to the guillotine. Do you understand?" He sat lifeless. I pinched his arm.

"Ow!" He jerked his head and looked at me, his eyebrows peaked high above his dark eyes.

"Do you?"

The taut skin around his eyes began to relax as he stared at me. "Yes." His voice was hesitant, like a child's.

A feeling of wanting to take him out of this hell swept over me. I should have thought he deserved this punishment after exposing me, but now my compassion surprised me. I gripped his hand. Although filthy, it was still the soft hand of a person who ordered others to do his work. "What's her name?"

"Magdeleine Corrié." He winced, as if hearing her name pained his heart.

"The message?"

He stared at the ceiling.

I squeezed his hand. "We have but a few minutes more."

He pressed his lips together, his nostrils widening as he sucked in the dank air.

I hated pushing him. I softened my voice. "Do you wish me to tell her of your love?"

He nodded, then pulled me close. "She is with child. Ask her…if she will marry me."

"That is honorable."

"It is not honor." The muscles around his mouth quivered.

I patted his arm. "I will bring her food and your message." I stood and prayed I would be the clerk to receive the list with her name. "Remember, say nothing. I do not wish to join you at the guillotine."

He squinted. "You leave me to rot in this hell?"

His words hit me like a slap. Why wasn't he grateful? I'd saved his life, and he was angry? "I'd think anyone would prefer to live, even if among rats."

He lifted his chin. "You get me out of here, or you will go to the guillotine with me."

I was a cowering bug beneath a rock, taunted by the snapping tongue of a warty toad dressed in a ruined golden silk waistcoat. If I could have felt one drop of sympathy for this arrogant bastard, I'd not feel so ashamed. He'd exposed me once, and he'd do it again."

Maybe Etty was right. Had I remained a helpless woman, I wouldn't be one now. I could write LaGarde's name on the next list, and he could be executed tomorrow. I shook my head. I couldn't do it—he'd be a father soon. I sighed. "How?"

He raked his hair. "There are tunnels beneath the prison."

I ran my fingers over the pouch, hanging at my waist, feeling the weight of the rusted, pitted key to the tunnels Henri had given me, telling me to use them if I ever needed to escape Paris. The cold damp air of the tunnels settled over me as a trembling moved up my legs.

I had to act like I could do as LaGarde requested. I had to give him hope. I lifted my chin above my neckcloth. "It will be my pleasure." I bowed to mock him.

He laughed.

The sound of footsteps neared. LaGarde scrambled to stand. "Why do you do this for me when I was so rude to you?" His voice was gentle, sincere.

"You treated me the way you'd treat any man you deemed inferior."

His cheeks reddened. "I never would have treated you so, had I known you were a woman. Nonetheless, I was a bully."

I nodded. "You still are. Yet, you treated me as a man, and I'm grateful to you for that. But I didn't fight fairly. Instead of a sword, I used my father's name as my weapon." It was not until that moment I realized the true reason I was there. "I am sorry."

He sniffed. "I deserved it."

"You don't deserve this." I waved my hand. "I don't believe being born a noble should be a death sentence."

He dropped to his knees. "If you can save Magdeleine and my child, instead of me, I will willingly go to the guillotine and be indebted to you for eternity." He kissed my hand and rose but remained bowed. The clank of keys sounded outside the door.

I squeezed his hand.

"Merci," he whispered. "Until we meet again, Mademoiselle."

As the guard slammed the door closed, dizziness swarmed me. I had promised to save another life. But how? The corridor shrank around me. A torch hanging from an iron ring in the wall sputtered and snuffed. My breath whooshed out of me, and I stumbled in the darkness. The guard's lantern bobbed ahead. I ran, reaching out for him and keeping my fingers within an inch of his shoulder until we reached the outer gate.

I squinted in the light and heaved for breath. Somehow, I had to find the courage to travel the tunnels and get LaGarde out of the most secure prison in Paris or face the guillotine myself. Even with torches, traveling the dark tunnels was terrifying. How would I rescue LaGarde through them?

I shoved my hand into the pouch and ran my fingers over the tunnel key. Henri had told me the key unlocked every door in the tunnel system, except for the Verzat mansion's wine cellar. I gripped the cold iron. I doubted I could convince LaGarde to rescue himself, but I could try. I could not face the dark alone.

Wiping sweat from my forehead, I straightened and squinted in the sunlight sparkling across the river. No one would suspect the daughter of the Public Prosecutor of saving people from the guillotine. Most would think me a useless female. Above, a robin sang and trilled. I could play the charade of a useless woman as an advantage.

I might not change laws for women, but I could change lives. I headed for the cemetery. I had to find more names of the dead.

7

MY DOVE-GRAY BONNET was my most fetching, so I wore it and my low-cut gown for the guards at la Bicêtre. I had no more bribe money. As I wanted enough time alone with LaGarde's mistress to ensure she understood my plan, I stole a piece of Papa's stationery, wrote my request, and forged his signature.

Less imposing than la Conciergerie, la Bicêtre was no less frightening. Prisoners' wails drifted into the courtyard, making me shiver. I forced myself across the cobbles and into the gate house.

I held out the forged paper. "Le Prosecutor requested I meet with Magdeleine Corrié."

"Identity Card." The long-haired guard did not look up as he stretched out his palm.

"Is le Prosecutor's signed request not enough?"

He squinted at the paper, making me think he could read only numbers.

"I wish to meet with her alone." I leaned over, giving him a view of my décolletage.

He looked up, his eyes roving over me until they stopped at my bosom.

"Shall I ask Prosecutor Fouquier-Tinville to appear before you himself?" I purred like a cat.

He jumped up and stood with his hands trembling at his sides. "Follow me, Citizeness." He yanked a ring of keys off the wall.

If my scheme worked, I'd be endangering this young man's life also. He wasn't gnarled or greasy or corpulent like the others. Although he'd undressed me with his eyes, he probably had a sweetheart who loved him. Guilt sat in my chest, thick like mud. I would learn his name on the way out.

"Would you be so kind as to carry my basket?" I oozed allure.

He grabbed the handle and led me through stone-walled corridors, stained with splashes of dried blood. I'd read that Revolutionaries slaughtered prisoners, including girls, in this place. A metallic scent hung in the air. Did the ghouls leave the evidence as a warning to new prisoners? I covered my nose with my handkerchief. I could be locked away in here tomorrow. I repeated what had become normal for me: I cannot be caught.

The guard stopped outside a large room where women and children huddled. Golden light streamed in from the narrow windows above, illuminating the filthy straw, making it glow.

The air was damp and fetid, stinking of vomit and urine. A queasiness moved in me, and I sniffed the handkerchief.

He cleared his throat. "Magdeleine Corrié."

The women and children turned toward a corner where a woman in a thin white gown sat rocking herself and humming.

A sinking sensation pulled in my chest. I'm too late. She's gone mad.

"Corrié!" the guard yelled.

The woman jerked her head up, stood, and walked toward us, wavering like a phantom.

The guard opened the gate, grabbed her arm, making her stumble, and shoved her ahead of us.

I poked him. "She is with child. Should she lose it, it'll be *your* neck on the guillotine, Citizen."

His mouth dropped open. "Pardon."

"Guide her gently."

He nodded and placed his hand on her back as he led us into a small cell with soiled hay and a filthy blanket.

"Give us half an hour, please." I put out my hand for the basket.

"Ten minutes." He dropped the basket, grinned, locked the gate, and left.

Bastard. I brushed the dirty hay from the linen serviette covering the food and picked up the basket. Magdeleine scurried into the far corner and shivered like a hunted mouse.

I unwrapped the tin cup and held it out. "Milk. It's good for the baby."

She ran her hand over the small swell of her belly but didn't acknowledge me. I thought her to be three to four months along. I took a step closer. Eyes filled with alarm, she backed into the wall, panting.

I stood still. "Louis LaGarde sent me to you," I whispered.

Her hands covered her heart. "He's alive?" Her cheeks trembled.

I nodded.

Quiet sobs shook her. I crept close and gave her my handkerchief. She pressed it to her face and inhaled. She calmed a bit and looked at me. "Your mouchoir is so white and clean and smells of lavender. Merci." She held it out.

"Please keep it." I was so accustomed to such luxuries I hadn't noticed the scent. "I'll bring you more if you like. I brought some food. Have some cheese." I pulled it and bread from the basket.

She trembled like a leaf in a windstorm. "You're not taking me for execution?"

I stepped back. "No."

"When will they come?" She gripped the handkerchief.

I swallowed back a foul taste. "Has your name been called?"

Tears dropped from her thick lashes. Little wonder LaGarde was attracted to her—her features were as fine and delicate as porcelain.

I put my hand on her shoulder as much to calm myself as her. "When?"

"Three days ago."

I held her hand, so thin and frail, like a bird's claw. A prickling ran up my back. Did the torturous imbeciles not tell her? No wonder she looked like she had gone mad. She *was* mad— mad with despair. "They cannot execute pregnant women."

She stretched her neck and looked at the ceiling. "They will after I've given birth." She gasped. "They could kill two with one whack! I want to go now, but they put me back in here." Her mouth opened, and her sob rattled my heart. "What will happen to my baby when they do kill me?"

Would a new list be created after she delivered her child? That was my only hope, for that was the only list I could change. I squeezed her hand. "Let us hope this insanity is over by then." I forced cheer into my voice. "LaGarde asked me to tell you he loves you and wants to marry you."

Magdeleine's eyes brightened, and she tucked a strand of hair up into her ragged mobcap. "Why did he not come?"

I swallowed hard. "He's at la Conciergerie."

She wrapped her arms around herself and rocked, making a high-pitched wailing.

My arms hung useless. Nothing in the basket could soothe her. I pulled her close. She smelled of sweat and fear. "You must promise not to repeat what I tell you," I whispered. "Do you?" She nodded. "He will not go to the guillotine. You must not ask any questions, but he will wait for you."

She clutched at me. "How?"

I shook my head.

"Why are you doing this?" she asked.

Why was I? Not only was I risking my life but also the life of every person I'd duped along the way. I wanted to help the Revolution, but not if it meant executing innocents. I was undermining the very thing I believed in. But I doubted my belief, along with my ability to save the people I'd temporarily rescued. All of us could be executed.

"Did Louis pay you?" She spat on the handkerchief and dabbed it along the red welts on her neck.

I shook my head. I'd bring her vinegar for the flea bites next time.

"Do you have a wish to die yourself?" She bit at her thumb.

"No." I could be in her place if I were caught. There was no one to save me should I be discovered. A stirring moved through me, and I pressed my hand over my stomach. "If I were in here, I'd want someone to help me."

"Merci." Tears dropped down her pale cheeks.

"LaGarde wants you to eat, so you will be strong when the baby comes." I rubbed her arms and helped her sit in the hay. She took the milk and gulped.

Were the lists of Bicêtre prisoners kept in my father's office? I took my dagger from my reticule, cut a piece of sausage and gave it to her. If another clerk copied the names, could I intervene?

Footsteps echoed. I stood, brushing hay from my gown and helped her stand.

She gave me the empty cup. "What's your name?"

I faltered. Could I trust her? I'd not give her my family name, so she could never identify me to the guards. "Geneviève." I wrapped the remaining food in the serviette and gave it to her.

"Patron Saint of young girls. Perhaps I shall have a daughter." She smiled. "Patron Saint of Paris, as well."

I sighed. If my predecessor saved all of Paris, perhaps I could save a few prisoners—no matter how much I doubted my abilities. I picked up the empty basket. "I'll return soon with more food and more mouchoirs."

She nodded. The ruffle of her cap shivered as she forced a smile.

The clanking of keys echoed in the corridor.

I'd need a thousand saints to help me get her out of here. I had less than four months to figure out how to keep her name from appearing on any list—if she didn't miscarry. Although I didn't believe God intervened, I needed all the help I could hope for, so I blessed myself as I left.

I followed the guard out into the sunshine. I wished I could write to Henri, ask his advice. I emptied my lungs of the stinking prison air, closed my eyes, and listened for his voice.

But I knew he'd tell me to do what my heart told me to do. My heart was filled with doubt and fear...and hope. Damn him. I'd have to figure this out without him.

Paris
August 1793

PAPA WORKED LATE into the night, so he was rarely home for dinner. In his absence, Etty sat at the head of the dining table, and I sat to her side, wishing Auguste was allowed to join me. When I was younger than Auguste was now, Maman sat me upon three cushions so I could eat at the dining table with the rest of the family.

I inhaled the rich scent of potato-leek soup. My stomach contracted. Etty's one good quality was her family recipes.

Triangles of rouge covered her cheeks, and she wore her graying auburn curls swept up to the crown of her head, displaying her enameled necklace, brooch, and earrings to best advantage. The jewelry shone in the candlelight—she wouldn't dare wear it outside the house and risk a mob attacking her for it. "Do you know anyone who has emigrated to America, my dear?"

She only called me *dear* when she wanted something. She must be talking about a letter. A sliver of excitement shot through me. I sipped some wine deciding whether I should take the bait. Henri was my secret—a secret I wanted to keep—yet I longed for news of him. "A few of the families of the girls I met at the Abbey, like Mademoiselle Jefferson, departed for America."

"I mean *French* families." She smoothed her serviette on her lap.

She used the same sweet voice with Papa when she tried to dissuade him from allowing me to clerk. If she was keeping Henri's letter from me, she'd use it to control me. I inhaled a steadying breath. "I can't think of a specific family."

"Pass your bowl, dear." She lifted the gilded handle of the Sèvres tureen and dipped a ladle into the steaming soup.

Clad in white linen, the dining table, accommodating eight, was vast and empty without Papa and my two brothers. The older was fighting the Prussians, and five-year-old Auguste, Etty claimed, wasn't mature enough to dine with adults. When I had children, I intended to dine with them no matter their ages, at every meal. *If* I had them.

I placed the bowl before her, staring at the intricately painted fox chasing exotic birds that swirled around the tureen's oval base. The serving dish was as over-embellished as she was. I retrieved my bowl and set it before me.

"Have you heard from *anyone* in America?" She served herself and replaced the lid.

It had to be a letter from Henri. I gripped my spoon. "No. Have you?"

"I don't know this Henri who has written. But you must." She sat back, dancing her fingers along her lace-covered bodice.

I had to act as if I didn't want the letter. Otherwise, she'd make me grovel to get it. I sat back, imitating Papa's ennui, and slurped my soup. "There was a clerk in Papa's office named Henri."

"This Henri knows you."

A snarl inched its way up my throat. Had Henri revealed my dressing as a man or attending University in his letter? He wouldn't be so careless. He knew his letter could be censored—I hoped. "Papa's clerk wrote you?"

Her high-pitched laughter sounded like a cackling hen. "He did not write *me*."

Why was she dragging this out? If Henri had written in English to trick the censors, she wouldn't be able to read it. She was challenging me, forcing me to admit he'd written to me. "This soup is salty."

She tasted it and straightened her back. "I shall speak to Agathe about it. I fear she may have omitted the wine. Dear Antoine loves this old family recipe. I shall have her add a glass of wine before he comes home."

I held back my smile. The soup was perfectly delicious, but I'd made her doubt herself—which was right where I wanted her. If she showed me Henri's letter, I could snatch it from her in her less confident state.

"Can you not think who this Henri is?" Her voice climbed high as her laughter.

I would not give her a shred of information. I shook my head.

She giggled, like a little girl.

I dug my fingers into the chair and forced a sweet smile. "What is it you really wish to say?"

"Why did Henri not take you with him, Geneviève?"

Her words were as sharp as the guillotine's blade. I should have braced myself, but it was too late. I would soothe the pain in my chest later. Right now, I would pretend and hope to confuse her. I laughed. "Who would take me where?"

She pulled a letter from beneath her plate and tapped its corner against her chin, her eyes gleeful. "If Henri did not care for you, why would he write about his château?"

Heat raced up my back and spread down my arms. She had read Henri's letter addressed to me. She had invaded my privacy. If I snatched the letter from her, she might hold it tightly, and it might rip. She would present the torn letter as evidence to my father. "Papa's former clerk owns a château?"

Her expression soured. "You know perfectly well he does." She placed the letter on the far side of her plate and took up her spoon. "You are looking a bit peaked, my dear; you should wear a bit of rouge."

The crimson powder made her look like an old salope. "I could never wear it as well as you do."

"Why did Henri not take you to America with him?" She made a clucking sound in her throat. "Does Henri not love you?"

I wanted to rake my fingernails across her rouged cheeks. Henri *had* asked me to go with him. I pictured his last day in Paris and sipped more wine, tasting a bit of mold. Henri's words clanged in my head. *I admire you, your strength, your courage. How could I not love you? But I cannot ask you to marry me. I have nothing to offer you.*

Nothing except himself, I thought, and he didn't think that was enough. Pride had stopped me from telling him that he *was* enough for me. He'd not said, *I love you*—not directly—but I regretted not telling him I loved him. I loved him more than anyone.

I pressed the wineglass against my quivering lips. Memories of my days in his arms sped through my mind. But had he ever actually said the word *love?*

"You did not throw yourself at him, did you, Geneviève?" She frowned.

I wiped my fingers on my serviette, stained from my past week's meals. Her serviette, no matter how many meals she'd consumed, was as immaculate as an altar cloth. I twisted the fabric, imagining strangling her with it.

A Bible verse played in my mind: *Do unto others as you would have them do unto you.* How strange I should remember it when what was being done to me was unkind. What did she hope to gain?

I smoothed the cloth. If she could get rid of me, she'd have my father all to herself. I could play her game. Another woman might snivel and beg for the letter. But I was a woman who dressed as a man—I did not beg for anything.

"If Henri loved you, surely he would have asked you to marry him."

I gripped the chair. She was a bitch, a floozy, a whore, a... pouffiasse.

I smiled as I reached for the tureen and ran my finger along its fluted edge. "Reading other people's mail is disrespectful, *Etty*."

"Etty is your father's pet name for me. Call me, Maman."

I dragged my fingernail across the painted gold, spraying flecks across the tablecloth.

She placed her spoon upon her plate. "Take your hands off that. It is a priceless family heirloom."

It wasn't old enough to be an heirloom. "Is it, *Etty*?" I inched my thumbnail along a bird's scarlet wing. A tiny bit of color flecked off. I pinched it up and examined it.

"My mother received it as a wedding gift and gave it to me and your father for our wedding." Her voice trembled.

I waited for her to tell me she'd give it to me as a wedding gift so I could tell her I'd use it as a chamber pot. "How nice. Reading other people's mail is rude," I whispered.

"Parents have every right to protect their children."

"I am not a child. And you are not *really* my parent. And you're not *really* protecting me, *Etty*."

"I am protecting you from becoming a vieille fille. Your father will be most disappointed to hear that you do not accept me as your maman."

"My maman died." I scraped my spoon against the hand-painted design at the bottom of the bowl.

She flinched.

"Who do you think he'll believe?" I smiled sweetly.

"He would never accuse me of lying!"

"He would never accuse me, either."

She lowered her chin. "He trusts me."

"He trusts *me* to work in his office." My sweet voice sickened me.

"You'll not be working in his office much longer." Her smile wavered, but she fluttered the letter. "He will not dispute *this* evidence."

I lunged.

The pouffiasse stuffed it down her décolletage. "Your father *chose* to marry me. He didn't *choose* you."

My pulse pounded. I imagined myself ripping her bodice and seizing the letter, but that would leave evidence she could show Papa. An image of crashing porcelain skittered in my mind.

Without looking at the tureen, I stood and lifted it.

Her arms flew from her bodice. "Put that down!"

"After you give me my letter, I'd be happy to."

Eyes wide, she stared at me.

I jostled the tureen, rattling its lid.

She pulled the letter from her bodice. "Put the tureen down gently."

I backed away from her. "Put the letter on the buffet."

Her face reddened as she sat still as the painted birds.

I took another step backward. "It's quite heavy." I exaggerated my shaking, rattling the lid.

She stood and, without taking her eyes off me, backed up to the buffet, and placed the letter on it.

"Now remove the brooch from your gown and place it upon the letter."

Her mouth dropped open. "Antoine gave me this brooch."

I shook the tureen, wobbling the lid.

Mouth pinched, she removed the brooch, placed it on the letter, and returned to her chair.

"Sit down."

She lifted her chin but remained standing.

I pushed the tureen above my head. "This is getting heavy."

She yanked her chair out and threw herself onto it.

"Lovely. Now, I advise you to stay seated while I place the tureen on the buffet."

"Of course, my dear." Her shoulders rounded, making her décolletage wrinkle most unattractively. She resembled a fallen soufflé.

I put the tureen down but lifted the lid and held it in one hand while I retrieved the brooch and letter and shoved them into my hanging pocket.

Etty stood.

"Not yet." I waggled the lid. "As this letter is no longer in evidence, I suggest, for the safety of all your heirlooms—especially the brooch Papa gave you—that you not mention your invasion of my privacy to my father." I was enjoying this power over her. "Brooches can so easily be lost."

I walked to the door and opened it. "I will place the lid upon the floor when you sit down, *my dear.*"

She clutched the chairback and sat. "Be careful with that priceless heirloom!"

Not wanting the tureen to be damaged—I'd need it to influence her again—I placed the lid gently on the table and slammed the door behind me.

Grasping my cloak, I hurried out into the night in search of a safe place to read my lover's words.

I ran down the street and stopped. On the next corner, a lamplighter brought his torch to a streetlamp, closed the glass door of the lantern, and moved on to the next. Clutching the letter to my breast, I dashed to the puddle of light spilling onto the street.

The dark green wax seal had been broken. Damn that pouf-fiasse. But the return address was legible. *Walnut Street, Philadelphia, Pennsylvania, America.* I pressed the letter to my heart. He's safe. He has a job. He wants me to join him. The paper had been refolded many times. By Henri, the censors, or Etty? The ink was dark, yet the letter edges were soft, and I squinted to read the words.

March 1793
Chère Geneviève,

I write in English with the hope the French censors will not seize this.

Joliette and I arrived in America in late December. We delivered the wine to the merchant in the city of New York and traveled on to the nation's capital, Philadelphia. Many émigrés and former courtiers, with whom Joliette served at Versailles, have settled here, and we hope these émigrés will assist us in selling more wine. It is a relief to converse in French.

The Americans are welcoming, still grateful to Lafayette, and you would find them agreeably forthright.

Joliette is still grieving the loss of her husband. She and I thank you for your kindness of visiting Guillaume before his execution.

Be grateful you refused my offer to accompany me, for we crossed the Atlantic aboard a slaver. The conditions under which the Africans are trapped by their own people, chained, and enslaved are unimaginable horrors. Although I urged Joliette to return to her cabin, she stood firm, determined to witness the plight of the Africans, so that she could tell others of the atrocity.

The French sailors treated these human beings worse than animals, as animals are fed and watered. The captain ordered the sailors to brand them, like cattle. The conditions were so vile at least one African died every day. Sailors threw their bodies overboard without—ceremony or shroud.

My repulsion has fueled my conviction to work as an abolitionist with members of the Quaker community to ease the suffering of the enslaved. I was shocked to learn that General Washington, now the president of this great nation, owns Africans. I am ashamed for him, and he has lost my respect.

The news we receive from France makes me fear for your life. I agree with Edmund Burke. (Remember reading his pamphlets in the Palais-Royal and writing essays on them for Père Sébastien?) Liberty is not an excuse for one to do whatever one likes. Violence may be the tool with which Revolutionaries destroy the Monarchy, but continued violence will destroy the country. I fear France has only begun its revolution, and the violence is sure to evolve with greater ferocity.

Geneviève, I beg you to travel to the château for your own safety. I know you wish to change laws for women, but you would be managing four-hundred families, and with your leadership—should you accept the job of vigneron—the women and girls would flourish. Please consider it. I have written my maman to expect and welcome you.

In the meantime, I have an important request of you. If I enclose an article that urges whatever French government is currently in power to outlaw the transport of Africans, would you deliver it to my printer friend?

Joliette prevented one of the African women from being abused by the entire crew by purchasing her freedom. The woman is mute, we suspect from the abuse she endured, but Joliette is teaching her to read and write. She is especially helpful to Joliette as my sister is with child. Joliette is thrilled to be carrying a part of Guillaume and expects to deliver in April. I am thrilled to be the babe's oncle!

I wish you safety, Geneviève. At least visit the château. It is beautiful and much safer there. Trust that I will write regularly and know if you do not receive my letters, they have been confiscated.

Je t'embrasse,

Henri

I caressed the soft paper. Memories of afternoons making love to Henri flitted in my mind, making me breathe quickly. Warmth flowed through me as I remembered our political conversations and the time we'd spent in the Palais-Royal. He was concerned for my safety. I felt like I could fly to America.

He'd written in English, so Etty could not have read it. But she had said *château*. It was the same word in English, but had she gotten someone to translate the letter for her? One more person privy to my secrets. Damn her, again. Yet, if she knew he wanted me to go to the château, she would have encouraged my leaving to get rid of me.

The soup sat heavy in my stomach. He'd not written the word, *love*. I scanned the page again. Not once. He'd written that the letter might be intercepted, perhaps he was afraid it would be Papa to receive it. Of course. He wrote he feared for my safety. He wouldn't write to his maman about me if he didn't love me.

I kissed the letter, crossed my arms over my heart, and spun around. *Henri, Henri, Henri. I love you. I am so glad you are safe. I miss you so.*

"Arrêtez!"

I jumped, jerking toward the voice.

A rotund gendarme with a drooping moustache marched toward me. I shoved the letter into my bodice and wrapped my cloak around my shoulders and stood tall.

"It's after curfew! Papers." He thrust out his gloved hand.

"Of course." I reached into my hanging pocket and extracted the papers.

The gendarme unfolded them, squinted, looked at me, and squinted back at the papers.

"Antoine Fouquier-Tinville is my father. I am a clerk in his office, and I am on my way there now."

"Why are you carrying the papers of a five-year-old boy named Auguste Tinville, Citizeness?"

My hand flew to my mouth. Where were my papers? I patted my hanging pocket. Had Etty taken them, too? "Excuse me. I took my brother walking this afternoon and must have kept his papers instead of mine."

He peered at me, then shifted his gaze to the house.

A carriage stopped. "That is my father. He can identify me. Come."

The gendarme returned the papers and quickly bowed. "No

need, Citizeness. I recognize the coach. Best get home and find your papers." He turned and walked on.

My legs were so weak I wanted to crumple to the ground. Had Papa arrived just five minutes earlier…he might have walked into the dining room and seen me threatening Etty with the tureen. He'd never trust me again. Had she planned that, too? Had he told her he'd be home earlier this evening?

I shook my head and watched Papa climb the steps to the house, enter, and shut the door.

Would that pouffiasse tell him about the letter? She could lock up all her precious heirlooms and tell him. But she had no proof. And I had her brooch. If she had read the letter, she'd know it was harmless, exactly as Henri designed it. She'd been speculating. She'd hoped to spin a story and force my father to believe her. If she knew that Henri was of noble blood and told Papa, they would have me married within a week, to any non-noble Etty could find.

I walked to the back of the house and climbed down the chipped stone steps into the cellar. Listening for servants, I retrieved the frock coat and stuffed the letter into the secret pocket and hid the coat behind the vinegar cask. I crept up the back stairs to my chamber.

I would write to Henri and tell him to send my letters to Pierre's printshop. Pierre would never violate my privacy or Henri's. With that security, Henri would feel comfortable writing of his love for me.

I lighted a candle and caught my reflection in the mirror. I was pale, thin, drawn. Did men like women who looked like Etty? I'd never fuss as much over my appearance as she did.

The soft light illuminated the jar of hair ribbons Maman had given me. I lifted the lid and inhaled her lavender scent. The only time I wore the ribbons was when I requested something of Papa. Perhaps that was my way of being a coquette.

I pulled out a yellow silk ribbon and pressed it to my cheek, remembering Henri untying it and running it over my breasts. Warmth rushed through me. How would I endure his absence?

I replaced the ribbon and imagined reading his words. Doubt gnawed at me: Did he love me? But I was worrying needlessly. I had to learn how to get to his château. With every breath I took, I hoped there was no reason to doubt his love for me.

ALTHOUGH I'D NOT yet found the guillotine list with Magdeleine Corrié's name, I began to look forward to days of rest, instead of the abolished Sundays. I packed a basket of food and visited her every ten days. No matter the prison, the odors were always the same: dried blood, unwashed bodies, infected sores. It was the stink of despair. I lifted my skirts from the filth and hurried behind the guard who led me into a small visitor's cell. At the clank of the key in the lock, I shivered. I did not want to be imprisoned even for a few moments.

Wearing a gown that must have been quite fine long ago, Magdeleine stood in a corner, in the only shaft of sunlight that penetrated the hay-strewn chamber. Her belly was straining the fabric. I vowed to bring her a skirt with a drawstring waist the next time I visited. I'd already used all the money I'd saved for my passage on my false papers, but I couldn't deny her a few luxuries.

I set the basket down and smiled like I was in a lovely salon, not a dank prison cell.

Magdeleine tucked curls into her frayed cap. "How is Louis?"

"Well."

She stretched out her hands. "Have you a letter from him?"

Her mouse-like demeanor I'd seen on my last visit had vanished. I'd be just as eager for a letter from Henri. I pulled LaGarde's letter from my reticule and offered it.

Her fingers trembled as she brought it to her heart and whispered, "Merci." She unfolded the paper and pinched the gold cross she wore on a chain around her neck as she read.

I uncovered the basket and brought out a bowl of tepid boeuf bourguignonne and a wooden spoon. "Our cook made this yesterday."

She wiped away tears, folded the letter, and placed it in her hanging pocket. She sat on the hay and took a bite. "Mmm, delicious." She patted the mound of hay next to her. "Come, join me."

I wanted to leave, but the loneliness in her eyes pricked my heart. I sat. The walls of the cell were too close, the chamber too dark. I wished I could leave, but I needed to return the bowl and spoon; otherwise, Etty would be suspicious—she inventoried the kitchen once a week. I shouldn't have brought the stew, but Magdeleine's pallor was ghostly, and I wanted her to be strong enough to deliver her baby.

I wrapped my shawl tighter. "I must leave in a few minutes. I promised my brother I'd take him to the park."

She stopped eating and tilted her head to look at me. "How do you know Louis?"

I couldn't tell her LaGarde had exposed my breasts when I dressed as a man to attend University. She knew me only as a woman. I also didn't think she'd want to hear he'd seen my breasts, even if mine weren't as full and lovely as hers. "My friend went to University with him. He introduced me to LaGarde one night at a café when—ah—they were students."

She took a spoonful of the stew, savored it, and licked her lips. "I know all Louis's friends. What's the name of yours?"

"Henri." Warmth rushed to my cheeks.

"You love Henri."

"How do you know?"

She licked the spoon. "When you spoke his name, your face glowed."

I should have lied. Henri was my secret, and I wanted to keep it that way. Why hadn't I said another name, like Pierre? Everyone knew ten men named Pierre.

"You go with Henri when he visits Louis?"

"Henri asked me to visit LaGarde for him, as he can't."

She ran her finger around the inside of the bowl and licked the sauce. "Why not?"

I took out the cheese, bread, saucisson, and wine from the basket and placed them on the straw in front of her. "He's in America."

She placed her hand on my arm. "You must miss him terribly."

I swallowed hard. She patted her long delicate fingers over my sleeve. Although dirt caked her fingernails and her knuckles were raw, her hands were lovely. My fingers were stubby, my palms wide, which I was grateful for when I dressed as a man. My hands would never be as feminine or lovely as hers.

"Henri asked me to visit all his friends who are in prison. LaGarde isn't the only one."

"Why did you not go with Henri?" Magdeleine asked, her voice soft.

"He…" I gazed up at the shaft of light, so warm in this dark place. "I…didn't want to go."

"Why not?"

She was so close I smelled her sweat.

"He said he had nothing to offer me." I closed my eyes against that day when we stood in the heat on the blood-stained paths of the Tuileries and saw Henri's sorrow, his hope-lessness, his weary posture.

"But he had himself to offer, and that is all you want, isn't it?"

My breath caught. How had she known? "That's not fair. He's an ocean away."

"Louis may as well be an ocean away yet, despite our both facing the guillotine, he writes of his love for me."

She was right. Henri hadn't written of his love for me—but that was because he didn't know if his letters would be read by my father.

She looked up at the window high above us. "The first time Louis sent me a letter, he told me he loved me to his sole! S-O-L-E." She giggled. "I asked him if he meant his boot or a fish."

I laughed with her.

"He said, 'fish!' He professed to have a pet fish he loved dearly rather than admit his misspelling."

Now that sounded like the LaGarde I knew. LaGarde had called her a whore, but she was educated. Had he lied?

She fondled the cross on the chain at her neck. "Have you written to Henri of your love?"

Her eyes were so compassionate I looked away, fearing I might cry, and shook my head.

"Oh, Geneviève. Are you afraid to tell him?"

I cleared my throat. "I should be going. My brother's waiting."

"Louis's letters bring me such joy—they make me want to survive another day in this place." Her fingers caressed my cheek. "I wish for you to have the joy of Henri's letters."

I pulled away, but she gently held my arms. "Are you afraid?"

I stared at my fat ugly fingers grasping the basket.

She lifted the bowl. "If you have the courage to enter prisons to visit me and Louis, you have the courage to tell Henri you love him. I know you do."

Magdeleine's eyes were violet, the color of Maman's favorite flowers. "You bring so much joy to me," she said smiling. "Not just because you bring Louis's letters, but because you are hopeful and kind." She rubbed the swell of her belly. "You do not see me as a prisoner. You treat me with respect. I'm sure Henri must see your kindness as well."

Something twisted inside me, making me want Henri to tell me he loved me all the more.

She gave me the bowl and her letter for Louis. "Promise me you'll write to your Henri?"

"Yes." I said it so rapidly she must have known I was lying. I put the letter in the basket and handed her two handkerchiefs. "I'll come back in ten days."

She closed her eyes and brought the lacey squares to her nose. "These mouchoirs smell of lavender."

Next visit, I'd bring ten mouchoirs, a clean one for every day.

Her eyes were moist. "Geneviève, promise you will write him of your love today."

I nodded and left her.

As I hurried out of the prison's gate and into the shadowed courtyard, I thought of Magdeleine's advice. I was certain Henri loved me. But Magdeleine was wrong. I couldn't tell him—because I wouldn't have the courage to know if he didn't love me.

I stopped and looked back at the towering prison walls. Magdeleine had talked to me about my problem, despite her dire circumstances. She'd made me laugh—inside a prison. She was thoughtful and kind, like the Abbess who sang me to sleep the night Papa left me at the Abbey. She was kind and gentle, like Maman had been.

Even if I found Magdeleine's name on the list, I'd have to ask Papa to release her. I couldn't watch her deliver a baby in this hell. How would I ever convince him?

10

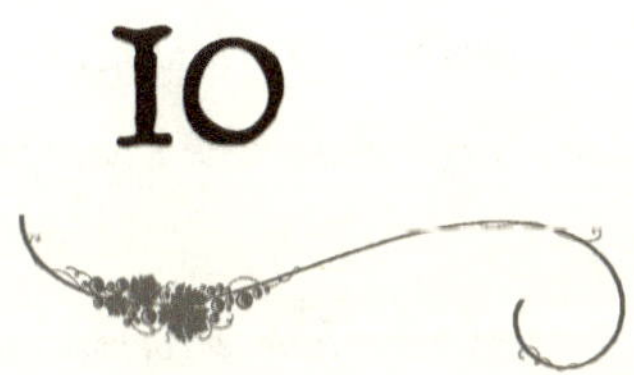

Paris
September 1793

THE CANDLEFLAME FLICKERED, daring me to bring the quill to blank paper. In my mind, Magdeleine's soft lilting voice encouraged me but, while I knew how to show my love to Henri, I didn't know how to write of my love. At least my profession wouldn't be censored. I longed for our old political discussions, and I wanted so very much to discuss Mary Wollstonecraft's, *Vindication of the Rights of Women*, but if I did, the whole letter would be held in evidence, and I'd be arrested as a traitor by the Committee of Public Safety. Papa would know I'd gone to the Palais-Royal, a place he'd forbidden me to frequent, to purchase it.

I could only hint.

The candle was but a stub. Whether or not I had the courage, I had to write him before the candle burned out. I dipped the quill.

Dearest Henri,

I find myself remembering the afternoons we spent in your room and feel myself tingle and blush. I long for the warmth of your arms.

Do you remember our long conversations in cafés at the P.R.? A book written by an English woman is for sale there, and I believe you have the freedom to read her book in America. Now I understand what you meant when you told me you admired me. You spoke of friendship—the most sublime and serious of all affections—and when relationships are based on friendship, they are based on mutual esteem. And that is why you urge me to the safety of your château. I shall go there after my work is complete here and await your return.

It saddens me to write that Olympe de Gouges has been arrested. I long to discuss this with you—remember speaking of her Declaration of the Rights of Woman? *Do you know that she offered to defend the King at the National Assembly? I fear her action may have brought unintended attention from her enemies.*

So that you can write freely, without worry about your letters being intercepted by my father, please address my letters in care of your friend's printshop. He's agreed to pass them on to me.

I treasure our shared affection and esteem, and I long to share it in person again, one day soon.

Yours,

G.

I stared at the ink, spreading into the paper. I wrote about our physical love, but I was a coward. If I didn't remind him of my love, it could fade along with the ink. I quickly added: *I send you my love until we can be together again.*

The candleflame snapped and began to gutter. It was the best I could do. I quickly folded the letter and brought the candleflame to a stick of sealing-wax, dropping a puddle onto the paper's edges. The flame snuffed as I pressed my seal into the wax. Sitting in the darkness holding my words in my hands and my wishes in my heart, I vowed to practice writing of my love until I received Henri's reply. I hoped he would write of his love soon, for I had no idea how I would battle my self-doubt until then.

II

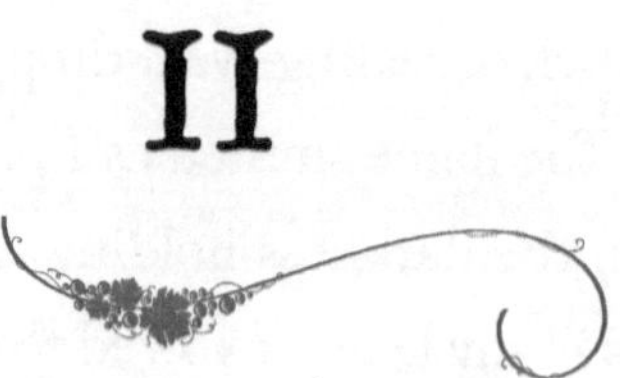

Paris
September 1793

ＴHE AROMA OF carrot-ginger soup heartened me. It was
Papa's favorite potage, and I hoped it would help make him
grant my request. I wove Maman's yellow ribbon through my
hair, pinched my cheeks, and quietly entered the dining room.
"Good evening."

"Good evening, my dear. We've already begun. Sit down."
Etty placed her hand protectively atop her precious tureen and
put out her hand for my bowl. She was on her best behavior
in Papa's presence. The smile I gave her sealed our pact. She'd
keep Henri's letter a secret as long as I had her brooch.

Pulling out my chair, I gave my bowl to her, and took my
place across from Papa who sat next to Etty. She petted Papa's
sleeve. If he often wore velvets or silks, I could understand the
temptation, but he wore scratchy woolens.

The flickering candles cast dark shadows under Papa's eyes, making him look worn out. He sipped and nodded at Etty who twittered on and on about the upcoming nuptials of her niece and the advantageous marriage.

Nearly choking on my wine, I cringed at the word, marriage, for I knew my spinsterhood would soon be the topic of conversation. I'd change it before it began. "Papa, do you remember the Corrié family?"

He shook his head and continued sipping.

I knew he'd not remember because he'd never known such a family. "Their daughter, Magdeleine, attended school at the Abbey with me."

He looked up at the ceiling for a moment. "Ah…the father was a lawyer?"

"No. He was an importer."

He shook his head and dipped his spoon.

"Is she married?" Etty's fingers searched her bodice for the brooch that sat in my hanging pocket.

I would lie to make Magdeleine's pregnancy legitimate. "Yes, but she is widowed, now, poor thing."

"There is no shame to widowhood. And it is usually a short phase in most women's lives." Etty caressed Papa's sleeve. "She was trained to please one man, and she will certainly please another."

I wanted to say, as a former whore, it was Magdeleine's trade to know how to please. But I gripped my chair cushion and smiled.

"Your dear papa was a widower when I met him." Etty's smile was so wide, she reminded me of a marionette.

The image of my mother's face flashed in my mind. Then

I saw myself waving a book at Etty and saying, Mary Wollstonecraft wrote *A Vindication of the Rights of Women* because of wives like you! But I kept my smile. "Papa, I visited her."

"That was kind of you, Geneviève." Etty sipped her wine. "Where does she live?"

She's being nice to me because Papa was there. "La Bicêtre."

Her inhale was sharp. "Prison is no place for a young woman of your class."

"I agree. Magdeleine should not be there."

"What crime did she commit?" Etty dabbed her serviette at the corners of her mouth.

"Magdeleine is accused of being a Royalist, but she is not."

"How was she accused of being one, then?" Etty asked.

I drank more wine. Maybe Etty could help my cause without realizing it. I cleared my throat as I searched for a lie. "She was married to a noble."

Etty's eyebrows rose.

"That could happen to anyone, could it not, Maman? It could have happened to you. It could happen to me, but I know you and Papa would not allow that to happen."

She caressed the pearls encircling her throat. "Rousseau said a woman's existence is to please her husband, no matter the consequences."

Rousseau believed it, and Etty grew up believing it. I toyed with asking Etty if she'd join Papa if he were in prison, but I wanted to save Magdeleine. I took a calming breath. I'd start with a simple request like I'd planned. "Papa?" I waited until he looked up at me. "Could you release Magdeleine?"

"No." He picked up his bowl. "Etty, more of that delicious soup, please."

I bit the inside of my cheek. He'd not even considered it. I sipped more wine, feeling its heat spread into my chest. "Magdeleine is accused of being a Royalist, but she's a true patriot, Papa. Surely you can allow her to defend herself and her cause?"

He ran a piece of bread around his bowl.

I looked to Etty. "It was an arranged marriage. The man was not her choice. You would agree, Maman, that she was being a dutiful daughter?"

"Yes, of course."

"But should she be punished for that?" I asked.

Etty patted her serviette over her lips and peeked at Papa.

I leaned forward. "She is not a Royalist."

Papa cleared his throat. "If she has been tried as a Royalist, there is nothing I can do."

I had to appeal to his sense of honor. "But Papa," I leaned across the table. "She is not guilty."

He swiped his serviette across his mouth. "Would you have me take her place?"

I sat back into my chair. "What do you mean?"

"For that is what will happen should I shirk my duty to the Républic."

"Oh, Antoine. Do not suggest such a horror." Etty patted her serviette over her face.

"You ask this favor when, should I grant it, I could be sent to the guillotine?" His jowls shook.

"No, Papa." I had to deliver my final plea. "It's just that… she's with child," I whispered.

"Oh, my dear!" Etty, pale as the tablecloth, collapsed back into her chair.

The crease between Papa's eyebrows deepened. His spoon clattered on the plate.

I placed my hands upon my heart. "Maman, can you imagine birthing a child in a prison cell?"

Etty sniffed into her serviette.

"You attempt to manipulate, daughter." Papa's voice was low.

"No, Papa. It is true."

He drew his fingers across the tablecloth, bunching the linen. "The law allows her execution date be delayed until she delivers."

"And after?"

He closed his eyes and exhaled. I instantly regretted my challenge. He rubbed his thumb across the knuckles of his fist. "You wished to clerk in my office to learn the laws." The air grew hot from his anger. "You should know this law."

I folded my hands in prayer. "I do, Papa. I also have learned the National Constitution passed a law that guarantees children an education. But if the child has no mother, what will become of it? Once Magdeleine gives birth, she will be forced to abandon her child and face the guillotine. Such a law is inhuman. Why does the Constitution not guarantee a child its mother?"

Etty muffled a cry.

He stood so quickly his chair toppled behind him. "You have learned nothing since your mother died." He threw his serviette on the table. "You've upset Etty." He glared at me, his jowls waggling.

What was he talking about? "Papa, I only asked if you could intervene for my friend."

"You go places you should not."

"I only visited a friend in prison. Is that what makes you so angry?"

"You interfere where you do not belong. Leave us now."

I pushed myself up from the table. My legs, my arms, my hands shook. "I am sorry I have upset you, Papa, and you, Etty."

"Get out. I wish to enjoy my dinner in peace."

His anger seemed far more than my request deserved. At least Etty was not gloating. I'd never seen her speechless or touched. She'd been sympathetic to Magdeleine.

I closed the door quietly behind me and climbed the stairs to my chamber. His words taunted me, *You have learned nothing since your mother died.*

I closed my door and looked out at the city. A breeze rippled the Seine in the distance and brought the cloying scent of roses into my room. Roses had been in my mother's room the night she died. I closed the window.

I must have done something very wrong after Maman's death, but what? What horrific thing could a four-year-old do? There'd been little time to misbehave. He'd taken me to the Abbey and given me to the nuns the next day.

He'd been so quick to anger. Like he was carrying his anger all these years.

I picked up the portrait of Maman next to my bed and ran my fingers around the silver frame. Papa had been so cold about Magdeleine's condition. Had I asked for a sister? If Maman had been with child, the baby could have caused her illness. Did he blame me for her death?

Wrapping the quilt around me I sat on the bed, shivering, but I wasn't cold. I was afraid. Afraid of Papa's anger.

I had to get Magdeleine's name off that list. If I didn't, I'd have to get her out of prison before she gave birth. There was no one else to do it. Only me. I didn't know how I would do it, but I couldn't let Magdeleine's baby be born in a prison.

12

Paris
October 1793

I KICKED THROUGH WET leaves and dodged puddles in a chill too early for the season. I looked forward to visiting my new, and only, friend, yet I was sad we'd met under such conditions. Color returned to Magdeleine's cheeks and her belly grew larger, but her smiles seemed forced, like she was pretending to be in good spirits for me. I still tried to imagine using the tunnels to get LaGarde out of la Conciergerie. If I could figure out the tunnel system, I wondered if we could use them to get Magdeleine and the baby out of prison.

Splashing through muddy water, I damned the Revolution. It forced my future husband to leave me, and it was murdering my friend. King Louis didn't send people to their deaths for no reason. He could imprison them and execute them if they were guilty of crimes, but he never slaughtered people—

especially for being loyal to him. And Revolutionaries had guillotined him.

I looked about, scanning for anyone following me. At least the Committee of Public Safety couldn't imprison me for my thoughts. If they could, I'd already be headless.

The thin young guard, Émile, recognized me, but as I always presented a forged request from le Prosecutor Fouquier-Tinville, he always addressed me as Citizeness. I prayed the forged papers never made it back to my father's office.

Émile's hand shook as he accepted my paper.

I rested the basket on my hip. "Are you well?"

He nodded and stared at the paper. "Citizeness Corrié…"

"Is she all right?" I gripped the basket.

"Her time…the baby—"

"Already?" I spilled the basket. I snatched up the food. "Hurry me to her!"

He jumped at my shout, grabbed the ring of keys and a torch, and ran down the corridor. The torch flared as we raced to a cell, its door ajar.

I pushed him aside and entered. A scream tore at my heart. Magdeleine lay back on a mound of hay, panting. Weak light and a rainy mist streamed through the high, horizontal window.

I knelt next to her and caressed her cheek. "I'm here, Magdeleine. I'm here. I'll help you."

She gripped the gold cross hanging at her neck.

"Have you clean cloths and water?" An older woman, her sleeves rolled up, her arm beneath Magdeleine's skirts, startled me.

"Get water!" I shouted at Émile. I yanked the serviette covering the basket and handed it to her.

I pulled out a handkerchief and wiped Magdeleine's forehead.

She grabbed my hand. "Don't leave me." She panted. "Please."

"I won't leave you. I'll stay right here."

Her eyelids fluttered. I gripped her limp hand. "Be strong for Louis; he loves you." Holding her hand, I leaned toward the old woman and whispered, "Are you a midwife?"

She shook her head.

Mother of God help us, I prayed. "Have you delivered babies?"

"My own."

"At least you have more experience than I. What is your name?"

"Camille."

Magdeleine screamed. Camille reached under Magdeleine's skirts and frowned.

"Be strong, Magdeleine." I bent toward Camille. "What is it?" I whispered.

"She's been at this all night, and she may be too exhausted to push much longer. The baby's head is slippery, and I can't pull it out. If it doesn't breathe soon..."

"What can I do?"

"Get me a cloth."

I searched the cell but saw nothing but filthy straw. I couldn't leave Magdeleine. I jumped up and pulled the hem of my petticoat out, bit the seam, and ripped it lengthwise until it reached my waist. I bit again, tearing it around me, and handed the cloth to Camille.

She twisted it around her hands and reached beneath Magdeleine's skirts. "Push!"

Hands shaking, I knelt behind Magdeleine and gripped her shoulders. "Push. I'll help you."

Magdeleine's scream cut the air like a wild cat's. She fell back into my arms, panting. Don't die, I prayed.

"Again!" Camille commanded.

I didn't think Magdeleine could do it; she was so weak. "Come. You must do this for Louis." I lifted her shoulders.

She grunted, low and long, and fell back against me. Sweat coated her neck making the gold chain of the cross stick to her skin.

"Once more!" Camille shouted.

"I can't." Magdeleine's face was white as milk, her breathing shallow and rapid, like she couldn't catch her breath.

"Do it for me, please." Words clogged my throat. I brought her hand up and kissed her fingers, so delicate. "I'm getting you out of here, Magdeleine. You're not going to the guillotine. I promise," I whispered.

She stared at me, her eyes searching mine.

I was not a good liar. I had to convince her. "My papa is the Prosecutor, Antoine Fouquier-Tinville," I whispered. "He promised me, he'll release you and the baby!"

A half-smile crossed her lips.

She thinks I'm joking. I should have told her long ago. "Louis waits for you and your child. He'll be so happy." I blinked back tears.

"One last push!" Camille shouted.

Magdeleine closed her eyes. I pulled her up, and she grimaced.

"Remember, Louis wants to marry you. Do this for him."

She struggled, grunted, and fell back, panting in my arms. Her heartbeat fluttered against my chest as I held her.

Her weak, high-pitched wail pierced my heart.

"You're almost done." I prayed I was right. "Just one more."

She grunted.

"One more. For Louis," I begged.

Her face reddened to purple. She grabbed my arms and squeezed so hard my hands grew numb.

"Ah!" Camille's face glowed, as if touched by a ray of sunshine. She lifted a blood-covered babe. "You have a daughter, Madame."

Magdeleine fell back into me.

I cradled her. "A daughter. You were right! You have a daughter." I kissed her cheek. God, help me to get them out of here.

Magdeleine struggled to smile, but she sagged against me.

"A knife. I need a knife to cut the cord." Camille urged.

"Rest now. I'm right here." I laid Magdeleine back on the hay, pulled out my dagger from my hanging pocket, and handed it to Camille.

Blood splattered the bodice of her gown. "Help me. Now!" Camille's eyes were wide with alarm.

I crawled to her side. Blood pooled in the straw. My breath caught. "Is all that blood normal?"

She shook her head. "Smooth the cloth for the baby."

Mother of God, help us. I pulled off the underlayer of my petticoat, shook it, and laid it on the straw.

Camille handed me the sticky blue infant—so tiny—I could

hold her in one hand. She weighed as much as a pot of tea. She lay motionless. I jiggled her, bringing her close to my chest. I'd do anything to protect her from the terrible world she had just entered. Anything.

Camille sawed through the cord and tossed the knife on the hay.

I laid the babe on the cloth.

"Clear her mouth with your fingers while I get her to breathe." Camille began stroking the infant's chest.

I gently swished my finger into the babe's mouth, pulling out mucous and clots of blood. "Is this normal?" My voice shook.

Camille nodded and stroked the baby faster. "Get it all."

I twisted the cloth and swiped around the inside of the baby's mouth. She lay still, blue and still. Her head was narrow and misshapen.

Before I could ask if the child was deformed, Camille cradled the infant's neck and head, bent over her, placed her mouth over the babe's, and puffed a tiny breath.

Please God, let us keep her. I will get them both out of here, I promise.

The babe's chest rose. Camille moved back. The baby's chest collapsed, air rushing out. Camille bent and blew again and again and again. A gurgling sound erupted, and the baby's wail rang out.

"Yes! She breathes!" I cried. "You have a strong daughter, Magdeleine, and she has Louis's fine straight nose." I looked back at her. She lay still, too still. I crawled to her. She had the look of an angel. I shook her. "Magdeleine."

Her eyelids fluttered. "Call her Louisa…after Louis." She grasped the cross. "For her." The light in her eyes dimmed.

Her head lolled to the side.

I shook her. "Magdeleine." Her skin was moist and looked waxy. "Magdeleine!" I cupped her face in my hands.

"God help her." Camille held the whimpering infant against her bosom. Her eyes flicked to Magdeleine's hands, one holding a pool of blood that streamed from a jagged wound across her wrist, in her other hand lay the handle of my dagger.

Tears dropped onto my hands, still clutching Magdeleine's cheeks. I fell back onto the hay, releasing her. The odors of blood and feces and urine and sweat sickened me. I had tried so hard. A rock sat in my belly. I should have lied better. She knew I was lying. I should have tried harder to convince her. I should have picked up the knife and put it away. Why wasn't I paying attention? I could have saved her.

I bent over, clamped my hand over my mouth, and screamed in my mind. Why? She was loved.

"Did you not hear me?"

I sucked in air to stop my tears. "No, Madame. I'm sorry."

"I said, you must find a wet nurse for the baby."

Magdeleine's face was pale, no longer creased with worry lines or despair or fear, yet how could she leave her daughter?

I nodded. My arms were heavy, my hands useless. I looked back at my dagger. Guards were paid to report people to the Committee of Public Safety. One of them could accuse me of killing her. I dragged my sleeve across my face. Leaning over Magdeleine, I picked up the knife, wiped the blood across the hay, and replaced the dagger in my hanging pocket.

She had become my friend—my only friend. If the guards saw her wrist, her body would not be buried in consecrated ground. Who were priests to judge whether this innocent loving woman should be buried in consecrated earth? Magde-leine didn't believe in a god who would put her in here, anyway. Despite my blind belief in God as a child, I was beginning to see her point. Nonetheless, I didn't want her in a mass grave. I wanted her in a place where I and LaGarde and her daughter could visit her. I wiped the blood from her wrist with a scrap of my petticoat.

I dug into the basket. "I brought you a clean mouchoir, Magdeleine. I know how much you like them." I took out the handkerchief and patted her face. "It's scented with lavender, your favorite." I wrapped it around her wrist and tied it, making the bow look like a blossoming flower. Lifting her arm, I placed her hand over her heart. She looked so peaceful. She wasn't frightened anymore. I couldn't let go of her fingers. Her pale, long, feminine fingers. I unfastened the gold chain and the cross from her neck and clipped it around mine. "I'll give this to Louisa when she is old enough."

I'd never told her my family name. She'd never really known me. If I'd told her long ago, she might have believed my promise. I hung my head, choking on breaths. A warm hand pressed my back, the spot on the other side of my heart. I bit my lips.

"You must have courage, my friend," Camille whispered.

I shook myself. I'd need courage to face LaGarde. How on earth would I tell him? His plea rang in my head: *If you can save Magdeleine and my child, I will gladly go to the guillotine for them.* He'd blame me. He'd expose my crimes, and I'd beat him to the guillotine. I couldn't blame him.

"Your water."

The voice made me turn.

The guard dropped a bucket, slopping water over the dirtied hay.

I jumped up. "You're too late, aren't you!" My arms trembled.

He looked down at Magdeleine. He removed his hat and placed it over his chest. "I'm sorry, Mademoiselle," he whispered and backed out of the cell. His footsteps echoed along the stone corridor.

Camille dipped the cloth into the water and washed the baby. "They will kill the baby if you leave her here."

She was right. I plunged my hands into the bucket, swished them, and dried them with my skirts.

The cell lightened. The rain stopped. A pigeon cooed from the roof. The baby cried feebly. I lifted my arms. "May I hold her?"

Camille wrapped her in the serviette and handed her to me.

The baby's arms jerked. I captured a fist and stretched out her fingers, long and dainty, like her mother's. I would tell her that when she was older. I would tell her what a good friend her mother was. How brave. A sob rose in my throat, and I swallowed against it.

Louisa whimpered.

"She's hungry," Camille said.

Where would I find a wet nurse? I couldn't take her home with me. Etty would worry the neighbors would think her mine. She would have me banished—even though I'd showed no signs of pregnancy—she'd convince Papa the neighbors would spread a scandal. I pressed the baby against my bosom and patted her back.

The cross poked my neck. I had not seen the nuns at the Abbey for at least a year. They would remember me, I had lived and worked there for years, but they, too, would think the baby mine. Despite my tarnished reputation, perhaps that was a good thing. As my daughter, she'd never face the Tribunal.

The baby mewled. Like a kitten. I looked up at the clearing sky. A beam of sunlight lit up the straw around Magdeleine, like a halo. She'd loved her daughter yet had never held her.

I knelt close to Magdeleine and smoothed her hair. Bringing her arm out, I placed the baby next to her and curled her fingers around Louisa. "This is your maman, little one." The baby nuzzled Magdeleine.

I blew out a long breath. Did you kill yourself to save her? Or could you not live with knowing they'd take her from you and send you to your death? I wiped my eyes. I couldn't imagine a mother facing death, not knowing what would happen to the child she left behind. God damned Revolution. "Oh, Magdeleine, I miss you so."

I sat back on my heels, watching Louisa rest in her mother's last embrace.

A darkness entered me. Louisa's safety was now my responsibility. I inhaled and lifted my shoulders. I'd put her in the basket and get her past the guard and out of this hell. He'd dare not stop me.

I gave Camille all the food from the basket. "Merci, Camille."

She smiled, bowed her head, and whispered, "God help you."

God. What kind of God allowed the guillotining of new mothers?

Getting LaGarde out of la Conciergerie would be far more difficult than getting Louisa out of here. But I had to do it—for Louisa and Magdeleine. I doubted my ability to get LaGarde out, but I couldn't possibly witness another death. I had to save him to save Louisa.

13

Paris
October 1793

I RAN MY FINGERS over hatchet gouges and black scorch marks, scarring the wood that had protected Pentemont Abbey for more than a century. The signs on either side of the entrance were gone as well as the crucifix, but the ghost of its shape was unblemished, as if the power of God protected it. I pressed my heart. The Républic had taken over all churches, convents, monasteries, and abbeys two years earlier. Why had I not checked on the Sisters? Why did I think they would still be here?

Because I had no other option, and I was stupidly hopeful. I pulled the bell rope—once, then three quick pulls—the ring of a student. The bell jangled. Mon dieu, please let them be here. Let them be safe. Why did I speak to God when he'd just let Magdeleine die? Rain pounded the cobbles, and I pulled the basket under my cloak. I swiped at the rain dripping down my face from my bonnet ruffle. If I'd dressed as a man, I'd be a lot drier. Ruffles were totally useless. Hat brims deflected the rain. All the stupid layers I wore and why was it that women's clothing did nothing to keep them dry?

I stared up at the two huge doors, which made me feel like I was four years old—when my father had brought me here to be cared for by the Sisters the day after we buried Maman. Their dulcet voices echoed in my mind. Their singing calmed me throughout my childhood. I surrendered to their loving care and, after a while, I missed Maman less.

Louisa cried, and I jiggled the basket to calm her, but she began to whimper. I pulled back my fichu, which I had wrapped around her as my scarf was the only piece of cloth that wasn't blood-stained. Her eyes stared. Her mouth searched for milk. I stroked her cheek, soft as a rose petal, and teased her lips with my knuckle. She sucked at it, and warmth flooded through me. I felt this way toward Auguste, whom I had loved since his birth. How could I become so attached to her after only two hours? Was this another part of being a woman that I had no choice about? Louisa had to eat soon, or she'd start wailing. Please, God, don't let me fail her. He hadn't helped Magdeleine, why did I think he'd help her child?

I pulled the bell rope signal again. Now that all the churches were closed, there were no more baby-wheels where one could anonymously pull a leaver and the infant disappeared beyond the wall and the nuns on the other side would care for it. Not that I would leave LaGarde's child at a baby-wheel, but I'd have no place to take Louisa but home. My stays dug into my chest as I imagined Etty's face and heard her call me a salope.

Would Papa let me keep Louisa? Doubt sat like a rock in my chest. He'd never let me keep the baby of a prisoner.

The wooden slat before the small grilled window slid open, but no face appeared in the opening.

"I'm Geneviève, here to see Abbess Marie Catherine," I whispered. The slat closed. If the Sisters fled, who was behind the door? I began to step back, but Louisa stirred. I had no other choice. My fingers trembled as I scratched at the metal grill covering the window. "Please?"

The grinding of iron against iron screeched. The door opened to a narrow wedge of space, and I pushed the basket ahead of me, slipping through. The door banged closed behind me and iron ground against iron.

The courtyard, once a riot of colorful flowers and spiraling green vines, was an empty muddy pool. In the center, where I envisioned myself as a little girl sitting on the fountain's rim, enjoying a cool mist in summer's heat, stood a pile of rubble. Shutters barred all the windows of the sprawling stone building. My chest ached. What had happened to my home?

I turned toward a gaunt woman wearing a maid's cap and ragged apron over a dung-colored gown. She lifted her chin. Her face, lined like the shell of a walnut, was familiar. I stepped back. "Sister Magali?"

"Don't call me that." Her mouth twisted, and I feared she would cry, but she pressed her lips to stop their quivering. She looked up at the top of the walls as she turned in a circle.

My arms grew heavy with my longing to be comforted by her. "Are you not Sister Magali?"

She shook her head, sending rain drops showering. "Call me Magali." She smiled a sad smile and lifted her arms toward me. "Geneviève, we've not seen you in so long."

I looped the basket handle over my arm and embraced her, searching for the scent of incense, but smelling a musty odor. She was stiff, not soft and warm as I remembered. "What happened here?"

Her bony shoulders rose. Tears sat in her dark eyes. I knelt, put down the basket, took her hands in mine and kissed them, readying myself for her usual blessing. Her ring was gone, as were her crucifix and rosary.

She jerked her hands from mine, grabbed my elbows, and yanked me to my feet. "I cannot bless you."

I picked up the basket and searched her face. Did she know of my crimes? My lies and sins? "Please, I need your forgiveness. Your blessing."

She shook her head. "I cannot."

"Why?"

Tears dropped onto her apron. "I am no longer a nun."

I nearly spilled the basket. "Why not?"

She pressed her hands to her stomach and whispered, "I pretended to swear the oath. Because of this, I am no longer a nun in the eyes of God."

I rested my hand on her arm. Being a nun was her whole life. Yet, pretending seemed an excellent idea. Surely God knew the truth. "But if you swore the oath, who desecrated the Abbey?"

"Sans-culottes."

The damned barbaric Revolutionaries. I shivered, shaking off an ominous force pressing on me. "When?"

She dragged her apron across her face. "After Abbess Marie Catherine made us all promise that we would pretend to swear allegiance to the Constitution, and we did, she refused. She alone remained faithful." A sob escaped. "God forgive me." She inhaled, and her arms shook. "She took our rings, gave them to Sister Josephine, and told her to have them melted and use the money to feed the children. We buried our crucifixes and rosaries in the garden." She covered her mouth. "During the September Massacres, they came for her."

I reached out and took her into my arms, her body shivering like a starving cat. I rubbed her back. She had comforted me like this so many times. All this had happened while I had thought the government was right to seize lands owned by the church and sell the properties to feed the poor, yet those people still starved. The money had gone to support the war, and no doubt into a few informers' purses. Why had I not thought of the Sisters, Abbess, and the Abbey when the Civil Constitution of the Clergy law passed? Because I had been spending those days in Henri's arms.

She struggled to inhale. "Before the sans-culottes got through the door, she made us take the children and hide in the tunnels." She moaned. "They hacked her to death." She covered her sobs.

I swallowed back the urge to vomit. My legs began to give way. I gripped the basket and leaned against the door, remembering Abbess Marie Catherine holding my hand and singing to me until I fell asleep my first night here. Revolutionaries had butchered her gentle soul.

"I am sorry to shock you." Sister Magali put her hand on my shoulder.

Cold rain ran down the back of my neck. At the end of the courtyard splashes of dark red stained the wall.

Sister's mouth trembled. "We lived in the tunnels for three days."

How had the Sisters and children endured? How had the nuns survived burying the Abbess's broken body? I inhaled against a sob and tried to calm my voice. "The Abbess sacrificed her life to save your lives."

Sister Magali jerked back. "But we wanted to die with her." Her voice was a raw whisper. "Not one of us is faithful to this nation." She spat and pounded her fist against her chest. "We are faithful to God, our Father." She blessed herself and kissed an imaginary cross.

A hollow opened in my chest. "Sometimes, God wishes us to be good actors in order to do his work." I tilted my head, hoping for agreement. Hoping she would understand my lying, deceiving, and dressing as a man—if she ever found out.

She swiped at her tears and nodded. "You must leave, Geneviève. It is not safe here."

The baby wailed. Sister's eyes flashed.

I jiggled the basket. "Is there a wet nurse here?"

The lines in her face deepened. "Yours?"

"No. Her mother died." I tickled Louisa's lips. "She has not yet suckled."

She nodded, held my arm, and guided me to the cellar. "As the sans-culottes have taken everything of value, there's nothing left to pillage. The cellar has been safe…so far…but there is talk."

I followed her through the mud and down into the cellar.

A tallow candle flickered light across the dirty faces of three parcels of children and three women whom I recognized as former nuns. A stink of stale wine, vinegar, and mold permeated the air. A young woman, a girl really, younger than I by a couple of years, sat in the corner nursing an infant. Jiggling the basket, I ran my finger along Louisa's cheek. The woman's face was angelic, but it no longer held the innocence of youth. I hoped she loved the father and not been taken against her will.

Sister Magali took the basket from me, placed it on a wobbly table, and pulled back the fichu. "Uh! So tiny!" She turned to me; her brow furrowed.

Her unspoken accusation burned my face.

"Louisa was born two hours ago, at la Bîcetre. Her mother…" I swallowed. Catholics thought suicide a mortal sin—would that sin reflect upon Louisa? If I told the truth, Sister might not take Louisa or help me. Forgive me for lying in a House of God. "Her mother died giving birth."

Sister blessed herself and whispered a prayer. She cradled Louisa and carried her to the young woman, who gave the babe she'd been holding to one of the nuns. The young woman brought Louisa to her breast and guided the baby's mouth to her nipple. The young woman smiled. "She's hungry. Her suckling is strong."

"Her name is Louisa," I whispered. Emptiness, helplessness crept up my arms. Maybe Magdeleine felt this. Did she end her life because this longing would have worsened? She could not have borne prison without Louisa.

Sister Magali held my elbow and guided me outside, closing the cellar door behind us. She scanned the courtyard and the top of the walls as she led me to the stables and unlocked the barred door.

Weak light filtered in from attic windows, illuminating goats crowding a pen on one side, a sow and piglets rutting in another pen on the other. The animal odors were a relief to the sour stench of the cellar. How had the sans-culottes missed these treasured animals? Knowing Sister Magali, she'd taken them to the tunnels, too.

Sister stopped between the pens and turned. "She is not yours?"

I shook my head.

She wiped her brow. "You want us to keep her here?"

"Until her father is released."

Her eyebrows rose.

"He's at la Conciergerie. I hope it will be soon." I pressed my hand to my heart.

She folded her arms and leaned against a post. "Are we endangering ourselves and the children already in our care?" Her eyes sparked with a wariness I'd never seen.

I began to shake my head and stopped. "Not if we have a false birth certificate for an identity card. Can you sign a baptismal certificate?"

She shook her head. "Baptismal certificates are no longer issued or accepted. The mother and father must apply for the child's identity card at city hall." She looked to heaven. "Mère de dieu, nous aider."

We needed more help than the mother of God could provide. My hands jerked. "If there is no mother?"

"The father must."

"The real father is Comte Louis de LaGarde; the mother, Magdeleine Corrié."

"Their crimes?"

"Royalists."

She inhaled sharply. "Could your father not intervene?"

I could not tell her my father refused me and condemned them nor that I eliminated LaGarde's name from the death list. My stomach burned. I was risking Sister's life as well as the lives of the other nuns and children. I squeezed my eyes against the image of all the people I had endangered lined up before the guillotine. I'd burn in hell trying to atone for my father's condemnations. I dragged my foot over the cobbles and shook my head.

Her shoulders dropped. "She will soon be an orphan."

I couldn't tell her I would be getting LaGarde out—if I succeeded. "I can give you real names for her identity card."

"You wish *me* to be sent to la Bîcetre?"

"No." What was I thinking? Did I expect everyone to risk their lives? I could buy a forged identity card from Pierre, but where would I get the money?

She leaned down and picked up a kid, cradled him, and scratched his head. He bleated, and she let out a small laugh. "Goats are safer than children in Paris."

I petted his silky coat. Goats were safer than anyone in Paris, and that was my father's fault. I nodded. "I will act as her mother."

"And if your father discovers this?"

"I will act surprised and lie. I'll race here and take her with me through the tunnels. I know of a place for her in the country."

She tilted her head. "Perhaps you should take her there now."

I paced between the two pens, biting at the dried skin on my thumb. Henri had told me to go to his château for my own safety. I had no doubt the people there would watch over Louisa. Henri's milk-mother would welcome her, as she had welcomed Henri when he'd been brought to her.

I rubbed the kid's horn buds. "When she is strong enough, I will. But it's a two-day journey. How will I feed her?"

"There is talk the République will requisition the Abbey as barracks for the military. We will be without shelter when they do." Sister's face lightened, as if angels arrived with sunbeams. "Is this place in the country large enough for four women and eight…nineteen children?"

I laughed. Henri had told me the château had forty bedrooms. But how would they get there? The gnawing in my stomach worsened. How could I possibly save more people? "All of you would need travel passes."

She kissed the goat's head and dropped him back into the pen. He shimmied and trotted to his mother's teat. "We can sell the animals for papers and hire a driver and wagon, if you can get Louisa an identity card."

The gnawing traveled up my throat. What if we were caught?

"What names for the baby and her parents for the pass?"

I cleared my throat. "Her name is Louisa…Her father is Jean Detré. Her mother is Geneviève Tinville."

"It will take a few weeks." She clapped her hands. "Can you spare some food in the meantime?"

I came here, searching for help. Now I was being asked for it. I rubbed my eyes. I didn't have the strength. I didn't have the courage. I'd lost my friend. I had to tell LaGarde.

Rain dripped through shafts in the roof. A damp chill seeped down my back, and I longed for my shawl. In my mind, I saw it wrapped around Magdeleine, and I was glad to have given her the comfort, as small as it was.

Sister Magali's warm brown eyes were so sympathetic I wanted to crawl into her arms. I didn't have the will to say no to the woman who'd raised me.

I shook myself. I wouldn't be spending money on the milkmaid or guard bribes anymore, but I'd also not be saving money for passage to America either. The image of Magdeleine flashed, and I squeezed my eyes. "I will pay the wet nurse and bring you food every other day." I sighed at the animals. "You don't need milk or cheese?"

"Not as long as we keep the animals hidden." She placed her hands in prayer before her. "Bread. The children are so hungry for bread. It is a comfort to them."

I would have to bribe our cook. She would keep her mouth shut; she bristled at Etty's interference in the kitchen. "I will try."

"If the military arrives, we'll have no shelter and will have to return to the tunnels."

Where would they go? I would have to take them to the château with or without papers. I could not wait to wear breeches and my tunic; my corset was tight as a noose.

Sister reached out and cupped my chin. "You've lost a friend, Louisa's mother?"

My throat closed around a sob. I swallowed hard. "It was my fault. I should have tried harder to get her out of there. I should have begged my father. She wouldn't have died if I had." Tears fell.

Sister held me close, patting my back. "It wasn't your fault. It was God's will. You were with her and a comfort to her. She entrusted her daughter to you. God loves you, Geneviève."

I shivered like a sapling in a storm. God loved me more than Magdeleine…and LaGarde? I didn't believe it or in the kind of God who left all those children in the cellar orphans. Or the kind of God who rewarded Abbess Marie Catherine for her loyalty by being hacked to pieces.

Sister dried my tears with her apron. "You are very brave, my child."

I shook my head. "Magdeleine was brave." She must have known that if she killed herself, I would take Louisa out of there. It was the only way she could ensure her child did not go to the guillotine with her. I would never have the courage to make such a sacrifice. I wrapped my arms around myself. I hoped never to face such a choice.

"God go with you," Sister whispered as she pushed me toward the door.

I reached out. I couldn't leave Louisa without holding her. "But—"

"She'll be fine. Go, now."

I walked out into the rain, empty and hopeless. I had failed. Failed Magdeleine, Louisa, and worse, LaGarde. What would he do when he learned Magdeleine was dead? What would he do when I asked him for money for a false identity card for his daughter? If I didn't visit him, it would be a matter of time until he exposed me, yet again. He'd promised I'd beat him to the guillotine if I didn't get him out.

I sloshed through puddles and stinking muck, realizing I'd

forgotten to hold up my skirts. I was not remembering when I was wearing a gown. Was I becoming more a man than woman?

God, give me the courage to tell LaGarde. Give me the courage to get him out of there.

14

Paris
October 1793

WITHOUT LOUISA'S BASKET, my arms hung useless. The fine mist soothed me until I remembered LaGarde. I scuffed the gravel. How would I say it? I wouldn't tell him about the knife. Magdeleine would have died even without her hastening act, as Camille had said.

Fear pumped in my veins. LaGarde might grow so enraged at my failing to get Magdeleine out of la Bicêtre, he might expose me right there in his cell. The guards would seize me and drag me before my father.

I trembled like the coward I was. I did not know how to face him. Although LaGarde was less likely to voice his anger to a woman, I couldn't dress as one for I didn't want the guards to associate my father's daughter with LaGarde. If I could muster the courage to face him, we might have a chance at getting him out, and I had to get him out for Louisa.

Avoiding Etty's questioning my bloodied gown and praying all the servants were busy, I climbed down into the cellar and changed into my breeches and frock coat.

I shoved two bottles of wine under my arm and wiped sweat from my face. God, give me the courage to tell him and make him understand it was your doing, not mine.

At la Conciergerie, I kept my face impassive. Instead of giving the old guard a cup of wine, I slid him a few sous. I shifted my weight as I waited to be taken to LaGarde's cell. I deserved his rage. I'd not gotten Magdeleine out. It was my fault she was dead.

Leaning against his cell wall, LaGarde folded his arms before his chest, his gold-flecked eyes glinting.

An acidic taste rose in my throat as I tried to find the right words. I hadn't gotten him out of here yet, and his lack of gratitude for saving his life continued to chafe. But he was about to learn the love of his life was dead, and for that, I pitied him.

I entered and stayed near the door.

"How is my Magdeleine?"

My jaw locked and, as I forced it open, pain shot up the sides of my skull. "You have a daughter."

He jolted toward me.

I set the wine near my feet, removed my tricorne, and gripped its brim. "Magdeleine named her Louisa, after you."

He squinted. "And Magdeleine?"

Magdeleine's cries filled my head. God, help me. I stepped back, closer to the door. God, make him understand. "I'm sorry. She labored all night." The tightness in my throat strangled my voice.

LaGarde's broad chest expanded as he inhaled. He took a step closer, beckoning me to continue.

The hat brim grew wet in my grasp. "I'm sorry."

"Tell me."

I swallowed air, nearly choking. "A midwife birthed the baby, and I…comforted Magdeleine. She wasn't alone." I stared at the stone floor, wishing I could fall through it. Wishing my friend were there with me.

The toes of his boots touched mine. I pressed my palm against the wall.

His eyes were red-rimmed. He squeezed my arms. "Tell me."

I blinked back tears. "I'm sorry. She died." A sob burst and I slumped.

He let me go and retreated into the corner.

My legs gave way, and I spilled onto the floor like an unstrung marionette, heaving for breath, the room blurred. "I'm…so…sorry."

He kicked and ripped the pallet and kicked and ripped and kicked and ripped as an explosion of straw rained over us.

Sobs wracked me, like they had been slammed out of me. "I did everything I could." I wanted to tell him I had tried my best, but my efforts had been so lame. Why hadn't I taken back the knife? I lay panting.

LaGarde punched the wall and shouted, "Dieu m'avait damné!"

I was sick of his selfishness. God had damned Magdeleine far worse. She'd left her child. LaGarde was still alive and a father. "You're not the only one God has damned."

His eyes slits, he glared at me.

My own anger surprised me. But if he was going to kill me, I was going to give him a good enough reason. "You're not the only one she left. You're not the only one suffering. Your daughter will never know her mother." I gulped for breath. "All your rage won't bring Magdeleine back." The anger washed out of me like the ocean's tide. I pushed myself onto my hands and knees. "She was my friend." I swatted tears. "I miss her, too."

Holding his injured fist to his mouth, he dropped onto his knees and moaned, his body convulsing.

I swallowed the instinct to comfort him, for his rage simmered beneath his tears and would strike out like a coiled snake.

I pressed my forehead against the stone wall, cool and hard. I should have gotten you out of there, Magdeleine. Somehow, I should've gotten you out. Damn you, Papa. I leaned back on my heels and pulled my handkerchief from my waistcoat, balled it up, and tossed it on the floor near LaGarde.

His moans diminished to whimpers, but he writhed and jerked, like a wounded animal.

Slowly, I got to my feet, uncorked the wine, took a long drink, and placed it near him. I backed up quickly.

He grabbed the handkerchief, wiped his face, and collapsed with his back against the wall. His fingers waggled for the wine.

I didn't move.

He leaned over, snatched it up, drained the bottle. He dragged his sleeve over his face. "When?"

"This morning." My throat was raw.

His head dropped until his chin rested on his chest. He

grabbed the other bottle of wine and took a swig. "At least she didn't face the guillotine."

My chest burned. I'd never tell him what she'd done. Never.

He jerked his head up. "Did she?"

"No! She…passed soon after the baby was born." His face contorted, and I backed up. "She held Louisa before—"

He snorted.

Heat arced across my shoulders. I wanted to punch him. "You find that funny?"

"Ironic. The baby will never remember it."

I wanted to slap the ingrate. "She was of great comfort to Magdeleine."

"And what comfort for me?" His eyes were that like those of a lost little boy.

I slapped at the hay clinging to my breeches. "You have a beautiful daughter, which Magdeleine gave you."

He leaned his head back and closed his eyes. "A lot of good she will do me in here."

I kicked his foot and startled him, making him stare at me, rage still smoldering in his eyes. "Just the thought of her should brighten every day of your selfish life." I snatched up my hat, slammed it on my head, and yelled, "Guard!"

"Do not leave me." He crawled to me and grabbed my leg. "Please."

My disgust poured out of me like sticky warm syrup. "You're pathetic. Do you think of anyone other than yourself?"

He sniffed. "Magdeleine."

"Louisa is of Magdeleine, and you'd better start thinking of her, now. She needs you." I banged on the door. "Guard!"

LaGarde wiped his face. "Where is she?"

I wasn't sure I heard him, so faint was his voice. "A safe place."

"Bring her to me?"

Frustration strangled me. I had gotten Louisa out of prison, now he wanted me to bring her back. My head tipped back, and air rushed down my throat.

"I am sorry I grabbed you. I saw you…as a man. I would never harm a woman. I lost my mind. Magdeleine was all I had. All I loved. Forgive me."

"I'm unharmed. You have a daughter to love now."

Tears dripped from his quivering chin. I refused to feel sorry for him.

"Bring her to me?"

I had no more patience. "Don't you want to know how she is, or if she is healthy?"

"Is she? Healthy?"

I glared down at him. "Was it not enough for her to be born in a prison? You want her to live in one?"

He shook his head. "I only want to see her. To hold her for a bit. To feel Magdeleine in her."

"You want Louisa to make you feel better. What a father you'll make."

He dragged his hands through his hair and stared at the floor. "Magdeleine was all I had."

He had a daughter, but I'd probably feel the same if Henri died. I wiped sweat off my face. Was I not doing enough? Enough for everyone? Why should I add one more danger to my life for this selfish bastard? I sighed. Because if I brought her, he'd at least stop hounding me to get him out of here—or he'd hound me more. But how would I sneak a baby in here?

The idea was stupid. If Louisa were discovered, her name would be placed on the list.

I needed to spend more time watching the Tribunal proceedings. As horrifying as they were, I needed to understand why my father condemned so many innocents. I needed to reason with him, get him to stop. I needed to confront my own father, not save the miserable excuse for a father that stood before me.

I rubbed my face and looked up to the window beyond which a bright cloud hovered in a deep blue sky. If I lived in this hellhole, could I bear a glimpse of such beauty?

My bringing Louisa to LaGarde would be good for her. She needed to know her father. I wasn't about to ask him for money for a false identity card today. Maybe he'd be more cooperative once he saw her. Perhaps he'd be more patient while I searched for a way to get him out of here. I should have copied his name on that damned list. Instead of trying to fight the world dressed as a man, maybe I should be satisfied with being a useless woman.

"Bien sûr." I shook my head, not believing what I was doing, not having any idea of how to do it. "Why the hell not?"

The keys jangled as the guard unlocked the door.

"By next day of rest," LaGarde growled.

"I'll do it when I do it." I left without looking back. Damn you, LaGarde. Damn you to hell. I didn't have to bring Louisa here. And I wasn't going to endanger her for his sake.

15

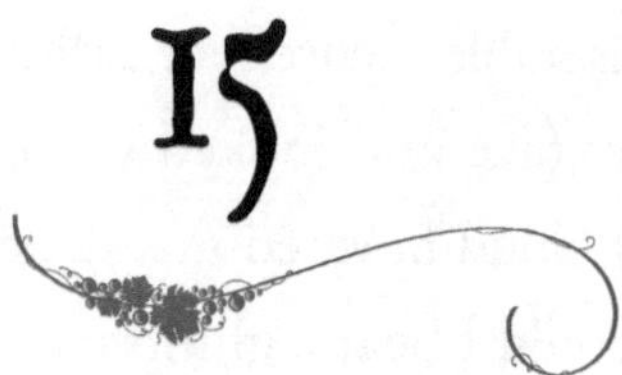

Paris
October 22, 1793

A TROOP OF SOLDIERS blocked our carriage as Papa and I approached the Châtelet. A guard on horseback raised his sword and yelled a command. The soldiers marched in columns out of the square. A crowd of red-capped sans-culottes swarmed after them, thrusting their pikes aloft.

The hairs on the back of my neck bristled as I remembered a similar scene we witnessed a year earlier. The stink of carnage filled my nostrils, and it seemed as intense as that day the sans-culottes sliced off the heads of priests and mutilated prisoners' bodies, drenching Paris in blood. We had escaped the mob, but Papa had restricted me to the house that very day, and it had taken me a year to convince him it was safe for me to return to my clerk position.

"I pray we do not see the murder of a thousand people like we did during the September Massacres."

Papa stared out the window.

If they began another slaughter, Papa would confine me to the house again, and I'd never save anyone. "Where are they going?" I asked.

His eyes were glassy, as if he were lost in a dream.

"Papa?"

He shook himself. "To find refractory clergy and people who have hidden them."

The sans-culottes wouldn't stop to ask if the nuns had taken the oath; they'd slaughter them and Louisa. A tightness gripped my chest. "For what purpose?"

"The Directory passed a law that makes all clergy who have not sworn the oath to the République and those who've harbored them punishable by death on sight."

I envisioned Sister Magali's pale, tired face. I gripped the bench. "Priests or nuns?"

"Both." He sighed. "If they bring back any alive, I shall have a busy day."

I jolted as the carriage rolled to the square and stopped. Martin jumped down from the driver's bench and opened the door. Papa got out, turned, and offered me his hand.

I gripped it but didn't move. "The Sisters and Lou—" I could not mention Louisa. "The children at the Abbey—they are in danger."

He blinked.

I pressed my thighs into the bench. "Do you not remember Pentemont Abbey? The nuns there cared for me when Maman passed."

He smiled. "Of course."

"You cannot let them be taken."

He shook his head. "You know I can do nothing if they've not taken the oath."

I clasped his hand with both of mine. "They have sworn the oath, Papa, but as you just saw, those men are out for blood. There will be no reasoning with them. Please, send a guard to protect them."

He patted my hand. "I do not have the authority to send a guard unless you want the guard to bring them before the Tribunal. You do not want that."

The image of the Sisters and children and two infants standing before my father tightened my throat, trapping my breath. I shook my head.

He beckoned me to get down from the carriage. "If they have taken the oath, they have nothing to fear. Come."

A hardness crept into my chest. The nuns had raised me, not him. He owed them more than whatever he had paid them. "Nearly a year ago, you and I and Etty watched from this carriage as sans-culottes chopped off the Princesse de Lamballe's head. They danced down the street twirling it by her hair, flinging blood upon bystanders."

He winced, but I wouldn't stop. "That same day, sans-culottes hacked the Abbess to death—the very woman who took me in her arms when you brought me to her. You trusted those women with my life. The sans-culottes will hunt them down. They are in hiding in the Abbey's cellar. Please, Papa, send someone to protect them."

He tilted his head. "My dear, I cannot."

"Cannot? Or will not?"

His shoulders drooped. "If I send someone to guard them under my authority, and they have not taken the oath, I will be held for harboring them."

How would I prove they had taken the oath? How did any member of the clergy? I doubted the government issued certificates. I lurched and grabbed his hand. "Then give me money to help them escape, Papa, please."

He yanked his hand away. "You are most unladylike, my dear."

His tone had the same intent to humiliate as Etty's. I lunged, snatched at his frock coat. "If not for those nuns nursing me through the fever, I would have died."

He shrugged me off and smoothed his sleeve.

I had to get through to him. "Please," I whispered, "I beg of you. Their lives are in your hands. Don't send them to their deaths. Not when they cared for me so that I did not die and join Maman."

He jerked his head up. Like a breeze rippling across water, warring emotions moved over his face as he stared at me.

"Without them, I would have died, Papa." I didn't want to hurt him, but it was better to cause him pain than to send the nuns and children to their deaths. "You would have lost Maman and me."

He stared at his feet as he pulled his handkerchief from his pocket and wiped his eyes. It pained me to force him to remember Maman, but I had to save the women who had mothered me.

"I need to get them far from the city." I held out my hands.

He dug into his purse. Running his tongue over his teeth, he pulled out a few coins and pressed them into my hands.

Not nearly enough. "I need every sou you have."

He freed his sagging chin from his jabot and turned the purse upside down, shaking it. "That is all I have. I am sorry." He turned and hurried through the archway to his office.

Martin stood holding the carriage door, looking after my father. He'd heard our entire exchange. His face seemed sympathetic. But I didn't trust him, and I didn't know why. Yet, I had no time to waste. "Would you take me back home, Martin, and wait for me there, please?"

He bowed his head. "Of course, Mademoiselle."

He snapped the whip and the carriage jolted.

I'd find more money somewhere. Etty must have some.

16

WITHOUT MAKING A sound, I opened our front door. Cook and our maid argued in the kitchen. Something metal clattered on the wooden floor. I slipped into my father's office, lifted the slanted lid of his secrétaire, and gazed at Maman's miniature portrait tucked in the back corner. I miss you, Maman. You would have welcomed Louisa with open arms. I pulled out the key hidden beneath it.

Hands shaking, I unlocked the top drawer. Stacks of louis d'ors glittered. Where had Papa gotten all these solid gold coins when he was paid in paper assignats, as were all true patriots? My heartbeat pounded in my ears. If I took one from each stack, the missing coins wouldn't be as noticeable. I plucked them up, wrapped them in my handkerchief, and stashed them in my hanging pocket. I relocked the drawer and replaced the key. As I closed the lid, it slipped. The bang echoed. Footsteps thundered down the hallway.

I flung open the lid and pulled out a sheaf of papers. The door opened. Etty stood huffing.

"Excuse me for disturbing you." I smiled. "Papa sent me to retrieve some papers he forgot. I didn't mean to make so much noise." I clutched the papers to my chest, closed the lid, and walked to the door. "I must get them to him as quickly as possible."

Auguste ran around Etty and wrapped his arms around my legs. "Fold some boats for me and take me to the fish-pond, please?"

My heart hurt. I ran my hand over his silken curls. I might never see him again. I knelt beside him. "I must help Papa with his work, but when I come home, we will go for a walk."

"Promise?" Tears rose in his eyes, and I feared I might give up my mission and stay here with him forever.

I pulled a paper off the desk, folded it into a boat, and handed it to him.

He pressed it against his chest, like it was the most precious thing in the world. His grin brought tears to me. I tucked a curl behind his ear. "Ask Maman to read you the story about the fox and the fisherman until I return." I looked up at Etty and smiled. I hated lying to my brother. I hoped Etty would show her son a soft heart and read to him.

Etty stepped in front of the door, her eyes pinched. "Antoine did not mention any papers to me."

I laughed. "As you often point out, he is so overworked. He only remembered as we arrived at the Châtelet. Please excuse me. He needs these now, for the trial he is conducting. It is urgent."

"He gave you the key?"

What was she talking about? I hadn't needed a key to lift the lid…but she didn't know that—she was forbidden to enter this room. "Of course. How else could I get them?"

She huffed an exhale and stepped aside. "Tell Antoine I expect him to join us for dinner this evening."

"Certainly." I kissed Auguste and ran back out to the carriage.

I whispered to Martin, "Rue de Grenelle and rue Bellechasse. Vite!"

He nodded. "The horses will fly, Mademoiselle."

I nodded my thanks. Inside the carriage, I placed the papers on the floor and spilled the coins from my handkerchief onto my skirt. Two hundred and forty livres—enough to *buy* a wagon and two horses. It was a two-day ride to Henri's château, and we'd have to sleep in the wagon. But outside Paris, no one would know they were Sisters.

I shut my eyes, envisioning all the louis d'ors. There had to be ten times that still in his desk. And gold, not worthless assignats. I was certain Papa was paid in assignats, so he must have gotten the gold some other way. A sick feeling moved through me. When nobles were condemned, what happened to their wealth? It was supposed to go to the République, to benefit widows and children.

Did the nobles' wealth enter the pockets of the members of the Committee of Public Safety? If the wealth entered the pockets of the informers, there was no question why informers were so eager to report their neighbors.

Was Papa keeping secrets—like I was? Perhaps he hoarded the money for bribes should the tide turn. I rubbed my arms. And should the tide turn, my brothers and Etty and I—we'd all be in danger if my father appeared before the very Tribunal he conducted. I would no longer be safe carrying his name.

I forced myself to inhale. That wasn't possible. That would be like Robespierre losing power. My father could be hiding huge sums of money for someone else. If so, my stealing two hundred livres might jeopardize their lives and Papa's. How would he replace it? I was taking far too many risks. And risking far too many lives. My trying to save lives was putting more at risk—but I couldn't stop myself.

I spilled the coins back into the handkerchief, put it into my leather pouch, and tied the pouch to my waist. I'd spend as little of it as possible and return the remainder. Merci, Papa.

The carriage rattled over the cobbles and bridges toward Faubourg Saint Germaine. The streets were unusually empty of people. Word spread fast. I hoped I wasn't too late.

I knocked on the ceiling of the carriage. "Slow down," I shouted up at Martin when we turned onto Rue de Grenelle. No sense in drawing attention to an Abbey everyone thought abandoned. "Wait here." I opened the door before the carriage stopped, jumped down, ran, and pulled the bell rope—once, a pause, and three quick. Constantly scanning the street and the windows in the nearby buildings, I listened for soldiers and sans-culottes.

Sister Magali might know of the danger—if so, they were already hiding in the tunnels. I should have asked her how to get to the entrance. A scraping sound stopped my breath. "It's me, Geneviève," I whispered.

The key rattled against metal and the door opened a crack. I slid past the door, and it hushed closed. Sister Magali relocked the door and, before she could extract the key, I grabbed her arm and tugged her close, whispering, "Is Louisa all right?"

"Of course."

I gulped a steadying breath. "Send two women with blankets and baskets of food and all the children immediately to the market. You and the other woman herd the animals after them. You must sell the livestock today. A man with wagon and horses will meet you at the market and take you all to a safe château."

"Who is this man?"

I leaned close. "I am that man. Trust me."

Her face grew white as an altar cloth. "I do not have the traveling papers for all the children."

"We've no time to get them." But how would we travel? I rubbed my forehead. I'd lie but wouldn't tell Sister. "I'll use my father's name if I must. Hurry. If the bell rings again, do not answer it." I unlocked the door, slipped through the opening, and ran for the carriage.

Martin stood next to his bench, pointing at the far end of the street. "Mademoiselle, soldiers."

I did not stop to look. "Take the carriage around to the Abbey's stable entrance and wait for me there. Hurry!" I raced back to the Abbey door and pulled the bell rope without pause.

Soldiers scattered from building to building, two strode toward me.

Think. They'll demand to know why I'm here. I must get them to leave—without entering the Abbey—the Sisters needed time to round up the children and animals and get out. But how? Think! I had no chance of getting rid of two huge men. But one thing I was certain about: they knew my father's name.

The two men stood before me. My hand froze around the bell rope, my heartbeat racing, images of the Abbess's hacked body flashing in my mind.

The older one, a curving scar running the length of his face, ripped my hand from the rope and pulled my arm behind me, making me yelp in pain.

"Public Prosecutor, Antoine Fouquier-Tinville, sent me here!"

The younger soldier laughed. "And Maximilien Robespierre sent us." He stuck out his hand. "Papers."

They need only see Papa's name to release me. I need not panic. I lifted an eyebrow at the guard clutching my arm. "If you do not wish to appear before my father, I suggest you release me."

The grip on my arm tightened. I winced.

I'll ask their names and remember not to take them off any lists. With my free hand, I reached into my hanging pocket, pulled out my identity card, and kept my voice as cool as spring water. "You are not the only ones looking for refractory clergy. My father sent me here. As I attended this place as a child, I know of all the intricate passages where one might hide."

"Pardon!" The younger showed the other my card. He released me, and both soldiers stepped back, standing at attention, their fingers quivering on their sword hilts.

"Of course, Citizeness Fouquier-Tinville. May we assist?"

asked the younger as he held out my card, which vibrated with his trembling.

"Your names?"

The younger paled. "Gasc, Citizeness."

The other looked far into the distance. "Pisier, Citizeness."

I snatched back my card. "I have lost the element of surprise thanks to you two. I can be of greater service to the République without you, Gasc and Pisier. I'll inform my father of your *assistance*."

They muttered apologies, backed away, and hurried down the street.

I wiped the perspiration from my upper lip. I was fortunate. I doubted sans-culottes would have been as civilized. I stood with my hand on the bell rope, not pulling it, until all the soldiers moved out of sight.

God, keep Louisa safe and let the women and children escape. I kicked a cobblestone. I had to stop asking God for help if I didn't believe in his power. I forced myself to walk slowly around the corner toward the stable entrance, the tension in my shoulders dropping when I spotted the carriage. I ran. Martin jumped down and tilted his head toward the stable.

In the doorway, all the children and women stood shivering as if it were snowing. The goats strained their ropes held by one of the Sisters.

I searched Martin's face. The faint lines at the corners of his eyes deepened. I had no other choice but to trust him. "Please take the women and children to the market and wait with them there."

He grinned, his eyes sparkling. Without complaint about

fitting more than twenty people in a carriage that had never transported more than six adults, he nodded and began organizing the children on the floor and benches.

Sister Magali gripped the sow's rope and a basket of piglets. She leaned near me. "God speed you, my child."

I ran to the cellar and my disguise.

17

THERE WERE TIMES when it was advantageous to be a woman, or at least my father's daughter, so I crammed my gown, bonnet, and reticule with my identity card into a leather satchel. I donned breeches and waistcoat, grabbed my older brother's frock coat, pressed his tricorne onto my head, shoved Jean Detré's papers into my waistcoat, and ran for the stables.

The stableman had horses and a wagon, the bed of which would easily fit twenty, for rent at a much lower price than the cost of buying them. I had learned to ride a horse but driving two attached to a wagon had to be different. I didn't want to endanger the people I was helping. If I asked the stableman, he might not rent the horses to me. Did I have the strength to handle two horses? Although I didn't trust Martin, I'd get him to show me. Needing the transportation back, I paid the rental fee and guided the mares toward the market.

As I passed la Conciergerie, I envisioned LaGarde in his cell. He'd be angry when I didn't show up within five days, but I'd be back within ten and force myself to explore the tunnels and find an escape route for him before I visited. My hands grew numb thinking of the dark tunnels, and I gripped the reins, forcing feeling back into my fingers.

Long shadows striped the market square by the time I arrived. At the entrance, a guard stood next to another whose back was turned as he pissed into a pile of rotting cabbages. Glad they were too occupied to notice me, I hurried the mares around the far side of the square where Martin waited with my father's carriage. The children's cries and frets clashed against the vendors' barks of their wares.

I wished there were more people about or a few hagglers, for a wagonload of twenty children would be remembered. I waved my arm through clouds of black flies, swarming the metallic stink of dried blood surrounding the butcher's stall. The intense afternoon light exposed bruises and rot on the courgettes and aubergines. I hoped the sisters had enough food with them.

When I brought the mares behind the carriage, Martin reached up for the reins, which I gladly released to him.

He pressed a hard object against my arm. "You may need this, Mademoiselle."

I stepped back. "How did—"

"Take it. You will need it."

I stared him in the eye, wanting to ask him: Where and how had I revealed myself? If I was that obvious, the guards might notice. I glanced back at them, but they paid us no attention.

I accepted his offering, which, by the feel of it, was a pistol he'd wrapped in his handkerchief. I had never shot a gun and didn't know if I'd be able to. But it would provide an excellent threat. I shoved it inside my waistcoat.

Worry pulled at the corners of his eyes. "Do not hesitate to use it."

"Should my father ask—"

"I haven't seen you since I delivered you home, Mademoiselle. After that I took the horses to have them shod."

My exhale burst. "Thank you, Martin." Maybe my distrust was just fear.

"I'll help you load the children and women. Thankfully, they've sold the pigs and goats."

I wanted to laugh but kept quiet.

A small blond boy, reminding me of Auguste, hacked a cough that shook his narrow shoulders. He reached for Martin who bent down, picked him up, and flew him like a bird into the wagon bed. The boy giggled.

I approached the wet nurse who held Louisa and opened my arms. I breathed in Louisa's sweet milky smell. Her eyelids were translucent blue, and her cheeks soft as rose petals. My heart ached with longing to tell Magdeleine her daughter was healthy. Louisa held her fists below her chin, and I uncurled one. Oh, Magdeleine, she has your delicate, long fingers.

Martin helped the Sisters into the wagon and handed up blankets, food baskets, and children. He fashioned a mouse from his neckcloth and scurried it from child to child, pinching their noses and cheeks and ears. Whining and crying stopped. Peals of giggles floated over the square.

A market woman, stooped and grayed, brushed close to me.

She held out two apples and whispered, "For the children."

I took them and began to thank her, but she blessed herself and ran off like a frightened rabbit. An uneasiness stirred in me. Everyone in this market knew they were orphans and nuns.

When it was time to give Louisa back, my arms stiffened. I reminded myself I could hold her again later and gave her up to the wet nurse.

Martin left them and whispered, "May I know where you are going, Mademoiselle?"

If Martin told anyone, it could get my father in trouble with the Tribunal. I couldn't risk it, even though it would be good to let someone know where we were headed—should sans-culottes murder us all. "I'm not sure but far from Paris. Far from a city where women and children are not safe."

The lines around his mouth hardened. "There are terrible goings in the Loire."

Straight where we were headed. I examined his eyes, searching for truth. "What sort of things and where?"

"The Vendée. They are rounding up people suspected of being Royalists and clergy, tying them up, putting them on barges, and sinking the leaky vessels in the Loire River, drowning them all."

His words hit me like a punch to the chest. Henri's château overlooked the Loire. I tried to keep my face impassive, but my lips quivered, and I pressed them together. Was my father aware of these murders? He couldn't possibly have ordered them. "I shall avoid the Loire."

"Do you wish me to come with you?" His gaze flicked from me to the children and back to me.

"No. My father needs you." Even though I didn't trust him,

I could not endanger this man who'd risked his job to help me already. I had to stop risking everyone's life. I had to stop. Today. I shook my head. "We will be safe."

"At least tell me where you are going. Should there be an uprising, I will try to find you."

His eyes seemed kind—but not trustworthy. He knew who they were. He could be an informant for the Committee of Public Safety. He could report me today, and I'd be standing before my father by dusk. I couldn't further endanger the Sisters. "Why? Do you know of a safe place for women and orphans?"

His mouth hung open. He shut it and shook his head.

It was dangerous to ask him to show me how to drive the horses. I'd figure it out myself. "Merci for your help, Martin." Turning away, I climbed up to the wagon bench.

He took off his hat. "God keep you." He hurried back to the carriage.

I sat on the bench and asked Sister Magali to join me. Her eyes were wary, but she nodded and sat. She would have to pretend she was me, in the event we were stopped, unless she wanted to wear the breeches and tricorne. Without a man, women and children would be in greater danger—hard to imagine.

I patted the pistol in my waistcoat, praying it would be a good enough threat, for I had no idea how to load or shoot it. Henri taught me the tunnels, but he hadn't taught me how to shoot a gun. It wasn't something I'd ask Martin to show me. Maybe a man at the château could. I might need it when I rescued LaGarde.

I snapped the reins. "Allez!" The horses jolted. I gripped the reins and pressed my feet into the floorboard.

As we traveled toward the city barrier, I wondered who I was, really. I dressed as a man who hoped he could drive this wagon yet couldn't shoot a pistol. I was a woman who charmed her way out of danger using her father's name yet endangered everyone around her, including her father. I was a man-woman who had fallen in love with Henri yet kept myself isolated, awaiting his return.

All my disguises and risks and lies and, now, stealing and harboring clergy, were rooted in the same person. But exactly who that was, I'd no idea. I slowed the mares as we neared the barrier gate. There'd be a time when even my father's name would not deliver me. God help me then.

Once we got through the barrier, I'd have to figure out how to get to the château. Once I found the Loire River, I'd follow it. I did not want to ask anyone for directions. They'd know we were lost and rob us blind.

18

WE TRAVELED FOR two days, stopping only to rest and feed the horses. Miraculously, we were not stopped by any soldiers. And brigands had the good sense to not waste their time with a wagonload of women and screaming, fretting children.

The river widened and ahead, a wooden sign carved with, *Château de Verzat*, stood at the foot of a hill. I slowed the horses and let out a long, low whistle.

Sister Magali turned and looked around her. "Have we arrived?"

I halted the horses. "I think so."

In the distance, a château of the same butter-colored stone of the greatest buildings in Paris stood at the top of the hill, glowing in the afternoon light. Red-golden leafed grapevines covered the slopes surrounding it. Men and women moved through them, clipping dead vines and pitching them into the wicker baskets strapped to their backs.

Henri owned all of this—all the land I could see on this side of the Loire River. Never would I have guessed the wealth this estate generated. Leaving it must have broken his sister's heart. When Henri and I were married, I'd be mistress of this place. I could scarcely breathe.

Sister Magali giggled. "There should be room for all of us." Her laughter was like birdsong.

I smiled. "Let's find out." I snapped the reins and drove the horses up the hill and beneath the porte cochère. Dark green wooden shutters covered every window. Two wooden beams crossed over the dark green doors. Although the brass Verzat crest glittered in the sunshine and the greenery had been clipped, the château appeared to be abandoned, or at least closed against intruders, or more likely, Revolutionaries. Henri had written his mother lived here and she expected me.

I handed the reins to Sister Magali and jumped down. "Wait here while I look around. Yell if anyone comes and I'll return."

"Be careful," she called out after me.

I walked around the towering home of my lover, imagining how overwhelmed he must have felt the first time he arrived here, knowing he would inherit it. When I reached the back, I followed a well-worn path that led through the vines. After walking a few minutes, I saw a limestone outcropping in the next massive hill, and below it two great wooden doors, emblazoned with the Verzat crest, covering a round opening in the rock. I figured it must be the wine cave, but those doors were barred also. Henri's sister was importing wine to America. I had expected much more activity. What was going on?

A horse whinnied, and I walked past the cave toward the sound. A chill breeze rustled dry leaves like a warning. Something wasn't right. I checked the hammer and flint on the pistol and held it at the ready. I doubted I could shoot it but hoped I would not need to.

A woman cried out.

Staying amongst the vines, I hurried toward the sound.

"This is a winery, not a monastery," a woman's voice cried.

I crept behind the vines and peered through the leaves. A soldier pinned an old woman, dressed in faded black silks, against the limestone. Her chin quivered and her eyes were wide with terror, but she held her head high.

I lifted the pistol and aimed it through the vines.

The soldier clapped his empty scabbard and looked around.

A boy of about fourteen years emerged from a cave cut out of the limestone. "You lost your sword when the buck charged. Don't you remember?"

The soldier reached into his waistcoat and withdrew a dagger.

Merde, I cursed. I'd have to shoot the bastard and that would bring other soldiers. Damn. Could I surprise and bluff him? Make him think there was more than one of me?

He grabbed the neck of the woman's gown and brought the dagger to her throat. "Noble scum!" he growled.

I couldn't get a clear shot, not without shooting the woman, too. Still, I kept the pistol aimed, watching for an opportunity.

She cried out, dropped her cane, and crossed her arms before her face.

The boy grabbed the cane and twisted the silver handle. A blade clicked out of its tip. He drew the cane back, shifted his weight to his back foot, lunged, and thrust the blade into the soldier's stomach.

I covered my scream.

The boy shoved the blade up, gripped the stick with both hands, and wrenched.

Blood oozed over the soldier's uniform, the stain flowing, blood dripping onto the dirt.

The boy began to pull the blade out of the soldier's gut, but it caught. With both hands, he gripped the handle harder and yanked.

Nausea rose and I swallowed it back. I'd never possess this boy's bravery.

The soldier's mouth gaped. Black-red blood bubbled down his chin. He clutched his stomach, staggered, and fell onto his back, his breath hissing like a snake.

The boy dropped the cane he'd used as a rapier. Splatters of blood stained his hands, breeches, tunic, like a butcher's apron. He dropped to his knees.

"Simon, are you all right?" The old woman knelt next to him and placed her hand on the back of the boy's neck. Her face was as white as a priest's cassock.

The boy pressed his forehead into the dirt. "Oncle didn't tell me about the blood." He started to cry. "I killed him." He punched the ground. "I killed a man!"

She pulled him up, pressing him close and rubbing his back. "You saved my life, Simon." She drew back and looked at him.

He dragged his fist over his eyes. "He was going to kill you."

"You saved my life." She held him close and rocked him.

He wiped his face and pulled away. "I did it just like Oncle Albert taught me."

I let out a breath. Simon had courage. We were going to be great friends.

"I am most proud of you." Her blue eyes were watery. "You have the courage of two men."

"But he didn't tell me about all the blood!" He sobbed and hugged her neck.

I pushed my way through the vines, holding the pistol high. "Did you see any other soldiers?" I whispered.

The boy grabbed the rapier.

"Henri Detré sent me," I cried. "I won't hurt you."

The old woman fell back against the rock wall. The boy steadied her and faced me, his eyes now holding excitement. "Is Henri here?"

Shaking my head, I forced myself to speak more calmly, "Are there other soldiers near?"

His arms trembled. "I…I didn't see any."

"They'll be looking for him. We've got to get rid of the body. Have you a hiding place?"

The old woman straightened to a regal posture. "Who are you?"

"Gen—Jean. Henri's friend. We attended University together. He told me to come here and that he'd write to his mother to expect me. Are you Madame Detré?"

"Madame is expecting a woman, but…" She peered at my face and by the glimmer in her eyes, I knew she knew I was one. "I'm certain you are Henri's friend."

"We must be fast. Where can we hide the body?"

"The cave." Turning to the boy she said, "You must never speak of this, Simon, never. You must tell no one, not Oncle Albert, not even in code to Henri. Do you understand?"

The boy wiped his nose and nodded. "Aren't you glad he's dead?"

"Certainly. But we can tell no one. Do you promise?"

"Yes. I promise."

"If his body is discovered, every person on this estate will be executed." The woman looked up at me. "We must hide him in an unused chamber of the cave and roll wine barrels before the door."

Flies swarmed over the soldier's bloodied body, his open eyes, his hand clutching the dagger.

I nodded and swallowed back the urge to vomit. I began to pick up the man's shoulders, hoping the boy could handle the feet. The soldier's blood leaked from the wound.

Simon stood staring, not waving away the flies landing on his face.

"Simon? Are you all right?" The woman held the boy's arm. "Can you help drag him?"

"I'm a bit dizzy, myself." I placed the soldier on the ground and wiped my sleeve across my face.

"Yes, Madame." Keeping his back to the soldier's body, Simon grabbed the soldier's legs and heaved his weight forward. He groaned, dropped the soldier's legs, bent over, and vomited.

I offered my handkerchief. "It's all right. I nearly did that, too. But I was inspired by your courage."

Simon spat, then wiped the handkerchief across his mouth. "I can do it," he insisted, grabbing the soldier's legs.

"Wait." I'd passed the soldier's horse, and it would prove he was here. "Was that his horse back there?"

The boy nodded.

"I'll get his saddle."

"I'll do it." The boy was off before I could protest.

"Forgive my manners," the old woman said. "This is an extraordinary circumstance. My name is Madame Bourran, I am a friend of Henri and his sister, Joliette. I help oversee the château in their absence."

"I am pleased to meet you, Madame."

"Thank you for helping us and not turning us in." Her eyes drilled into me, seeming to question my loyalty. "What is your name?"

"It is safest if you know me as Jean. I would do just about anything in the world to help Henri's friends."

Her smile was tranquil, like she had lived a lot in her lifetime. I supposed what I saw was wisdom. I took the opportunity of her gratefulness. "Might you have room here for a few more children, Madame?"

Her eyes grew wary. I should have waited until we'd hidden the soldier, so she would trust me. But I trusted her. "They are orphans…and former nuns, Madame."

"Friends of Henri?"

I stopped my impulse to lie. "Henri does not know them, but they would be his friends if he did."

"Your name?"

"Gen…Jean…Detré."

Her eyebrows arched.

Simon returned dragging the saddle, bridle, reins, and the soldier's haversack.

"Smart of you to remember those things, they could be identified." I took my place at the soldier's head.

A smile lightened Simon's face. He tossed the saddle and other things atop the body and grabbed the soldier's feet. "Let's get him in there."

Madame Bourran carried the haversack and held a torch as Simon and I dragged the soldier deep into the caves.

Grateful for not only their company, but also the light Madame carried, I inhaled a musty wine scent. I had traveled two days to arrive at the château, a place Henri believed to be safe. If soldiers found this body, I'd be held for murder. In addition to having committed crimes in Paris, I now had to be on my guard in the Loire Valley. Was there nowhere safe? Maybe, once Henri got a job, he'd send for me rather than returning to France. America had to be safer. It couldn't possibly be as dangerous as France.

My arms grew weary, dragging the man farther and farther down into the endless caves. I couldn't write to Henri about this soldier. Nor LaGarde's mistress and child. Nor the nuns and orphans. The cave narrowed and my heart beat faster. Henri probably thinks I'm calmly copying files and reading political pamphlets. He'll be so surprised to learn how much I've helped his friends. He'll be so proud of his future wife.

Sweat pooled at the small of my back. I was glad for the coolness of the caves. I only hoped Madame Bourran would shelter Louisa and the others. I couldn't take them back to Paris. I wondered if people could live in caves. They lived in the tunnels of Paris.

I had to get LaGarde out of prison. Once I gave Louisa to LaGarde, I would do everything I could to leave France and join Henri in America.

19

Château de Verzat
November 1793

T HE CHÂTEAU'S KITCHEN was bigger than a church and
warmer too, with two huge fireplaces, each of them bigger than
the cellar the Sisters and children had been living in. All the
children, the wet nurse, and four former Sisters sat on benches
at a long battered wooden table in the center of the cavernous
stone-walled room.

Sister Magali tied the children's serviettes below their chins.
The children, wide-eyed, whispered their surprise and delight
at the warmth, which came not so much from the fires but
from the people gathered at the table. Although not related
by blood, they were all family.

"Would you like to hold Louisa?" Madame Detré handed
Magdeleine's daughter to me.

My arms were aching for her. I wiped my hands on my breeches and snuggled her to my chest, listening to the contented slurping of the children as they devoured their soup.

A boy's dark eyes followed Madame Bourran as she ladled more apple-parsnip soup for everyone. He lifted his bowl and said, "S'ilvousplaîtmerci," as one word.

"What fine manners you have." Madame ran her knuckle along his cheek.

His smile revealed two missing front teeth. She filled his bowl, and he brought it to his mouth and drank until it was empty. He pulled her sleeve as she finished serving the next child and offered his bowl again.

She laughed and refilled it, seeming to enjoy her role as adopted grand-mère to the children as much as they enjoyed her. She turned to the sideboard and placed more bread in a basket. The boy jumped up, picked up the basket, and offered it to each of the Sisters and then each child.

The Sisters sipped their wine and closed their eyes as they murmured prayers of thanks.

"Hold her over your arm, and gently pat her back after she feeds." Madame Detré positioned Louisa along my forearm.

I imagined how happy Magdeleine would be if she saw how Louisa had gained weight and grown. I patted Louisa's back, which she seemed to like, because she let out a loud burp.

I laughed and lifted her so her delicate face was near mine. Her eyes were so trusting. I worried I might not live up to her expectations, but I knew I'd die trying. I laid Louisa in my lap as she clutched her fingers to her mouth.

Madame Detré placed her hand behind Louisa's head.

"Always protect her neck and head." She smiled at me. "You'll be a wonderful, loving mother. Henri will be so glad you've joined us."

I pressed my lips against a gasp. I wore breeches and a waistcoat. How had she known? If I was this obvious, I was taking greater risks than I imagined. I placed my jittering hand behind Louisa's head, the other under her back, and handed Louisa to Madame Detré. "I must speak with Simon. Do you know where I can find him?"

Madame Bourran stood. "I'll show you how to get to his home, my dear."

I cringed at the words, my dear. She must have told Madame Detré who I really was. I followed her into the vineyards.

She pointed at a path. "Follow this until it curves near a lamb shed. He lives with his maman and stepfather in the third house on the left." She looked out over the vines as if she were watching the past unfold. "Henri brought them and Madame Detré here when I needed assistance. I am very fond of Simon and Henri." She placed her hand on my arm and waited until I looked at her. Her gaze was unwavering. "You love Henri, do you not?"

My cheeks burned. But her eyes were so kind.

She laughed softly. "I know you are a woman. No man would have been so caring to Simon when he killed that soldier. You are most brave."

"Thank you." It was my actions. I would have to change those. But how could I stop showing care for a child? I gripped my frock coat.

"You love Henri?"

I stared at my boots. Etty didn't pry quite as much, yet I felt this woman's warmth and concern, neither of which I'd ever felt with my stepmother.

Madame stomped her walking stick. "He has excellent taste." Her eyes glittered.

A thundering caused us both to look toward the road along the Loire. A soldier on horseback turned from the roadway toward the château.

My heartbeat pulsed in my throat. "Do you think he's missing his comrade?"

She slowly dipped her chin. "I would think them too busy drowning clergy and Royalists in the Loire."

A squirming in my stomach nauseated me. Martin's warning had been no rumor.

The soldier charged up the hill through the vines toward us.

I reached into my waistcoat and placed my hand on the pistol. As soon as I got LaGarde out of prison, I would make him teach me how to shoot the thing.

The young soldier, missing buttons on his stained and dusty frock coat, pulled his horse to stop before us. He swept off his hat. "Bonjour, Citizens." He was younger than the one who'd died but no less cocky.

Madame and I uttered an unwelcoming bonjour.

"I come on behalf of the République. Have you seen any other soldiers, today?"

We shook our heads as we looked at each other. I was certain we were both praying he wouldn't discover the dead man.

"Do you know of a…" he shoved his hat under his arm, reached into his frock coat and pulled out a wrinkled paper. "Simon Amoulin?"

I could honestly say I did not, for I only knew of a Simon.

Madame Bourran leaned on her cane and looked with imperiousness upon the lowly soldier. "I know every tenant on this estate and there is no Amoulin."

He nodded. "Should you meet an Amoulin, notify the authorities immediately. He's a clergy-loving Royalist." He spat, turned his horse, and galloped toward the river.

I wiped sweat from my neck. The child was in terrible danger. "Do you think Simon might wear my gown, carry my real identity papers, and accompany me to Paris—where I can get him false papers?"

She put out her hand to grab my arm for stability. "I'll convince his mother." She leaned her head near mine and whispered, "Whose name, before she married Étienne Chastain, was Amoulin." Her eyes twinkled.

I was feeling less guilty about the crimes I'd committed. I was in good company. For a moment, I longed to stay here, amongst these warm people who cared for one another. But I had to get LaGarde out of prison. Louisa needed her papa.

20

AS WE HEADED for Paris, Simon fidgeted on the wagon bench next to me, pulling at the gown's sleeves and bodice. "How do women wear all these things?"

"You've got it easy. Wait till it grows hot." I breathed in a muddy scent. With the winter rains, the river flooded its banks, forcing me to take back roads, roads traveled by starving people. I had a basket of carrots and a few turnips and cabbages and hoped it would be enough. Unlike soldiers, starving people I understood and could reason with. It was the Revolutionaries I feared. My pistol would stop only one, should any discover Simon's real identity.

He flounced the gown's skirts. "I'll never be able to run in this."

"That's one of the reasons I dress as a man." I snapped the reins and urged the horses up a hill. "Simon, you must never reveal to anyone that I am a woman. It's against the law for a woman to dress as a man."

"Is it against the law for a man to dress as a woman?"

"No." Another inequality. "You'll have to wear that disguise until we reach Paris, where I hope you can get lost in the crowds until you get false identity papers."

He pulled at the bonnet. "And this?"

"Especially that. Why are soldiers looking for you?" I asked.

"I wrote Henri that I took the Marquise to the cave where we attended mass."

"You told him you were hiding clergy?" I cried, nearly dropping the reins.

"But I thought really fast and told the soldier that was my code for mating the goats because Henri reads my letters aloud to Madame Joliette and I didn't want to shock her. The soldier didn't believe me and made me show him the goats and I took him to the pen where I'd put the doe, I named the Marquise, and her kids." He pressed his fingers to a smile, making me think he was rather proud of his foil.

"Then I heard the buck's hooves, and I pulled Madame Bourran into the pen and the soldier drew his sword—" He looked up at me, his eyes bewildered. "Was he so stupid he thought he could duel with a goat? And Madame forbade him to harm the buck because he sired more than two hundred kids, and then the buck rammed the soldier and knocked him out!" He crowed a laugh, and I joined him.

Simon slapped his skirts. "We dragged the soldier outside

the cave and when I realized he had dropped his sword I went back and got it. And that's when you got there." He lowered his voice. "But there really was a priest hiding under the hay in that pen—I fell on top of him."

"Where's the priest now?" I whispered, thinking I had not seen any clergy in the vineyard.

"He pretends to be a farmer and lives in a cottage on the estate."

The Sisters would be glad to meet him. I prayed they wouldn't celebrate mass.

"Wasn't that quick thinking to make up the goat story?" Simon's posture was that of a young rooster.

"Yes. But!" I used a warning voice. "It would have been better not to have told Henri about the clergy in the first place. You could have gotten everyone on the estate killed. And now, you're a wanted man."

His shoulders dropped. "I won't be that stupid again."

"I hope not."

Cranes flew over the gray ribbon of the Loire, reflecting the morning light and reminding me of the Seine. I had a two-day ride to scheme a way of getting LaGarde out of prison, but a year-long ride wouldn't have been enough. The Royalists couldn't rescue Marie Antoinette, why did I think I could rescue LaGarde? But I had to. Otherwise, he'd send my neck to the guillotine ahead of his.

"What're you thinking about?" Simon's voice sounded far away.

I pushed out a sigh filled with hopeless ideas. "I must get Louisa's father out of prison, and I've no idea how to do it."

"Which prison? I'll tell you which tunnels to take."

"How—"

He snapped his fingers and grinned. "Henri taught me the tunnels."

Why had I not spoken earlier? Simon had proved his quick thinking. Why did asking for help never occur to me? I pulled out the leather string out from around my neck and showed him the key. "Henri gave this to me before he left. It opens every gate in the tunnels—except the door to the Verzat mansion wine cellar."

Simon whistled. "Formidable! You are so lucky. You can go anywhere."

If I wasn't terrified of the dark, I could, but I didn't need to spill that secret. "La Conciergerie."

He laughed. "That's an easy one. There's three tunnels. They open to the kitchen and the storage cellar and the dungeon—but that's filled with rats. Where's your friend's cell?"

Darkness and rats. Formidable. I closed my eyes, imagining the corridors I took to LaGarde's cell. "Past the main guard gate, then the guard room on the second floor, to the right, past two huge cells with high windows looking out onto the Seine, down that corridor to the end, up another flight of winding stairs, to the next floor, straight ahead, third cell on the right." I opened my eyes.

Simon stared. "You're as good as Henri remembering the tunnels."

"Why did Henri teach you?"

He leaned forward, resting his elbows on his knees. "He didn't want what happened to my papa to happen to me."

I gentled my voice. "What happened?"

"Papa joined the Revolutionaries at the Bastille, and Maman

asked Henri to find him and stop him. Henri left right away, but when he found Papa," his shoulders slumped, "he was already dead."

I placed my hand on his back and felt him take a shaky breath. I quickly looked around but saw no one but a pair of fishermen casting their nets on the river.

"Henri promised Papa he'd look after Maman and me. I don't think he expected me to be so much trouble."

I laughed. "You're not so much trouble."

"Madame Bourran wouldn't agree." He jumped around on the seat and faced me. "Let me help you."

Help me? He was just fourteen. A child wanted for murder, but nonetheless a child. His mother would kill me if anything should happen to him, but then again, I'd already helped save his life. But I had to find a place for him to sleep in Paris. "How would you help?"

"I'll go with you." His eyes shone bright as a puppy's.

"I cannot take you into a prison!"

"The tunnels." He grinned.

That might work. I wasn't as terrified of the dark when Henri had taught me the tunnels—I wasn't alone. But if Simon and I were caught…I shivered. I would not take Simon into the prison, though, just the tunnels. We only had to avoid the gendarmes that were usually looking for thieves. Thieves that could kill us, as well. The pistol might threaten them, but…"We should have borrowed Madame Bourran's walking stick."

He grinned and reached under the bench. "I did." He lifted it up and laughed.

He was a little thief as well as a murderer. But I was a thief and much worse. "You're formidable."

Dressed as a man, I could enter the prison just by passing the guards. We'd need the tunnels to get LaGarde out. If Simon were waiting for us, it just might work.

All I needed to figure out was how to get LaGarde out of his cell. I glanced over at Simon, wearing my gown. A lady of the night might have a better chance of it. The slam of the cell door and screech of the lock echoed in me. If I got caught, I'd have to be prepared to play the part. Now all I needed was courage. And LaGarde's cooperation. And he wasn't going to be too agreeable since I wasn't bringing Louisa. I would have to depend on his desire to meet his daughter.

21

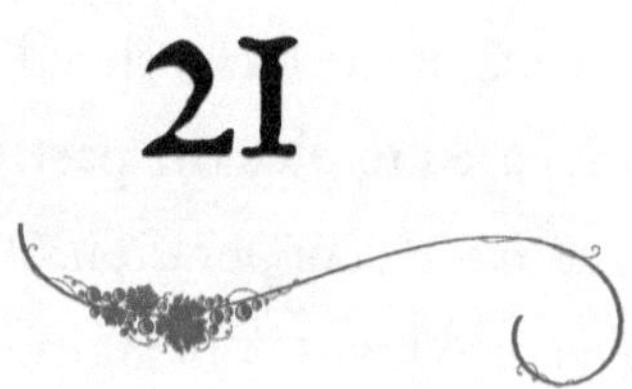

Paris
November 1793

Despite the cold fall day, I sat sweating at the Paris gates until the guards, bored by their task, glanced at our papers and waved us through. I guided the horses back to the stable and returned the wagon. A few louis d'ors remained, enough, I hoped, to pay for Simon's false identity papers.

"There weren't so many people when I lived here." Simon walked backwards and faced me. "What happened?"

"Many are starving and came to Paris looking for work." I cupped his elbow, and he stopped, his eyes questioning me. I placed his hand on my arm. "Act like a woman, while I act like a man. We don't want to draw attention," I whispered.

"Oh."

He began walking, but I pulled him back. "The man leads."

He looked toward heaven and sighed.

"It's not a game, Simon. Act like a girl," I whispered.

"It's frustrating."

"If you only knew just how frustrating, you might want to change the laws like I do."

We wound our way through alleys until we reached Pierre's printshop. I opened the door, spilling light into the small dark room. The clattering of metal against wood made me want to cover my ears. I tasted the sticky ink, thick in the air.

Pierre stood reviewing a tray of type and looked up as I closed the door behind us. He shoved the tray at another man and fled out the back door.

I ran out the front door, around the corner, and down the alley just as he was backing away from the shop, right toward me.

I strode forward, tipping my hat, just as any man would. "Bonjour, Pierre."

He spun around, looking up, searching the windows, and past me. "No."

I smiled. "It's so nice to see you again."

He stood, legs rigid and arms crossed before his chest as his eyes continued to rove the windows and alley. "No."

"You don't know why I've come."

"I can guess." He jutted his chin. "Who's this?"

I turned to see Simon had followed me. "Simon," I whispered. "Henri promised his papa he would take care of him."

"We lived next door to Henri and his maman." Simon dipped a wobbly curtsey. "Bonjour, Monsieur."

Pierre's eyebrows rose. "Whatever you need, the answer is no."

"Please. Simon only needs papers and a place to stay for a few days. I can pay."

"Henri brought my papa's body back from the Bastille."

I turned to Simon. "He did?"

Simon nodded. "Henri tried to stop Papa, but he couldn't, so he went after him. He found him and brought him home to Maman and me."

Henri had never mentioned his act of selfless bravery. I missed Henri more. No wonder Henri felt Simon was his little brother.

Pierre frowned. "If he needs papers, he's a danger. No." He looked up at the windows above the alley. Had a curtain swayed?

What was Pierre looking for? What did he fear? "He's only fourteen."

"And what shall happen to my son if I am sent to the guillotine?" Pierre's voice was harsh.

I was risking another's life besides my own. I rubbed the back of my neck. I had to stop endangering people by helping others. Right after I secured Simon's papers. "You have the opportunity to save a boy, a boy whom Henri loves and would entrust to your care. Henri would ask the same of you."

He dragged his thumb across his chin as his eyes scoured the alley. "I am being watched."

I looked about but saw no one. Then again, the curtains could hide many. "By whom?"

"All my neighbors starve. Any one of them would turn me into the Committee of Public Safety for the reward money."

"We are all in danger of that."

He leaned toward me. "Maybe it is I who should report you to the Committee."

A prickling ran across the back of my neck. Papa would be so ashamed of me if I appeared before him. I would not be able to look him in the eye. I would force my own father to sentence his daughter to death. I shook off the thought. "Please, do it—for Henri."

"You are using Henri's name unfairly." He glanced about and brought his fist to his chest. "You would be sending me to my death."

I brought my face to his and whispered into his ear, "I work for my father, Antoine Fouquier-Tinville. If your name ever appears on his list of the condemned, I promise you, I'll replace it or go to the guillotine myself."

He jerked back and looked at me for the first time since I'd arrived. I stared back.

He leaned in close. "You have access to the lists?"

"Yes."

"Can you save someone?"

"I've saved many." I covered my mouth. What an idiot I was to brag about my crimes. Why did I not keep my mouth shut?

His fingers vibrated as he reached out. "My brother, Alphonse, is at la Force."

I swallowed my self-disgust. Would I never learn? I closed my eyes, inhaled, and looked into his eyes. "I will try."

His fingers wrapped around my arm as he mouthed a merci. He turned to Simon and looked him up and down. "What name, Mademoiselle?"

22

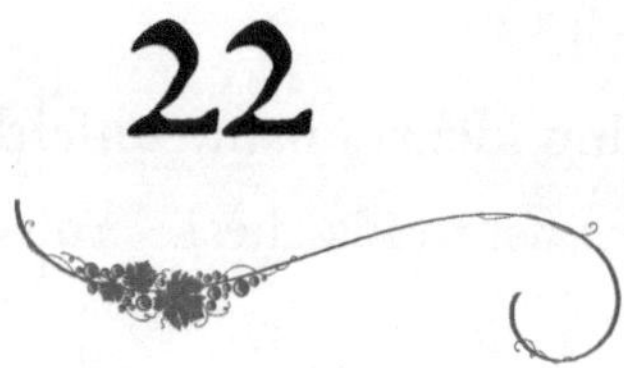

Paris
November 1793

Relieved Pierre had agreed to shelter Simon, I stood before the front door of my home, wondering if I should knock. I was much more comfortable wearing breeches and a frock coat, but I had reluctantly changed into my gown and hid my disguise in the cellar. I'd been gone for a week. Etty was probably hoping I was dead, Auguste was missing me, and my father was worrying. At least I hoped Papa was worried. I knocked.

The door opened and our maid's hands flew to her face. "Mademoiselle Geneviève!" Agathe grabbed my hands and pulled me inside. "You are safe!"

"Bonsoir, Agathe—" I stopped. Etty stood at the top of the stairs, hands on hips, scowling. I'd best offer an olive branch. "Etty, how nice to see you. Is Papa home?"

She descended, step by imperious step. "You have worried

your father terribly."

I had to get her on my side before Papa returned. I gripped my hands in prayer. "I am sad to tell you, Magdeleine passed away in prison after delivering her baby. I took the baby to a wet nurse at a farm in the country." I braced myself.

When she was within an arm's length from me, she whispered, "Salope."

A laugh burst from me. "Do you think I've been whoring for the past week?"

"If not for your father needing a wife after your mother died, I would have been a vieille fille. Do you not understand I am trying to spare you the same horrible fate?" Her hand slammed my face, knocking my head against the balustrade and sending me sprawling across the floor.

Sparks of light swirled. My cheek burned. I lay on the carpet, smelling burnt onions and stale wine. A spiral of heat wound down my back. I dug my fingers into the carpet, trying to stop the dizziness.

The door opened, cool air sweeping over me.

"Geneviève!" Papa's voice shouted. He knelt next to me, pulling me to sit up. "Are you all right?"

"She's drunk." Etty's voice sounded like how I imagined a viper might speak if it could.

First, I was a whore now a drunk? A growl worked its way up my throat. Would telling the truth cause more or less trouble? I relished having power over the pouffiasse, even for a moment. I trembled as Papa helped me stand.

Papa steadied me. "Drunk?"

I straightened my skirts. "No, Papa."

Etty backed away, the muscles in her cheeks flinching.

"I was so excited to see Maman, I slipped and fell." I smiled sweetly at her.

He caressed my cheek. "You fell on your face, by the redness of it." He turned. "Etty, get her a cool cloth." He stepped back, examining me. "You've been helping the nuns all this time?"

I nodded.

Etty glared at me, like I was something vile on the sole of her shoe. She threw her skirts to the side and left us, dragging Agathe after her.

"I took them and the children to the country, to a vineyard on the Loire River where they can tend goats and chickens and a garden. They will be safe there." I would never tell Papa about Louisa, for she had LaGarde's noble blood.

He smiled. "You have the courage of a man, ma petite. Come, you must be as hungry as I." He led me to the dining room.

The table looked enormous in the absence of the Sèvres tureen. I smiled. I'd had some effect on Etty, and I planned to have much more—the Sèvres candlesticks still stood on the mantel.

I sat across from Papa as Etty entered carrying a decanter of wine.

I wanted to drink the whole thing. I'd need courage to face the tunnels again, even with Simon. I'd need courage to face LaGarde. Dressed as a man or a woman, I doubted I could get him out of his cell—not with guards who could be waiting at every corner.

Agathe entered carrying the tureen.

I smiled so sweetly, I hoped to sicken Etty. "What kind of soup are we having this evening?"

23

 HE TORCH SIMON carried was but a speck of light in an eternity of darkness in the tunnels. Every time it flickered my heartbeat galloped. I'd shoved four candles into my binding and brought two char cloths and steel. I feared even four candles might not last until we got out of this hell.

Simon gripped my hand. "You're all wet."

"I'm sweating."

"It's cold down here, how can you be hot?"

"Keep moving." I tightened my grip on his hand. The last thing I wanted to do was spend any more time in these tunnels than I absolutely had to.

"I like living with Pierre."

I wanted to kiss him for trying to keep my mind off my fear. "Why?"

"Little Pierre treats me like a big brother. I'm important—like Henri's important to me."

I grinned but kept my voice serious. "You are important, Simon. To me, too."

"Maybe, but Little Pierre follows me around like a puppy. I always wanted a brother. I'm going to ask Maman for one when I get back."

"I hope you can go home, soon." I was panting. "You must miss her."

"Take slow breaths, Gen. I won't let anything happen to you."

I gripped a candle and tried to inhale slowly.

"We're getting close, so I have to douse the light."

"What? No!" I dug my fingernails into the candle and wrapped my hand around his.

"We don't want to be discovered." He snuffed the torch.

I closed my eyes and pressed my shoulder along the rock wall, trying to convince myself it was dark because I had my eyes shut. The idiotic plan did nothing to calm me. I opened my eyes and swallowed back a scream. My throat ached. I was such a baby.

"I think this is it." Simon stopped.

I pressed against him, panting.

"Are you all right?"

"Yes, let's get going."

"I think these stairs lead to the door to the kitchen. You stay here—"

"No. I'll go. You stay here."

He shrugged. "Okay, but if I'm wrong, and it's the dungeon, you better not scream if you see rats. The guards'll come after us."

I preferred rats over darkness. Panic swelled in me, shoving my breath out in tiny puffs.

"Keep your hand against the stairwell and feel for the door and lock. If anyone is on the other side when you open the door, stand in the door's shadow, you don't want them to see you."

My legs vibrated, but my feet wouldn't budge. I reached forward, patting my hands on the stairs. Holding onto a rock ledge, I peeled my foot from the ground and placed it onto the first step. Like a child learning to climb, I crawled up to the door and felt for the lock. My lungs ached as I sipped in the cold air. I pressed my hands together to quell their shaking and inserted the key. I'd take a quick peek around. If anyone was there, I'd force myself to close the door against the light, the beautiful, warm light. The lock clicked.

A hand gripped my arm. I slammed my hand over my mouth, fearing my scream would be heard above ground.

"Wait to see if anyone has heard," Simon warned.

I wiped my face and rested my forehead against the cold rock wall. "How long?"

"Two minutes."

Two minutes! I doubted I could wait two seconds. I counted, rapidly. I squeezed his hand. "If I get caught, you run."

"Never. Don't worry. No matter what, I'll get you out." His feet shuffled down over the steps, leaving me alone.

His kindness and belief in me made me want to weep. My legs cramped from my trying to still their shaking. Gripping the latch with both hands, I opened the door a crack. I relished the sliver of light like a starving woman feasts her eyes on bread. I blinked in the brightness. The door yawned open, and my legs could no longer hold me. I fell forward. Simon, run. Run!

"What do you want?" A woman with the stature of a wine

barrel stood before me, feet spread, hair corkscrewing around her head from beneath the edge of her mob cap. Her red hands wrapped around a huge wooden paddle she held above, ready to smash me like a fly.

I brought my shaking hands before me in prayer. "I'm looking for a printshop. Is this it?"

She aimed the paddle. "Get out of here before I add you to the soup!" She pulled the paddle back, and I dove into the darkness. The door slammed shut behind me.

"Simon?" I whimpered. "Please, Simon, don't leave me here. Come back." I sat with my back pressed against the wall. "Simon?" Please, please don't leave me. Please. Maman, help me.

"Gen! You all right?" Simon's voice was far away. I couldn't determine the direction.

"Where are you?" I shouted.

"Shhhsh!"

Sweat burned my eyes. I was going blind. I'd be in darkness forever. "Where are you?"

"Walk toward my voice."

I simpered, held my breath, clung to the wall. "Simon. I can't." My voice quavered like I was four years old. "Please, come and get me. Please."

Simon's rough hand grabbed mine, and I clasped it.

"You're shaking. Were there rats?"

I shook my head and realized how absurd that was since he couldn't see me. "Yes, yes, lots of rats, and a woman with a paddle. It was a kitchen."

"I told you to let me go. Did you see the room? Will you be able to figure out where the door is from the other side?"

I shook uncontrollably. "Get me out of here, please. We'll talk later."

He helped me up and began leading me through an eternity of hell. I started crying and hated my cowardice. "Light the torch," I begged.

"Too dangerous. I hear people in the distance."

I clutched his arm with both my hands and bit my lips against the pressure of a scream that would be heard all through Paris. I had to calm myself. Think. I tried to remember the kitchen and the memory of light warmed me.

I had no idea where the door was in that kitchen—except—there'd been a huge fireplace with a black iron pot hanging over a blinding fire across the kitchen, opposite the door.

It would be simple to find the fireplace; it would be bright and warm. If the same woman was there, I'd let LaGarde charm her. He'd have some way of getting her to show us the door to the tunnels. I'd let him worry about it. And I'd let LaGarde and Simon get me out of the tunnels.

I was so desperate to get out of the dark, I was looking forward to going home and having some of Etty's soup. I needed wine, too, to fortify myself for visiting LaGarde and convincing him of my plan. There in the dark an idea bloomed. If I did not visit LaGarde, he could not make demands of me. I had told him I'd be back when I was good and ready. And I wasn't ready yet.

I wondered if I ever would be.

24

Paris
April 1794

Etty stood at the door, buttoning Auguste's frock coat. "Do not let go of his hand for an instant." She hugged him and kissed his forehead.

"I promise." A stiff breeze whipped my skirts, making me feel less stable than when I wore breeches and a frock coat. I squinted at the sunshine glinting across the iron-picket fence and gripped Auguste's hand. "Hold tight, or the wind might whip you away."

His eyes shone with mischief. "Could the wind make me fly?"

The breeze lifted his tricorne, and I pushed it down. "Not today. But you must eat all your soup so you grow big and strong—then the wind can't lift you."

He thumped his fist to his chest. "The wind won't ever take

me from you, Gen." His cloak billowed and snapped behind him as he regripped my hand.

"I put your paper boats in my hanging pocket. The wind will make them fly like kites!"

Martin pulled the carriage in front of the house. Papa was already at the office, so why was Martin here?

He jumped down, leering at me as if I were wearing only my shift. Opening the carriage door, he asked. "Where shall I take you, Mademoiselle?"

My arm stiffened. "You risk both our lives by not calling me Citizeness."

He gave a courtly bow, which was another idiotic habit of a Royalist. "Citizeness."

"Thank you, but my father must need you. We do not."

"Your father will be in court until late this evening." He closed the carriage door. "I'll stable the horses and accompany you." He walked over to me and stood close, too close.

He smelled of stale sweat, his frock coat had too few buttons, and his blue, white, and red cockade was too big for his lapel. I resisted stepping back. We were the same height, and he was slight of frame. I would show no hint of intimidation. "No need. We're not going far and will return within the hour."

He returned to the carriage and jumped up onto the bench. "There are dangerous people about, Mademoiselle. It is not safe for you to be alone. I shall join you in a moment." He snatched the reins.

I wanted to slap him. "Your job is to be of service to my father." Dressing as a man had made me more commanding. I wouldn't have been able to refuse Martin a year earlier. "Please attend my father, Citizen."

Martin worked his jaw, then cracked the whip, and drove off.

I descended the steps. "Let's walk to the park, shall we Auguste?"

"Yes!"

I led him down the street and into a market teaming with people. I wove between stalls, redolent with odors of ripe cheeses, the briny scent of fish, and the sweet rot of cabbages. A woman tipped a huge jug and poured coffee into a wooden cup, calling out, "Café."

Curiosity yanked Auguste from stall to stall. "Gen! Look at the rats!"

I pulled him to me. People backed away from a man gripping a staff with a dead rat dangling from its point. A wicker cage tied to the man's back held half a dozen squirming, squealing vermin. He stomped his staff, calling out, "I kill the rats!"

I pulled Auguste away, out of the market. "Let's run the rest of the way, shall we?"

"Yes!"

Confident we had lost Martin, I led Auguste across the Seine, down an avenue, and around small alleyways. I was desperate for Henri's letter—it had been a year since his last. To conceal my mission, I had convinced my pouffiasse stepmother to allow me to take Auguste to the Luxembourg Gardens. Once far from the house, I planned to walk Auguste to Pierre's printshop, where I hoped Henri's letter awaited.

Breathless, I stopped and bent to Auguste's level. "You run very fast!"

"I could beat you!" Sweat beaded on his upper lip.

"I believe you."

He pulled a breadcrust from beneath his cloak. "Can we feed the fish after we sail the boats?"

I wanted to squeeze his plump red cheeks and grant him anything. But I was eager to read Henri's words, to let them play in my mind, to feel his hands through the paper. I wanted to retrieve the letter before we went to the gardens. Now that Henri knew his letters were safe from my father's eyes, he'd feel free to write of his love.

"Can you keep a secret?" I whispered.

Auguste pinched his lips.

"Papa asked me to pick up a document for him, but we can tell no one. After I get it, we can feed the fish for as long as you like."

"Let's race!" he cried, yanking my arm.

Holding hands, we ran through Faubourg Saint-Marcel, the stench of animal excrement and decaying flesh of the tanner's vats sitting over the river like fog. Wanting to avoid attention, I slowed to a walk as we turned onto a boulevard where filthy boys dressed in tattered breeches and tunics shivered with outstretched hands. I imagined Henri as a boy Auguste's age, trying to survive in these stinking streets. We arrived and entered the stuffy printshop. I hoped Pierre recognized me— he'd never seen me dressed as a woman.

"What's that rusty smell?" Auguste grabbed his nose.

"Ink. Printers use an ink made from iron and oak galls."

"The air's sticky."

"Does it smell like the books in Papa's library?"

He cocked his head, thinking. "I guess."

Pierre approached. "How may I help you, Citizeness?"

I winked, hoping he'd recognize me, but his face showed only confusion. Leaning close so that Auguste could not hear me, I whispered, "Might you have a letter for Jean Detré?" I mouthed, From Henri Detré?

A corner of his mouth lifted. He reached into a cubbyhole and offered a letter.

I reached for it, resisting kissing it, before I thrust it into my hanging pocket. "Merci."

"De rien, Citizeness. Please let me know how our friend is faring."

I led Auguste out onto the street and stopped before the printshop window. A prickling crossed my neck. It couldn't be a warning. It was the chill wind. My fingers curled around the paper. It would take but a moment to quickly read it, and I could savor it all afternoon. A cloud scuttled across the sun, darkening the street. Did I dare? I let go of Auguste's hand, reached into my hanging pocket, broke the seal, unfolded the paper, and brought it out from between the folds of my cloak.

"There's Martin!" Auguste called out.

I nearly let go of the paper as I twisted around to see Martin striding down the street toward us. I folded and creased the paper as if I were making a boat and slipped it under my cloak and into my hanging pocket. My arms thrummed. If he knew it was a letter, he'd tell my pouffiasse stepmother and, because Etty couldn't control my receiving letters, she'd have me married off within a week.

Martin pulled his ear. "Your maman insisted I accompany you."

He always pulled his ear when he lied. He'd obviously followed me. Why? I had ignored my instincts and let my guard down. Stupid of me. I'd never let that happen again. The print-shop's bitter stickiness coated my tongue. I'd been too eager for Henri's letter.

"I told you we didn't need you," I snapped.

He tipped his head, as if accepting my chastisement, and yanked his ear again. "Your maman was so concerned for your safety, Mademoiselle, I could not refuse her, could I?"

The last thing Etty was concerned with was my safety. But he knew I wouldn't check with her.

He thrust his hand toward Auguste. "I'll take you to the park."

Before I could speak, Auguste pulled his hand to his chest. "Gen and I will go. You go home."

I pressed my lips against a laugh.

Martin crouched down. "But your maman—"

"We go to the park, alone." Auguste stomped his foot. "You go home now."

I wanted to pick him up and kiss him. What a confident man my brother will make.

Martin backed off. "Very well, Monsieur. I'll follow at a discreet distance."

Auguste looked up at me. "What's discreet?"

"It means he's spying on us." I took Auguste's hand, turned, and headed for the Luxemburg. Maybe I couldn't control Martin, but at least he'd heard what I thought of him. I'd be extremely cautious and never let my guard down again. I couldn't read Henri's letter, for Martin would report every-thing to Etty. I plunged my hand into my hanging pocket and felt the warmth of Henri's words in the paper.

Etty greeted our return without the slightest bit of suspicion or curiosity. She knelt to unbutton Auguste's frock coat and listened to his animated tales of the frenzied fish and how far the paper boats had sailed and the sparrow that had fallen from a branch. Because she didn't ask about the printshop, I knew she hadn't sent Martin after us.

My anxiety over Martin's interest in me made my mouth sour. Remembering his gaze burned my skin, but I suspected he had a reason, other than lust, to follow me. He'd seen me commit two crimes: dressing as a man and harboring clergy. He could inform on me for both and receive a handsome reward from the Committee of Public Safety. How ironic that a government group dedicated to safety could be so dangerous.

Martin could also tell my father of my adventures. A sticky feeling slid down my back. Martin was getting too close, like a spider weaving a web. I had to misdirect him.

After kissing Auguste good night, I joined Papa in the dining room where he awaited his meal. I ate quickly, discussed nothing, and counted the minutes until I could excuse myself with politeness that would not raise their suspicion. I scurried to my chamber, closed the curtains, retrieved a hidden candle stub and lighted it. I pulled Henri's letter from my hanging pocket.

Dear Geneviève,

*I hope this letter arrives at your new address and you may read
it in privacy. Please send my warm regards to my friend.*

I am an oncle! Joliette delivered a boy, Guillaume, named after his father. He brings us joy, a greater joy I've never known.

I apologize for my delay in writing. Late in the summer, I contracted yellow fever, requiring me to convalesce for months, during which time I was weak and my vision blurred. The fever swept the city, and I am grateful to be alive, due in no small part to being nursed by the African woman Joliette hired to help care for Guillaume. We had agreed that should one of us fall ill, the other would take Guillaume to the country. Joliette kept her son safe by traveling north to New York.

After I recovered, Joliette and Guillaume returned. I have resumed my activities with the Quakers. I deeply wish America would outlaw slavery. The Africans live through unimaginable horrors, and abolitionists work to assist them in gaining their freedom. Much like women of France have been denied an education, the Africans are forbidden to read. This must rile your blood; I remember your passionate nature.

Working toward emancipating enslaved Africans gives me great purpose and enables me to learn much about laws of both America and France. I hope to become a lawyer in both countries.

Geneviève, knowing you are safe at the château would quiet my concerns for you. Please go there and write me when you arrive. My mother expects you.

Until I can once again embrace you, I remain yours,

Henri

Merci God, for saving Henri. I pressed the letter to my chest, remembering his hot hand cupping my breast, his thumb circling my nipple. Heat flooded me as excitement as intense as the first moment he'd touched me rushed through me.

He remembered my passionate nature. He was concerned for my safety and wanted me to go to his château. He would not urge me so, if he did not love me. He will be so pleased when he learns I've met his maman—and that she likes me.

I kissed the letter and fell back upon the bed. Henri loves me. He loves me, he loves me, he loves me.

Now it would be much easier to write of my love for him. His maman had told me I'd make a loving mother. I hoped she would tell him.

25

Paris
July 1794

Papa's steps were slow and heavy. He did not greet me as he sat.

My hands shook as I poured coffee for him. I had no idea how I would talk to him of his condemning so many people. I only knew I had to.

He spooned confiture across a piece of bread. "You are up early." Dark circles surrounded his eyes and flaps of skin folded over his jabot. He'd lost weight.

I pressed my shaking fingers against the tablecloth. He was usually more receptive to me when I was caring, so I acted as Etty would. I poured hot milk into the coffee, added two teaspoons of sugar, and stirred. "I wish to speak with you, Papa, and the carriage to the office is the only place you are not working." I offered the cup.

He took a sip. "Let us go." He drank the remainder, picked up his tricorne, and led the way to the carriage.

I folded my shawl over my trembling arm and followed. If he didn't agree to stop the slaughter, I hoped to convince him to at least slow the pace and send fewer to their deaths.

He got in and sat opposite me, placing his tricorne on the bench beside him.

The horsehair stuffing pricked through my gown scratching the back of my legs. I inhaled, hoping I'd not stumble over the words I wanted to say. "I attended yesterday's session."

"That is what you wish to discuss?"

The carriage jolted. "The proceedings. I want to understand the laws better."

He closed his eyes, as he always did when he was collecting patience for me.

The clattering of the wheels against the cobbles reminded me of the shouting crowd at the trial. The image of the condemned women's faces swarmed me, and I inhaled against the pressure building in my chest.

"The nuns of Compiègne." I clasped my hands in prayer. "You sent all to the guillotine, even the novices."

He let out a gruff sigh. "Those Carmelites refused to take the oath and obey the law of the Civil Constitution of the Clergy." He rubbed his eyes and looked out at the river as we rode over the bridge. "Refusing to take the oath is proof of counter-revolutionary activities."

The carriage swayed, and I pitched forward in my seat, leaning toward him. "But you did not allow witnesses to appear in their defense."

"Since the Law of 22 Prairial, and according to Articles Five and Seven, defenses are suppressed."

I gripped the bench cushion. "But you did not allow them to speak in their own defense."

"I did not disallow it. It is the job of Coffinhal and Dumas to advise them. As they were found guilty by the jury, I applied the law. That is my responsibility as Public Prosecutor. What do you not understand?"

The flash of anger in his eyes shamed me. I smoothed the blue silk of my gown. I did not understand how those innocent women, who dedicated their lives to helping those less fortunate, could be guilty of anything but living in poverty. I searched his face for a sign of compassion—and found not a trace.

He pressed his index finger between his gloved fingers, stretching each finger to smooth the leather. "Etty gave me good news last night." His lips smiled, but his eyes held back a secret. "She has found an appropriate suitor for you, who will consider the modest dowry I have allotted."

The air left my chest like the whoosh of a fleeing bird. I supposed a cow would fetch more than my hand. Etty had been far too kind to me of late. Now I understood why.

I gripped my reticule. I would not be diverted. "Did you know the Carmelite nuns sang *Salve Regina* as each faced the guillotine, until the last voice was silenced? It is said tears streaked even Sanson's cheeks." I had made up Sanson's reaction, but surely the executioner was moved by such faith. He couldn't be as heartless as my own father seemed to be.

"He is the son of a deputy and studying to be a lawyer."

"The executioner?"

"The suitor." Papa glared at me, making me feel like a stupid four-year-old.

"Papa, when I visited the woman, whom I knew when we were students at the Abbey, at Bicêtre, I saw a boy of about six years of age. Surely, Papa, a little boy, the age of Auguste, cannot be an enemy of the State."

A crimson rash spread across Papa's cheeks. "He is part of the conspiracy. Parents use their children to pass traitorous messages. He is as guilty as the parents."

"He is a child, Papa. Could Auguste be guilty of such a crime?"

"Of course not. He is my son."

"And I am your daughter. Did you not see my face when you condemned the nuns?"

He waved me away. "You would take the oath."

"Would I?" My words escaped before I had time to think. I had to convince him, stop him. "Papa, you try people in batches, like a cook selecting bundles of carrots for stew. Do you not see each human being as a creature with a soul?"

"The trying of people in groups make trials more efficient." He punched the bench. "Each of those souls has committed a crime against the Républic and is deserving of punishment."

"Must punishment always mean death?"

He rubbed his forehead. Light blue veins throbbed at his temples. He sighed and stared out the window.

My father was a butcher of human souls and the Tribunal an abattoir.

I was already sorry for what I was about to say, but I had no other choice. "What would Maman think of your condemnations of thousands?" I whispered.

He tipped up his head, gazing down his nose at me. "Your maman would know that I am an Executive Agent of the Revolutionary Tribunal. It is my job to follow and uphold the laws of France." His jowls trembled. "If I did not, what would become of me? What would become of my family? And you, my dear daughter?" He thrust a finger at me. "You are a clerk in my office. You, more than anyone, should understand the laws—the laws you said you wished to know more about by clerking!"

"I understand the laws, Papa. It's just that there have been so many deaths. Orphans crowd the streets calling out for their dead parents. How can thousands of children dying of starvation be good for France? What if Auguste were one of them?"

His eyes glinted in the gray morning light.

Please, God, let him reflect upon his condemnations. I, alone, could not convince him. I was useless.

He shook his head. "All are guilty of counter-revolutionary acts. Of which you are guilty by questioning the laws."

Did he know I'd replaced more than one hundred names? I swallowed against the coffee sitting in my throat. "No, Papa. My work supports you and the République."

"Let us hope the suitor believes that." He picked up his tricorne. "As my daughter you should not doubt me, you should believe and trust in me—without question. I have been overly patient with you. You disappoint me greatly. I fear I must dismiss you as clerk."

"No!" I grasped his hand, but he shook me off. "Papa, I

only wanted to understand why so many are sentenced to the guillotine. You've explained the laws thoroughly. Articles Five and Seven. I am eager to continue my efforts in supporting you and the République."

He stared out the window. I'd pushed him too far. His eyes were as cold as flint. I pressed my fist against my bosom. "Please Papa, let me prove I am a true patriot."

Still staring out the window, he ran his finger between his neck and cravat. "You may continue to clerk until you are married, which I trust will be soon. Etty believes it can be within the month. She has invited the suitor to dine with you on the next day of rest. You will behave as a proper lady and be polite." He spat the words through tight lips.

My tongue dried. I pushed the words. "I look forward to meeting the suitor, Papa. In the meantime, I will do my duty to you and my country."

"Your duty is to please the suitor and accept his proposal, should he extend it." He grabbed his hat and readied himself to get up.

The carriage stopped and, before Martin could jump down, Papa kicked open the door, got out, stormed across the square, under the archway, and into the Châtelet.

I sat, my chemise clinging to my sweating back. I'd not touched his heart in the least. He would send just as many batches of people to their deaths this afternoon as he had the day before.

What was I thinking? I rubbed my eyes. I was a coward. The moment Papa threatened to dismiss me, I backed down and rushed to accept his explanation. Was I insane to doubt my father? The Tribunal would condemn him if he didn't do his job, of that I was certain. Would the Tribunal come after Etty and my brothers? And me?

Outside the open door, rows of red, yellow, purple, and blue flowers lay on a wicker basket held by an old vendeuse who walked across the square, singing out, "Les fleurs!" She was Maman's favorite seller. I pulled my reticule strings. I'd buy violets for Maman. They would cheer me.

Martin appeared next to the door, offering his hand. His eyes were merry, like he was delighted in my embarrassment. "Mademoiselle?"

"Citizeness," I growled. Ignoring his hand, I stepped down. My legs wobbled. I pressed my toes into my shoes, searching for secure footing. I no longer trusted my father. I no longer trusted myself. I took a step.

Martin's hand steadied me. "Are you quite well, Mademoiselle?"

I shook off his hand. "Quite. Thank you."

His eyes shone. "Certainement, Mademoiselle."

I didn't trust Martin. But I did trust myself not to attend dinner with a suitor. Etty would be most pleased to entertain him and praise my graces for me.

I had to replace more than two names on every list and save as many innocents as possible, while I still held my position as clerk.

26

Paris
July 1794

"A BEAUTIFUL DAY, MADEMOISELLE." Martin held
the carriage door open, stretched out his hand, and smiled a
too-big smile.

I tied my bonnet ribbons under my chin. "Indeed, Citizen."

He stood so close, I wanted to push him away. But he could
report me for dressing as a man. I didn't know exactly what
he wanted from me, but I knew I wouldn't give him anything.
I gripped his hand tightly hoping he would back away, but
instead my grip encouraged him and, as I stepped down, his
arm encircled my waist and guided me a few steps. A damp
cold crawled up my back.

"You are looking especially pretty today, Mademoiselle."

"Merci, Citizen." I forced a polite smile while wanting to
shake his presence from me like a dog shakes water from its

fur. I hurried across the square toward the Châtelet's archway. My head ached. I'd not yet found the name of Pierre's brother on any list. Perhaps that was good.

"Your father has a long docket today," Martin called out after me.

A prickling ran down my back. How did he know anything of my father's work? I pretended not to hear him and hurried under the archway and into the building.

"Gen! Gen!" I recognized Simon's voice and searched among the people hurrying about the shadows of the huge hall. Simon stood below the winding staircase. I forced myself to walk slowly, calmly. He'd not be here unless there was trouble.

His face was pinched, his hands tugging his tunic.

I pressed my hand below my ribs, forcing myself to calm. "What is it?"

"I know who's been watching Pierre." His gaze darted at the people passing behind me.

"Who?"

"I saw him watching from around the corner when they came and arrested Pierre."

"What?" I lunged forward and grabbed his arm. He looked up at me, tears about to spill from his dark eyes. "When?"

"Early this morning. They took him." His voice cracked. He dragged his sleeve across his eyes. "Pierre told us to be calm, not to resist or fight, so they wouldn't destroy the printshop."

A heaviness sat in me, pulling at my chest. "Who was it?"

"Your groom."

I jerked. "How do you know?"

Simon kept his eyes on the crowd. "I followed him after they arrested Pierre. I didn't know he stopped in front of your house until you came out." He sucked in a breath. "After you got in the carriage I followed and ran in here when he stopped."

I pressed my lips together until my mouth ached. I knew I shouldn't have trusted Martin when he was so helpful with the Sisters and children. But what could I have done differently? I couldn't have rescued them without his assistance. He'd seemed happy to do it; like we were working together for the same cause. He'd even given me the pistol. Why hadn't I pressed him when I asked where he'd gotten it? I knew then he was doing illegal things, but I hadn't wanted another problem to solve.

I rubbed my forehead. Why hadn't I questioned him?

I looked around, fearing I'd find Martin sporting his smug expression among the men in the entry hall. The echo of his words, *Your father has a long docket today*, taunted me. Bastard. He knows Pierre will appear before my father today. I had to get that list.

"Gen?"

I shook my head and looked back at Simon.

"Pierre's son…" Simon looked like he might burst into tears.

My chest burned. Pierre had feared for his son. I had promised Pierre. Why, why, why had I risked his life? The answer stood before me. To save Simon's life. I reached out and rubbed his arm. "Yes?"

"Little Pierre screamed for his Papa when they took him away." A tear overflowed and trickled down his cheek.

"Was he with his mother?"

Simon nodded. "But he screamed. It was terrible. He's only six."

I had promised Pierre I'd save him, and now I had to make good on it. The list wouldn't be ready until tomorrow, if then.

It could take a week or a month. "I'm going to them, now." I dug into my reticule for one of the louis d'ors I'd stolen from Papa and pressed it into Simon's hand. "Go to the Auberge Mouton Blanc, around the corner from Saint Merri."

He nodded. "I used to live near there."

"Get a lodging room and wait there. I'll bring Pierre's wife and son."

"What are you going to do?"

I wanted to say, Kill Martin, but instead, I whispered, "I'm going to get Madame Lochot and her son. Martin could turn them in, too."

His eyes darkened. "I wish I had Madame Bourran's walking stick."

"Where is it?"

"At Pierre's shop."

"I'll get it." I patted his back and sent him out into the sunshine.

I waited for a few minutes, looked about for Martin, and then slipped out the servants' entrance. Twisting my reticule strings, I imagined wringing Martin's neck with my bare hands.

27

Paris
July 1794

I OPENED THE PRINTSHOP door and stood quietly waiting. Clerks moved about in the shop, working like Pierre was on an errand and would return soon. I hoped no one would recognize me. They could turn me in to avenge Pierre's arrest, and I wouldn't blame them.

An elderly clerk, with gnarled, blackened fingers looked up.

"Where can I find Madame Lochot?"

He lifted his eyes to the ceiling. "Top floor."

As I headed for the stairs, I spotted Madame Bourran's cane in the corner. I picked it up like it was mine, twisted it, and the blade clicked. I reset the blade. Simon needed this sign of manhood, to remind him of his own courage, and he could use it to defend himself and Pierre's family. I wished I had one myself.

I climbed the stairs to the top floor and knocked on the only door. There were no cooking smells, no sounds. "Madame Lochot, I am a friend of Henri Detré," I whispered.

The door opened and sunlight spilled across a boy, his arms clinging to a petite blonde woman, his face buried in her skirts. The woman held the door and looked around me and then at me. "Where's Henri?"

"In America," I whispered. She began to push the door, but I slid inside and closed it.

She backed up, her thin arms wrapped around her son, her tear-stained face creased with worry. She wore no cap, no jewelry, no shawl. She shivered in the heat.

I leaned on the cane, like I needed it and to appear unthreatening. "Henri asked me to help you. That is why I am here."

She lifted her chin. "Can you get my husband out of prison?"

"Maman!" The boy lifted his arms and gripped her shoulders, nearly pulling her over.

"Shh, Papa will be back soon." She rubbed his back. The boy sobbed. His auburn curls glinted in the sunlight.

"Madame, the man who reported your husband, could report you. You're not safe here."

Her shoulders sagged. "No matter. Where would we go without Pierre?"

"He would not want you in prison. He'd want you to be safe."

She jerked her head toward me. "Why should I trust you?"

"Because I am Henri's friend, and I give you my word of honor."

She smiled for a moment. "Pierre never accepted help from anyone, except when Henri brought bread, when there was none to be had. We might have starved without Henri's help."

Her eyes were so filled with sorrow, I looked away. A small table and three unmatched wooden chairs. A cold fireplace. Broken metal letters from the printshop littered the mantel. Worn damask curtains hung on the windows and before a doorway that I figured led to a bedroom. I wondered if Pierre's shop had been successful, for the money he made on false identity papers apparently had not been spent on luxuries or food.

She cupped her hand around her son's head. "We cannot leave without Pierre."

"I understand. But until he is released, you can't stay here. I've sent Simon ahead with money for lodgings at an inn in the Marais. I will take you there now, where you can wait safely until Pierre is released. Then you can all go to Henri's château."

She tilted her head.

"Madame, do you know that Henri has a château on the Loire? He gave me money to help his friends and told me to take them there—if they were in danger. Henri would help you now if he were here. Let me help you. Pack a small bundle of things and come with me now."

She remained straight and stiff. "What's your name?"

"Geneviève."

"Geneviève, what?"

I smiled, hoping I looked confident. "Knowing only my first name will be much safer for you and your son."

She bent and kissed Little Pierre's head. He whimpered. "I've no other choice, do I?"

I shook my head. "Pierre would want you both to be safe."

She began placing clothing in a pile on the table.

At least I could keep Pierre's family safe until I could get him out of prison. I'd have to be on guard against Martin. He'd just used Pierre to show me he had power over me. I shook my trembling hands.

First, I had to get Pierre's name off that list. Then I'd worry about getting him out of la Conciergerie. LaGarde wouldn't be happy when I told him we'd have to rescue another prisoner while I was getting him out, but LaGarde would have to help me. None of us had a choice.

28

Paris
July 24, 1794

IMBERTON STOOD AT his desk, straight and unbending as a plane tree, scribbling away at a long document.

Every morning I arrived earlier and earlier, only to find all thirty clerks already at their desks. If I were not my father's daughter, I suspected I would be reprimanded for my tardiness.

I peeled off my gloves, placed them in my reticule and stored it under my desk. I scanned the first paper on the pile atop my desk, the list of names of prisoners at la Conciergerie. My breath caught. Second name from the end, Pierre Lochot.

The room closed in around me. I pressed my fingers to my eyes until sparks of light flurried. I opened my eyes and reread. Pierre's name was written in a different hand and bolder than the rest. Was that on purpose? Did someone know to look for his name? I scanned the room. Did anyone suspect me of changing the lists? I searched my memory of names I had collected at the cemetery, but all I saw were the faces of Pierre's wife and son. I had to replace Pierre's name with a similar one.

Imberton appeared before me and cocked an eyebrow. "Is something wrong, Citizeness?"

"No." I picked up the quill.

"I wish to review your work today. Bring every document and its original to me as you finish it. Do not give anything to the delivery clerk."

My corset was so tight. "Has my father changed protocol?"

"Spelling errors have been noticed by the Tribunal. It is now my responsibility to ensure those mistakes do not happen again. Get to work."

I took the blade from under the inkwell and sharpened the quill. I never misspelled anything. Were other clerks required to give Imberton their work? I glanced around the room. Armand placed a finished document in his basket, picked up another, and began copying. Denis wrote with a fury, as if a deadline approached. Neither brought their documents to Imberton. A delivery clerk wove through the aisles between the desks, collecting documents from everyone's basket but mine.

I watched Imberton as he scanned a paper and frowned. He was setting a trap. If I could delay copying the guillotine list by a day, I could make two copies this evening, after Imberton left, and burn the original. But how could I hide the original list from Imberton?

I began returning the blade to its place when a loud slam of a door made me jump, and I sliced my finger. I pressed a blotting cloth around the wound, but the nick continued to bleed.

I had no other choice but to hide the list. Holding the cloth against my finger, I lifted the sheaf of fresh paper from the shelf under my desk and placed it atop the guillotine list. I slid a piece of fresh paper onto my desk. Keeping the guillotine list at the bottom of the sheaf, I returned the fresh paper to the shelf.

I took the next document, a list of witnesses, and began copying it. I scanned the room, watching for anyone else bringing their work to Imberton but spotted none.

I brought the first document and my copy to Imberton. The people on that list weren't in danger…yet.

He glanced at it. "This document is not urgent. Where is the guillotine list?"

I blinked. "I did not see such a list in my documents."

"I placed it at the top myself." He grabbed the pile and quickly reviewed page after page.

"Perhaps another clerk copied it?"

He shook his head. "I put it right here not thirty minutes ago." He glared at me. "Did you move it?"

I tipped my head. If he found the list at the bottom of my fresh paper, would he dismiss me? Worse, would he tell Papa? "Maybe you assigned it to another clerk. Or the delivery clerk already collected it?" I walked to Armand's desk. "Did you copy the guillotine list?" I asked.

Armand scratched his jaw with his ink-stained finger. "No."

I hurried to every desk, questioning each clerk, until I reached the end of the row.

Imberton stood before me, his face red against his frayed white jabot. "Return to your desk." His heels clacked down the corridor toward the Court.

I rubbed at the ink staining my middle finger where a callus had grown. I could not let Pierre die. I should have prepared for this. Was there another original list held by my father? If Imberton requested it, my father would know I'd caused a problem. Acid rose in my throat. I copied another document, dutifully placing it and the original on Imberton's desk.

The clacking of Imberton's heels made my hand jerk, spraying ink. I stared at my work.

He stopped before me, holding up the guillotine list.

"I'm so glad you found it." I hoped I sounded convincing and reached for the paper. "Where was it?"

He snatched it away. "You will no longer be copying these lists, Citizeness." He took it to his desk and began writing, his finger inching down the paper, name by name.

Bastard. A drop of blood from my cut splattered on my document.

I gripped my quill. Damn Martin. Why had he turned Pierre in? It couldn't be just the money; my father paid Martin well. Greed? Was Martin using me to get more people to report? Papa might fire Martin if I concocted a story about Martin's improper behavior. But Martin would be paid far more if he informed on me to the Committee of Public Safety.

I had promised Pierre I'd get his name off the list or go to the guillotine myself. The witnesses' names I'd written blurred on the paper before me. I had to get Pierre out of prison. There was no other way to save him. And I had to, for his son's sake.

I'd have to get Pierre out of la Conciergerie the next night when I got LaGarde out. LaGarde wouldn't be happy about the added risk, but as a noble of the sword, he'd be happy to use his rapier to skewer Martin.

I dipped the quill. Blood had seeped through the blotting

cloth. I imagined writing Martin's name in blood. I felt no remorse about my desire, as any other lady would. But I was a woman who impersonated a man, and I imagined a man would feel just as vengeful.

29

WANTING TO MAKE certain none of the guards—who knew me as the man who visited LaGarde—would recognize me, I pulled my hair up into my bonnet and lowered my neckline. After tucking a few sous in my reticule for a bribe to see Pierre, I hurried to la Conciergerie. I had to reassure Pierre I'd get his name off the guillotine list.

A long line of visitors crowded the stone chamber before the gate, unusual for it was not a day of rest. I whispered to a woman standing before me, "Why are there so many people here today?"

"You haven't heard? Le Proscecuteur," she spat the word out like a bad seed, "has stepped up executions. We all want to see our loved ones before they're headless, don't we?"

My heartbeat thundered. I prayed, Please, Papa, don't send

him today. I knotted the strings of my reticule around my fingers, silently repeating my plea.

My hands trembling, I stood before the guards.

The same, yellow-eyed guard stuck out his dirty hand. "Papers."

I presented them and pitched my voice high. "Lochot. I'm here to see Pierre Lochot."

The guard checked his list. "Not here."

"There must be some mistake." I reached into my reticule for the sous. "He was brought here yesterday."

"And he was taken out this morning."

"To where?" I pressed my hand against my pounding heart.

"Where else? Madame la guillotine! Next!" he yelled.

A floating sensation pulled me from the room. I fell back, grasping at the damp wall as I slid onto the stone floor. I lay there, my lips and nose numb, a roaring filling my ears, darkness pressing around me.

"Citizeness!"

Something stung my face. Who was slapping me? Where was I? A crowd of people hovered above.

A woman with a white lace-trimmed bonnet framing her face like a delicate halo pulled me up and leaned me against a wall.

"Where am I?"

"La Conciergerie," she whispered. "You fainted. I am sorry, Madame."

How had I gotten here? An image of Pierre rushed at me. I blinked and blinked, but he remained before me, his face ablaze with anger as he shouted, *My son. My son.*

I pressed my cheek against the cool stone. I had promised

him. My chest felt like a boulder was crushing it.

A hand touched my back. "Shall I help you outside, Citizeness?"

I looked up and quickly turned my face away as I balanced myself against the wall. It was the young guard who often led me to LaGarde's cell. I could not let him recognize me.

I spoke in a high, breathless, feminine voice. "No, merci." I rushed for the street, people and sounds spinning as I ran.

At the Quai de l'Horloge, I fell against a tree. The fighting currents of the Seine dizzied me. My hands trembled as I pulled my shawl to my nose, trying to block the stench of rotting flesh and offal from the abattoirs upriver.

The prisoners inhaled this putrid miasma every time they walked out into the courtyard for a breath of fresh air. It was a wonder they all didn't die while waiting to be guillotined.

An ache throbbed in my chest. I had broken my promise to Pierre. My arms hung useless. It was my fault. I shouldn't have enlisted him to save Simon. I couldn't save Pierre just like I couldn't save Magdeleine. Why did I even try?

Across the river, the black turrets of the Châtelet pierced the deep blue sky. Why, Papa? Why was it so important to put a man to death so quickly? What law told you to do that? If there was such a law, it was an insane one. And you're more insane for obeying it.

Martin's words filled my head. *Your father has a long docket today!* He'd been taunting me. If not for Martin, Pierre would still be alive. I stomped my foot in the dirt. Damn you, Martin. If I were a man, I'd kill you. Maybe I'd kill you anyway. Why shouldn't a woman exact revenge just like a man? It would be a delicious satisfaction. But it would not bring Pierre back.

I dragged my hand over my face. How would I tell Madame Lochot?

The shadow cast by la Conciergerie chilled me. I had to get LaGarde out. Imberton suspected me, and he could review every document I had copied and discover every name I'd substituted.

LaGarde could take Simon and Pierre's family to the château, and I wouldn't have to worry about anyone anymore. LaGarde might relish helping me kill Martin, too.

I couldn't tell Madame Lochot, yet. I'd tell her after Simon helped me get LaGarde out. I kicked at dried leaves that flew up and scurried away with the breeze. I'd have to face the darkness of the tunnels—again. But that might be easier than facing LaGarde. I had not visited him in months. He would be furious, livid. But I would get him out.

30

Paris
July 25, 1794

L aGARDE PACED HIS cell like the trapped bull he was.

"I told you to bring her to me," he snapped, jerking his head toward me.

I shrank inside my frock coat and gripped the brim of my tricorne. "Her hiding place was no longer safe. I put her safety before your request."

His shoulders dropped. "You were right to do so."

His voice was so soft; did I hear correctly? "I moved her out of the city, to the country," I whispered.

"Who cares for her?" His eyes watered, washing away his anger.

"Former nuns who cared for me when I was a child. I trust them."

"Merci." Anger sparked in his eyes again. "When are you getting me out of here?"

I crept close to him, trying not to breathe in his body odor. "Can you get out of this cell and into the kitchen?"

"For a price."

I swallowed. I had no more resources. Nothing to sell.

"I have the money." His breath was hot on my neck.

I dared not ask. There wasn't time. "When do the guards change?"

"You think like a man." He grinned.

"Is that a compliment?"

His eyes sparked. "They change after delivering the moldy bread they serve as dinner."

He had complimented me. I drew my boot through the dirty straw. "If I visit you before the dinner, the second guard, who accompanies me out, will not have seen me arrive."

His smile broadened.

"When I call the guard to allow me to leave—"

He interrupted. "I will overtake him, exchange clothes and, dressed as the guard, lead you out. But, once I pass the main guard room, I'll take us both down to the kitchen." He gnawed at his thumbnail. "Can you act the part of a salope, so the guards think I'm taking you for a pleasant interlude and allow us some privacy?"

Damn. He'd come up with my plan. But letting him think it was his idea would give me more control. "My stepmother already considers me one, so it shouldn't be too difficult."

His face grew serious. "She does not know you at all, does she?"

I shifted my weight and shrugged.

"Stupid woman, your stepmother."

I laughed. "You know her very well."

He raked his hair. "You'll arrive as a man, but leave as a woman?"

I nodded.

"You know the tunnels from the kitchen?"

"From the other side."

"We'll have only a few minutes to find the door."

"It's across from the fireplace." I hoped. Sweat dripped from the binding wrapped around my breasts down my belly. If we didn't find it, we'd both be trapped. The guards would not take us to appear before my father. We'd be added to the batch for execution the next morning.

31

THE NEXT DAY, the yellow-eyed guard sat picking at his teeth with a piece of straw. I stood before him, trembling in my frock coat and breeches.

I'd brought an entire bottle of wine, just for him. But I had to make him work for it, otherwise, he'd suspect I was up to something. "LaGarde."

"Not here."

Same game. "You say that every time I visit, Citizen. And I always ask, 'Have you a cup?' I'm feeling generous today." I rested the bottle on the desk. "I've brought a whole bottle, just for you."

He grinned and waggled his fingers.

"First, call the guard who takes me to LaGarde."

He jangled his brass ring of keys, and a new guard came from around the corner. A small young man with a rash reddening his face appeared. He fidgeted like a cornered mouse. If he were the guard who showed up to let me out, LaGarde would never fit in his uniform. My binding tightened as I tried to inhale. If the new guard showed up, would he remember I was a man when I left as a woman? Not if LaGarde knocked him out. And that would be the easy part. Where would we get another uniform to fit LaGarde?

The old guard belched and drummed his fingers on the desk.

I slammed the bottle on the desk before him, like I was angry. "Enjoy, Citizen. It's a very fine vintage."

"Who are you here to see?" the new guard asked.

"Louis LaGarde," I pronounced it clearly, precisely, seriously.

This time, we walked down a spiral staircase not up. I began to object, but I stopped myself. If I protested, he'd realize I knew where I was going, which might make him suspicious. LaGarde had charmed the guards into telling him where the kitchen was. If they'd changed LaGarde's cell, how would we know how to get there?

Sweat collected on my brow. I counted every step and memorized every turn. LaGarde would rely on my remembering: down one flight, no two flights, straight, past a large, overcrowded cell stinking of rot, down a corridor of wooden doors, right, up a flight of spiral stairs, left into a corridor, fifth cell on the right.

The guard unlocked the door. I passed him a few assignats and whispered, "Merci," as I entered.

He nodded and closed the door behind me.

A man crouched in the corner. He was not LaGarde.

"Guard!" I screamed. "Guard! This is not the man I wish to visit. Come back!" My voice was high, screeching.

The man in the corner looked up and grinned. He knew I was a woman.

Not taking my eyes off him, I kicked my boot heel against the door. "Guard. This is the wrong prisoner!" I kicked and kicked like a terrified horse. "Guard!"

The man crept on his knees toward me, his filthy hand grabbing for my leg. I brought my knee to my chest and kicked forward, hitting him in the jaw and sending him sprawling on his back. He let out a grunt, rolled over, and pulled himself onto his knees. He licked his lips.

I kicked and pounded on the door. Keeping my eyes on the man, I clutched the doorframe to put more power into my leg for the next kick to his head. I had to knock him out before he had the chance to overpower me. "Guard!"

A pounding filled my ears. Other prisoners were banging against their doors and shouting. Perhaps they were trying to help me; perhaps they were trying to drown out my cries so the guard would not hear me. I would become their entertainment. The prisoner crept on his belly toward me, one arm protecting his head.

I reached into my waistcoat and pulled out the pistol Martin had given me. I inhaled, steadied my wide stance, pulled back the hammer, and aimed.

At the click of the hammer, the prisoner looked up, fear flooding his eyes. He backed into the corner, trembling.

A jangling cut through the prisoners' pounding. The key

grated in the lock. I gently released the hammer and shoved the pistol into my waistcoat. The door opened.

I pushed my way past the guard. I had to act like a man. I slammed my fist into his shoulder, knocking him back. "That's not LaGarde!"

"Pardon." His face blushed crimson. "It's my first day. I'll take you there now, but I must find out where he is."

My head spun. I wanted to tell him how to get to LaGarde's cell—he was waiting, and he'd be furious—but I kept quiet and memorized every twist and turn of the maze. After endless turns and retracing of steps, we arrived. Before the guard unlocked the door, I looked through the metal grate and shouted, "Is that you, LaGarde?"

"Who else would inhabit these luxurious surroundings?" LaGarde growled.

His sarcasm made me want to kick his teeth in. I scowled at the guard, like an impatient man. "That's him."

The guard opened the door and held out the assignats I'd given him. His eyes were innocent, like a boy's.

"Pah." I made my voice gruff. "Keep it. It's your first day."

"Merci." He smiled and locked the door behind me.

LaGarde stared at me while the guard's footsteps receded. "What happened?"

"The new guard took me to the wrong cell. I couldn't correct him; he'd have been suspicious."

His jaw muscle pulsed. "That short, small guard?"

I handed him a wedge of soap and damp serviette. "You'll never fit in his uniform."

He rubbed the cloth over his face and dragged his fingers

down until he clutched his neckcloth. "A new guard makes it too dangerous for you."

"It has to be tonight."

"He already made one mistake. Another could put your life at risk. I will not do it."

"The head clerk at my father's office is suspicious of my omissions and has taken the guillotine lists from me. If he exposes me, I'll be in prison, and I won't be here to help you. Besides, Simon is waiting for us in the tunnels."

His eyes flashed. "Simon?"

"He owes me his life. He knows the tunnels like the inside of his pocket. He'll get us out, even if every guard in this place should follow us." I rubbed my arms, thinking of Simon waiting in the dark.

LaGarde looked to heaven and blew out a sigh.

I crossed my arms and glared at him. So, I wasn't perfect. But I was the only one getting him out of this hellhole.

"If the new guard returns, we'll have to find another one, more my size. That will be two guards to overpower."

I pulled out the pistol. "Do you know how to shoot this thing?" Its weight set my hand trembling.

"Why are you shaking?" He took it and checked the flint. "How many bullets do you have?"

"One."

"Powder?"

"Powder...for the gun?"

He shook his head. "Let us hope we need only threaten." He tucked it into his waistcoat.

I'd had no powder when I aimed the pistol at the prisoner or the soldier Simon killed. Thank God I hadn't needed to fire it.

I opened my frock coat and pulled my skirts out from my breeches. I began unbuttoning my waistcoat but realized LaGarde was smiling at me. I pinched the edges of the waistcoat. "You've seen them before. Remember?"

"Indeed, I do." He quickly turned his back.

Men were men—no matter the circumstance. I unwrapped the shawl binding my breasts and dropped it. Shaking my bonnet from my tricorne, I rolled up the hat and crammed it beneath my breasts. I doubted it gave me enough décolletage, so I crumpled the binding and added it, and tied the bodice strings. My breasts bulged over the lace neckline. "How's this?"

He turned back to me and chewed the corner of his lower lip. "Pas mal."

Not bad? I couldn't wait to be rid of him. I opened the reticule tied at my waist, pulled out a vial of perfume and doused myself with it.

LaGarde clamped his hand over his mouth and nose. "Ugh. Do not ever wear that again. I smell better than you."

I loved annoying him. "I want to be a convincing lady-of-the-night." I pulled out a pot of rouge I'd taken from Etty's dressing table and began smearing it on my cheeks.

LaGarde put up his hand. "Eh, eh, eh! Allow me."

His fingers brushed my cheeks so softly I thought he'd conjured a feather to apply the rouge. My face grew warm. He was so near I felt the heat of his body. He was wrong—he did not smell better. I searched for the lily scent I'd poured all over myself, but his stink overpowered it. I couldn't blame him. He'd not bathed in more than a year.

He stepped back, his eyes appraising me. "It will work."

I picked up the bonnet and, before I could put it on my

head, LaGarde grabbed it and placed it at an angle, so the brim dipped over my right eye. He stepped back, admiring his work.

I wrapped the shawl around me and made a circle before him.

"Now you not only smell, but also look like a salope." He grinned.

I sighed. That was the easy part. "How do you know how rouge and hats should be worn?"

"I dressed Magdeleine often enough." Pain struck his face, and he looked away.

I struggled to inhale as the air grew thick with the odor of blood when she'd given birth.

Loud footsteps sent a shiver through me. They were not the steps of the new guard—they sounded like the steps of a giant.

LaGarde stiffened. He pressed his back against the wall next to the door and nodded.

I adjusted the shawl to reveal my décolletage.

"Time's up." The lock screeched. The door opened.

I smiled, trying not to listen to the voice inside telling me I couldn't do this.

A man, the size of a tree, ducked his head in, swept a torch around, and stepped inside. LaGarde moved behind him, aimed the pistol, and cocked the hammer.

At the sound, the guard gripped the edge of the door and turned toward LaGarde.

LaGarde lunged, thrusting the pistol into the man's gut.

The guard crumpled. Had LaGarde shot him? Was the sound of the shot muffled by the man's bulk?

LaGarde handed me the pistol, which felt cool, not hot as I

expected. He rolled the guard over and began stripping him. The guard's face was white, his arms limp, a wet spot growing at the crotch of his breeches. The guard had fainted.

The pistol wavered in my hand.

"I am grateful I have no need of his breeches." LaGarde thrust his arms through the guard's frock coat sleeves, donned the guard's cap, grabbed the keyring, and pushed me ahead of him out the door, slamming it behind us.

The sound of the key locking the door made me joyous for a second, but from that point on, we were targets until we were swallowed by the tunnels. I did not think I could fear anything more than the darkness of the tunnels, but I was eager to reach their safety.

LaGarde grabbed my arm, and we raced toward the guard-room—the only way out of the cells. LaGarde had to pass as a guard by walking through a room filled with them. Trial by fire.

He slowed. "Act like your life depends upon it, for it does." He barked an actor's laugh that rumbled along the stone corridor. Still laughing, he pulled my hand and entered a chamber where four hulking guards sat on benches, drinking wine before the hearth of a huge fireplace harboring a snapping fire. One guard tugged off his boot. Another brushed dirt from his frock coat. The other two drained their cups.

"I'm the lucky one tonight." LaGarde grabbed my ass, making me jump. I squealed a high nervous laugh. He roared his laugh and dragged me along.

The men looked up at LaGarde, then at me.

"You the new guard?" one asked.

My heart thumped in my throat.

LaGarde brought up my hand and waved it. "Yes. I am celebrating!"

"Better be back before we change," the bootless one called.

I forced myself to sway my hips and smile, turning my head like a preening peacock.

"I want to take my time with this one, but I won't be late." LaGarde pulled me close. "Do something to make them laugh," he whispered fiercely.

I smacked my hand against his backside and grabbed his ass.

The guards roared.

LaGarde shouted, "She's hungry!"

The guards banged their metal cups. One yelled, "Save some for me."

I dug my fingernails into LaGarde's hand. He yanked me out of the chamber, slamming the door behind us. We ran along corridor after corridor, down spiraling steps, and through another long corridor to huge wooden doors, with a lock. Smells of roasting meat and potatoes emanated from the large crack beneath the doors. This had to be the kitchen I'd seen from the tunnel door. I blew out the breath I'd been holding since we left his cell.

LaGarde stopped. He peered at the lock and then the keys.

I prayed, Please, God, we've come so far, please.

LaGarde inserted a key, it didn't turn. Another, another, another.

Every part of my body trembled. I wiped my hands on my skirts, grabbed the keys from him, pulled out the longest, plunged it into the lock, and turned it until it clicked open.

LaGarde stilled my hand as I withdrew the key. "When we get inside, where is the door to the tunnel?"

"Across from the fireplace." My words skittered against each other.

He pushed open the door to shouts banging about the cavernous room. A whack, whack, whacking noise made me think of a butcher hacking meat apart. I pulled back. There were two fireplaces.

LaGarde peered around the door. "Stay close to me." I clung to his frock coat with both hands, stepping in time with him as we entered the kitchen. The heat of the room made me light-headed. I could not faint. I pressed my lips together until they hurt. He kept us against the wall, creeping in the shadows.

I searched the room for a door across from one of the fireplaces and spotted the door to the tunnels, halfway across the chamber. I tugged LaGarde's sleeve. He glanced back, and I pointed. He nodded. We'd have to cross the chamber to the other side. We'd be totally exposed.

"What're you doing in here?" A deep male voice thundered.

LaGarde pushed me behind him. I clung to his frock coat.

"Ha!" LaGarde boomed and pulled me before him. I shook, nearly collapsing. "Need to take this little minx to the tunnels, for a bit of privacy." He laughed and yanked my arm.

I knew I'd better go along with him, but as I stared at the man wielding a cleaver and wearing a bloodied apron, I froze.

The butcher frowned and whacked the cleaver into the top of a wooden barrel.

I dropped my voice. "I can't wait." I forced a husky laugh. LaGarde captured my fingers with his mouth and made a loud sucking sound.

Did any woman find that appealing? I gave a dazzling smile, like I was thrilled.

"Let us pass my friend. I've not much time before I return to duty." LaGarde forced another laugh.

The butcher's bloodied hand seized my arm. "Me, first." He yanked me toward him.

A scream clogged my throat.

In one quick movement, LaGarde released the cleaver from the barrel and touched the blade against the butcher's neck. He whispered, "I found her first. You can have her after."

The butcher dropped my arm.

I ran across the chamber to the door, unlocked it with my key and yanked it open. LaGarde's footsteps thundered behind me.

Keeping my shoulder along the wall, I fled down steps into the darkness and turned toward the light. Still holding the cleaver, LaGarde backed into the darkness. "Key," he hissed at me.

I ran back up and gave it to him. He slammed the door, jammed the key, and the lock clicked. Pitch darkness surrounded me.

"Simon?" I screamed.

"Right here." A spark flared and caught a torch, which sputtered into flame, illuminating Simon standing at the bottom step. He held the light high and grabbed my hand. "Hurry."

Shaking as if a strong wind blew, I grabbed LaGarde's hand.

He resisted my pulling. "Why are you so fearful?"

"Everybody's afraid of the dark." I yanked his hand.

"Not like this."

"Let's go!" His hand slid from mine. I fled into the darkness.

LaGarde captured my hand; his breath was hot on my neck. "Trust me. I will not let anything happen to you."

I did not trust LaGarde. I ran. I had no idea where we were going, but I was rushing to get there. As soon as I got out of the tunnels, I would find a way to join Henri in America. There would be no escaping this crime.

32

Paris
July 26, 1794

Simon entered the lodging room first. "Madame, I brought friends to help us."

Madame Lochot sat on a straight-backed wooden chair before an empty fireplace. Her son stood beside her. A candle burned on a small table next to a pallet in the corner. Stiff brown linen curtains sliced the sunlight, like roof thatching.

I followed, taking off my hat. "Madame," I whispered. "I was dressed as a woman when we met. I am Geneviève. This is Louis."

LaGarde took off his hat and bowed to her like she was a noble. "Madame."

Madame Lochot worried a rosary with one hand and patted her son's back with the other.

I crouched before her son. "Pierre, this is Monsieur Louis."

The child sucked his thumb and did not look up. I squeezed my hat. He was too old for such comfort, but at least it was something. Please, God, help me tell her. I looked up at his maman.

Her face was white, nearly translucent, like melted wax, her eyes unfocused, not seeing us. "My husband?" she asked.

I swallowed against the knot in my throat. The image of Pierre's name on the guillotine list flashed in my mind. I gripped my hands in prayer. "Madame," I began. Tears sat in her eyes and, I wanted to look away, but I forced myself not to, for I knew Pierre would want me to look her in the eye. I owed him that honor. "I am sorry, but Pierre was tried for conspiracy—"

She covered a cry with both her hands.

"Papa!" Little Pierre called out.

Simon put his arm around Little Pierre's shoulders.

"I am so sorry. Pierre has passed." I tried to stand and teetered. LaGarde grabbed my arm and steadied me.

Her sob made my chest cave. I stared at the cold hearth, rubbing my arms. Like a fist was squeezing my chest, I struggled against it to inhale. Pierre's son wailed. I hated my father. If I could, I'd have traded his life for Pierre's that very moment. I hoped the entire Tribunal burned in hell.

Madame curled over her son and rocked him as her body heaved silent sobs. Simon stood behind them, tears rolling down his cheeks. Pierre had treated Simon as a son, also.

The air grew thick and heavy. I longed to open the window, but I couldn't risk any one of us being discovered. My arms hung numb, useless. I couldn't save Magdeleine or Pierre. I might have dressed like a man, but men didn't fail like I did.

I rubbed my burning eyes. I couldn't save any more people. I couldn't fail again. I had to stop impersonating a man. I didn't measure up. I had no strength. No courage.

Madame and Little Pierre cried softly. Simon bent over their hunched bodies, rubbing the boy's back. Simon had become a man at fourteen.

LaGarde stood at the window, late afternoon light crossing his face and the grime encrusted in the lines around his eyes. I wondered if he was remembering Magdeleine and his own family.

The lone candle guttered. Below it sat a sketched portrait of Pierre in a rough wooden frame. He wore his stained apron, yet his eyes shone. There was no keepsake of a lock of his hair attached to the frame. Now there never would be.

I couldn't save Pierre, but I could protect his family. I would be abandoning them, something I promised myself I'd never do to anyone else, but I had no other choice. I couldn't risk their lives by failing again.

I was exhausted. My eyes burned, my head throbbed, my heart ached. I longed for the safety of the château for myself. But I couldn't leave Auguste—to be away from him would be torture.

I knelt again. "Madame, I know Pierre would want you and your son to be safe. Monsieur Louis and Simon will take you to Henri's château, where the informants can't find you."

Behind me, LaGarde's footsteps were sharp. "I am not leaving—"

I jumped to my feet. "Your time in prison has done nothing to change you," I hissed. "You're just as selfish as ever. I saved you, LaGarde. You owe me this one favor."

If I didn't know better, I'd say hurt flashed in LaGarde's eyes, but that was impossible for one so heartless.

Simon touched my arm. "I'll take them, Gen. I'll use the money you gave me for lodgings and take them by coach." He picked up Madame Bourran's walking stick. "I have protection."

I wanted to kiss Simon. I glared at LaGarde. "Thank you, Simon. That is kind and manly of you."

LaGarde's gaze smoldered.

I took Madame's hand in mine, but she kept her eyes closed. "You and Little Pierre will be safe with Simon. He is fearless and brave." Unlike some people I knew. "I hope I will see you all there, very soon."

I whispered to Simon, "Please write to me as soon as you arrive—in code?"

He nodded and continued to comfort Little Pierre.

I shoved my hat on and walked out. I began to slam the door behind me, but LaGarde caught it and closed it silently. He pursued me down the steps and into the dusk.

"Wait." He grabbed my arm and turned me toward him.

I pulled my arm back and slapped him. So hard, he released his grip on me and pressed his hand to his jaw.

My hand stung. But I didn't regret hitting him. I hated him. "Don't you want to see your daughter? She's at the château. You're going there anyway. Would it be such a hardship to take a widow and her son?"

"She will be safe there. But you—"

"Yes, thanks to me. I've saved not only your life, but also your daughter's and you do not even say, merci."

His eyes glinted like ice. Whatever he was feeling, whatever he wanted to say, he wasn't going to reveal it.

I smacked his arm, hoping to shame him into apologizing. "You shirk your responsibility to your own daughter. So long as she's safe at the château and someone else is caring for her, you can do whatever you please." I heaved another breath watching his face.

His lips moved, but no words came out.

"I don't know why I impersonate a man. They're all cowards. You disappoint me just like my father did."

His eyebrows jumped.

Why did I say that? I shouldn't have. But it was true. LaGarde was abandoning me just like my father left me at Pentemont Abbey when I had begged him not to. I heaved for breath. "I never want to see you again."

I turned and ran toward the river, into the light of the setting sun casting a dark red stain across the water.

I would not save any more people. I would not try to be a man, nor dress as one. I would save myself from now on.

The pressure in my chest burst, and I slowed my steps. At least women could cry.

33

I RAN UP THE steps, pushed open the door, and yelled, "Etty!" I slammed the door closed. "The Committee has issued a warrant for Papa's arrest!" I ran to the parlor and stopped, panting.

Papa sat on the chaise longue, next to Etty, holding her hands.

"Papa!" I rushed to him and dropped on my knees before him.

Etty picked up a cup from a tray on the low table. "Would you like some tea, my dear?"

Was I dreaming? "Guards are searching for you, Papa."

He patted my shoulder. "Etty made tea. Would you like some?"

"No. I want you to escape, Papa. I can save you."

He reached for my hands and pulled me up. "Trust your father, Geneviève. I do not need saving."

I lurched to my feet. "You do! They'll take you to la Conciergerie. I can take you through the tunnels, beyond the city barriers, to a château. I can get you to Nantes and arrange passage for you on a ship for America. You have the money. I've seen it."

He nodded. "I thought it was you who took the louis d'ors."

"Where did all that money come from?"

"You took it to save the nuns?" He smiled like an understanding priest, unnerving me.

This man was not my father. I shook my head to clear it. "Yes, for the nuns. I'm sorry I stole the money." I gripped the sleeves of his frock coat. "But you've got enough left to get out of Paris before they find you."

He peeled away my hands and brought them together. "As I have told your maman, this is all a misunderstanding. I shall go to la Conciergerie later this evening and give myself willingly to the charges for the express purpose of clearing my name."

I shook off his hands. "Like Robespierre? He was The Incorruptible, and he was guillotined—yesterday!"

"I did my duty in sentencing Robespierre. My dear daughter, have faith in your Papa. I have obeyed the decrees of the Committee of Public Safety and the Convention. I have followed and upheld the laws with diligence. What can I possibly be tried for when I have carried out the laws to the letter?"

My father's eyes had always reminded me of a confused loveable bird, as they did now. Surely, in his heart, he must have known he was murdering people with Robespierre's encouragement.

He'd sent thousands to the guillotine—including women and children—not allowing evidence, witnesses, or self-defense. Did he think he would be granted the privileges he'd denied them? Something rock-hard lodged between my ribs.

My father could be found guilty of my crimes. "Papa, what if your clerks did you wrong? Their errors could send you to prison." A ribbon of shame wound through me.

"I reviewed every document in my office. There have been no errors."

I grabbed my skirts. I had to confess, even if it meant losing his love. "It was I."

He tilted his head and blinked.

"I…" I placed my hand on my heart. "When I copied the guillotine lists, I replaced names of people you condemned with names of those already dead." I stared at the carpet. "It's my fault. I am guilty."

He stood, his finger caressing my cheek; his eyes so full of love I thought my heart might shatter. "You are my daughter, Geneviève, you could never dishonor me so."

I sank onto the floor. All this time he had faith in me? I wanted to throw myself at his feet, but I straightened. "No. I speak the truth."

He placed his hand on my head, as he had when I was a little girl. Tears dripped off my chin.

"I know you confess this lie only because you love me, and you want me to be safe."

A groan cracked the hardness between my ribs. He'd always believed in me—even though he'd never said it—he'd believed in me. Long after I had stopped believing in him. I had betrayed his trust. I was unworthy of his love. "I do love you, Papa. I do."

"Then rise and make me a promise."

"Anything, Papa."

He took my hand and Etty's and pressed them together. Etty smiled tightly.

Papa looked from her to me. "Promise that while I am clearing my name, you will protect and care for Etty and Auguste."

A tremor rippled across Etty's cheeks as she tried to hold onto the smile I knew she was forcing. She had never forgiven me for confiscating her brooch.

"I promise, Papa. I promise."

"Good. Now, be a good daughter and trust in me."

"Yes, Papa."

"Leave us now. I wish to be alone with Etty." He sat caressing her hand. "Trust your papa, Geneviève. I will say goodbye before I leave for la Conciergerie."

The rose-colored silk of the drapes reflected afternoon sunlight upon his face, erasing lines, making him look as young as he'd been when Maman died. Etty stirred her tea, the ring of the spoon against the china cup tinkling.

Papa would find none of these luxuries at la Conciergerie.

I bowed my head. "Yes, Papa." I backed up to the door, turned, and stumbled up the stairs to my chamber. I had to get those papers out of Papa's files. But how? I separated the curtains and peered from my window. Martin stood at the carriage bench, watching.

Bastard. I turned and headed for the cellar and my disguise.

34

Paris
July 29, 1794

Gone! the tricorne, breeches, waistcoat, and frock coat. My false identity papers. Henri's letters—gone!

They had to be here. I pulled down the vinegar cask, swept my arms across the dirt ledge. Nothing. Who would have taken them? I tilted the wine barrel from the wall and knelt next to it, reached behind it, and swept my arm, scattering rat turds to the floor. The only people who came to the cellar were Cook and Agathe. I picked up casks of vegetables, jars of confiture, baskets of potatoes and leeks, checking behind each. I found nothing but spiders and rat skeletons. I'd kept my disguise behind the vinegar cask for three years—now the clothes and my papers were gone. Who took them?

I collapsed into the dust and wiped sweat from my face. Pouffiasse Etty. She was so calm at the news of my father's arrest because she'd found my disguise. After Papa left, she would report me to the Committee of Public Safety and present the evidence. Not only that I'd impersonated a man but also carried false identity papers. I rubbed my neck. I also confessed replacing names in front of her. I groaned. That would condemn me without a trial.

She had planned this. I couldn't report her first—who would care for Auguste?

But what about Martin? He turned in Pierre. He knew I dressed as a man, and he was following me. If he turned me in, I'd have no chance to help Papa. I kicked a rat turd. Bastard.

Bunching my skirts in my fists, I folded over my legs. All my crimes would send Papa to the guillotine. It's me that should face death. I balled up my skirts and yelled into them, "I'm guilty. Not him!"

My head throbbed. Whether I went to Papa's offices or remained here, guards would come to arrest me—once they found the false names on the papers I'd copied. Names of people the Tribunal had condemned. Not only that, but I'd gotten LaGarde out of prison.

Think! All this time, Papa had believed in me. And I had betrayed him. I thought I was saving innocents, but my actions sent Papa to prison. The thick humidity made me feel like I was trapped under water. The only way I could rid myself of shame was to take responsibility for what I'd done. I had to get the files I altered as proof before anyone else found them and blamed my actions on Papa. I would have to break into the offices.

I would wait until Papa kissed me goodbye, and he left for la Conciergerie to turn himself in. Martin would drive Papa and not be able to follow me. I'd leave by the back door before Etty noticed I was gone.

35

AT DAWN, I brushed the white dust from my skirts and peeked out from the cellar. I ran through alleys to the back entrance of the Châtelet, crept up the servants' steps, crossed the hall to the clerk chamber, and stopped to gather my wits. Please, God, help me find the papers I copied. If I could present them to the Tribunal, they would be forced to release Papa.

I edged myself around the doorway and stepped back to see the clerks already at work. Instead of copying, they were sorting documents into piles lining a table before the fireplace where Imberton stood, straight as a pike.

Armand held up a paper. "Roland?" He lifted another. "And Delignon?"

Imberton indicated two piles. Armand deposited the papers and returned to his desk where a stack of documents teetered. I wished Armand had already sailed for America.

Denis, holding folders, called out, "Widow Capet." Imberton pointed at the tallest pile. Denis deposited the folders and hurried to my father's office. Denis's twins were four now, and his wife with child. I hoped he would be safe.

Imberton noticed me. His face reddened as he pointed and shouted, "Guards! Arrest her!

My heartbeat thundered.

"Guards!" Imberton shouted.

I ran for the servants' stairs. My legs shook so hard, I careened off the walls as I clambered down the steps. Where could I go that was safe? The château, but I'd be stopped at the city barrier. I could no longer use my father's name—the day I'd dreaded since the first time I used it as protection had arrived. The only way past the barriers was through the tunnels. My skin felt too tight, like it was suffocating me.

I stood panting at the side door. Once I opened it, I'd be exposed. But if I went through the side exit, I could make it to the square and blend in with the market people. I would have to walk past the morgue. The tunnel was dark, lit only by holes in the ceiling protected by metal grates embedded in the streets above, which I had stepped over a hundred times. I'd never traveled the passage, but I'd no better choice.

I wrapped my shawl around my face, took a deep breath, and ran. The moans from prisoners in the dungeon echoed along the stone passage. The air was thick with the stench of blood and death. I shoved open the wooden door, not caring who was on the other side. Stopping in the alley scattered with rags stained with blood, I wrapped my shawl around my shoulders and forced myself to walk calmly. I peeked around the corner.

The square wasn't much longer than the copying room. I inhaled, stood tall, and headed for the biggest knot in the crowd.

Rioters swarmed the arched entrance, raising pikes and screaming. Men and women wearing red caps charged across the square. A woman pounded the closed main doors. "Give me back my husband!"

I tottered and pressed my feet to the cobbles.

"Join your victims, you man-eater!" yelled a man, wielding a sword.

A rotund man, his beard and hair wiry and disheveled, bellowed, "Send Tinville to hell! Let him wallow in the blood he has shed!"

I fell back. They were screaming revenge against my father. I bent over, nauseated and dizzy. Clutching the building, I forced myself to stand straight.

A guard came out of the entryway and yelled, "He's at la Conciergerie!"

The crowd of red-capped sans-culottes turned and flowed like a stream of blood across the square and over the bridge toward the prison. I could get Papa out, like LaGarde. I just needed men's clothing, a place to hide, and a plan.

I forced myself to breathe calmly, descend the steps, and intermingle with the crowd, while trying to remember the tunnel entrance nearest the prison. The flower seller stood at the edge of the market. I headed straight for her and hoped I could make it without anyone recognizing me.

A powerful hand grabbed my arm, pulled me to the bulk of a man, his warmth penetrating my sleeve. I opened my mouth, but his other hand covered it. The square spun around me.

"Be quiet and act like you are happy to see me, for you should be."

LaGarde's voice made me want to fall to my knees and weep. But it wasn't jocular. Its seriousness yanked the dizziness from me. I was so happy it was him and not a guard, I wanted to kiss him.

I shook my head to clear it. "Have you a death wish?"

"Stay close to me, no matter what happens," he growled and tightened his grip.

My feet scarcely touched the ground. He guided me along to a carriage, opened the door, and placed me inside as easily as if I were a leaf caught in a breeze. He jumped in, closed the door, and rapped on the ceiling. The carriage jolted.

Shades covered the windows, and we sat panting in the semi-darkness, yet the crowd's jeers taunted outside. The carriage jostled me as it banged over the cobbles. I gripped the cushion. After a moment, LaGarde pulled a bundle from beneath the bench. "Quickly, change your clothes. We are headed for the barrier."

The tricorne, breeches, waistcoat—all mine. I shoved my hand into the secret pocket of the frock coat and pulled out my papers and Henri's letters. "You!"

His profile was sharp, his mouth pursed. The carriage hit a bump and I nearly fell. He remained tall and still.

Anger surged through my fingers. Not caring if he saw my flesh, I ripped off my shawl, skirts, and bodice. I pulled on the breeches, boots, tunic, waistcoat, and tied the neckcloth, imagining I was strangling LaGarde with it. He stared straight ahead.

I shoved my arms into the frock coat sleeves, secured Henri's letters, creased the folds of my papers in my lap, and sat panting, squeezing my eyes against the image of my father kneeling before the guillotine. I could force LaGarde to help me rescue Papa—I'd blackmail him. The carriage jolted, knocking me into LaGarde. I pushed myself away from him. I was losing my mind. I couldn't force LaGarde to do anything. Damned bully.

LaGarde opened the shades. Light illuminated his straight nose, gold-flecked eyes, blonde hair tied in a leather string. He smelled of a hayfield, and I wanted to lean into him. He made me feel safe, and I hated him for it.

I must have smelled like damp and piss and blood from the dungeon. I scooped up my gown and sniffed sweat. Damn him.

He'd saved my life. Why was I angry? He'd saved me, just as I'd saved him. And he'd been angry with me too. Now I understood. It would be better to face the guillotine now, before they killed my father.

I hated knowing LaGarde controlled me, yet I was grateful. I'd nowhere else to turn. But, if LaGarde hadn't stolen my disguise, I'd be on my way and wouldn't need him.

Jeers of death to my father blared outside the carriage.

"I thought you went to the château after I shamed you into being a father to Louisa."

"You never let me finish my sentence that day." He looked at me then. "I tried to say, 'I would not leave without you.' But you did not allow me to speak."

Without me? Heat rushed up my face. "Why? Louisa needs you. She's your daughter."

Something flickered across his face. Pain? Hurt? Disappointment? I couldn't tell.

He looked away. "As you said, I owed you."

"Ah. You finally realized it, but not in time to help Madame Lochot and her son."

"I could not follow you and travel with them. Besides, I trusted Simon."

"You followed me? Is that how you knew where I hid my disguise?" The horses slowed. Outside, sunlight glinted across the Seine, and I shrank back from the brightness.

LaGarde worked his jaw side to side. "I knew they would come for you after you got me out of prison. I have followed your every movement since then."

I sat back. We'd parted days earlier, and I'd never seen him, not once. I'd been so nasty to him. Yet, he thought I'd need saving. He was right. Nevertheless, he was wrong. "Why'd you steal my clothes?"

He stared straight ahead. "Because you would have gone to your father's office last night, and they would have arrested you."

How had he known what I'd do? Was I so obvious? "Papa's innocent of whatever charges they serve."

He quirked an eyebrow. "You are not."

I lurched forward, teetering on the edge of the bench. "I must save him."

"Be my guest." He opened his arm toward the door. Jeers for my father's head were as loud as if the sans-culottes were in the carriage with us. He tilted his head. "They will condemn you within hours, and then you will be of no use to him." He sat back, working his jaw. "You should know your groom spies on you. The bastard is probably turning you in right now. Should he, I will not be able to help you, then, either."

He was right. I was teetering on bursting into tears, and I hated it. "I must get Papa out. Prove he was doing his job, what the Tribunal required of him."

"There will be a long trial. You can do much more for him as a free man than an imprisoned woman."

He was so damned smart, it was irritating. I crossed my arms. "You had no right."

"You had no right to save my life, either. But you did." He leaned close and whispered, "Now we are even." His eyes sparked.

I laughed. I slapped my mouth, horrified I could laugh when my father was in prison, but another laugh burst like a bubble. I laughed long and hard, the tensions of the last days spiraling out of me like a rolling ball of yarn. The carriage bounced and I fell on the floor laughing.

LaGarde pulled me up and put a finger to his mouth. "We are nearing the barrier." He wiped his fingers across his mouth to regain his serious expression. "Ready to be Jean Detré?"

I pressed my fingers to my lips. He'd gotten me this far, which was further than I'd imagined I'd be in a week. I didn't trust LaGarde, but I didn't trust myself, either. Right now, I'd no other choice.

"Who else would I be?" I prayed being Jean Detré would be safe enough.

36

Paris
July 30, 1794

"Wake up," a male voice commanded.

I bolted upright and squinted in the golden light streaming through the carriage windows. The last thing I remembered was being angry with LaGarde, and that didn't surprise me. He sat opposite me, wearing a very satisfied expression. Then I remembered my father was in prison. I was headed for the guillotine. So was LaGarde. Why was LaGarde so happy?

Beyond the window, wind skated through fields of ripening wheat. In the distance stood a château of cream-colored stone with a blue-slate roof and three rounded turrets. Countless chimneys pierced the afternoon sky. It was châteaux like this one that Revolutionaries targeted, and I wondered why they hadn't burned it, along with its gardens, orchard, and crops.

I rubbed dust from my eyes. "Where are we?"

"Frazé."

I let out a low whistle. "The poor noble who owned this has got to be dead."

"He was almost guillotined." LaGarde chuckled, looking quite smug.

"What? The République owns it?"

"No. It is an orphanage, now."

I closed my eyes, praying for patience. "How can this estate be an orphanage?"

A corner of his mouth rose. "Louis LaGarde is the director of the Magdeleine Orphanage."

He loved shocking me. I waggled my fingers, beckoning for more of the story.

"Magdeleine came to me one day with a street urchin in tow. She wanted to take care of Gilbert and would not listen to my objections—I pointed out we were not his parents." He gazed out the window. "Out of desperation to spend time alone with her, I suggested we take him to my château and ask the servants to look after him. This appeased her for the moment. The next day, she had two urchins with her. She blinked those eyes at me and said, 'Gilbert needs playmates and so do these two.'" He laughed at himself, and I imagined him reliving that day.

"After that, she found a few children every week, and they were overwhelming my servants." He let out a sigh and looked back at me. "The Assembly had already taken my noble title and the 'de' from my name. I knew they would seize my property within the year. Instead of the proceeds going to corrupt officials' coffers, I established the Magdeleine Orphanage, gave my estate to it, and made Magdeleine and myself directors."

He looked out over the gardens, shaking his head. I imagined he still marveled at the power she'd had over him.

The golden afternoon light glinting off the brass handles inside the carriage reminded me of the gold louis d'ors I'd found in my father's desk. I'd wondered if they'd been owned by imprisoned nobles. But my papa was ethical. He'd never steal from the République. I pointed to another château beyond the first. "Who lives in that one?"

"Horses. It is the château's stables."

His calm irked me. The stables could house thirty families. My chest tightened as I remembered walks in the Versailles' Gardens with my parents on Sundays—something I'd never do again. This estate wasn't much smaller and no less grand than the palace of the King, our dead King. That was the real reason LaGarde gave it up—not because he was generous—he probably thought if he gave the estate away, he'd keep his head. I was being too hard on him. He'd done it for Magdeleine and now the orphanage was a fitting memorial. Pressure built in my chest. I missed her. She had been the best female friend I'd ever had.

Our carriage slowed under the porte cochère. LaGarde jumped out and offered his hand.

I grabbed my filthy gown and reticule from beneath the opposite bench, tucked the bundle under my arm, and got down, unassisted. The carriage door banged shut.

LaGarde led me to two huge pale blue doors and pulled a bell rope. He shouted back at the groom, "Merci! Please stable the horses. I will join you after dinner, and I will bring the brandy."

"Bien sûr." The groom clicked his tongue and snapped the reins and the carriage rumbled down the hill.

A noble drinking with a groom? Had prison knocked LaGarde from his lofty perch?

A willowy man, his gray hair tied in a shiny black ribbon at the back of his neck, stood in the entry hall and opened his arms widely. "Master Louis!" He bowed deeply.

"Ah, none of that nonsense, Adrien." LaGarde embraced the man and hugged him fiercely, making the old man's eyes bulge. "We are equals. Remember?" LaGarde released him.

Adriene wavered and kept his head bowed.

LaGarde pulled my arm. "This is my friend, Gen…Jean Detré."

I removed my hat, offered my hand, and lowered my voice. "Pleased to meet you, Adrien."

Adrien shook my hand timidly and nodded as he stepped back. I imagined it was hard for him to change a lifetime of subservience.

"Please have the housekeeper make up my room for Jean." LaGarde asked, politely.

"Of course, Ma—mmm."

"Louis. Say Louis." LaGarde tugged at Adrien's sleeve, playfully.

Adrien's face wrinkled and grew scarlet, reminding me of a baby about to burst into tears. "Louis. She'll do it immediately…Louis."

LaGarde had been kind and forthright with Adrien, which I admired, but I was skeptical. What was LaGarde's motive in being friendly with the servants? He'd been a bully to the only two non-nobles at University, Henri and me. Maybe prison had changed him.

"Come. You must be as hungry as I." He gave Adrien our hats and my bundle of clothes before I could protest and pulled me toward two gilded white doors. He flung them open onto a vaulted room so long and ornate, it had to have been a ballroom.

Screeches and laughter of at least forty children made the crystals on the chandeliers tinkle. I laughed at the irony between the elegance of the room and the raucous children.

Long wooden trestle tables, topped by white linen and flickering candles in silver candelabras, ran the length of the room. Children sat on benches of halved logs on either side of the tables.

"Oncle Louis's back!" screamed a boy of about eight who jumped up on the bench and pointed.

I stepped to a side wall as every child swarmed LaGarde. He threw his head back and laughed. I'd never imagined him capable of such joy. His hands tousled hair, pinched cheeks, playfully yanked braids. His laughter boomed and his arms searched to hug every child—individually and affectionately.

A tall boy who had hung back walked forward and reached his hand out to LaGarde, who swatted it away. "You have grown, Gilbert, but you are never too big or too old for a hug." LaGarde embraced the boy, cupped his hands around Gilbert's head, and kissed him. The boy blushed as tears dropped. I grew teary myself.

After their embrace, Gilbert wiped his face and stepped back. "You've grown too thin, Oncle."

LaGarde roared. "I shall fix that immediately."

Who was this man? Where had he been when LaGarde was

in prison? A tingling ran across my lips, and I feared I'd cry. Not even the Sisters had been this affectionate to me. Only Maman had loved me as LaGarde was loving these children.

LaGarde clapped. "Let us be seated."

Four women stood along the tables and wrangled the children into their places. They didn't dress like governesses or nurses or servants. They wore colorful gowns that at one time must have been elegant, but now were worn and frayed. Their curls sat atop their heads, held in place with glittering pins and feathers. Taking their places on the benches amongst the children, they laughed and joked with them. Who were these—ladies?

LaGarde stood at the head of the table behind a large red, damask-covered armchair, which had been empty, and I wondered if it had remained so during his imprisonment. "Say bonjour to my friend, Monsieur Jean Detré." He quirked an eyebrow at me.

The children shouted, "Bonjour, Monsieur Jean!"

I cleared my throat and forced my voice lower to shout, "Bonjour," and waved. I looked at every face—each radiating love and joy. I blinked at tears. Etty had never allowed Auguste at table with us. She and Papa and I had missed this wonderful chaos.

LaGarde hunched over the table and scanned every child's face until he got to the last. He growled like a bear. "What is for dinner?"

"Oncle Louis's lentil soup!" they screamed. They pounded their silver spoons upon the tables. "We want Oncle Louis's soup. We want Oncle Louis's soup!"

LaGarde instructed the children to his right to scoot over

and make room for me. He grabbed my shoulder and pushed me onto the bench, and he sat in the red chair.

"Where did you come from?" the little blonde girl next to me asked. She was about Auguste's age.

I swallowed tears realizing I didn't know when if ever I would see my brother. "Paris." My voice broke. "Where did you come from?"

"My maman's tummy."

My mouth dropped open, and she laughed. I laughed with her.

One of the women, wearing a faded aubergine-colored gown, brought a tray with two bowls, serviettes, and silver spoons, her décolletage jiggling with her every step. "Welcome home, Louis. I am so sorry about Magdeleine."

He nodded and brought his finger to his lips. "Let us not tell the children yet, Suzanne."

She nodded and left us.

"How does she know?" I whispered.

"You are not the only person who visited me in prison."

I sat back. "Why didn't you have her get you out?"

"She did not remove my name from any list."

His wit was always faster than mine.

Another lady, wearing a white plume in her dark red hair, brought two crystal wine goblets and a decanter. She placed them on the table and tucked a curl behind her ear. "I am so sorry about Magdeleine, Louis. Will you bring your daughter here?"

I shot a look at LaGarde.

He tilted his head. "Thank you. Perhaps."

She nodded and then glanced at me and adjusted her dangling earring like a coquette. Was she flirting with me? At least she thought I was a man. I pulled at my tight neckcloth.

The gold griffons running around the bowl's pale blue border confirmed my suspicion: it was Sèvres porcelain. Etty would be terribly jealous and outraged that these fine dishes were used to serve orphans.

LaGarde poured wine and glanced at me.

"Are you not afraid the children will break these expensive dishes?" I asked.

"I broke a few when I was a child." He grinned. "Why should they not enjoy what I have enjoyed? Besides, we have settings for two hundred of this pattern and another two hundred with white stags in place of the griffons. Better the children enjoy them than the Revolutionaries steal or destroy them."

Etty would faint dead away, but he had excellent logic.

Doors at the other end of the room opened, and kitchen servants brought out huge pots of steaming soup and ladled it into the porcelain bowls.

After I was served, I inhaled a rich earthy scent, and took a taste. It was delicious. I looked at LaGarde. "Why do they call this 'Oncle Louis's soup?'"

He blushed. It was the first time I had seen him blush, and I felt a tug of fondness for him. I gulped my wine.

"When the children first came here, they said the lentil soup tasted like chamber-pot slops." He laughed and leaned close to me. "They had been starving, so I thought they were probably right. The next day I went to the garden and picked things I had liked as a child: sweet carrots, nutty parsnips, tender greens. I instructed Cook to dice and sauté and add them to the lentil soup—" he dropped his voice, "I did not call it chamber-pot slops. I also poured in some wine when she was not looking." He grinned. "That evening, I told the children I added magic to the soup. They were tentative, but in the end, they licked their bowls clean. Now they call it 'Oncle Louis's soup."

I laughed with him. I wanted to stay in this place forever, a place where people made others happy, a place where everyone belonged to this family, a place where everyone felt safe. I felt safe. And it was all because of LaGarde's generosity. I hoped he'd be as generous helping me help my father.

I finished my soup and drained the wine in my goblet.

LaGarde refilled my glass.

I ran my fingers down the crystal stem and watched the children. They'd finished and were waiting quietly. LaGarde nodded. They all folded their serviettes and placed them on the table, then folded their hands and whispered what I thought was a prayer. In unison, they looked up and called out, "May I be excused please?"

LaGarde nodded.

The children got up quietly and lined up on either side of LaGarde. Each placed a kiss on his cheek and said, "Bonne nuit." LaGarde wished them each a good night by name. How had he remembered forty names? When the last little girl arrived, she reached her arms toward him. Louis picked her up and sat her on his lap.

She squealed in delight. She whispered, "I'm Sophie, and I'm five."

He hugged her. "You have grown so much I almost did not recognize you."

She flung her arms around his neck. "I love you, Oncle Louis."

"I love you, Sophie!" He set her down and she ran to join the others.

Louisa came to my mind. How he must be longing for her.

The women waiting at the doors ushered the children out. They turned in unison, leaned forward, revealing their ample bosoms, and blew LaGarde a kiss and closed the doors.

How bizarre. "Who are those women?"

"Magdeleine's friends." He laughed. I suspected he was laughing at my shocked face.

Mistresses? I couldn't say the word. "Did they...work with her?"

He puffed an exhale. "They are former prostitutes who could no longer work because they were with child. Magdeleine invited them to live here with their children and help take care of them all."

The silence hurt my ears. How had this man kept himself from his daughter? He'd make a wonderful father. My chest tightened. My father had been affectionate and playful before Maman died, but after her death those qualities had never returned. I drank more wine. My father loved me. He told me he believed in me. But I'd never felt the warmth I'd just felt amidst Louis and these orphans.

LaGarde's eyes shone. He poured more wine and drank deeply.

My father had missed all that LaGarde had created. Papa never played with Auguste. I had to get my brother. I had to get Papa out of prison. I had no idea how, but I had to return to Paris.

I folded my serviette and placed it on the table. "You must be eager to meet Louisa."

He nodded. "We will go tomorrow."

A wriggling worked its way down to my stomach. He'd go. I was leaving tonight for Paris. "Will you bring her here?"

He shrugged. "She has been with the Sisters for nearly a year. She does not know me. I will do what is best for her. I do not want to make her feel unsafe."

I closed my eyes, and in my mind, I saw Magdeleine lying in the straw, with Louisa cradled in her arm. I spoke to her in my mind: *I understand why you loved this man, Magdeleine. Is that why you left Louisa? Because you knew that Louis would care for her?*

LaGarde folded his serviette and stood. "I will show you to your room."

I got up but backed away. "I cannot take the director's room. I'll sleep in the stables."

"I am sleeping in the stables to ensure you do not steal a horse and ride to Paris."

I pressed my lips together. How did he know me so well? "If I wanted to go to Paris, you couldn't stop me."

He smiled. "That is why I am locking you in my chamber."

Fine. I'd enjoy a good night's sleep and go to Henri's château in the morning—LaGarde couldn't possibly stop me from leaving then. There was no rush to return to Paris. I expected Papa would be in prison for a long time. Besides, I missed Louisa.

37

The Loire Valley
July 31, 1794

WE LEFT AT dawn. Birdsong, something I'd not heard much in Paris, thrilled me for a moment, until I remembered my father was in prison and Pierre was dead. Wisps of fog rose from the Loire, making me think of spirits. I hoped Pierre's spirit was untortured and free. I had to get back to Paris, but escaping LaGarde's protection would be tricky.

"You didn't actually lock the door last night, although you made it sound like you did." I held the reins tightly. The horse LaGarde had given me was huge and skittish and terrifying. I resisted hanging onto the saddle, for I feared he would find my lack of skills entertaining.

LaGarde was as comfortable on his mount as he'd been in his red chair. The reins looked like strings in his bearpaw hands. "I thought you would test the door before jumping out the window and breaking your neck."

My horse lost its footing, and I leaned, reseating myself. Could I hide nothing from him?

"Those thoughts of yours are worse than reality," his tone was gentle.

A breeze rippled the hayfields. I laughed. "And what thoughts are those?"

"You blame yourself for Pierre's death. Was he not making false identity papers before you met him?"

I huffed a sigh and squinted in the bright dawn. The sun wasn't fully up, and already we were arguing. Yet I supposed Pierre was. Henri had sent me to him years earlier. I shrugged.

"The Tribunal considers that crime proof of being a traitor, Geneviève. A crime he committed long before you met him." LaGarde squinted at me.

The horse strained, and I pressed my thighs tighter around the beast. "I told him I worked for my father, and I'd get his name off the list or go to the guillotine in his stead. I promised."

"Why?"

"It's my fault, don't you see? I couldn't get his name off the list. When I went to la Conciergerie the next day to tell Pierre we would rescue him, he'd been taken to the guillotine." The horse stepped into a dip in the road, and I felt his muscles tense, preparing to break into a gallop. My legs ached from squeezing the beast.

LaGarde's horse stepped ahead. He looked back. "Thank you for volunteering my life, yet again."

My horse snorted. My thighs burned. I wouldn't give LaGarde the pleasure of watching me fall.

"Absolve yourself of that guilt." He pulled to the side of the road, holding his horse while waiting for mine to catch up. "You have taken care of his family, when you did not owe him anything."

My horse yanked his head and leaned down to tear some grass along the road. "But Martin, my father's groom, followed me and turned Pierre in. I led him to Pierre."

He swatted at a fly. "That is what informants do. Martin's actions are beyond your control."

Damn. My horse lurched for more grass, and I slackened the reins a bit. Before I could pull back, the horse bolted. I yelped, clinging to the horse as it galloped up a hill. I pulled back on the reins so hard, my arms burned. The horse continued to fly. I dug my heels into the stirrups and let up on the reins, letting him think he had free rein, and then I yanked. The horse reared, tilting me back, but I leaned forward until I stood, shortened the reins, and pulled with all my might. He whinnied, danced round in a cloud of dust, snorted, and stopped.

Clinging to the reins, I fell into the saddle and leaned over, gasping for breath.

LaGarde brought his horse up to mine. "Where did you learn to ride like that?"

"Just now." I dragged my sleeve over my sweating face and sat up. "I learned just now."

His laughter rang out over the fields.

"Why..." I panted, my arms trembling. "Why did you give me such a spirited horse?"

"A spirited horse for a spirited woman."

I jerked my head. "You gave him to me on purpose?"

"Her. Riding her requires undivided attention. I hoped you would not have an opportunity to think about Paris." He brought his horse close and took the reins from me. "It worked."

My arms were too tired to hit him. "What's her name?"

"Kate."

"Ah. Shakespeare's *Taming of the Shrew*." I slowed Kate. "You think you can tame me, LaGarde?"

"Never. Nor would I want to. I admire your spirit." He chuckled and led my horse to walk beside his mount.

A tiny bit of pride warmed my chest. The scent of lavender reminded me of Maman, and I looked about for it. Up ahead, a field bloomed purple. I wanted to lie down in it.

I dragged my arm across my face wiping away sweat. "My father was arrested for my crimes. I must return to submit evidence and confess."

"You said the clerks were filing stacks of papers. Should you be able to obtain evidence, and I do hope you do *not* present the list upon which my name appeared," he cocked an eyebrow, "your confession would be looked upon as merciful compared to the thousands your father condemned."

Merciful? I hadn't seen my action like that when I'd substituted his name, but it was. I rubbed my burning arms. If I hadn't saved LaGarde, he wouldn't have saved me, and I'd be in prison right this minute—if I were still alive.

"You must realize you are wanted for altering court documents, getting me out of prison, carrying false papers, and dressing like a man. Any one of those crimes will send you to la

Conciergerie. And three of the four will send you to the guillo-tine. Do you think if you are caught, they will spare your life?"

I didn't confess to being a thief and a liar as well.

He adjusted his pristine neckcloth. "If I were your father, I would prefer facing my own death to witnessing the death of my daughter. I imagine your papa is that type of man. No?"

Was he? Papa was so convinced he had done his job as required and instructed. Yet that hadn't kept him out of la Conciergerie. Doing one's job should keep one out of prison.

LaGarde gently gripped my arm. "Look at me."

I squinted up at him. He'd washed and trimmed his hair and it lay in waves across his wide shoulders.

"In your heart, do you really believe your father did nothing wrong in sending nearly three thousand people to their deaths?"

I pulled away, but he wouldn't let go. His horse was still; mine shifted from hoof to hoof.

"You love your father. You want to believe he is innocent," he whispered.

LaGarde's eyes were kind. Sunlight made the golden flecks in his green eyes shine like amber. He stared into me, and heat rushed up my face. I nodded. He let go of me, clicked his tongue, and the horses walked.

I had trusted my instincts when I challenged Papa about sentencing the Carmelite nuns. I was grateful not to be wearing a corset, as my chest ached so I could not inhale. I had enraged Papa; he'd threatened to fire me. He had insisted he followed the laws without fault. If that were true, he wouldn't be in prison. LaGarde was right. I couldn't control Martin or the Tribunal.

I rubbed my hand along the horse's neck. I detested feeling helpless and useless. I had to figure out how to help my father before returning to Paris.

LaGarde smiled. "I would like to propose a gentleman's agreement."

I peeked up at him. His face was still, his eyes serious.

"If you agree to stay at Henri's château for a while with Louisa and me, I will accompany you back to Paris and attend your father's trial whenever it begins."

"I don't need you to accompany me. I can go myself."

His eyes flashed. "I am a noblesse d'épée. Do you know what that means?"

"You are a noble of the sword." The words tasted like sour wine.

"And the meaning?"

"You live and die by the sword, which, in this case, is your word."

He nodded. "Do we have an agreement?"

Good thing I wasn't a noble of the sword. I had no intention of keeping my word. I'd just add it to my list of crimes. I did long to see Louisa. After playing with her for an afternoon, I'd escape—without LaGarde—but I'd pretend for now. I'd broken my word a hundred times and wasn't finished. "Only if we trade horses."

38

A STIFF WIND WHIPPED dust into our faces as we crested a hill. We stopped the horses and gazed across the dark green valley. Atop the next hill, a château glowed in the golden afternoon light. "All the vines and orchards we can see," I brought my arm out, "and then some, are owned by the Verzat estate."

LaGarde whistled. "Did Henri inherit all this along with his title?"

Henri's château was huge but not ornate. Yet it seemed to me LaGarde was still impressed. "He wasn't happy about it; he wanted to remain a Deputé and help his neighbors of Faubourg Saint-Antoine." I let my horse stretch her neck to reach a patch of grass. "He accepted the inheritance for his sister's sake. Joliette runs the wine business from America and advises the man who manages the vineyard now."

"Impressive. There are very few businesswomen."

"She's a widow."

"Unfortunately, it is the only way women can own businesses. Henri surrounds himself with powerful women."

Did LaGarde think that women having power was good or bad? My horse shifted, and I reseated myself. "What do you mean by that?"

"His sister seems as insistent about changing the world as you are."

A bit of pride pricked at me, but a queasiness followed for I could not tell if LaGarde was serious. The wind was hot, making me sweat. "Are you mocking me?"

He gazed at the river, watching, thinking. "The world needs changing, and women are just the people to do it."

Did I hear him correctly? "But how can women change the world if they have no rights?"

"That has not stopped her or you." He grinned and the light caught the golden flecks in his eyes, making them sparkle. "Let us go. I wish to hold my daughter before she is another minute older."

I led LaGarde down into the Verzat estate, past small farms, and along a creek. When we reached a cottage surrounded by a vegetable garden, I slowed my horse and called out, "Bonjour?"

Simon ran out, waving furiously. "Gen! I wrote. Did you figure out the code?" He crossed the small yard and helped me dismount.

Simon and his codes. I hoped his letter hadn't been intercepted. "I didn't get it. What did it say?"

He hugged me, holding on for a moment. I hugged him hard, so grateful he was safe. I rubbed his back and let him go.

"I wrote, 'The chicks arrived safely.'" His smile was broad. "Wasn't that smart?"

I couldn't ask if he had included his name, which could be traced. I didn't want to spoil his moment of triumph. I playfully swatted his hat brim. "Very smart. Thank you for bringing them here."

Simon looked questioningly at LaGarde.

After my outburst in Paris, I didn't blame Simon for not trusting him. "LaGarde wouldn't let me stay in Paris, alone. That's why he couldn't bring Pierre's family here. He saved my life."

Simon tilted his head, chewed his lip for a moment, and nodded. "That's fair. You saved his."

LaGarde roared a laugh and so did I.

"LaGarde is Louisa's father."

Simon stood, hands on hips, squinting at LaGarde. "I carved a rattle for her."

"I thank you." LaGarde tipped his hat.

"Will you stable the horses? LaGarde's in a hurry to meet Louisa."

"Sure." Simon grabbed LaGarde's reins. "Can you teach me to shoot a pistol?"

LaGarde smiled. "Certainement."

We walked through vines up a gentle slope toward the château. In the distance, a layer of mist gathered over the Loire, and pink and violet clouds scuttled above it. The butter-colored stone walls towered above as we approached the massive wooden door at the back. Excitement ran through me as I envisioned the Sisters huddled by the cooking fire and the wet nurse rocking Louisa.

Madame Bourran opened the door. "Geneviève!" she cried, stepping outside to embrace me.

Her arms were so warm and loving I feared I might cry. I released her. "May I present Louisa's papa, Louis LaGarde?"

Before I could turn, she reached out and captured his hands. "I remember Comte de LaGarde from Versailles. Welcome, Louis."

LaGarde bowed deeply and kissed her hand. "Marquise, you are as beautiful as I remember."

"You do flatter me." She squeezed his hand. "Please, continue."

We all laughed as LaGarde and I entered the cavernous stone-walled kitchen. Candles flickered from sconces and candelabra, illuminating the room with a soft golden light, redolent of roast chicken and garlic. The aroma of baking bread and rosemary made my stomach rumble.

The Sisters and wet nurse sat in a circle before the fireplace, mending children's clothing. Sister Magali rocked Louisa who waved Simon's wooden rattle.

I led LaGarde to her. "Sister Magali, this is Louis LaGarde, Louisa's papa."

She pulled Louisa to sit up in her lap. "You have a beautiful, healthy, and happy daughter, Monsieur."

LaGarde tossed aside his tricorne as he dropped to his knees and stared at Louisa. The baby pulled back, pushing into Sister Magali's bosom, appraising LaGarde with her deep violet eyes, Magdeleine's eyes. Louisa's face reddened.

LaGarde pulled back, and whispered, "Geneviève, help me here."

I knelt beside him and waggled my fingers before Louisa, trying to get her attention. She grabbed one of my fingers, tightly. "This is your papa, Louisa." She smiled and gnawed on my finger. My chest warmed as her sweetness melted all the tightness that had imprisoned my heart.

"You remember your Tante Geneviève!" LaGarde rested back on his heels, reached into his waistcoat, and pulled out a silver teething ring with dangling bells that tinkled as he shook it. "I am your Papa," he whispered.

Louisa's eyes widened, let go my finger, and pulled the silver ring into her mouth. I saw the flash of a stubby white tooth and laughed. How had LaGarde known she'd be teething?

LaGarde reached his hands out to her, and she tilted toward him. He picked her up and clutched her to his chest, nuzzling her neck. She cooed. Tears welled in his eyes. "Thank you, my dear, sweet Magdeleine. Thank you," he whispered so softly I knew he'd not meant for me to hear him.

I sat on a bench at the long table in the center of the room, the memory of Magdeleine holding Louisa as real as if she lay before me. Sadness crept up my throat. I swallowed hard, trying to make the image fade. I was so very tired of losing people.

LaGarde brought Louisa up and held her above his face. "I love you, my angel, and I will never leave you." He cradled her in his arm and uncurled her tiny fist. He looked around the room until he spotted me. "Geneviève! She has Magdeleine's delicate long fingers."

The candlelight wavered as I smiled. "Yes, she does, LaGarde."

The wet nurse and other Sisters left us and, while Louisa slept in LaGarde's arms, he and I sat at the table with Madame Bourran. Sister Magali brought a plate of cold chicken and platter of cheeses and bread. She poured wine and placed the carafe on the table. "Shall I put Louisa to bed now, Monsieur LaGarde?"

"Louis. Please call me Louis. No, I shall keep her with me until she needs the wet nurse. Thank you, Sister."

She blushed and touched the place where a cross had once rested. "Please, Louis, call me Magali. It is safer. They drown clergy in the Loire."

LaGarde shifted on the bench and cleared his throat. "Magali, thank you for taking such excellent care of Louisa. I am indebted to you and your," he mouthed the word Sisters, "for eternity."

Magali bowed her head, pressed her hands together in prayer, and left us.

Madame Bourran sipped some wine. "You both must call me Tante Nicole. Never Marquise or Madame. I do not wish to call attention to my nobility."

"Tante Nicole." LaGarde brought up his glass. "A toast."

We lifted our glasses.

"To Geneviève. Neither Louisa nor I would be alive without her." His eyes sparkled.

Heat rose in my face. I wasn't a hero. If I could have saved Magdeleine, she'd be here with us, now. My arm trembled. I missed my friend more than ever.

Tante touched her glass to mine, drank, and poured more all around. "I know Geneviève is courageous, but that is a story I would like to hear."

I wanted to forget Magdeleine's death. I stabbed a piece of chicken and devoured a mouthful.

"Ma...Tante Nicole," LaGarde began, "first, help me convince Geneviève to stay here until her father's trial begins. I do not think Louisa and I can keep her here alone, and she is a wanted woman in Paris."

Another person privy to my crimes. I groaned and gulped more wine.

"Wanted for what?" Tante Nicole asked.

I kicked LaGarde's foot, and glared at him, hoping my expression would silence him.

"Where shall I begin?" LaGarde kissed Louisa's head and smiled.

Resigning myself to the fact that I'd have more control if I told the story, I began. "My father is Public Prosecutor Fouquier-Tinville. I must attend his trial. Surely you would agree?"

"Attend the trial, which may not begin for months. But you wish to leave as soon as possible." LaGarde sipped his wine. "And it would be dangerous as you are wanted for crimes against the République."

"What crimes?" Tante Nicole refilled our glasses.

"Are we not all guilty of them, Tante?" LaGarde replied. He drained his glass. LaGarde could probably drink a barrel of wine and feel no effects.

"I also promised my father I'd care for my stepmother and brother. They are alone, and I should help them."

Tante stood. "No father would wish his daughter to risk her

life for anyone. Louis is right, Geneviève. You must remain here."

"I also promise I will go with you to the trial, whenever it begins," LaGarde said.

"You just promised you'd never leave Louisa." I hadn't meant to be so sharp.

"She will not mind if I protect the woman who saved her and her father's life." LaGarde looked down at Louisa, asleep in his arms. "Will you, mon petit ange?"

"May I please hold your little angel?" I wiped my hands on my serviette and reached.

LaGarde gently placed her in my arms. "Always support her head."

I pressed my lips together. A former bully, LaGarde, was a mother hen.

Louisa had gained weight, as she should, she was nearly a year old. She had LaGarde's strong jaw and Magdeleine's long eyelashes. She smelled of sweet milk and lavender and, something elusive, innocence perhaps.

I'd never be able to leave her in the morning. Perhaps LaGarde and Tante were right. Maybe I should wait until the trial began before returning to Paris. Perhaps Martin and Imberton would cease looking for me by then.

I cradled Louisa to me and felt the gentle rise of her chest with her every breath. Holding her filled a place in me left empty by Magdeleine. My friend would want my love for her child to heal me. I held Louisa tighter. I didn't even try to hold onto my heart.

LaGarde placed his hand on my shoulder. It was steady and strong. "Is she not an angel?" he asked.

"Un ange. Bien sûr." I didn't want LaGarde to take his hand away. His breath, close, his voice intimate—they stirred something in me I didn't want to feel. I began to shrug the sensation off, but I stopped myself. I fully intended to remain faithful to Henri. But LaGarde's hand was so reassuring. And for the first time since Henri left, I didn't feel so alone or helpless.

I'D BEEN AT the château for a week. My heart and arms ached at the thought of not holding Louisa, but it was time to return to Paris and get Papa out of prison. I shook off the image of him in a cell and opened the armoire. A gown, bonnet, slippers, a shift, and bodice. Where were my breeches, frock coat, and boots?

Not again. I slammed the door. Damn LaGarde. He knows I can't go back to Paris dressed as a woman.

Someone knocked. Who else but LaGarde would be looking for me? I'll hit him. I grabbed a large book, strode across the room, and flung the door open.

Tante Nicole, eyebrows raised, took a step back. "Am I… interrupting?" She held a stack of men's clothing, my tricorne atop it, and a bouquet of lavender.

"No. I was just reading. Please, come in."

She placed the clothing on a chair and handed me the bouquet. "Lovely scent, is it not?" Her swollen flesh nearly enveloped her thin gold wedding band, glinting in the morning light.

The scent took me to Maman's chamber, where I had stood next to her, watching her brush and powder her hair. "Yes."

"Louis and Louisa picked them. Just for you."

My scalp itched. He hadn't taken my clothes and, worse, he'd given me flowers. "I'll have to thank them."

"Louis is such a devoted father."

I nodded and poured a glass of water from the pitcher.

"Do you not agree?"

"Yes. He is." I placed the flowers in the glass.

"And so handsome."

A warm frisson shot through my body. Damned handsome. At least she didn't ask if I found him attractive. I placed the lavender on the bedside table, inhaling Maman's calming scent.

"Is there something you are not telling me?" she asked gently.

A great deal, I thought, but I rushed my reply. "No."

"Louis told me how you saved him and Louisa…and you tried to save Louisa's maman."

I shelved the book. "Magdeleine was my friend. I loved her."

"How long have you known Louis?"

My fingers jittered. I didn't want to reveal how I knew Louis, but he'd already told her his half of the story. "Both Henri and I met him at University."

"You…attended?"

I shrugged. "Dressed as a man."

"Ha!" Her pearl earrings quivered. "You've been dressing

as a man for a long time."

"It's been…necessary."

"I should have liked to attend University. You are far more ingenious than I." She sat on the chaise longue before the fireplace. "You have known Louis a long time."

"I know a man far different from the one you know, Ma—Tante." I gripped my hands. I should not have let that out.

She cocked her head. "Tell me about the man you know."

I'd already said more than I wanted to, so why not tell her everything? "LaGarde was an arrogant brute at University. He disdained both Henri and me, simply because we were the only two non-nobles. Angry that I had showed him up in class, LaGarde, thinking me a man, attempted to challenge me to a duel and sliced open my waistcoat with his rapier, exposing my breasts."

"Heavens!" She flicked open her fan and waved it.

I hadn't meant to horrify her, and I put out my hand to calm her. "He didn't know my sex at the time." I rubbed my forehead. I just defended him, why? "When he threatened to report me, I told him my father's name. LaGarde was so scared, he never returned."

Fluttering her fan, she frowned. "Then why did you remove Louis's name from the execution list?"

Shame burned in me, but I might as well admit to my actions. "I didn't fight fair—frightening him with my papa. I knew LaGarde's only crime was being born a noble, same as Henri. I didn't believe he should die for it, so I replaced his name."

She ran her fingers over the ribs of her fan. "But you got him out of la Conciergerie."

I didn't want to tell her, yet the concern and confusion that filled her eyes made me want to tell the whole truth. I sighed. "He threatened to expose my substituting names on the list if I didn't, which would have put my name on the list."

She stood and whapped her fan on the chaise longue. "I do not blame you for not being fond of him." She neared me. "But you could have left him to rot there. Why did you not?" Her voice was soft.

I walked to the glass-paned door and looked out over the workers moving through the grapevines, thinking I should be out there picking with them, earning my keep. "Magdeleine loved LaGarde. She entrusted Louisa to me. Louisa needs a parent. Even if I don't like LaGarde, he is her papa."

She walked to the window and wrapped her arm around my waist. I wanted to wiggle away, but I couldn't. A warm presence—Maman? I didn't know. But I felt Maman was there, hovering next to me, making me stay in Tante's embrace.

Sunlight caressed Tante's face, softening her wrinkles, making her gray hair shine like silver. She had been a gorgeous woman and still was. "You are the kindest and bravest person I have ever met, Geneviève."

The merciless stays poked my ribs. I pulled away and opened the glass-paned door onto the balcony, letting in a breeze that brought the scent of ripening grapes.

"You are right. You know a different Louis. But people change. He saved your life."

A prickling ran across the back of my neck. Had he bragged about that? "If he had not taken my male clothing, I may not have needed saving."

She stared at me so long I wondered if she believed me.

"Has he apologized?"

"In his way. I think Magdeleine and Louisa changed him. LaGarde is a different person around children. Nonetheless, I am wary of trusting him."

"You have every reason." She sat on the bench and patted it. "Sit down, ma chérie."

I joined her, grateful for the cooling breeze.

"Have you heard from Henri?" Her cheekbones and strong jawline had rounded, but her eyes sparkled.

My breath sat heavy in my chest. I shook my head.

"How long has it been?" Her words were as soft as velvet.

"Months…six."

"Storms would delay ships for a few months, but not six. Perhaps the ship carrying his letter was lost."

Despite the fragrant air, my lungs were leaden. "Before he left, Henri asked me to join him."

She fluttered her fan. "Why did you not?"

I pulled at a stay. "He could not marry me because he could not support me, and I didn't want to go as his mistress."

She rested her soft hand on mine. "Would you join him now, as his mistress?"

Would I? "Henri is a student, without an income."

"The estate produces one."

My hand grew warm beneath hers. "Henri feels the estate is Joliette's. He wants to make his own way in the world."

"And you remain loyal to Henri." She patted my hand.

"I will always remain loyal to him." I removed my hand and stood. I needed to dress as a man and leave Henri's château. "Has he written to you? Is there something you're not telling me?"

She tapped the fan on her lips. "No."

I gazed at the clothing on the chair. No wonder I was more comfortable pretending to be a man. Men weren't questioned about their feelings like this. Why could women not mind their own business? If we both were wearing breeches, would she be interrogating me?

She stood and adjusted her shoulders. A Marquise stood before me, one who could command an army. "Try to get to know the new Louis and forgive him. He spent a great deal of time in prison, and I believe that changed him, also."

I turned away from her and picked up the tricorne. But will he change back to the man I knew at University? The air in the room grew heavy.

"Louis did not want me to return your clothes. He said you would leave if you had them. But I told him I trust you." She touched my elbow. "Am I wrong to trust you?"

I wished the cooling breeze would fill my tight lungs. "No, Tante. LaGarde promised to take me and going with him would be safest for me."

"It takes time to build trust. Louis will have to work hard to earn yours."

A million years, I thought.

"I know you have good sense, Geneviève. I will leave you to your book." She closed the door softly behind her.

His words taunted me: *If you give her the clothes, she will leave.* I threw the tricorne across the room. Damn you, LaGarde.

I stood before the mirror. I was too thin. Lines crisscrossed my forehead. My hair had no luster. Etty had lectured me on using an egg yolk to restore silkiness and shine to my hair. I had thought her vain. I ran my fingers through what had been curls, but which now felt and looked like straw. Perhaps I should try an egg yolk. I wanted to look my best when I was in Henri's arms once again.

I placed my breeches, waistcoat, and tricorne in the armoire. I'd prove LaGarde wrong. I was trustworthy, far more than he was. I'd remain here until Papa's trial started, however long that took.

How I would put up with LaGarde until then, I had no idea. Joliette needed me to act as the vigneron, and it was time I started doing my job.

40

Paris
March 28, 1795

AFTER A TWO-DAY ride back to Paris, I stood before a chipped mirror in a lodging room, buttoning my waistcoat. Imberton wouldn't recognize me dressed as a man, but that weasel, Martin, would.

LaGarde pinched a burned candlewick and patted the soot on my eyebrows.

I inhaled his fresh scent, like a hayfield after a spring rain. Why did he have to smell so nice? My face warmed and I stepped back. "Quite menacing. My own eyebrows scare me."

"When we return, I shall have Tante Nicole instruct you on the proper application of maquillage." He held out a powdered wig with two horizontal rows of curls on either side.

"You jest."

"No. You may feel you look ridiculous, but that is exactly the point. Martin Garat would never suspect you would wear such a thing."

"Aren't you afraid of being remembered and exposed as a noble?"

He pushed out his lower lip. "Even my posture has changed since I was a courtier. I doubt anyone but a fellow noble would recognize me, and only then if he looked very closely. And to expose me, the noble would be exposing himself, no?" LaGarde dangled the wig.

I pinned my hair up and pulled the thing over my head. "I suppose the former owner of this had no need of it for the guillotine?"

"Courtiers thought me quite handsome when I wore it."

"It's yours?"

LaGarde frowned and tapped his finger on his chin.

I dreaded attending my father's trial, yet I was a loyal daughter. I could not let him pay for my crimes. I ripped the wig off and fell onto a wooden chair, scratching my scalp furiously. "It's infested with fleas."

He took the dusty thing to the window and examined it. "There are no fleas. It scratches because you are unaccustomed to it." He fitted it on my head. "I joke to help you relax, but you must be anxious."

Anxious? I was terrified. I waved my hand like it didn't matter.

He crouched before me. "Tell me what you intend to do at the trial."

His eyes had not been so full of concern since he'd asked me to save Magdeleine. I exhaled to push away the image of her laying in the hay. "If, and only if, the documents I changed are presented as evidence, I will stand and tell the court I altered them." I inched my fingers up under the wig and scratched my temple. "They will then take me and release my father."

He tipped up my chin, forcing me to look at him. "For eight months, they have collected evidence. Surely, they have more than the documents you changed."

Sunlight reflected off the gold specks in his eyes. "I changed hundreds." My voice squeaked, but LaGarde's gaze did not shift. "My father assured me he followed laws perfectly. They can't execute him for upholding laws they created." LaGarde looked so deeply into me, I squirmed.

"Your crimes would be looked upon as saving graces compared to the mountain of evidence they have amassed against your father. Geneviève, reports say he sent a son to the guillotine instead of his father—who was the man your papa condemned."

I had read that report and others, many others. My chest tightened, like when I wore a corset. I had to know if he was guilty of those crimes. "Regardless, I want to be there for him."

He captured my hand and held it, lightly, tenderly. "That is reason enough, yet I must request a promise."

I tried to pull my hand away. "Will you never stop with this noble-of-the-sword-word-of-honor business?"

He chuckled.

I stared at his massive hand encircling mine, making mine look as small as a child's. Powerful, yet gentle. I wanted to feel his hands all over my skin. I sat back.

His eyes sparked. "What is it? I have not yet asked."

Heat raced up my face. "Nothing, just a bad thought. What is it you wish?"

"Promise me that you will not offer a confession—even if the papers you altered are presented as evidence." He looked deep into me, his eyes clear and intense.

I began to pull my hand away, but his grip tightened. I was a loyal daughter—wasn't I? If my father was condemned for his own crimes, would I join him out of loyalty?

"Your confession could not possibly save him. There is no practical reason to attach your fate to his. No father would want you to." He whispered, "Promise."

My heartbeat quickened. I yanked my hand away. "Do you think I'm looking forward to having my head chopped off?" I jumped up and walked to the window.

"You saved hundreds of lives, now save your own," he whispered.

I stared out at the filthy alley. I missed the vineyard, its bright light, its calm, its hope.

"I think you fear your father going to the guillotine more than going yourself."

Damn him. "Right now, my father is alive, and I hope we'll both be when this trial is over."

"Promise. Your word of honor." He crossed his arms before his chest.

I swallowed against the nausea building in me. Maybe he was right. If I couldn't change my father's fate, there was no reason to join him. But I didn't know that yet. My word was worthless, so I might as well give LaGarde what he wanted. But wasn't it about time I made my word mean something?

"I can't."

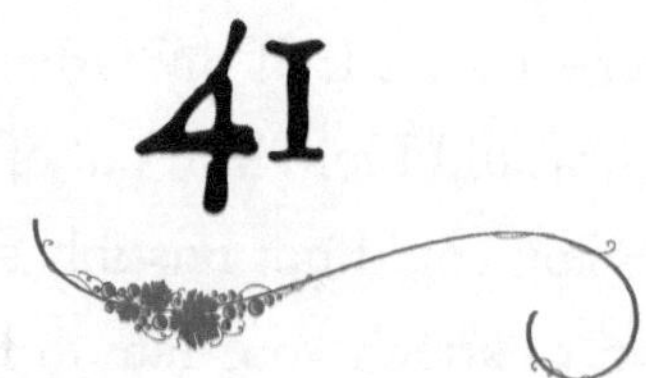

41

THE BINDING AROUND my breasts tightened as we climbed the steps and walked through the arched corridors of the Palais de Justice. Although I felt off balance in the men's boots LaGarde insisted I wear, I tried to keep my stride equal to LaGarde's, while watching for Martin and Imberton.

The Tribunal held court in the Freedom Hall, which accommodated hundreds of onlookers in the vast gallery overhanging the audience below. Guards bearing pikes lined the walls of the main floor. Mottled gray light seeped in through smudged windows running the length of the hall. The air was thick with sweat, the stink of wine, and a sour stench I feared was vengeance.

People spoke in hushed tones, but some words sliced my

heart like a knife blade: *About time he joined his victims.*

Scanning the spectator gallery above, I searched every woman's face, but I did not find Etty's. The image of Papa tenderly stroking her hand that last afternoon wavered in my mind. She was too fragile to handle this and, as he always protected her, he'd probably told her to remain at home. She must be out of her mind with fear. A surge of sympathy came over me. How had she endured the past eight months of his imprisonment? Who was minding Auguste?

A long, tall desk for the Tribunal judges stood on a raised platform—where my father once sat. To one side, stood an empty witness box, on the other sat a chair encircled by a waist-high wooden fence—a cage for my father.

I tugged at the wig. LaGarde poked me, and I stopped fidgeting.

The spectator benches, but an armlength apart, were pushed toward the front of the hall enabling many more people to stand at the rear. LaGarde directed me to sit on the end of a bench in the back, so we could easily flee.

People streamed in until guards shut the doors. Objections and murmurs from the people left outside joined the voices of the crowd inside, which grew ominous.

Eleven jurymen entered and sat to the left of the Tribunal desk. A guard led my father, shoulders rounded and hands bound behind him, to his cage.

The image would never leave me.

Papa's jabot, pristinely white, was tied in an elegant knot, reminding me of the mornings we rode together in the carriage to his office, our private time alone.

He'd lost so much weight his clothes hung in wrinkles. If

there were money for a tailor, he would have had his clothes altered. What had happened to all the louis d'ors?

A deputy untied Papa's binding and locked the box's gate. Papa sat and looked around. His hairline had receded, and his nose appeared sharper. He sat blinking, like the confused loveable bird I used to see across the dining table.

Even if Papa could see me at this distance, I doubted he'd recognize me. I willed him to feel my presence, my loyalty, my love. Etty must have promised not to attend. But I was here, even if Papa didn't realize it, I was there for him.

Shame washed over me for not having written him but doing so would have sent the Revolutionaries to the château, endangering everyone on the estate for harboring me. And I couldn't keep my promise to protect Auguste and Etty if I were dead.

I dug my fingernails into my leg, trying to feel something—love, loyalty, hope—but numbness seized my body. Would I have the courage and strength to stand and confess my crimes to save my father?

The men of the Tribunal filed in and sat behind the tall desk.

A man I recognized as a lawyer, I thought a friend to my father, stood before Papa, and read from a sheaf of papers, "I charge you, Antoine, Fouquier-Tinville—" Boos and hisses erupted from the gallery. "Former Public Prosecutor, with having transformed ordinary deeds into counter-revolutionary offenses, betraying every function of your office, having been at least one of the principal agents of the former Committee of Government, and conspiring against the security of the State and the French people."

A woman's voice screeched, "Now *you* can face Madame Guillotine!"

I shook the image of the guillotine's blade from my mind as a prickling ran down my neck. Could LaGarde and I outrun this mob?

The lawyer continued for more than ten minutes, outlining the various crimes Papa was to have committed.

I prayed they would not be able to prove my father had committed even one.

The lawyer paused, looked around the hall of spectators and announced that four-hundred and nineteen witnesses would appear.

LaGarde's eyebrows jumped.

Hope flooded through me. If Papa had more than four hundred people to defend him, he'd not need my confession.

"No witnesses were allowed for those he condemned!" A male voice shouted.

The man was right. I thought back on that morning in the carriage when I asked Papa why he'd not allowed the Carmelite nuns to have witnesses. He'd been adamant in his reply, Since the Law of 22 Prairial, and according to Articles Five and Seven, defenses are suppressed. Why was Papa allowed more than four-hundred witnesses when thousands had appeared and been condemned without one? Had the laws my father upheld been repealed?

Nausea roiled in my stomach. The government had changed, but Papa was being tried for crimes committed against the République.

A judge yelled for silence as voices shot across the hall. The lawyer paced, his hands thrust out and pressing down, trying to calm people, shouting something about the defense.

A sinking feeling pulled in me. I closed my eyes.

Four-hundred and nineteen people would be testifying *against* my father.

42

Paris
May 5, 1795

O N THE THIRTY-NINTH day of the trial, I wanted Papa to see me there for him. I convinced LaGarde to sit at the end of the second row from my father's cage. Despite my disguise, surely a father would recognize his daughter's eyes. When my father was brought in, I stared at him, hoping he'd look my way, but he stared far beyond the walls of the room.

Imberton was called.

LaGarde leaned near me. "Calm your leg."

I hadn't felt my leg bouncing, jittering the whole bench. I pressed my palm to my thigh, forcing my heel to the floor, trying to feel my foot in my boot.

"What is it?" LaGarde asked.

I whispered, "If he produces the document that your name originally appeared on, they'll hunt you down."

He puffed out his lower lip and shrugged. "No one will recognize me. I ask you again, give your word of honor."

I wished I could, but I shook my head. Wanting to hide from Imberton, I slouched behind the tall man sitting in front of me.

Imberton entered the witness box and stood straight as a pike.

"Citizen Imberton, you worked for the Prosecutor?" the lawyer asked.

"Yes, I was his head clerk." The morning light shone against the worn patches on his black frock coat.

"What duties did the Prosecutor require of you?"

"I managed all the clerks who filled out forms, copied, filed, and delivered documents."

"Were you and your clerks thorough in this documentation process?"

Imberton wiped his handkerchief across the back of his neck. "We worked until all hours of the night. If the clerks did not finish, the Prosecutor threatened to lock them up. He yelled obscenities when documents were not ready. He threw and broke things as he gave orders. Under those conditions, clerks made mistakes and had to start all over, taking more time than expected. But all documents were in perfect order when we delivered them."

I'd never heard my father yell at clerks, but I had always left the office before dark. My binding grew damp. At least stays weren't digging into me.

The lawyer handed Imberton a sheet of paper.

Please don't let it be one I altered. My hands jittered. LaGarde cleared his throat. Especially the one with LaGarde's name. I interlaced my fingers to stop their shaking.

"What is this document?" the lawyer pointed.

"A list of people designated for the guillotine."

A sob worked its way up my throat, and I coughed. LaGarde gripped my shoulder, pressing down on me. I wasn't sure I could stand or speak if I wanted to.

"Why is a name crossed out?"

I never crossed out anything. It would be an extreme violation—and would be more noticeable than a substitution. Someone else had altered that document. I flashed a look at LaGarde.

He squeezed my shoulder.

Imberton looked down his nose at my father, as imperiously as he had when he stood before my desk. "The Prosecutor scratched it out."

My chest caved as my breath rushed from me.

"Why?"

Imberton inhaled, making himself taller. "To write another name in its place. He often crossed out names from the list of the condemned and added others."

Gasps ripped through the spectators like a knife through cloth.

My father's face was impassive, as if he'd not heard a thing. I squeezed my eyes. Imberton had testified my father had sent innocent people—people who had not been tried—to their deaths. Yet, Papa did not object…or show remorse.

LaGarde clicked his heal against mine. I looked up to see alarm in LaGarde's eyes.

My father had professed following the law to the letter, yet he'd altered court documents. Just as I had, but I'd not replaced the name with the name of an innocent. My father, who'd built his life following rules to the letter, did this? My head, my heart ached.

The lawyer took back the paper and strode to stand before my father. "Did you, Antoine Fouquier-Tinville, scratch out a name and insert another on this document?"

Papa took the paper, examined it, and handed it back. "Yes."

My head jerked to the side. I must have misheard.

A rumble moved through the crowd.

"And why did you do that?"

"I knew one man was not guilty and another was, so I replaced one with the other. I have that right as Public Prosecutor."

My mouth dried. It was *not* his power. Substituting a name was no one's power. Revolutionaries had dethroned the King because he had had such power.

People in the gallery above stomped their feet so hard, I feared the ceiling would cave on top of the audience. Spoiled fruit splattered on the wooden fence around my father. A rotten potato hit him in the head, and he jerked back. The room filled with a fusty stink.

The lawyer waited for silence. "This new name, did that person have a trial?"

Brushing potato bits from his frock coat, Papa replied, "There was no need. I knew he was guilty of counter-revolutionary activities."

"That man was my husband," screamed a woman in a tattered apron and cap. "And he was innocent! Even if you go to the guillotine my husband will still be dead." She broke into sobs as another woman comforted her.

I wiped my eyes. That woman and her children would die

of starvation. And it was all my father's fault. Shame burned in me. Shame for my father and shame for my own name, a name I despised.

The chandeliers trembled from the stomping of feet in the gallery. People in the audience leaped up and tried to climb over the benches to get at my father. Guards raced from the sides wielding pikes, blocking people from killing my father with their bare hands. Yet my father sat still as an owl, his gaze glacial.

The last time I was with him glimmered in my mind, his finger caressing my cheek. His eyes so full of love I thought my heart might shatter. *You are my daughter, Geneviève, you could never dishonor me so.* My shame for having committed that which he did not believe me capable of was embedded in my mind like an insect in amber. Was I not just like my father? I too had altered documents. But there was a difference. I had done it to save people. He'd sent innocents to a mass grave and left their families to starve.

Perspiration sat on my upper lip, and I blotted it with my neckcloth. They had not presented any documents I had altered. Yet my elation of the document not being one I touched was eclipsed by my father's undeniable guilt. I wished I were sitting in the back. I could not meet my father's eyes even if he looked my way.

"Do you wish to leave?" Concern creased at the corners of LaGarde's eyes.

I shook my head.

He drew a flask from his waistcoat, uncorked it, and handed it to me.

I took a swig and another, liking the burning sensation that flowed down my throat and into my chest. I wiped my sleeve across my mouth and returned the flask. "That's not Verzat wine."

"No. It is brandy." He tucked it into my waistcoat. "If you should need it, you have it."

"I hope you have another flask." I sat looking at people's faces. A woman whose graying hair sprung from her cap held a babe to her breast and clutched three little ones to her legs. They wore rags and looked like they hadn't eaten in days. Had my father murdered her husband as well?

A brief recess was called to quiet the spectators, but everyone stayed where they were.

My arms and legs were numb, feeling totally useless. Shame over the mounting evidence against my father burned in me. Not only had he sent entire families to the guillotine, he had also sent fathers in place of sons and sons in place of fathers. My chest ached when a dead man's wife produced the birth certificates of her son and husband. How had my father mistaken a sixty-six-year-old for a twenty-two-year-old? Had he been overworked? Worried? Confused? The document in which he'd crossed out one name and replaced it was undeniable proof of his wrongdoing. His actions were cruel, heartless, evil. How would I ever make amends? I would never use the name Fouquier-Tinville again.

A judge stood, waving his arms to quiet the crowd. A hush fell over the room. The Court Clerk called Martin Garat to witness.

Clutching the edges of my frock coat, I tilted my head toward LaGarde and lifted my eyebrows toward Martin. LaGarde nodded.

"You were employed by Public Prosecutor Fouquier-Tinville?"

Martin tugged the hem of his silk waistcoat. "I was his groom and drove his carriage every day."

"Another witness, Jean Baptiste Tavernier, previously testified that sums of money were given to the Public Prosecutor instead of the Registry." The lawyer stepped close to Martin. "Did you ever witness Public Prosecutor Fouquier-Tinville accept money that should have been deposited to the Registry?"

"Many times." Martin smiled.

The crowd buzzed like an angry hornets' nest.

My mind raced, images clanging together, as I tried to make sense of them. I grabbed handfuls of my tunic, pulling it so tight the fabric began to tear. The solid gold coins I'd found in the secret compartment of my father's desk blazed in my mind. I'd suspected my father had taken the money from nobles. The lawyer and Martin were accusing my father of the same crime. Why had I doubted my instincts? I blew out a breath to still a tugging in my chest. Because I wanted to believe in my father. I didn't want to suspect him of being greedy or taking advantage of his position.

Martin brought out his arm, as if to stop the lawyer. "I saw him accept bribes many times." He lifted his chin, freeing his neck from a too-fancy jabot. "I also saw and heard him bribe jurors." He turned toward the jury box, looking at each face as every man returned his glare.

The lawyer leaned toward Martin. "Did he ever give you any of that money?"

"Oh, no!" Martin's face contorted with the effort of his objection. "Certainly not."

The crowd erupted in laughter.

Martin had answered a bit too quickly, too forcefully. Perhaps my father hadn't given money to him. Perhaps Martin had stolen it.

I let go of my tunic and wiped my sweaty palms on my breeches. My father sat, motionless, chin jutted forward, eyes alert. All these years I feared I'd done something that prevented him from loving me. I'd feared it was my fault he'd left me with the Sisters. Now I realized I'd done nothing to cause his rejection. The man who was capable of sending thousands to their deaths was incapable of loving me. It was *his* fault he couldn't love me, not mine.

I ran my fingernail along the edge of my waistcoat and pulled at a loose thread. I had felt so imperfect. But I should not have had to be perfect to be loved.

I twisted the thread as the crowd and sounds blurred around me. All this time I denied my instincts because I wanted to be a loyal daughter worthy of being loved, because I thought I had to earn it. I glanced at LaGarde. He required nothing of Louisa, nor of the orphans he sheltered. I'd been pursuing something that should have been given freely.

My father wasn't the man he'd pretended to be. He wasn't the man I'd needed him to be.

Another recess was called. Conversations buzzed.

LaGarde leaned close. "Geneviève, they have undeniable proof."

My hands twitched.

"Which shocks you more? The men who have worked for and witnessed against your father to save themselves or the evidence?"

The truth, I mouthed.

He plucked the flask from my waistcoat, took a gulp, and handed it to me.

I drained it. We would have to wait for the jury's decision, but their judgement was already clear in my mind. I hoped I'd have the courage to witness the verdict. And look my father in the eye.

43

A TORRENT OF RAIN beat against the wall of windows, a harsh rat-a-tat foreboding the execution drums. Men moved through the dark hall, lighting candles in the chandeliers and sconces. The scent of melting wax thickened the already dense, hot air.

Again, I insisted on sitting in the second row, this time, directly before my father. I still hoped to catch his eye, to see some glimmer of his recognition of me and my loyalty to him—despite his crimes.

The lawyer announced that the witness my father had called in his defense had sent a message claiming illness and would not appear.

People in the gallery applauded and a male voice shouted,

"His own witness won't defend him!" Laughter clattered like a flock of crows.

My father's eyes grew glassy.

A good daughter would be sympathetic. But with the presented evidence echoing in my mind, contempt sat in me like a pool of fetid water. If he showed one shred of compassion for those he'd wronged, I'd at least have one tender memory to treasure. If he apologized to even one of his victims, my heart might burst with love for him.

The lawyer stood facing the audience until the crowd quieted. Then he called my father to make his statement.

Ignoring the people in the gallery, Papa stood and gazed out, not at the faces, but into the distance, above the heads of the audience. No longer looking like a confused loveable bird, he now resembled a haggard vulture.

He squared his shoulders. "It is not I who should be arraigned here," his voice cracked, and he lifted his chin from his tightly knotted jabot. "…but the men whose orders I have executed. I was the agent of the Committee for the Government." He pounded his fist on the gate's wooden rail. "What would you have done in my place?"

My breath sat in my chest cold and solid as ice. He still believed he was innocent. He'd go to the guillotine professing it. But really, what choice did he have? Admit to his heartless cruelty? At one time, I'd thought him insane. But I'd told myself that lie so I could keep loving him and remain his daughter. He wasn't insane—he was a monster.

The silence of the room and my desire to hear an apology dulled my hearing. Snippets of my father's words hovered in the hall like a hoard of insects.

"...a conspiracy I have never known..."

He was blaming others. I yanked at my ear, but a buzzing filled my head. The hall closed in around me.

"...men of ill-will find what I say..."

Sparks of light spun, and I loosened my neckcloth.

"....men eager to find...guilt."

I bent forward over my knees. The floor rose like a wave. Sparks of light showered around me. Men didn't faint. I wiped sweat from my forehead. I couldn't faint. I inhaled slowly, willing the specks of light swirling around me to stop.

Cool metal pressed against my cheek.

LaGarde whispered, "Have a sip of brandy."

I took the silver flask, drank, coughed, and pushed myself to sit up.

My father's face was red and swollen, his jowls shook as he threw himself down into his chair. His posture of defiance embarrassed me and solidified my contempt for him.

A deputy brought a rope and tied my father's hands.

The lawyer called the jurymen to make their decision. They filed out, followed by my father, hands bound before him.

A man from the gallery called out, "They'll be back in ten minutes." People laughed and jeered.

One of the judges announced they would reconvene the next morning.

We sat while people filed out, quiet in their exhaustion. As the last person exited, LaGarde placed his hand on mine. I wanted to fall into his arms and stay there.

I turned to him. His eyes carried the same concern he'd shown earlier.

"Let us have dinner and wine. A lot of wine." He tipped the flask. "The brandy is finished."

For the first time since the trial began, I inhaled deeply. I no longer suffered guilt for my crimes contributing to my father's fate. LaGarde was right. My crimes were mercies.

I'd not heard one apologetic word from my father. Not one syllable of regret. He truly was a monster. There was only one more thing I owed my father—witnessing his death.

44

Paris
May 7, 1795

THE NEXT MORNING was glorious. Outside the lodging room, rooftops glinted in the sun. Nature was punishing my father who, sure to be found guilty, would bid adieu to such beauty. Like an encroaching dark cloud, my thoughts turned. How many people had he sent to their deaths on similar days?

LaGarde handed me the wig.

I shook my head. "You've paid for our rooms and all our meals and never complained or left my side, except to sleep, for the past forty days. Why?"

He pushed out his bottom lip. "For the same reason you took my name off the list."

Despite my dislike for him, I cared about him. Did he feel the same way about me? I shoved the wig on my head. "Let's get this over with."

We arrived to find people mobbing the square before the Palais de Justice. We entered through a backdoor and walked to the great hall.

The atmosphere crackled. Were people as confident as I that my father would be found guilty? Was it their impending celebration I felt? Or their fear that he might be found innocent?

LaGarde tried to lead me away from the first row, but I sat and glared at him, daring him to challenge me. I wanted my father to see me, to recognize his daughter.

A guard led Papa to the witness box. Judges took seats at their desk. The jury filed in.

Dark shadows encroached from the walls and ceiling, shrinking the room until all I saw was my father, hands tied behind him, his eyes focused on the back wall.

I closed my eyes as the verdict was read.

"Guilty!"

The cheers rattled the chandeliers.

My eyes snapped open. Waves of relief and sorrow rushed over me like a hot and cold waterfall. My heartbeat thundered.

Feet stomped. People clapped one another's backs. A woman cried out, "Now you'll drown in the blood of your victims, you monster."

Gulping a breath, air rushed in, filling my lungs. My chest expanded, as if a rope that had coiled it had unwound. I was happy for the people rejoicing and, instantly, guilt coated my skin like syrup. I forced myself to look at my father, willing him to look my way.

He sat motionless, eyes deadened, face reddening until it was the color of beetroot.

The deputy pulled my father to his feet. My father shook him off. The deputy slapped him and dragged him out.

I rose. People shoved and pushed past me. The windows and benches shook with their stomping and cheers. I looked at LaGarde. Not once had he shown the contempt he must have felt for my father—the man who had sentenced him to death.

"Do you wish to witness this?" LaGarde's voice was soft.

I placed my hand over my chest where some tiny thing gnawed at my heart, like a worm on a grape leaf. The woman was right. My father was a monster. But now that he was on his way to his own grave, images of him flowed through me: his knuckle lifting my chin, his voice expounding upon laws, his sorrow-filled eyes with every mention of Maman.

I scratched my scalp under the wig. Papa had dishonored me. I had dishonored him, too, but there was a difference. A shiver ran through me. My father was a cruel monster. Yet, despite everything, just one look of remorse would enable me to forgive him. If I got close enough, I'd remove the wig so he would recognize me. I had to give him that chance.

Compassion filled LaGarde's eyes.

"I'm not sure I want to, but I feel obligated." I whispered, "He is my father."

LaGarde placed a hand on my shoulder and led the way.

The tumbrel—that had carted thousands to their deaths— awaited. I wondered at the irony. Had the Tribunal purposefully chosen carts that had once been used to haul manure for transporting prisoners on their last journeys?

People jammed the streets. Not since the royal family had returned from Versailles, six years earlier, had I seen such joyous, vengeful people. LaGarde kept me close to the building until we broke free of the entangling mob. We hurried down back alleys to a street where we'd be able to see the tumbrel roll by on its way across the Seine. My heartbeat thundered as the distant roar grew louder. Jeers clashed, the loudest, "Join your victims!"

Although Etty had been unkind to me, I hoped she could not hear this. It was so loud, if the windows were open, she would. Yet, I suspected someone had already delivered the news, and she'd not hear the crowd over her weeping. I hoped Agathe was distracting my brother. I wished I had folded many paper boats for Auguste before I'd left.

LaGarde gripped my elbow as people shoved and pushed past. I wanted to clasp my hands to my ears, but there wasn't room to move my arms. The press of sweating bodies and the stink of stale wine dizzied me.

The horses pulling the tumbrel snorted. The tumbrel and my father were before me. In my mind, I saw the child I'd been reaching out for him at the Abbey. She was frightened and needed his protection, his reassurance that all would be well. My arms ached.

A woman grabbed at my father's sleeve. He yanked it away and shouted, "Filthy riff-raff." He spat at her.

My chest grew cold. The first day of the trial, I had thought I'd rip off my wig and wipe the soot off my eyebrows so that my father would recognize me and see my love for him. Now I stood, my arms limp at my sides. All these years I had worked for and tried to earn the approval and love of a man I could no longer respect. A man unworthy of respect.

His eyes roved the crowd. I wasn't sure if I wanted him to see me or not. His eyes glinted like cold hard metal. He tilted his head back, looking down his nose at LaGarde. Was my father remembering that he had condemned LaGarde and wondering why he still lived?

I wanted to slap my father. LaGarde rescued orphans. My father killed their parents.

LaGarde wrapped his arm around my shoulder, drawing my father's attention to me.

His gaze fell upon me. I yanked off my hat and wig, expecting his face to soften, as it did whenever he greeted me for, despite my darkened eyebrows, surely a father would recognize his own child's eyes, the shape of her face, the color of her hair. But not a flicker of recognition crossed his stone-hard eyes.

I turned away, staring at the filth wedged between the cobbles. I had hoped, like the child I'd been. The woman I had become stood in silence. Anger and contempt raged in me like a fever. I shoved the wig and hat back on my head.

People pushed past us.

LaGarde whispered, "Do you wish to follow?"

"You may think me a coward, but I do not wish to witness it—he does not deserve such an honor."

"I do not think you a coward." His eyes were so kind I wanted to fall into his arms. "You have never been braver."

I didn't feel brave. I felt like going home. But where *was* my home? "I want to say goodbye to my brother first."

The corner of LaGarde's mouth jerked. "They will be watching for you."

"I know. But Etty won't want Auguste in the house. He'll be in the park with the housekeeper."

45

 THE CARRIAGE SHUDDERED as we headed toward the park. "Why have you never spoken of your brother?"

I didn't want to answer questions. I wanted to give Auguste a secret way to find me, tell him goodbye, and get back to the château. "He's my half-brother."

"You must love Auguste dearly if you are risking your life to see him."

My eyes burned. He was seven now. I hadn't seen him in nearly a year. Dust covered the plane trees, making them more gray than green, as if they, too, had been condemned to die by the almighty Committee of General Security and Public Safety. "I do."

LaGarde ran his tongue over his teeth. "Why not bring him and his mother to the château?"

"She is penniless."

"As were the Sisters and the orphans, but you gave them shelter."

I felt his unwavering gaze on me like the rays of the sun. Street urchins, clamoring for sous, ran alongside the carriage. The children, the cobbles, the water, the air—everything in Paris was filthy.

"Did your father not provide for her?"

"I took the money," I snapped. "To save Louisa and the Sisters and orphans." I scratched my scalp. "I thought I was just stealing from Papa, and I would return it, but I didn't."

He suppressed a smile. "I will have money delivered to her anonymously to pay for their travel."

"You are kind, but she won't leave the home she shared with Papa." I didn't want to admit my stepmother could be so cruel, but LaGarde had to know. "I think Etty reported me to the Committee. She'd turn me in if she hasn't already."

"Then bring Auguste, alone."

I wanted nothing more than to do just that. I wiped the perspiration from my face. "Etty just lost her husband. I cannot take her son."

He pushed out his lower lip, like he usually did when he accepted things beyond his control. The carriage entered our old neighborhood, and I pulled back into the shadow.

He leaned over and rested his elbows on his knees. "You know gendarmes will be at the house…watching for you."

Auguste's voice sang in my mind. *Make a boat for me, please.* "Do you have a pamphlet?"

He frowned. "You wish to read gossip?"

"I want to fold the paper into boats for him." I pointed

across the small meadow of dried weeds to the pond where Auguste and I had sailed hundreds of boats. An ache throbbed in my chest. Auguste stood alone, at its edge, dragging a stick through the murky water. "There he is."

LaGarde pounded the ceiling of the carriage, and it slowed. "Go to him. I will bring a newssheet to you."

He was so damned kind. I grabbed the door handle. "Merci."

LaGarde's hand covered mine. "Be careful. The carriage will remain here."

"I won't be long." I jumped down and straightened my frock coat. At the end of the pond, a hill rose. Agathe sat on a bench at its top, totally absorbed in gossiping with two old biddies dressed in black, no doubt discussing my father's execution.

I hoped I wouldn't frighten Auguste with my disguise and scrubbed the soot from my eyebrows. I hurried through the prickly grass and crouched a few feet from him. "Would you like me to make you a boat?" I whispered.

He jolted. "Gen!" He furrowed his brow and peered at me. "Is it you?"

I took off my hat, shook my hair loose, and opened my arms.

He threw himself at me. Crying, pummeling me with his fists. "Where were you, Gen?"

I hugged him, pulling him close, breathing in his soft scent, not wanting a thread of air to come between us. I rubbed his back. "I'm here. Quiet, now."

He pulled back and brushed the hair from my face. "Why are you dressed like a man?"

I put my finger to my lips and whispered, "I'm hiding from bad gendarmes. Will you help me?"

He nodded fiercely. He was taller, thinner, his cheeks sallow.

He wasn't eating enough. My arms ached to take him with me. "You must not tell anyone, not Maman nor Agathe, that you saw me. Do you promise?"

He put his hand to his chest. "On my heart. I promise." He pressed his forehead against mine. "Where were you? Papa is gone and Maman cries all the time. No one reads to me."

"Not even Maman?"

"She doesn't have the words."

"Do you mean she doesn't know some of the words?"

"She doesn't have any of them."

Could Etty not read? Is that why she always asked me to do it? If she had told me, I could have taught her. A pressure built in my chest, squeezing my heart. "I'm sorry. Do you remember the stories?"

"It's not the same as when you read them." He gripped my lapels. "Come home, Gen."

I shoved my hat on and ran my fingers through his auburn curls, streaked with gold, glittering in the sun. Why had I not noticed he had Papa's heart-shaped face? I wanted to scoop him up and carry him all the way to the château. He would love it there. He could play with the other children and the animals. He would have plenty of food. And we'd be together, safe. I rubbed his back. "I can't stay here. Bad men would come and take me away. But I'll visit."

"No! You stay with me!" The heat of his body sent a throbbing through me that I feared would shake me apart. His sobs soaked my tunic. A better sister would stay. But bad men would not be after a better sister.

A pair of boots stopped next to Auguste.

"Mademoiselle!"

Heat shot up my back.

Martin's obsequious voice dripped like syrup. "How nice to see you again."

My thighs burned from crouching. Had he brought guards to arrest me?

"Stop spying on us!" Auguste shouted.

I pulled Auguste close and stood. Forcing a smile and gripping my brother, I stepped back. "Bonjour." I gazed beyond him, searching for gendarmes, hoping to spot LaGarde.

His eyes glittered like the brass buttons of his frock coat. He caressed the embroidery on his silk waistcoat, which was far too elaborate for a groom. His hand shot out and snatched my wrist. "Before I deliver you to the Committee, I have a surprise for you."

If he hadn't brought guards, he would kill me himself or, worse, make me wish I was dead. I yanked my wrist from his grasp.

Auguste squirmed in my arms. "Go away, Martin. We don't want you here."

Martin sniggered. "Your papa—"

"Stop." I glared at him, warning him not to continue. "I will return Auguste to his nurse, and then we can depart. Do not follow me."

He winced. "You do not trust me? After all the years I devoted to your dear papa?" He grinned.

He knew I had been at the trial. He knew I'd go to Auguste. I wanted to spit in his face, but I needed to ensure Auguste's safety. "Wait here."

He clasped my arm and jerked me so close his lust rose like a stink. "If you don't return, I'll come back for your precious brother."

I swallowed back rage that thrummed in me and yanked my arm back. I hurried Auguste halfway up the hill near to where Agathe was sitting, but not so close that she would notice me. I crouched to face him. "Do you remember the printshop where I took you?"

He nodded. "Through the market with the rats and across the river?"

"Yes. That's right. If you need me, you go to that shop and tell them you are a friend of Henri Detré. Can you remember that?"

"Of course. Henri Detré."

I hugged him. "They will get a message to me, and I will come for you. It must be our secret. You must tell no one—ever."

"I promise." His breath was warm on my neck. "Please don't go, Gen."

I ached to stay with him. I inhaled against burning tears and steadied my voice. "Run to Agathe and tell her you want to go to Maman right away. Cry, pout, yell, do everything to make her take you home. Do you understand?"

"I'll protect you. I won't let Martin take you away."

"I know." My throat was so tight my words squeaked. "But I must do something now, and I want you to be safe. Will you make Agathe take you home?"

"When will you be back?" His eyes were pools of trust. I had never hurt him, never betrayed him, never made a promise

I had not kept. He patted my cheek, and I feared my heart would splinter.

"Very soon. I promise. And I'll bring boats." I kissed his neck, his forehead, his nose. "Will you go home now? Do not look back for me. Promise?"

"All right. I love you, Gen." He kissed my cheek. "Hurry back?"

"I promise. I love you." I gave him a little push and watched him run to Agathe. As I rose, I pulled the dagger I kept secreted in my boot and slipped the blade up into my frock coat sleeve. I had to outsmart Martin, but how? I didn't see any gendarmes. If he hadn't brought them, I would have only to escape him. I straightened and walked down the hill. Searching the park, the path, the road, I hoped no gendarmes lurked in the shadows and LaGarde would appear within the next second.

Martin slumped against a tree with a grin as greasy as his lanky hair.

A snake of hatred curled in my belly. I wiped my sweaty palm against my breeches and gripped the dagger's hilt. I had to surprise the viper, lure him, catch him off guard. I would have to act in the opposite way he expected me to behave. I would act the helpless female. When he was sure he had me where he wanted me, I'd stab him. I hoped I had the courage and the strength.

He lunged and grabbed me, turning me and pulling my back against his chest. I gave a little scream and no objection. My unexpected compliance unbalanced him. He stumbled and clutched me. I leaned back into the disgusting stench of his body, reeking like the sweat of a hard-ridden horse. I fought every urge to struggle.

In the distance, Auguste tugged Agathe's hand and hurried her over the hill. My heart thudded as, in my mind, I urged him not to look back and to run to safety.

Martin scratched his fingernail along my neck. "I'll take my time with you before I send you to the guillotine." He flicked his tongue along my ear and bit my earlobe.

"Ow!"

"I like when I hurt you." His breath was hot. "I want to hurt you more. Make you scream and beg."

I swallowed back a wave of nausea. LaGarde, where are you? Think. How can I get far enough away to use the dagger? Pretend to give Martin what he wants, then turn on him.

I let my body go limp, rested my chin on my chest, pretending to faint. I moaned.

He twisted me toward him. Acting as limp as a ragdoll, I gripped the dagger hilt, brought it up, and slashed the blade across his cheek. Easy as drawing a knife through butter. Tiny droplets of blood showered his face.

He yelled, clutching his cheek and stumbling backward. Blood streamed down his jaw.

I ran across the meadow, jumped in the carriage, and shrieked, "Allez!" Where was LaGarde? "Allez!" The carriage lurched. How would LaGarde find me?

Martin's shouts echoed, "Gendarmes! Gendarmes!"

I could not see Martin through the window. Had he followed me? The door banged against the opening. "Damn you, Martin!" As I lunged across the bench to pull the door, it was yanked from my hand. LaGarde threw himself across my lap, shouting at the driver, "Allez, vite!"

The horses charged, careening around a corner. I caught the image of Martin clutching his face, blood covering his hands.

LaGarde pushed himself up and reached out. "You're bleeding!"

"No." I heaved for breath. "I stabbed Martin. It's his blood."

LaGarde took the dagger, wiped it clean with his neckcloth, and watched out the window.

I leaned over my legs and gagged.

He sat next to me, held my forehead, and pulled back my hair. "Take deep breaths."

I tried, but my breath sat hard as rock beneath my breastbone.

The carriage rumbled over cobbles, through neighborhoods no longer familiar to me. The nausea began to fade as the ache of missing Auguste etched my heart.

LaGarde rapped on the ceiling of the carriage. "Pull over!"

"No! Martin alerted the gendarmes. They could be following us."

"I have been watching. They are not." As the carriage slowed, LaGarde jumped out and flung the dagger into the Seine. He yelled to the driver, "Allez," and jumped back in. "Best be rid of that before we give papers at the city barrier. The gendarmes might be waiting there."

"Merci." I gripped the bench and struggled against the nausea.

He sat next to me and held out a flask. "Drink."

I sipped the brandy, took another, and another until the warmth spread through me.

"You did not kill him?"

The words burst. "Damn it, no."

He rubbed my back. "When we return to the château, we will train in knife fighting."

Most women trained in embroidery, managing a household, and arranging social dinners. But I dressed like a man. I might as well learn to fight like one. Martin wouldn't give up his chase. The next time he came for me, I'd be ready.

46

Paris
May 7, 1795

LAGARDE SAT DOZING opposite me in the carriage, allowing me my solitude. I spat on my handkerchief and rubbed Martin's blood off my hands, his stink rising. I balled up the handkerchief, lowered the window, and threw it, hoping his blood did not kill anything.

I ripped off the wig, tossed it on the bench, and rubbed my scalp, scratching the memory of Martin from my mind. Golden afternoon light reflected off the river, but its beauty blurred behind the image in my mind of my father, his hands tied, collar ripped, and hair chopped short, exposing his neck. He had the neck of a wild boar, my father.

The horses' hooves beat a tattoo, echoing the executioner's drum, hammering the image of the guillotine into my memory. The constant chirring of insects did not drown out the mob's cries, pounding in my head. A sharp breeze raked fields of green wheat. How would I ever make amends? Would I fall to my knees and beg forgiveness every time I met someone who had lost a loved one to the guillotine? I would spend the rest of my life on my knees.

We arrived at the Magdeleine Orphanage long after the children had gone to bed. I pinned up my hair and donned my hat, as everyone there knew me as the man called Jean.

Exhausted, we sat before a cold fireplace in the salon. I wiped dust from my eyes, but my vision blurred, and I wondered if it was from not wanting to see the images that played in my mind.

A woman I recalled from my first visit, entered. Wearing a faded aubergine-colored gown, she carried a tray of bread, cheese, fruit, and wine.

"Merci, Suzanne." LaGarde reached up for it and placed it on the low table before us.

"De rien." She leaned over him, nearly spilling her breasts in his face, and kissed him on both cheeks. "Welcome home, Louis. I hope you stay a long time." She drew her fingertips along his jaw.

"Merci." He gently brushed her hand away, then reached for the bread and broke off a piece.

She no longer had to be a whore, but she still acted like one.

Suzanne poured the wine and offered me a glass.

"Merci." I stood and, as I reached, I upset it, spilling wine down her gown.

She stepped back, her mouth open, her hand flying up.

"Oh, I am so sorry." I grabbed a serviette and began to pat the stain.

She snatched the cloth. "That is not the way to remove wine. The stain must be salted." She straightened and turned to LaGarde. "Bonne nuit."

"Bonne nuit," he replied.

"Again, I am so sorry." I added a weak, "Bonne nuit."

She hurried from the room; I suspected in search of salt. Etty would be glad to know of that remedy. How clumsy of me. Had I done that on purpose? My cheeks burned. She prized that ratty old gown, and I'd made it worse. I sat staring at the food, knowing I should be famished, but I had no desire to eat or move. "I am so tired, I am not thinking or seeing things clearly. I didn't mean to spoil her gown."

LaGarde leaned back and stretched his legs out. "I shall buy her a new one, and she will be happy."

I wanted to suggest he buy her a gown with a higher neckline, but he'd think me jealous. And I certainly wasn't. "Where do you get all the money? You paid for our lodgings, our meals, and the food to feed all the people here."

He drank deeply. "Henri's father was not the only noble who wisely put his estate to use. My father gave the tenants their own homes on the condition they work the land. They are very productive and keep a portion of what they harvest. No one starves here."

Oh, to be born a noble—no commoner inherited a guaranteed income. Little wonder the revolutionaries wanted to kill them.

LaGarde drew a knife through a paté and offered a slice. "You will feel better after you eat something."

I accepted it and took a bite. Rich, silky, redolent of pepper and rosemary with a hint of cloves. The pastry encasing the paté was light and flakey. Divine. I took a sip of wine, rich and smooth as velvet. "Verzat?"

"Bien sûr. You think I would serve you anything less than the best wine in France?"

I was glad one of us could afford it. I took another bite.

"You are troubled."

I wiped crumbs from my lips. "I promised my father I'd protect and care for Auguste and my stepmother. I cannot return, and I have no money. Well, I suppose I could sell my hair to a wig maker."

He laughed.

I pulled a lock from under the wig. "But it is not the fashionable blonde."

"Never sell your hair. It is at its most beautiful upon your head…and about your shoulders."

Was he flirting or was I just tired? I shrugged. "I cannot invite them to Henri's château, for there are too many who might wish to take revenge for my father on my stepmother and his son."

"This château will shelter you for the rest of your life, Geneviève. If you wish it, Auguste and your stepmother as well."

"That is kind of you, but I believe she may turn me in. If it weren't for Auguste, I'd abandon my promise." I leaned back. "I call her Pouffiasse."

He laughed. "A bitch, a floozy, a whore? She must be quite a woman."

"Not really." I sighed.

"What do you wish to do?"

Had I any other choice? "Perhaps I can find a job and send money to her for Auguste. Until then, I will return to Château de Verzat, apprentice the vigneron, and await Henri's return."

LaGarde's heels clacked sharply on the parquet as he walked to a side table. He lifted a carafe and a glass. "Do you care for brandy?"

"No, merci."

He poured a glass and stood staring above the fireplace at a portrait of a man who I took to be his father. "Why has Henri not sent for you?"

There it was, like a storm advancing across the horizon, the question I'd been too afraid to ask myself. "He's been working as an abolitionist in America. He has no income."

"Pah. The winery is doing exceptionally well. War makes everyone thirsty."

"If I know Henri, he doesn't feel the money and the château are his."

LaGarde cocked his head. "One thing the Revolutionary government did do was make both women and all illegitimate children equal to men as heirs. The estate is half Henri's."

"Like you, Henri and Joliette didn't want the government to seize their property, so they sold the tenants their homes and property for one livre. The proceeds from the winery pay the taxes for the entire estate, the château's upkeep, and provide the tenants a small income."

"They were wise to do so. But there must be some profit to pay one passage to America."

My face grew warm. He was as persistent as a dog with a

bone. Why was he asking this when it was none of his concern? I got up and looked out the glass doors, but the dark reflected my sorry image. He'd know I was avoiding the question. How did LaGarde see right through me? It was his most annoying habit. My skin prickled.

"If he does not have the money, I will give it to you, if that is what you wish." His voice was soft as a breeze.

I stared at him. Was he so eager to get rid of me? Did he not just say I could stay here forever?

"Geneviève?"

He wasn't going to stop questioning me. I took a gulp of wine. "A lady does not ask a gentleman to marry her." Why had I said that? Did I wish to be asked? I thought back to the day Henri had left and winced as I remembered my accusation: *Accompany you as what? Your mistress?* I could have gone, but I'd wanted him to tell me he loved me. If only he'd said he'd wanted to marry me but couldn't afford to and would when he earned a living.

LaGarde pushed out his lower lip. "You are no ordinary lady."

I reached behind my back and tugged at the binding squeezing my breasts. "Nonetheless. A lady likes to be asked."

He grinned. "I shall remember that."

Did he never tire of teasing me? The binding cramped my breath. "I am weary. Shall we leave in the morning? You must be missing Louisa. I know I am."

"Yes."

"I'll sleep in the stables. You've no worry I will leave during the night."

He neared me and placed his hand on my arm. "There is plenty of room here. Before I show you to your chamber, I wish to extend an offer."

The binding tightened. Now what? I already felt naked before him. My arm tingled from the heat of his touch. I tilted my head toward his hand.

He let me go. "As director of the Magdeleine Orphanage, may I write to your stepmother? I will tell her that after her husband's arrest, he arranged for her and Auguste to live here, in the event something should happen to him."

Warmth flooded my chest. "That is most kind and generous...and thoughtful of you."

"The other ladies could keep her busy when you visit Auguste without her knowing."

I stepped back, laughing. "I can just imagine how my stepmother would get along with the other women and children here."

His smile fell.

I pitched forward. "I cast no aspersions upon the ladies, it's my stepmother who would be the problem. She is accustomed to being waited upon. She finds fault with everyone and everything. And she pays little attention to Auguste. She is insufferable and would have these kind women and orphans fleeing."

He laughed. "They are more resilient than you think. She would be the one fleeing."

"You are most kind, LaGarde."

"Is it not the least I can do for the woman who saved not only my life, but also my daughter's?" He was so close I felt the heat of his body.

"That debt has been paid. You saved my life. Remember?"

"I still owe you one life."

Why was he so damned handsome?

LaGarde picked up a candelabrum, its candleflames flickering. "I will leave this in your chamber. You might wish to write Henri before retiring."

I was wrung out from the trial and fending off Martin, and now he brought up the question I'd succeeded in avoiding for years. Why didn't Henri send for me? His last words played in my mind. *I've nothing to offer you.* Yet, he had asked me to live in his château while he was an ocean away. I'd been clerking to save money for passage, money I'd spent rescuing people. But did I still want to sail to America? Women could own businesses, but what sort would I own? They could own land, but I had no money to buy it. And what would I do with property? The country held no allure. I didn't speak English very well. I'd only go to be with Henri.

I drained my glass. If I asked and Henri refused, what then? And if he sent for me, but didn't want to marry me? I loved Henri. But it had been three years. He must have changed.

I followed LaGarde to the same chamber I had used the last time we visited. A white gown with stripes of tiny blue flowers and a blue silk sash lay on the bed. It was of a fine quality linen and of the new fashion, with the waist raised to just below the bosom, requiring no corset or stays. What a relief, but what was he telling me? I lifted the gown and looked at him. "Where did this come from?"

"Paris. Your false identity papers put Jean Detré between the ages of eighteen and twenty-five?"

I nodded.

"Should we be stopped by the Républican Army, they would immediately conscript you. Better you dress as a woman."

"How old are you?"

"My Papers show me married and my age as twenty-eight, so I am doubly safe."

"You're..." My heart thumped like a landed fish. "You're married?"

He roared a laugh. "Afraid I am already taken?" He slapped his leg. "No, nor am I yet twenty-eight. But both those facts keep me from being conscripted."

My heart calmed. One day I would trick him as he tricked me, and I wouldn't be so quick to right his thinking. I dropped the gown on the bed.

He placed the candelabrum on the desk, opened a drawer and withdrew paper. "Send Henri my regards." He placed the paper on the desk. "Bonne nuit." He left.

His persistence would surely drive me mad. I stood looking between the soft inviting bed and the desk. I unbuttoned my waistcoat, unwound the binding, and inhaled deeply. On a table in the corner, a crystal decanter sparkled in the candlelight. I poured a glass of brandy and sipped. Why had I reacted so stupidly when LaGarde said he was married? He had loved and wanted to marry Magdeleine. I must have reacted to thinking he had lied to her.

I sat at the desk, took up the quill, dipped it. The weight of the damned censors sat heavily on my shoulders. Their interference or destruction of my letter made writing cumbersome.

Dearest Henri,

After six weeks of trial, Antoine Fouquier-Tinville was found guilty and guillotined. I am relieved and pray his death stops the executions.

At least I could hang onto that hope. I tossed the quill down, picked up the glass, and opened the multipaned double doors. I stood on a small balcony overlooking the gardens. Silvery moonlight bathed the land. A tall muscular figure, unmistakably LaGarde, carrying a brandy bottle and two glasses, strode from the château toward the stables. He whistled a jaunty tune. Probably on his way to have a drink with the groom. An owl screeched, waking me to my own naïveté. A man like LaGarde would be on his way for a tête-à-tête with the buxom Suzanne.

I drained the rest of the brandy, slammed the doors, marched to the desk, and dipped the quill.

I have loved you all these years we've been apart, Henri. I still long for your tender touch, your gentle gaze, the whisper of your breath along my neck. You once asked me to go with you to America, and I regret deeply I did not join you. I have no money for passage, but if you arrange it, I will join you immediately. Being once again in your arms is my heart's desire. Until then, I remain at your château, assisting the vigneron.

Yours,

G.

I reread my words, wondering if I should give him a graceful way to decline. Should I offer to remain at the château and continue assisting the vigneron for Joliette? LaGarde's words thrummed in my head: *You have more courage than any woman or man I know.*

No, I wouldn't give Henri an easy way to reject me. I had the courage to face—I sighed. Perhaps I didn't have the courage, but I would find it. Now I had only to wait. And hope.

I ran my fingers through my hair. My scalp felt like I was still wearing that flea-infested wig. I would busy myself in the vineyard, increase production, and surprise Joliette.

47

Château de Verzat
November 1795

I PICKED AT GRAPE stains underneath my fingernails as I headed for the château kitchen. I would never have the hands of a lady. It had been nearly six months since I'd written to Henri and, all through the harvest and crushing, I'd awaited his answer. His sister's letters of instructions for Joseph, the vigneron, arrived twice a month. I took over responding to Joliette everyday—but those letters were about the vendanges, the crushing, the tastings. I was becoming a vigneron while waiting to become a wife.

A freezing wind whipped fallen leaves across the dirt road and, in the distance, whitecaps skittered across the river. I wondered if the Loire would freeze this year. I hoped not. Woodsmoke from the cottages on the estate reminded me that everyone here would not go hungry. Henri, your father would be proud of you for keeping them safe.

The breeze delivered the aroma of Oncle Louis's lentil soup as I approached the kitchen door. I smiled at the memory of all those orphans cheering for their Oncle Louis. I hoped Auguste would soon be among them.

Tante Nicole, Madame Detré, Louisa, and all the Sisters and orphans sat at the scarred wooden table. LaGarde ladled up bowl after bowl and laughed as he explained, "It is only Oncle Louis's soup if it has wine in it."

I closed the door behind me and hung my hat and cloak on a peg. The room quieted. The fire snapped. The children squirmed and ate their soup. What were they keeping from me? I looked at Louisa—her face never hid a thing. So much like her mother. A sliver of pain ran through my chest. Magdeleine's face shimmered in my mind. You would be so proud of your daughter, my friend.

Louisa wiggled on the bench, pressing her fingers to her mouth. She'd been told to keep a secret. And teasing it out of her would be great fun.

"Is there any soup left for me?" I sat on the bench across from Louisa.

Her fingers still pressed to her lips, she nodded.

LaGarde held his face and posture in all seriousness and placed a bowl before me. I inhaled the steam and picked up my spoon. It was mean of me, for I knew she could not keep a secret, but I smiled at Louisa. "How do you like your papa's soup?"

Her shoulders rose to touch her ears. "A letter came for you." She pressed her hands over her mouth and blushed crimson.

Giggles erupted from the children.

I laughed, hoping it seemed like I thought this funny, but the letter had to be from Henri, and I was overjoyed. "You tried very hard to keep the secret." I looked around, all eyes staring at me. My joy slid and crashed into the pit of my stomach. They would all want me to read the letter aloud, just as Madame Detré and Tante Nicole did.

This was going to take more calm than I possessed. I'd have to act happy—no matter the news. "Well, are you going to give it to me or have you hidden it?"

Louisa jumped up. "Let me!" She hopped over the bench, ran to a basket, grabbed the letter, and stood next to me, holding the letter over her heart and panting. "Out loud, Tante Gen?"

LaGarde scooped her up and thrust her above his head. She giggled. "Tante's letter is private." He took the letter from her and handed it to me.

If the news was bad, I could pretend. But if Henri was sending for me, everyone, would be sad—as I would be to leave them. Why had I not thought of that before? I would miss every single person surrounding me with their love.

I turned the letter over. The seal was unbroken—the censors had not edited it. My heart was thundering so loudly, I worried everyone could hear it. I peeked up at Tante Nicole. Her face was kindness itself. I couldn't stand it. I cracked the seal.

Louisa clapped.

I held the letter before me, quickly scanning, swallowing against the squirming in my belly when I did not see the words *join me*. Very well. I could and would act. I cleared my throat and spoke in a loud voice, for everyone to hear.

"Dear G,

As I have not heard from you, I fear you did not receive the letter I sent in July."

I looked up at Tante Nicole. Her face was soft with compassion, like she knew what I was feeling. She shook her head. I gazed at Henri's mother. "Has Henri written to you about me?" Madam Detré tapped her fingers against her chin before shaking her head. I continued reading aloud.

"I am so very sorry to learn of the passing of your relative. You have always been so courageous and never more so than now. I pray you are right, that the killings will stop. France has lost far too many of her citizens.

Thank you for caring for Pierre's family. You did the right thing by giving them shelter, and I am indebted to you.

My mother tells me you have brought a beautiful little girl whom everyone loves, most of all you. My neph—"

"Is that me?" Louisa's eyes glittered.
"Indeed it is." I continued.

"My nephew delights me daily and you must experience the same. I cannot imagine leaving him."

My throat tightened. Could I leave Louisa? I'd promised Magdeleine I'd care for her, forever. I cleared my throat and read aloud,

"Joliette is indebted to you for assisting old Joseph with the ven-danges and responding to her with such detail and regularity. She hopes that he is teaching you all he knows should he not be able to carry out her instructions. In such an event, she and I, as well as everyone on the estate, would be eternally grateful to you if you would continue until she can once again fulfill her dream of returning to the Verzat Estate.

There are many émigrés in Philadelphia. We hear all the latest news from Talleyrand, who believes former nobles will be able to return to France under the new Directory, to which he has petitioned for his own return. Both Joliette and I treasure that day and hold hope in our hearts for our return, which may be soon, as I am certain you hope as well.

Please write and let me know if you received my previous letter."

I stopped my voice, but read:

Until then, I trust your courage, my friend. Yours, Henri.

Friend? I folded the paper, pressing my finger along the edges, creasing it and its veiled message. I'm not sending for you. Don't come.

I could not look at Tante Nicole or LaGarde. I could not bear their looks of pity.

Madame Detré stood and walked to the fireplace, muffling a sob in her handkerchief. If I missed Henri, his mother must miss him just as much if not more.

"I remember Talleyrand from Court, before he was ordained

as a bishop. Do you remember him, Louis?" Tante Nicole whispered.

LaGarde nodded.

Madame Detré turned toward LaGarde. "Do you think they'll come home soon?"

"I suspect so, Madame." LaGarde placed Louisa on the bench. "Eat your soup before it gets cold." He sat at the head of the table, between Louisa and me. "This new Directory needs the money held by émigrés. And I believe the new government will want Talleyrand as a diplomat or minister. He turned against the church and, with his personal ties to the Americans as well as the British, he would be a powerful ally to this new government."

What did I care of Talleyrand? I closed my eyes, seeing Henri's words. What had he written four months ago? It had to be in reply to my letter, telling him I wanted to join him. Why did he not repeat his previous letter in this one? My pulse pounded in my ears. He held hope in his heart for the day he could return. He wrote of Talleyrand because he trusted him and his predictions. He was telling me to stay here because he would be returning soon. That had to be it, he couldn't write it for fear the censors—

The slamming of wood against stone made us all jump. Simon stood waist-deep on the stairs below the trapdoor to the tunnel connecting the kitchen to the wine cave. He waved his arm. "Gen, Louis, come quick. Hurry!"

LaGARDE HANDED LOUISA to Tante Nicole. "Take the children and the women to the secret room. Stay there until I come for you." He thrust a torch into the fire and caught a flame.

Secret room? I opened my mouth, but LaGarde grabbed my elbow and led me down the stairs to the tunnel.

The torchlight flamed and flickered as I ran after Simon, shouting, "What's happened?"

"A Chouan rescued some drowning Catholics and brought them here."

The cold air of the tunnels plunged down my chest. The Revolutionaries feared the Catholics would return the monarchy to govern France. We all had read the horrible reports that Republican soldiers hounded Catholics, slaughtered their animals, burned their crops and homes, stripped people of their clothes and jewelry, chained them together on leaky barges and scuttled the vessels in the Loire, making the river a mass grave. All for believing in a God most Republicans wouldn't admit they, too, worshipped.

In retaliation, the Catholic Royalists had formed their own army and called themselves Chouans. If they had come to us, they were being hunted, on the run, desperate. I prayed no one was injured, but I also prayed Revolutionaries hadn't followed them here. The entire estate would be turned over to the government should Chouans be discovered here.

At the end of the tunnel, Simon scratched his fingernails on the trapdoor above and waited. Three stomps sounded. Simon pushed up the door. I climbed the steep wooden steps into the fermenting room where huge casks, their circumferences greater than LaGarde was tall, lay on their sides. Breathing in the sour musty smell, I peered into the shadows, seeing no one. LaGarde climbed out holding his pistol. Good thinking. I wished I had mine, now that he'd taught me to use it, but I was grateful my dagger was in my boot.

Simon took the torch and led us behind the casks and through a narrow winding cave into a smaller chamber lit by a single candle held by the largest man I'd ever seen—a Chouan. He wore a round floppy hat of brown felted wool, trousers and boots of deerskin, and a goatskin thrown over his shoulders like a cloak. A small white patch with a red cross topping a heart was sewn to the lapel of his frock coat. *Dieu le Roi* was embroidered below the sacred heart. God the King were traitorous words. He held a musket like a staff, resting the butt on the stone floor. The stink of sweat and fear reminded me of the cells at la Conciergerie.

LaGarde's lips pressed into a grim line. The torchlight revealed two women and two small children, all dripping wet, shivering, cowering behind the Chouan. Auguste's face flashed in my mind.

I stood before the man. "What's happened?" He stared at LaGarde who pointed at me.

The Chouan looked me up and down. "They survived the drowning. They've nowhere to go. They beg you shelter." His sunken cheeks looked chiseled by wind and rain.

I thought the drownings had stopped. "But the Convention granted the right to religious freedom."

His knuckles grew white on the musket barrel. "Revolutionaries line them up outside their churches and execute them." His eyes were black, hard, cold, like a crow's. "Especially women—since they give birth to us Rebels." He spat his disgust to the side.

I swallowed against a bitter taste in the back of my throat. My father wasn't the only monster of this Revolution.

LaGarde stood next to me, his breathing deep. "You know Henri. What would he do?"

My shoulders rolled forward, like a giant hand was pressing down on me. If Revolutionaries discovered we were harboring Chouan soldiers or Catholics, they'd confiscate the entire estate. Henri would never forgive me, yet…he wouldn't be able to refuse them help. I inhaled trying to relieve the pressure. "Henri would give them food and offer shelter until they could find safety." The words scraped my throat.

LaGarde nodded. "I will support whatever your decision.

But we must warm these children." He shoved his gun into his belt, took off his frock coat, and wrapped it around the boy and girl. He crouched down, pressed them against his chest, and stood.

I looked up at the Chouan, and I thought his eyebrow quirked. My breaths grew rapid, shallow. "More than four hundred families are safe, here, Monsieur, and I will do whatever I must to keep them safe."

"They don't have to stay here." Simon crouched down, picked up a chip of chalky tufa stone, and drew on the floor. "There are caves in the hills. Troglodyte caves—where people lived hundreds of years ago—there are staircases and fireplaces and shelves and basins for water built into them. They're all connected. Two of them," he underlined a section, "connect to the Verzat wine caves."

"The dwellings are abandoned?" I asked.

Simon nodded. "The ones connected to the Verzat caves are. There's others in the valley where people live and raise mushrooms."

"How do you know this?" My voice cracked, thinking of the trouble Simon could cause us all.

"Henri taught me to explore the tunnels of Paris." He stood up and slapped his dusty hands on his breeches. "I figured he'd want me to do the same here." He scuffed his boot over the drawing, erasing it.

LaGarde chucked Simon' shoulder. So strange how men showed affection by slugging one another.

I blew a warm breath into my hands. "So, we can use the tunnels that connect the Verzat caves to get them to the caves in the forest, where they can live?"

Simon nodded.

"What happens should the soldiers discover this system?"

"The entrances to the Verzat tunnels are small." He pointed at the Chouan and LaGarde. "They wouldn't fit through. But the others will. Once we get them there, we could pile rocks, hiding the Verzat entrance, unless you knew where it was. If they're in danger, they could quickly remove the rocks, go through the passage, and replace them. Also," he grinned, "you'd have to know the Verzat cave system, otherwise, you'd die before you found your way out."

A shiver charged through me. I'd have to help these people through the dark. Formidable. I wiped sweat from my neck. I looked to LaGarde, but he busied himself rubbing the backs of the children in his arms.

LaGarde was not interfering, not controlling me. How unlike him. He'd ordered me to get him out of prison, made me promise not to admit guilt at my father's trial, which proved to be the right things to do, but on this he had no opinion. Was it because of Henri's letter? Did LaGarde understand that, even though Henri and I were separated by an ocean, we were partners? I chewed at the dry skin on my thumb. No matter why, now when I needed LaGarde's advice, he was letting me make my own decision. That was no partnership.

"Would this be agreeable to your group?" I asked the Chouan.

He nodded sharply, never consulting the huddling shivering women behind him.

Glad he didn't speak for me, I lifted my chin and looked at the women. "Your religion is your own affair. But should you practice it anywhere near this estate, I will report you myself. Do you understand?"

They nodded.

I stepped behind the Chouan and looked in the older woman's eyes. "Do you swear never to endanger anyone on the Verzat estate?"

"Yes, Monsieur, upon my life." She gripped a wooden cross that hung from a leather string around her neck.

I pointed at it. "Hide that until you're in your own cave."

She shoved it into her bodice.

I took the little boy from LaGarde, rested him on my hip, and looked him in the eyes. Tears and snot ran down his chin, his lips were blue, his teeth chattered. An unearthly terror sat in his dark eyes, and I wanted to look away. I hoped Auguste was never as frightened. "Do you know what it means not to show your religion?"

"Never to do this in public." He blessed himself.

I nodded and looked to the little girl I took to be his sister. Her blonde hair was plastered to her head, and she shook like a leaf in a windstorm despite LaGarde's tight grip and rapid rubbing of her back and tiny feet. "Do you know?"

Her fear-filled eyes looked at her maman. "Can I say…" Her teeth chattered. "…my prayers…before bed?"

I wiped water from the girl's face. "You must learn to pray silently. God can still hear you. Do you promise to do that?"

She nodded.

I returned the boy to LaGarde and took off my frock coat and gave it to the girl's maman. The woman shared it with the other woman, who I took for her sister. "And you?"

She brought her head up. "You need not worry about me, Monsieur. I do not believe in a God who would allow men to drown women and children."

I wanted to agree with her, but this wasn't the time. "LaGarde, what do you think?"

"I think we should feed them before they freeze to death." He turned and carried the children toward the trapdoor.

I looked at our refugees. "You must remain quiet. We'll give you hot food and drink, dry clothing and blankets. After you rest, we'll give you supplies and take you to your new home."

The maman of the children sobbed and whispered, "Merci."

The women followed LaGarde and Simon.

I stood before the Chouan, his eyes dark and alert as a hawk's. "Come, you'll have some soup and wine and warm yourself."

He removed his hat and placed it over his chest. "I thank you, Mademoiselle." As I opened my mouth, he put up a hand and smiled. "No man is as beautiful as the angel of mercy who stands before me."

I stomped to the trapdoor and climbed down the steps into the dark, my mind racing. I'm not man enough to keep doing this all alone.

At the other end of the tunnel, LaGarde opened the trapdoor, lifted the children into the kitchen, and helped the women climb the steps. Simon raced to add wood to the fire. I pulled out bowls and ladled soup for everyone.

"I will return with blankets." LaGarde left us.

I poured wine and offered it to the Chouan. He drained the cup, dragged his sleeve across his dark moustache, and walked toward the trapdoor. "I leave now."

"What?" I cried. "I thought you were going with them to the caves."

"I must rejoin my men."

"Wait, please. You must eat." I handed him a bowl, and he slurped, hungrily.

Holding a stack of blankets, LaGarde returned and gave one to each of the women and children.

"I must speak to you for a moment." I pulled LaGarde's sleeve and called out to the Chouan, "Please, Monsieur, wait for just a few moments, and I will give you food for your men." I led LaGarde to the grand dining room.

Although not used, the room had been kept sparkling by Madame Detré's daily cleanings. A huge fireplace stood at the far end, above it hung a portrait of Henri's father. Help me, Henri.

"What is it?" LaGarde asked.

"The Chouan is leaving." My throat tightened, and I choked on my words. "I can't…" I pressed the heels of my palms into my eyes. "Can't…"

LaGarde placed his bearpaw hand on my shoulder. "Let it go."

My words burst. "I can't take those women and children to live in some cave with no protection."

He pulled me to him, my face pressing into his chest.

I wanted to wrap my arms around him, but my arms fell limp at my sides. "I can't endanger everyone here."

"You care with all your heart, Geneviève. It is one of the qualities I admire most about you." His voice was soft, warm.

I dragged my sleeve across my face and pulled back. "But I can't save everyone."

He shook his head. "No, you cannot. But every life you do save, saves more lives." He wrapped his hands around my upper arms, holding me until I looked at him. "The day you arrived in my cell, I hated myself. I was an arrogant, selfish, bastard who bullied you. I realized that you risked your life to save mine. You are the most selfless person I have ever known. After you left me, I promised God and myself that if I got out of that hellhole, I would try to be more like you. You could not abandon those people if you tried. Caring for others and honor run in your blood."

The Tribunal certainly didn't see me in that light.

He rubbed my arms. "Let me help you help them."

"Where can we hide them?"

"We could hide them in plain sight. We have eighteen orphans. The children would be two more. And the women could be nurses, like the nuns." A sly smile came over him. "They will fit in well, as they are all Catholics."

A little laugh escaped me. "But papers. We don't have identity papers for them."

He patted my arms and stood back. "Let me take care of that. Shall I ask Tante and Madame Detré if we can add to the orphanage?"

I nodded. "But—"

He'd already left, his footsteps thundering on the grand staircase in the hall. I gazed at the portrait. Henri did not know the things about me that LaGarde knew. But Henri had not seen me in nearly four years. I hoped when he did see me, he'd know everything LaGarde knew.

I returned to the kitchen where the Chouan stood like a giant chestnut tree between the pale-faced women. "I will

pack some food for you, Monsieur. It will only take a moment. Have more wine."

I could not use a serviette as they all bore the Verzat crest and should the Chouan be caught, the crest could be traced. I wrapped bread, cheese, sausage into my neckcloth and offered it. The Chouan gave a small bow and thrust it into his tunic.

I put up my hand. "Mesdames, I didn't know this man would not accompany you. I don't want you to live in the caves, alone." The children's mother began to moan. I put out my hands. "Please, Madame, we wish for you all to stay here, in the château."

She sobbed and rocked herself. The other woman patted her back. "Shush. We will be safe here. We will live like kings."

I smiled and looked at the Chouan. "Please let their families know where they are."

He shook his head. "They have none."

I cleared my throat. "When it is safe, Monsieur, I hope you will join us for a grand feast."

"Merci." He bowed and headed toward the trapdoor.

LaGarde returned and whispered to me, "Do not allow anyone to enter the house. If you need to, hide everyone in the tunnel until we have returned."

I nodded. "I wish you a safe journey, Monsieur."

Simon led the Chouan and LaGarde down into the tunnel. The trapdoor slammed shut. The women and children jumped and looked to me, their eyes filled with fear, sadness, hope.

A heavy force settled around me. What would my harboring all these people bring upon every person on this estate?

49

Château de Verzat
June 1796

$\mathbf{M}$Y HANDS TREMBLED, splashing ink over the paper. I dropped the quill, shook the excitement from my fingers, took a steadying breath, and dipped the quill again.

Dear Henri,

You and Joliette may return!

The Directory has repealed the death penalty for returning émigrés and decreed their confiscated property is to be restored to its rightful owners, but only if owners return within twelve months.

Come home so we can be married!

I await you.

Yours,

G.

I kissed the letter and folded the paper around a sprig of lavender and sealed it.

Pressing the letter to my heart, I danced around my chamber. He's coming home. And we'll be married.

50

"**I**F THE REPUBLICAN soldiers stop you, they will conscript you," LaGarde shouted. "And when they discover you are a woman, they will guillotine you."

"I won't let them catch me," I yelled back.

He marched toward me. "You allow your excitement over Henri's return to overwhelm your normal common sense."

I waved as I walked away. "I carry a pistol and a dagger, and Simon is coming with me."

"Another impersonator. Two for the guillotine."

I flung my arms up. "Only one. It's legal for men to dress as women."

"And when they discover Simon is a man, they will know he is wanted!"

"I won't let anything happen to him," I growled as I headed

for the stables. Why didn't LaGarde mind his own business? I looked back at him, his shoulders hunched, his steps pounding away from me. He was jealous of Henri.

Simon, shawl askew, strained against his laced bodice as he hitched the horses to the carriage. "How do you move in these clothes, Gen?"

"Now you know why I wear breeches." I buckled the belly-band of the horse's traces.

Although the carriage had not been used since before Henri's departure four years earlier, the groom and stable boy had removed all the gilded fittings and painted everything a dull black, obscuring the Verzat crest, making it look like a common coach. Tante Nicole had placed hampers of food, bottles of wine, blankets, and tiny pillows of lavender amongst the green silk-cushioned benches inside.

It was the first day Henri's ship was expected, but there was no telling exactly when it would land. I hoped to reach Nantes by high tide.

Dressed in breeches, frock coat, and cloak, I climbed up next to Simon on the driver's bench. Would Henri recognize me? I smiled at the memory of his look of surprise when LaGarde had sliced open my waistcoat, exposing my breasts. Henri would recognize me.

I hummed a tune the workers sang while harvesting the grapes. Perhaps Simon would drive us back to the château so Henri and I could get reacquainted on the silk cushions. The thought sent my heartbeat racing.

I shook the reins to calm my thoughts and trembling hands.

Hoarfrost coated the ground and barren grapevines. The cold breeze held the odor of dead leaves and a metallic scent of impending snow. I hoped it would hold off until the ship arrived. I pulled Simon close and folded a blanket over our legs.

He smacked my arm. "Not taking liberties, are you?" His voice cracked.

I laughed. "You hate wearing my gown and bonnet, but you like hiding in plain sight." LaGarde's warning voice echoed in my mind. "Keep your voice higher, or it'll give you away. Remember, you're still wanted for conspiracy and, if they discover the soldier's body, they'll execute you for murder."

Simon dabbed his handkerchief at his nose, much like the affected way Etty had. The day Papa had been arrested flooded my vision. Had Etty followed through on her threat the day I'd left? I squeezed my eyes against her image but heard her voice. *If your father goes to the guillotine, I'll report you to the Tribunal and you'll follow him.* I'd never be able to return to Paris.

"Geneviève?" Simon breathed into his hands and rubbed them.

I shook off the memory. "What?"

"Do you think Henri will recognize me?" He batted his eyelashes.

I laughed. "If you act the coquette, I doubt it."

"Do you think he'll realize I'm a man, now?" He pulled more of the blanket, and I let him take the whole thing.

"Not in my gown."

"Ha!" He clapped, like the boy he had been. "Do you think we'll have to wait long for the ship?"

I shrugged. "If it hit bad weather, we could wait a week or more."

"A week? Sleeping in the carriage and shivering in this gown? I'll freeze." He wrapped the blanket around him.

"The only false identity papers you have are for a woman, so you have no other choice." I blew out my frustration in a sigh. "Besides, now you're getting a taste of what women must endure."

"I never thought about that." He gazed out over the river. "That's why my maman always wears a shawl?"

"It's also fashionable."

He rubbed his eyes. "Women have so much to worry about. All I worry about is eating and staying alive."

"That's quite a lot."

"Just two things."

"You'll be fine. There are blankets and food and wine in the carriage."

"I'll still freeze. Will you trade clothes with me?"

Despite the ice-covered puddles and frigid air, I was sweating. I had to stop thinking of reuniting with Henri. "Not on this trip, sorry."

"Did you like the mushroom soup we had before we left?" he asked, his eyes sparking with mischief.

"What are you up to?"

He slapped his leg. "The Chouan ladies and children have been growing mushrooms in the Verzat caves that are too narrow to store wine casks."

"That's very resourceful of them."

He thumped his chest. "It was my idea, and I showed them the tunnels. But they do all the work. They sell the mushrooms, but they make them into soup for all the orphans."

"The soup was delicious. It's good for them to have work and feel they are contributing."

"They're making some for Henri's welcoming feast." He leaned back and pushed his feet against the floorboard.

"That's not very ladylike."

He pulled the skirts over his legs. "Will you speak English with me? Oncle Albert was Henri's tutor, and he told me Henri spoke English poorly, so I want to impress Henri." His words tripped over each other.

Simon wasn't the only one wanting to impress Henri. "Certainly. That's how Americans say, Certainement.'"

"Certainly." He laughed. "This is going to be easy."

I hoped reuniting with Henri was easy, but something I couldn't identify nagged at me.

51

The Loire Valley
November 1796

IN THE DISTANCE a spire loomed, and a floating sensation ran through my arms. I squinted at the harbor of Nantes, but we were too far away to see the ships' flags. Willing Henri's ship to be there, I snapped the whip and kept the horses at speed until we came to the edge of the city.

A muscular sailor, knotting a length of rope, walked toward us.

I slowed the horses. "Monsieur, has the *Eliza* arrived?" I shouted.

The man glanced at me but stared at Simon, his eyes roving like he was watching a beautiful woman undress. Men never stared at me like that. Was a boy wearing my clothes more attractive than I was in the same gown? Would Henri still find me attractive? I'd grown so muscular. He had always enjoyed my legs—wrapped around him—I hoped he still would.

Simon smiled coyly. He'd get us killed. I elbowed him. He dropped his flirtatious smile, looking at me in surprise.

I shouted, "Monsieur?" He glanced at me. "Any news of the *Eliza*?"

"She's a day out."

My shoulders tightened. How would I be able to endure waiting another day? But at least the ship had not gone down.

The sailor made a kissing noise at Simon and lunged for the traces.

"Damn you." Aiming for the sailor, I cracked the whip.

He yelped and fell back.

A little thrill moved through me—I'd made a man jump. But the horses bolted, yanking me from the bench onto my knees. The reins slipped, and I grasped at them. Still, the horses raced.

My arms burned, but the reins slid again. I couldn't hold them. "Help!"

Simon wrapped his hands around mine, pressing them harder. The reins cut into my palms as Simon shifted his weight, pulling me back. My hands throbbed.

I didn't care who saw a woman driving a carriage, my hands were raw. "Take the reins."

Simon reached forward, and I let go. He pulled the horses to a stop.

Calming my breath, I pushed myself up onto the bench. Blood dripped onto the floorboard, but I'd no time to pamper myself. I patted my palms on my breeches. Being a man demanded being a hero. I didn't have the strength. I dragged my sleeve across my face. Did men ever feel this way?

"You're wearing that disguise because you're wanted, not to get attention," I yelled. "This isn't a game. You'll get us both killed!"

The Loire Valley
November 1796

W E REACHED NANTES by nightfall and drove the carriage into a stand of trees outside the city where we took turns sleeping and watching for soldiers and thieves throughout the night.

The scent of salt air awakened me. Simon and I drove the carriage and stopped the horses near a bridge at the edge of the port. We sat on the driver's bench and scanned the harbor, hoping the sunlight would illuminate a ship's sails as it came into view. A furious wind tossed the anchored ships. Dark clouds gathered on the horizon but, for a second, the clouds parted and a patch of light glowed.

"There!" Simon jumped up and pointed. "Over there!"

"Make your voice higher," I hissed. My heartbeat raced,

but a tiny image grew into a three-masted ship, its sails taut, sailing toward the harbor.

"It's huge! And flying an American flag." Simon jumped down and ran toward the dock, his skirts billowing behind him.

The icy wind stung my eyes, and I swiped at tears. Welcome home, my love. In my mind, I saw Henri leap down from the ship, run to me, scoop me up, and spin me around, laughing and crying and shouting, I love you Geneviève. Marry me!

I shook my head. I was dressed as a man, and he couldn't very well greet me in that fashion. I pictured us in the confines of the carriage, his hands hot on my breasts, his lips finding my nipples, his voice whispering his love for me. In my daydream, I had no words in return, for I was laughing and weeping.

An icy gust grabbed my hat. I climbed down, retrieved my tricorne, and tied the horses to a tree.

As I walked to the waterfront the ship entered the harbor. When I neared the end of the dock, a sailor smiled down at Simon who was holding onto his bonnet with both hands. I adjusted the pistol tucked in my belt, ready to defend Simon's honor and grateful to LaGarde for teaching me how to shoot.

My hand trembled, and I reminded myself that men defended women all the time. When Henri finally arrived, he could take over. I never wanted to wear breeches or a gun again.

Sailors scrambled along the yardarms, furling the canvas, yet the ship cut through the water as if still powered by the sails. The anchor chain rattled, water splashed, the ship slowed, and the foam behind it ceased. Waves crashed against the ship's hull, and the boat bobbed. The rigging of the ships filling the harbor looked like a forest of leafless trees.

I shouted, "Geneviève!"

Simon looked about, the wind nearly tearing off his bonnet.

I rubbed my hands to warm them until he tightened the ribbons. I waved, and he ran toward me. Three dockhands boarded a large longboat and rowed toward the ship.

"We should get out of the way of the stevedores. Let's wait up there." I pointed to a railing running along the boulevard, a few feet above the dock and offering a better view.

Simon picked up his skirts and raced ahead. He could move faster in sabots than any woman. I'd have to warn him he ran like a man. By the time I reached him, I was breathless.

From the ship's deck, sailors dropped lines down to a man in the longboat.

I gripped my hat so tightly my hands ached. My eyes watered as I searched the people crowding the deck. Sailors scurried around the passengers and dropped a rope ladder down to the longboat. I guessed the small boat would ferry the passengers from the ship to the dock, but with one wind gust, I feared the waves would swamp the longboat and drown the passengers.

Sunlight burst through the clouds and sparkled across the water, making it difficult to see the passengers' faces.

"Henri!" Simon jumped and pointed. "He has a boy with him."

My heart beat fast as a bird's wings. I whispered, "Welcome home my love."

Upon Henri's shoulders sat a curly-haired, dark-skinned boy, about Louisa's age, wearing a green frock coat and breeches. The boy gripped Henri's ears.

My laugh flowed through me, warming me. So like Henri to look out for children. He'll be a wonderful father.

With the boy clinging to him, Henri climbed down the ladder and handed the child to one of the men in the longboat.

I shoved my hands into my pockets, praying, *Please, God, don't let him fall.*

Henri quickly hurried back up the ladder, helping each passenger. The ship rose and fell, and the longboat rocked, but neither deterred my Henri.

The crowded longboat pulled up to the dock where two guards waited to check the passengers' papers.

I walked along the top of the hill and stopped directly above the guards who stood on the wharf. Clouds passed, darkening the water and sending a chill through me.

"Let's get the carriage and bring it around so we can leave right away." Simon's voice was high, but it cracked again.

I didn't want to lose sight of my love for a second. The sound of sloshing waves and the slamming of crates upon the docks forced me to shout, "Just a minute."

I gripped the railing to stop myself from waving like a frantic fool. I leaned forward, hoping Henri would look up and recognize me. I longed to reach down and feel his hands clasping mine.

"Let's meet him at the end of the dock," Simon cried, grabbing my sleeve and yanking.

My knees had locked, and I nearly toppled over.

"Hurry!" Simon ran ahead.

Not able to pry my eyes from my love, I walked as if in a trance.

When Simon reached him, Henri threw his head back and

laughed, no doubt recognizing Simon's disguise. They hugged and slapped each other on the back, as men do.

Henri turned and spoke to an African woman, dressed like a lady in a sky-blue gown and dark-blue woolen cloak and bonnet, standing next to him. He was protective and gentle toward her.

I shrank inside my frock coat.

She held herself like a queen. Her skin was smooth and her cheekbones high. I wished I had her thick black eyelashes. Sunlight lit up her amber-brown eyes. Who was she? My hand trembled as I wiped my face.

Simon dipped a wobbly curtsey to the woman. She smiled and brought the boy out from behind her skirts.

Simon crouched down to play with the child. As Henri caught sight of me, his smile stiffened, like he was bracing himself. His eyes were hiding something—a great deal of something. He raised his hand.

The joy I'd felt plunged to the pit of my stomach. I forced my feet forward, my heart racing like a chased rabbit.

"My old classmate!" Henri shouted as he opened his arms, as if to embrace me.

I stopped. The cold wind slid into me, chilling my breath, my legs, my heart. My mind held an image of Henri's younger face, his dark blue eyes roving mine as he bent over me, kissing me, loving me. That same man considered me an old classmate? What had happened to his love for me?

If he had stopped loving me, why hadn't he written about it? I dug down inside me and shoved pride up my back as I stepped forward and thrust out my hand, giving him no other option than to shake it.

His smile waned as he clasped my hand.

I broke his grip and pulled back.

He placed his hand on the woman's back. "Gen—"

"Jean." I removed my hat and gave a slight bow. "I am Jean. Enchanté, Madam."

Henri cleared his throat. "I would like to present Aurélia. She cannot speak but understands French and English and can write both."

She smiled, lowered her head, and peeked up at Henri. He leaned closer to her and whispered. She glanced at me, her eyes filling with pity. She reached out and ran her fingers gently along my sleeve.

My arm flinched. No one pitied me.

She lifted a small book, dangling from a ribbon tied at her wrist. She wrote on a page, tore it out, and offered it.

I nodded, feeling like the action came from outside me—as if I were a marionette, someone else was pulling my strings. I read: *I hope we will be friends.*

I smiled with closed lips and, crumpling the paper, shoved my hands behind my back. Was Henri expecting me to figure out she was his mistress? The coward couldn't tell me, even now as she stood before me? "I trust you had a pleasant voyage?"

Henri nudged the boy toward me. "This is our son, Charles Henri."

That tiny word, our, scored my heart like a rapier.

Simon's mouth gaped open. "An African?"

I shoved my elbow into Simon's side, while images of Henri making love to this woman whirred in my mind and anger burned in my stomach. Henri had cheated on me.

"Pardon! I mean, I thought…white men can't marry Africans in America." He dragged his hand beneath his nose. "Oncle Albert said France abolished slavery years ago, but not America."

Aurélia looked questioningly at Henri.

Pulling Charles up to his hip, Henri grinned. "We can marry in France."

Aurélia's eyes glowed like stars.

My breath turned to stone, heavy in my chest. Thunder rolled in the distance, echoing along the water. Rain dropped like a curtain. I welcomed it. I wanted to stand in the freezing rain until it washed me away.

"Let's get out of the rain." Henri brought his cloak up around his son.

The raindrops were sharp, stinging my face and neck.

"Did you bring a carriage?" Henri held Aurélia's elbow and began guiding her up the incline toward the road.

"I'll harness the horses." I forced myself to run. This couldn't be true. This was a nightmare. Why hadn't Henri written about her long ago? My fingernails dug into my palms. Why hadn't he wanted to tell his maman she was a grand-mère?

The rain soaked through my cloak, its weight slowing me. I untied the horses and hugged one around the neck. I buried my face into my sleeve. A heaviness settled in my stomach as the last words Henri had spoken before departing clanged in my mind, *How could I not love you.* It had been the only time he'd ever said or written the word love. He'd never said, I love you. He'd never said, I'll miss you. He'd never said, Wait for me. I rubbed my face against the horse's warmth. He'd never sent for me.

"I'm sorry, Gen." Simon stood close. "He should have told you."

I blew out a breath, instantly regretting it as a sob clogged my throat.

Simon gripped my shoulder. "Do you want me to harness the horses?"

I shrugged him off and swallowed the sob. "Yes."

When I wrote of my love for him, Henri never responded in kind. Had he not received my letters? He'd never mentioned them or my professions of love in his letters. My face burned. Etty's voice taunted me: *You didn't throw yourself at him, did you?* I had thrown myself at him. He didn't want me. My neck-cloth was strangling me. I tugged it loose.

The traces jangled as Simon fastened them.

"Papa, horse!"

The word papa released the tightness in my chest and my sobs. I pushed myself from the horses and began running, the ground blurring beneath my feet. I flew across the meadow toward the stand of trees, rain slashing my face like icy daggers.

"Gen, where are you going?" Simon called.

I had no idea. All I *did* know was that I couldn't stay there.

53

"GENEVIÈVE!" HENRI'S VOICE called after me.

My chest afire, I ran into the woods.

"Geneviève!"

I slipped on wet leaves, pulled on a branch to right myself, and ran. Henri's voice grew louder. I had to get away. I'd run all the way to Paris if I had to. I'd not stop. I'd never stop.

"Geneviève!"

His hand gripped my elbow. I stumbled and fell against him. "Let me go."

His grip tightened. "No. Please, listen."

I tried to yank my arm away, but he held me tightly. "No." I squirmed to get away, but his hands closed around my upper arms, pulling me to look at him. Lines he hadn't had before he'd left ran down either side of his mouth. I wanted to fall into his deep blue eyes. "I said, let me go."

"I'm sorry." He pulled me to him. "I am sorry."

His scent of cedar made my heart ache. I punched his chest. "Do you not love me because I dress as a man?"

"I admire you for dressing as a man."

"You admire me, but you don't love me?" I punched him again. "You're an idiot."

He wrapped his arms around me. "I know I am. I'm sorry."

I heaved in cold damp air stinking of mushrooms. He didn't love me. Sobs poured out of me, infuriating me.

He ran his hands up and down my back, reminding me of afternoons making love in his room. "Stop that!" I pressed on his chest, pushing myself away, but he wouldn't let me go.

"I wrote you of my family, but I fear the letter was lost at sea."

I pulled back. "Then why did you not write again? That's big news to keep to yourself. You should have at least told your maman, she's a grandmaman!"

"I wanted you to hear the news from me, not her. I'm so, so sorry."

"You sent treatises on slavery, but you didn't write of her? Of your son?" I screeched like a hunting owl.

"I did. But when you didn't write back, I thought I'd broken your heart and you were too angry to write back."

"Then you should have written again."

"I know I should have, but I didn't know how."

"Paper and ink would have worked." I pushed away. Icy rain streamed down the back of my neck. "I've lost my hat."

He looked around, but grabbed my arm, like he feared I'd run away. I acted like I was scanning the ground but watched him. He was more muscular now and more handsome, in a rugged way. Damn him. I kicked at a pile of leaves, disturbing a shrew that dove beneath a bush.

Henri spotted my tricorne, scooped it up, and returned it to me.

Shaking his hand off, I snatched it and pressed it low over my eyes. My arms and legs were useless, like they'd been rung out. The memory of the last time I saw him in Paris raked me. He looked as confused now as he had the day he'd left. Had he not wanted to hurt me then, too? I looked up through the rain.

"I hope you and Aurélia can become friends."

A gust of wind sent wet leaves raining down. Friends? The cold air knifed through my frock coat. With the woman who took my place? My fingernails clawed my breeches.

"I hope you can be happy for us."

Dark clouds further dimmed the weak light. As if a velvet drape had fallen on me, I wanted to push myself out of the darkness, but my arms wouldn't move. I was four years old, back in the hallway, calling for Maman. I shook myself. Anger arced across my shoulders and pulsed down my back, making me think I might kill him. "Happy." The word soured my mouth.

"Happy for our happiness." He smiled.

My hand flung itself out and slapped him.

His hands flew to his cheek. He doubled over.

"You were so happy, you forgot to tell me?"

"No." He coughed. "I…" He reached up, but I pulled away.

"I didn't want to hurt you. If we never returned, you'd never know, and I would have saved you the pain."

"You're an imbecile. I wrote of my love for you." I wanted to shove him.

He stared at his boots.

"You asked me to join you before you left. Didn't you think I was waiting for you to ask me again?"

He shook his head.

"You said you couldn't marry me because you had nothing to offer me."

He stared out toward the river.

"Did it not occur to you that I thought, once you got a job, you'd ask me to join you and be your wife?" I was screaming, and I didn't care. "Don't you think I want to have what you have? You selfish lout."

I pushed him against a tree and lifted my arm like I had a horse whip. He closed his eyes. His resignation snuffed my rage.

"Froussard." I let go of him, and he sagged against the tree.

"You asked me to go to America with you—I thought—because you loved me."

"I did ask you. I remember." He exhaled long and slow. "Be glad you didn't go, Geneviève. It was a terrible crossing—aboard a slaver."

Nausea climbed up my throat. "Is that where you met her?"

He looked down and dragged the toe of his boot through withered leaves. "The horrors of that trip were too much to tell." He looked at me, his eyes deep, deep blue, the lines around his mouth curving his lips down.

I pitched forward, the stink of rotten mushrooms filling me. Had he fallen in love with her out of pity? Sparks swirled. I pushed my hand against a tree, struggling for breath, slid down, and sat.

"Like you, my sister is brave. Joliette convinced the captain he'd get a better price for unbranded women, preventing them from that pain and indignation. She protected Aurélia from worse."

I could not imagine what could be worse…unless…I shook my head trying to clear the image of a woman being branded. "How?"

"Joliette bought Aurélia's freedom. It took nearly all the money we had, but she did it."

"Aurélia wasn't a slave in America?"

He shook his head. "She is free, but it was safer for Aurélia to act as one in America. She is free in France."

A sinking sensation pulled at me as I remembered his hands on my lips, my breasts, my thighs. "Why does she not speak?"

"She has been wounded." He crouched next to me. "Can you imagine being dragged from your home, then forced to march for weeks, thrown in the hold of a ship to sail for a month across an ocean you never knew existed, and sold while you stood naked on a platform for strangers to judge your worth?" His hands jittered in his lap.

"Joliette and I took her to doctors. All of them said there was no physical reason she can't speak." He smiled a bit. "One time, I thought I heard her humming to Charles Henri when he was sick." He shook his head. "Perhaps I imagined it."

The tenderness on his face made me want to weep, but I

forced myself to be angry. "You asked her if she could speak before her capture?"

He nodded. "She did." He stood and offered his hand to help me up. "You'll be soaked."

His kindness was infuriating. I batted away tears and stood on my own. "I'm sorry Aurélia has suffered so."

"I wanted to return to France for her and my son's sake."

I tilted my head.

"American children won't play with him because they think he is African. The African children are afraid to play with him because they think he is white." He swiped at a tear. "Charles is lonely." He inhaled and his shoulders rose. "I hope the people on the estate will come to love him as they loved my father."

I wanted to snap at him, tell him that French children would want to play with our child, had we had one. But I couldn't gather the cruelty to say it. Shame washed in like the tide. I turned away. "Charles deserves to be loved and respected—no matter his skin color."

I walked out into the meadow and strode through the sleet. Henri's love for Aurélia and his son made me love him more. I huffed. How did I fall in love with a coward? Worse, why was I still in love with a damned coward who'd kept the truth from me for years? He didn't want to hurt me. Ha! More likely, he feared my wrath. At least in that, he was wise.

I tipped my head back and opened my mouth, catching the sleet and swallowing it, letting the iciness cool my ragged throat. I wanted to hurt Henri just like he'd hurt me, but I felt drained. Vengeance wouldn't make him love me. I looked across the meadow and down at the carriage.

Despite the wind and sleet, Aurélia stood holding her son's hand, her cloak sheltering him. Facing her love for her child and future husband would help me fall out of love with Henri.

A gust of wind snapped at my tricorne. I gripped the brim and slowed my steps. I'd envisioned myself as Henri's wife, mistress of his château, mother of his children. I'd no more time to waste on illusions. I was a nobody, with nothing and no one. But where was I going? Wherever it was, I'd be going alone.

54

WHEN WE ARRIVED at the château, I commanded
Simon to stay with the others, and I returned the horses to the
stables. I could not stand one more moment amongst people.
And I certainly wasn't going to any welcoming party.

How could Henri love an uneducated woman? He couldn't
discuss politics or philosophy with her. He *couldn't* love her.
She was beautiful, far more than I was, and I understood he
had lust for her. But the image of his face as he gazed at her
taunted me. He *did* love her.

Refusing help from the stable hands, I unharnessed the
horses and stabled them. I brought out the beast LaGarde had
given me and began saddling her.

I was being ridiculous. Henri had had a child with Aurélia,

but he would never marry her. But he'd told Simon he could marry her in France.

"Where are you going?" LaGarde leaned against the stable wall.

I cringed at his voice. He was exactly the person I never wanted to see again. I adjusted the saddle strap under the mare's belly and shrugged.

"You were looking forward to Henri's return. Every lady on the estate is helping to prepare a feast. Are you leaving before the celebration?"

"I heard the Rebels are headed for Quiberon. I thought I'd join them."

His bearpaw of a hand covered mine. "That is not the reason."

Despite his success at farming, despite his raising chickens and goats and sheep, despite his harvesting the grapes and caring for his daughter, he still had the soft hands of a nobleman. Not a hangnail, not a speck of dirt, not a callous. Were nobles taught to keep their hands looking like they didn't perform work? His were strong, powerful hands, hands that took whatever they wanted.

Yet the gentleness of his touch sent a shiver through me. I shook free from him.

"Why are you going?" His voice softened. "Really."

I shifted the saddle. I had no idea. Maybe I'd just ride. Maybe I'd swim to England, just me and the horse. I'd no money. I couldn't return to Paris, well, I could if I wanted to face the guillotine. I had spent the last four years awaiting Henri's return and, now that he'd arrived, I had nothing. Absolutely nothing. No home, no lover, no dreams. I'd even had to become my fake identity: Jean Detré. The irony of it. I thought I'd get the name Detré via marriage. Stupid. I'd been so stupid. And here I was still hoping Henri would realize he loved me.

"Henri's son is nearly the same age as Louisa. Have you seen them play together?" LaGarde laughed. "Charles kissed Louisa, and she pushed him away."

"That's funny to you?" My arms jittered.

"Seems our children took up where Henri and I left off." He let out a howl of laughter.

Men. Why in God's name did I dress like one? I led the mare out of her stall.

LaGarde cupped his hand around mine. "I am sorry, Geneviève. You must be in pain."

I yanked the reins. "You know nothing about me."

He pried loose the reins and dropped them. Pressing my fingers together, he brought them to his lips, and kissed them. His eyes, so warm, so luring. "I would like to know everything about you."

I felt a tearing in my chest and pulled my hands free. "Know this: I don't need you to tell me anything about me. Get out of my way."

He stood before me, legs spread, hands resting on hips. His bulk filled the doorway. "Tell me the real reason you are leaving."

I was feeling like a marionette again. Some strange force controlled my limbs. I could try to kick the brute, but he would grab my foot and upend me. "I saved your life, and now you're stopping me? Ungrateful bastard."

"You not only saved me, but also Louisa and Simon and the Chouans. Now it is time to save yourself."

"Save myself from what?"

"Loneliness."

A rushing filled my ears like I was under the river. I couldn't feel my feet in my boots or my weight on the ground. I steadied myself against the wall but could not feel the rough wooden boards. My hands buzzed.

"If you do not allow people to love you, you will be alone, Geneviève." His voice was soft as a whisper. His jaw line ran to a square chin with a dimple in its center. Why had I never noticed that small depression before?

"I am sorry you are hurt. But Henri is not worthy of you. You deserve a man who cherishes your strength and courage and intelligence, and your vulnerability. A man who values and reciprocates your love. A man who will love you and not leave you."

The stables spun around me like I was in a rowboat caught in a current. His words roared in my head. All the words I had longed to hear—from the wrong man. I collapsed onto the hay, sparks of light swirling above me.

LaGarde crouched beside me. "You have the courage of ten men. But you must tap your courage as a woman." He smelled of a newly mown hayfield.

"My courage encompasses that of a man and a woman."

He shook his head. "It takes tremendous courage to allow yourself to be loved. And you lack it."

Tears burned, but I willed myself not to cry. I would die before I cried in front of LaGarde. Why was it that of the two men in my life, one was a coward and the other a bully? I was an idiot. I was more a man than either of them, even when I dressed as a woman. I would never find an equal. I was a fool for trying.

He sat beside me. "When Louisa brought you a bouquet of daisies do you remember weaving them into her hair?"

What was this lunatic talking about? I shook my head. "Daisies?"

"Yes, daisies. Last summer, she had picked them for you, to show you how much she loves you. You did not accept them. Instead, you wove them into her hair. You did not see the disappointment in her face. You did not accept her gift or her love."

His eyes were like warm chocolate. Damn him.

I dragged my fingers through my hair, remembering that day. He was right. I had done the same thing to Auguste. When he had sketched a picture for me, I'd placed it on his nightstand, when he'd meant it for me. Why? I wished I had accepted it. I wish I had it now. Darkness fell, like a black curtain had dropped over me.

I was running down a dark corridor, toward a flickering light, calling, Maman! Maman! I ran into her room, climbed up onto her bed, and pressed my cheek against hers. She was cold. So cold.

"Geneviève?"

I squinted in the light. LaGarde's face was inches from mine, but I looked past him. I was still in my mother's chamber. I rubbed my arms. She was so cold because she was dead. Had I known that when I was a child?

"Geneviève." LaGarde's voice was a whisper. "What are you thinking?"

Was I protecting myself from the same loss? Is that why I didn't accept the gifts of Auguste and Louisa? Why hadn't I accepted their love?

Straw poked my legs. I wiped sweat from my forehead. What was I doing on the ground? The hay cracked beneath my knees as I struggled to rise.

"Geneviève." LaGarde clasped my hands. "You are worthy of love. Let the people who are worthy of your love, love you."

My mind scrambled to make sense of his words. Worthy, love, people. What was he talking about?

Shaking off his hands, I screeched, "Mind your own business."

"At least allow my daughter to love you." He pressed his lips into a line and stepped back.

I stomped out of the stables toward the caves. I hoped I'd find a Republican soldier to shoot on the way.

55

I HAD TO GET away. I had no idea where I was running, stumbling over rocks, falling, losing my hat, scraping my knee. I got up, whacked my hat against my breeches, and pushed myself up the hill.

"Geneviève! I need your help." Tante's voice was urgent.

I dreaded stopping, but I couldn't pretend I hadn't heard her. I would never hurt the old woman. I gulped calming breaths. Tante Nicole stood at the entrance to the wine cave, waving her walking stick.

"What can I do for you, Tante?"

"I need your opinion on the tables for Henri's party. Come." She waved me toward the entrance to the tasting room.

The thought of Henri's party made my skin hurt. It was going to be dark in there, and I just didn't think I could take one more scare, but I sighed and followed her, scuffing my boots in the loose gravel.

Flaring torches hung from iron rings that had been driven into the walls of the largest chamber of the Verzat caves. A pitch-black hole at the opposite end yawned, leading to the fermenting room. The image of the Chouan flashed in my mind, and I prayed he was safe.

Candelabra marched down the middle of waist-high tables clad in fine white linen cloths. A huge chandelier of iron hung from the ceiling. The tasting room glowed like a ballroom.

I turned in a circle. There had to be forty tables, seating twenty people each. Rough-hewn benches sat on either side of the tables. "Where did you find all those cloths?"

Tante laughed. "From the château. There are plenty more should we need them."

"And the tables?"

Her smile grew sly. She lifted one of the cloths with her walking stick, revealing wooden boards topping upright wine barrels. "Should we run out of wine there is a convenient supply at hand."

I laughed. "This must have taken days to set up. It's beautiful."

"We started preparing the day you and Simon left to fetch Henri." She walked to the corner and stepped up onto a platform. "This is where Henri shall greet everyone," she pointed to the opposite corner, "and that is where the musicians will perform."

A sharp ache ran through my chest. I should be standing next to Henri. "You've thought of everything."

She frowned.

"What is it?"

She stepped down and sat on a bench. She patted the spot next to her. I joined her.

"How old were you when your maman passed?"

The walls of the cave closed in around me like the dark hallway of my childhood. My skin itched like insects were swarming me.

"Geneviève?"

I shook away the sensation. "Four."

Tante nodded. "If you will forgive me, I wish to speak to you as your dear maman would if she were here."

My breath sat in my ribs, solid, unmoving. I blinked and stared at a torch flame to keep the encroaching darkness away.

"Henri should have told you of his love for Aurélia and the birth of his son. I am certain they were quite a shock to you."

"He told me he did, but the letter was lost at sea."

She stabbed the stone floor with her stick. "He should have told all of us."

"He said he wanted me to hear it from him." I resented my quick defense; he didn't deserve it. He was wrong to have hidden them both from everyone.

"Nonetheless, he was not honest with you, nor any of us, including his maman. She deserved to know as did you." Her voice sounded tired.

I lifted my chin. Grooves in the ceiling made me realize that stone masons had enlarged the natural caves long ago.

"He misled you. That was not noble, caring, courageous, or kind."

My breath rushed out. She was right. I scuffed pieces of hay beneath my boot. Why hadn't I thought the same?

"You deserve a man who is your equal."

I looked up. She stared at something far in the distance. Creased with wrinkles, her fleshy neck reminded me of an old tortoise. Yet, the torch flames behind her lit up the soft downy hairs on her cheek, making her face youthful.

"I had thought I was Henri's equal, but I'm not."

"He is not *your* equal. You are both intelligent and kind and courageous. But you are selfless, often self-sacrificing. And most important, Henri lacks your passion." She stabbed her stick on the stone floor with every word.

A bitterness like grape skins sat in my mouth as I remembered Henri admitting he admired my passion, but I hadn't understood he admired mine because he lacked it.

"Henri will have to work hard to fill his father's shoes. He will begin that task this evening, when everyone on this estate welcomes his return, his future wife, and his son. I would wager he will be wishing he had your courage."

I wasn't sorry to miss that chaos.

Tante rested her cool dry fingers on my hands. "Do you ever dress as a woman?"

I snorted a laugh. "It's been a long time."

"Magali and I found a lovely gown that will accent your gray eyes and dark hair. And Louisa has a gift for you. They are waiting in your chamber to help you dress for the party."

I jumped up. "I couldn't—"

Tante held my hand. I pulled away. She stood, reached out, and gripped my arm. The formidable marquise she'd been now stood before me. She had the presence of a lion.

My heartbeat galloped. "Everyone will know..." My voice

cracked. "I threw myself at Henri…embarrassed myself. Every-one will pity me." My face burned. Why had I said that?

She wrapped her hands around mine and held them tightly. "No one pities you. Everyone admires you. Many people love you."

I pulled back, but she wouldn't let me go. I was trapped, like when Papa locked me in my room when Maman died. I couldn't get out then, and I couldn't get away now.

"You are the bravest person I know, Geneviève. It will take far less courage for you to attend the party than it will require of Henri. Besides, Louisa has been waiting to give you her sur-prise. Do not disappoint her. She adores you." Her soft fingers gentled my hands.

I blew out a breath, my throat constricting. In my mind I saw LaGarde's face and heard his words. *At least let my daugh-ter love you.* If I did let Louisa love me what would happen to me if she died? Or if LaGarde took her away? I would have nothing. I would be nothing. I would feel just like I felt right this minute—empty, worthless, helpless. My heart tightened like LaGarde was squeezing it in his fist.

"My dear, you kept the flame of love alive all the time Henri was in America, and I know the pain of extinguishing that flame seems unbearable. But do not let your broken heart make you blind to the man who *does* love you."

I yanked my hands from hers. "And who might that be?" I hadn't meant to shout, but why did she think LaGarde loved me? He was grateful. That was all. Why did I ever save that bully's life?

A trace of hurt flashed in her eyes and then kindness emanated from them. I preferred anger, judgement, ridicule, anything but kindness. Her lips lifted into a coy, little bow. "He'll be at the party this evening." She turned and walked toward the entrance, waving her walking stick. "Do not keep him or Louisa waiting."

The torch flames snapped, taunting me. I'd have to show up here and endure a slow humiliation for everyone on the estate to witness as they laughed at my folly. I swatted my hat against my leg. Fine. Let them gossip about pathetic, desperate Geneviève. I would leave by dawn. Dressed as a man, I might be able to work as a deckhand for my passage—to anywhere. I didn't give a damn, so long as it was far from France. I stomped out into the falling dusk. And I would not wear a gown to the stupid party.

56

I STOPPED IN THE hallway. Excited voices and giggles came from my chamber. I tore off my neckcloth and dragged it over my sweaty face. Although I wanted to run away, I would never hurt Louisa, no matter what the cost. I would just have to put up with the surprise and get it over with as quickly as possible. I balled up the cloth, stuffed it in my waistcoat, and peeked in.

"Tante Gen!" Louisa ran into my arms.

I picked her up, held her to me, and nuzzled her neck. She smelled so sweet, like lilacs. "Did Tante Nicole give you some of her perfume?"

She nodded and wiggled to get down.

Wearing a lace-trimmed white bonnet and gown with a wide blue velvet ribbon at her waist, Louisa looked every bit an angel. She reached for my hand. "Tante Magali and I have a surprise for you."

Sister Magali stood smiling, her hands clasped before her long white apron, her face reflecting the soft firelight glowing around a folding screen, no doubt hiding the surprise.

"What is it?" I looked from Louisa to Sister.

Louisa led me to the dressing table where a dove-gray and sky-blue striped silk gown lay across a chair. It shimmered like silver in the twilight coming through the tall windows. Next to the table sat a pair of gray silk slippers. I'd never be able to walk in such flimsy things.

My feet stepped back of their own accord. Stay, I commanded myself. Look surprised. I brought my hands to my cheeks. "How beautiful." I hoped the gown wouldn't fit.

Sister Magali lit a candle from the fire and brought it to the clutch of candles in the candelabra on either side of the dressing table. The tall mirror reflected us, the gown, Louisa's shining face. Magali's face seemed less lined with worry since she'd left Paris, and I was glad of the change in her. She looked like I remembered her when I lived at the Abbey.

From behind her back, Louisa brought up a silver ribbon, twirling it before me. "Papa gave this to me, and I will weave it into your hair. You will be so beautiful."

"Oh, I couldn't." I laughed.

Louisa's eyes filled with tears. Sister frowned and pulled Louisa to her, placing her hands across Louisa's chest, protecting her little heart.

Merde, I've done it again. I rushed to calm them. "I mean…I must bathe first. I'm wearing all the dirt and dust of Nantes on me. I would get the beautiful ribbon dirty."

Louisa screamed with glee and clapped. "A bath is ready for you Tante Gen!"

I wished I had made a different excuse.

Sister Magali opened the screen to reveal steam rising from a copper bathing tub.

Louisa pulled my arm. "Hurry. We don't want to be late for the party."

I wanted to sink under the water and stay there.

Magali shook out a linen cloth, gave it to Louisa to hold up, and held out another before her, affording me privacy while I removed my filthy clothes. They giggled behind the wavering cloths.

I sat on the stool. Chunks of dried mud tumbled over the carpet as I pulled off my boots. I would have to sweep it up before I left. Did men care or even think about such things? I left my clothes in a pile, held onto the sides of the tub, and lowered myself into the hot water. For privacy, I unfolded a linen towel over the water. The thin linen billowed out, and I smoothed it down against my skin. The scent of lavender swirled around me, reminding me of Maman.

Louisa peeked around the cloth. "Want me to scrub you, Tante Gen?"

My lips formed the word, no, but I could not hurt this sweet angel. I nodded vigorously. "Please."

She dropped the linen cloth and pulled a bar of soap and a bathing sponge from her hanging pocket. "Madam Detré makes this soap with rosemary. It smells delicious."

Sister Magali peeked out. "Shall I wash your hair?" The firelight danced in her eyes. She looked younger than her forty years.

I began to shake my head, but some force within stopped me. "Yes, please."

Sister tiptoed to the dressing table, picked up a bottle, and poured some liquid into her palm. She knelt near my head. "I haven't washed your hair since you were a child. Do you remember?"

I didn't remember any baths at the Abbey, but I wanted to please her. "Yes. You were always so gentle, like now. Merci, Sis—Magali." I submerged my head, wanting to stay there in the safe warmth, all alone, but I couldn't disappoint either of them. I emerged and inhaled the scent of rosemary.

Magali's fingers massaged my head, the room darkened and sparks like fireflies swirled around me. I closed my eyes and sank up to my neck in the warm water. My leg jerked; water splashed.

"Hold still, Tante Gen. You're filthy." Louisa soaped the sponge and began scrubbing my toes. Her tiny fingers tickled, and I laughed.

We laughed together and, as if a ball hit me in the chest, tears came. I cupped the water and splashed my face. Why was I crying? I covered a sob with a laugh. I had to get out of here. I splashed my face until I could calm myself. "You've much work to do!"

They giggled. I had no memory of having been bathed, but perhaps my body was remembering. Sadness washed through me but why? I had been sad about Henri, but now, I was angry with him, as well as LaGarde. Why this melancholia?

Finally clean and rinsed, I wrapped a sheet around me. Magali brought a shift, chemise, stockings, bodice, petticoat, hanging pockets, and garters. As she laced up the corset over all the layers, I couldn't fully inhale. I sat to tie the garters around my stockings and had to exhale and stretch to reach my knees. The clothes already restricted my movements, and I had not donned the gown yet. With longing, I spied my filthy breeches and frock coat. Was something wrong with me that I preferred those clothes to those I wore? I wanted to tear the tight garments off, and I'd not yet finished dressing.

Magali held out the bodice with long gray silk sleeves trimmed in lace. How would I lift my arms in that without tearing it? I shrugged it on. It fit like a glove, a too-short, too-tight glove as the top of my bosom bulged from my corset. Where did the décolletage come from? I had tiny breasts. I pulled at the fabric, but it gave not an inch. "This is too low, Magali."

She cocked her head. "No, it is not." She held out the lovely, iridescent overskirt, shimmering in the candlelight like drag-onfly wings. "It is the height of fashion." She waved the skirt, her face bright with excitement.

I swallowed and opened my arms as she tied the ribbons at my waist and knelt to fluff the skirt. I could take it all off as soon as they left.

Louisa squealed. "The colors change when the skirt moves!"

"What colors?" I asked.

"From pink to gray to silver to blue."

At first, I thought another woman had appeared in the room and then realized that it was my reflection shimmering in the mirror. I ran my fingers along the delicate fabric. "Is it not vain to wear such a gown, Magali?"

"You compliment God's creation by being so beautiful."

She was lying. I'd never heard such a thing in any church.

"I have never felt such fine silk. Where did this come from?"

"The attic." Magali straightened the lace at the sleeves. "Tante Nicole and I think it belonged to the Comtesse de Verzat because it is the gown she wears in the portrait that hangs in the Comte's chamber."

Louisa held out her ribbon. "This will match it perfectly." Sit down, Tante Gen."

As I took a step back, I heard LaGarde's warning echo in my mind. I pushed myself onto the chair and watched, reflected in the mirror, Magali pinning my hair at the top of my head and Louisa, standing atop a footstool, winding the length of ribbon between the curls.

I'd not worn many ribbons in my hair since Maman died. I longed for the jar of them I'd left on my dressing table. She had allowed me to pick out the ribbon for every day. I wished I had brought them with me. Along with the portrait in Papa's desk. They were all I had left of her, and I had lost them.

Her creation complete, Louisa stood before me, looking terribly serious.

"What is it?" LaGarde's voice reprimanded me, *At least let my daughter love you*. Had I not allowed Louisa to love me? I'd agreed to everything. I prayed I had not disappointed her. My heart throbbed in my throat. I would make a terrible mother.

"You are so beautiful, Tante Gen." She grinned, reminding me of the pranks her father played upon me.

I laughed. "And so are you."

A soft knock fell upon the door. "I am missing an angel. Has anyone seen my angel?"

Louisa put her finger to her lips and shushed me. "Don't let Papa see you until the party."

I nodded and took her soft hands in mine. "Thank you for the beautiful ribbon, Louisa. It is very kind of you to give it to me." I kissed her hands and saw Magdeleine's delicate long fingers.

Louisa kissed my hands. "Do not keep Papa waiting." She tiptoed to the door, opened it a crack, and slipped out. "Let's go to the party, Papa!"

His laughter and Louisa's giggles faded with their footsteps.

Love for Louisa swelled in me. Allowing her to love me had increased my love for her. Why had I stopped it before? Could I allow her to show her love for me again, and Sister Magali, too? I pressed my heart and promised I would force myself to allow them both to love me. But that was it. No one else. Ever. Except for Auguste.

Sister Magali placed her hands on my shoulders and smiled at our reflection. "You look so much like your maman."

My hands flew to hers. "You knew her?"

"We were schoolgirls together at Pentemont Abbey. I attended your parents' wedding before I took my vows."

That was why Papa had brought me there. I turned around and gripped her hands. "Why have you never told me this?"

"I was so sad when she passed. I could not imagine the grief overwhelming her little girl." Tears sat in her eyes. "And I never wanted to remind you of that grief." A tear slid down, and she blotted it with her handkerchief. "You are so much like her, Geneviève."

I wanted to know in what ways I was like my mother, but to speak would break the dam in my throat, releasing tears for her and the papa I had known then.

"She would be so proud of you. We are all so proud of you."

She smiled through tears. "You carry her beauty. Your light eyes, your dark hair, your proud posture," she laughed, "especially when you dress as a man."

I laughed and a little sob came out with it. "Did she ever dress as a man?"

"Oh, no. Your maman was a lady and would never have thought of fighting for justice as you do."

She was right. I was no lady.

"I do not mean you are not a lady. You are. But you have great courage and strength, Geneviève." She rushed her words. "Your maman was delicate and fragile. She was not able to fight the illness that took her."

I nodded and stared down at my wide hands and stubby fingers. Maman's had been delicate. I had my father's hands.

Sister knelt before me. "She loved you more than any mother I have ever known to love a child. She adored you…like Louis adores Louisa." She smiled and patted my cheek. "Time to go to the party. I must change my apron and cap. I will see you there." She left me.

I looked at my reflection, not seeing myself, but imagining Maman. Warmth flowed over me, like I was still in the tub. Maman must have bathed me when I was a little girl, and my body must have remembered, for now sorrow sat in me. It had been nearly twenty years, and I still missed her. Would Louisa miss Magdeleine for her whole life? I hoped not.

I sighed. I could not disappoint Louisa or Magali by not going to the party. I'd just have to find the strength somehow.

I clasped my mother's locket at my neck, tied a lace fichu over my décolletage, and tucked the ends into the bodice. After sliding my feet into the gray satin slippers, I stood, wobbling. Now I really couldn't run away. Was that why women wore all these delicate things? To make them appear helpless and dependent upon men? Maybe I'd get permanent identity papers as a man.

I folded a shawl over my arm. People could make fun of me for throwing myself at Henri. I didn't care. I would leave by dawn. A hot force clogged my throat again. I looked back at my reflection, the ribbon shimmering, the echo of Louisa's laughter floating in the air. Letting her love me made me not want to leave Château de Verzat.

I inhaled, stood tall, and opened the door. But I would force myself. I couldn't live with the constant reminder that Henri didn't love me. I couldn't live on the estate knowing everyone pitied me. I had embarrassed myself enough.

57

THE SHAWL WRAPPED tight around my shoulders, I slid on the icy gravel path, lit by lanterns, to the cave. I longed for my boots, but then I would be tempted to head for the stables. Music and light flared from the cave entrance. The aromas of roast chicken, warm bread, and plum tarts reminded me I hadn't eaten all day. I stood shivering and pulled at the corset to take a full breath.

I would get this over with fast. I'd greet Henri, Aurélia, their son, Tante, Sister Magali, Madame Detré, and Louisa and leave. The sooner I got out of these ridiculous clothes, the faster I could escape. I would figure out where I'd go later. I stepped inside the tasting room and stood against the wall.

The sweet musty scent of the fermenting room wafted out of the dark arched doorway and over the crowd.

In the far corner, a man played a fiddle, another thumped a drum, and a woman played a vielle à roue. I'd seen men play the complicated instrument in Paris, but never a woman. The muscles in her strong arms flexed as she wound the crank that made a buzzing sound while her gnarled fingers danced across the keys, striking wooden flute-like notes. She was brave. I liked her and, if I were staying, I would befriend her.

I searched over the heads of people, where I thought LaGarde would stand out, and then I would travel in the opposite direction. My delight in the music drained at the sight of Henri, his arm about Aurélia's waist. She was nearly as tall as Henri, but far more regal. She appeared the noble, he the simple commoner.

A warm hand touched my elbow. "There you are." Tante Nicole wore a powdered wig, a dark green silk gown, and emeralds sparkled at her ears and neck. Her eyes glistened. "You are so very beautiful, my dear."

I tugged at the neckline. This gown was making me into something I was not. "Thank you," I squeaked.

She wrapped her arm in mine and began walking toward Henri. People turned to watch and, I feared they pitied me.

I stumbled. "Pardon. I'm not accustomed to these slippers." There was no unlocking her arm. I was trapped. Where was LaGarde? Tante propelled me through the crowd. My heart hammered against my ribs. Everyone was looking at me, witnessing my humiliation. My face burned.

"Marquise de Bourran." Henri smiled and bowed to Tante.

She swatted his arm with her fan. "Tante Nicole. No titles unless you wish to lose your head."

"Excuse me, Tante Nicole." He laughed. "We continued

to use titles in America, out of honor and politeness. May I present my future bride, Aurélia?"

His future bride. The words pricked my empty stomach.

Aurélia dipped her head and smiled sweetly. Not too much, not too little. How did she know exactly what to do? Joliette had grown up at Versailles, she must have trained Aurélia.

Tante took Aurélia's hands in her own. "Welcome to France. I hope you will be most happy here."

Aurélia smiled serenely as she placed her hand over her heart and nodded.

I backed up, hoping Tante would be caught up in conversation and not notice, but she gripped my elbow. "Henri, there is something you should know. While you and Joliette have been away, there is one person without whom this estate could not have survived." She pulled me before her. "Geneviève has ensured the safety of every family here. She has rescued those in need, and because of her enthusiasm in the vendanges, working as hard as everyone else, she is loved and respected by every person here."

I closed my eyes and prayed, Please, God, open a hole in the floor so I can fall through it.

Henri chuckled. "You are not the first person to tell me this." He looked to me. "I know nothing of running this estate and even less about the winery." His smile faded. "Geneviève, Joliette and I owe you much, as does everyone here. Joliette and I hope you will make Château de Verzat your home, forever."

What did Aurélia think about that? I glanced at her, already writing in the little book, hanging on a ribbon tied at her wrist. She tore off the sheet of paper, offered it to me, and smiled.

The paper was thin and fragile, but her writing was as graceful as a jasmine vine. I read, *I hope you make your home here and we become good friends.*

Her penmanship, her grammar, her French, all perfect. She was far better at being a lady than I. If I were in her position, I'd scratch my eyes out.

Tante poked me with her fan and raised an eyebrow.

I folded the paper and tucked it into my hanging pocket. "Merci. I hope we will be good friends, also." I smiled like an empty-headed marionette.

Henri cleared his throat. "This evening I learned that the Châtelain, the man who manages this entire estate, would like to train you to take his position when he vacates it."

I barked a laugh and immediately pressed my fingers to my mouth. Had my contempt shown? I was good enough to be Henri's Châtelain but not his wife. What a lovely offer.

"Is he that old?" Tante's words were sharp as glass. I'd never seen the disappointment that sat in her eyes. "He must have great faith in Geneviève."

Her disappointment was in me. Heat washed down my chest and sat burning in my stomach. She found me ungrateful. I supposed I was. The role of Châtelain was my consolation prize, not having won the role of Henri's wife.

"You must forgive Geneviève, she is overwhelmed by the honor you present, Henri."

I struggled to take a breath against the damned corset stays. "You are right, Tante. It's a great honor, Henri...I'm speechless." I squirmed, wondering how much of an apology Tante expected of me. "It's a tremendous responsibility—a man's responsibility."

"Ha." Henri laughed. "That you usually are, but for this evening."

At least he had noticed some difference. I forced a sweet smile. "May I think it over?"

Looking at me, Tante ran her fan down her tortoise-like neck and tapped it on her bodice.

"Bien sûr." Henri poured us each a glass of wine and raised his. "To Geneviève. May she be successful in whatever she pursues."

Glasses clinked.

I sipped my wine, warm and thick and cloying. In my mind I retorted, I wasn't successful at winning you, was I, Henri? I glanced around. Where was LaGarde, and why wasn't he saving me from this catastrophe? I drank another sip and held the glass up to examine the color. Was this Verzat wine? A rustling of skirts and a giggle announced Louisa. Thank you, God.

I bent down. "Are you having fun, mon ange?"

She nodded, grabbed my hand, and began dragging me away. I was so grateful I nearly forgot to excuse myself.

She led me to the edge of a crowd surrounding a group of dancers as they shuffled, skipped, and leaped a lively gavotte. My eyes followed every move of the most fluid and lively gentleman. LaGarde? He put his hand at Magali's back and led her around the floor. Her cap askew, her cheeks bright pink, Sister threw back her head and laughed with glee as LaGarde twirled her before delivering her to a new partner.

LaGarde devoted himself to making every woman look like she was born to dance. A pious old widow, Simon's Maman, the Catholic mother we'd rescued, and Madame Detré, who pinched LaGarde's cheek after he bowed to her. I peered back at Henri, standing stiff as a sail in the wind, and next to him, Aurélia moving like a graceful willow in time with the music.

The dance over, Louisa cried out, "Papa, my turn!"

LaGarde looked over, and his eyes flashed as they caught mine. He gazed at me for so long, I wished I had a fan to cool the heat rising in me. He smiled, a rather roguish smile and, never taking his eyes from mine, he strode to us, picked up Louisa, and held her against his chest.

He loudly whispered into Louisa's ear, "Who is this beautiful lady?"

I coughed a laugh. Who was he kidding besides himself?

Louisa giggled. "I said you wouldn't recognize her, Papa. It's Tante Gen."

"No." He shook his head and pushed out his lower lip. "Cannot be. She is lovely, delicate like a flower, her lips glisten like honeyed nectar, she shines from within to make the stars jealous. This, this is not a man. This," he arched his arm, "is the most beautiful lady in the land."

Louisa crowed giggles.

She was adorable. I laughed, straining against my corset. How did LaGarde make me laugh when I wanted to be angry?

He whispered to Louisa, she nodded, and he put her down.

She grabbed my hand and her father's and joined them. "Dance with Papa, Tante Gen."

Oh, no. My legs vibrated. I didn't know how. Everyone knew I pined for Henri, and dancing with LaGarde would be the height of my embarrassment. My feet scuffled back. LaGarde's fingers tightened on mine, and he pulled me out from the crowd, my slippers trailing my feet.

The musicians started an unfamiliar rhythm. Dancers moved back into the crowd, clearing the center of the floor.

LaGarde raised his eyebrows and grinned. He took my hands, bringing my arms away from my sides and placed my left hand on his shoulder, his strong, muscular shoulder. "Count. One-two-three, one-two-three."

"What are you…"

But we were off, gliding in the open space, his hand pressing against the small of my back, moving my body in directions my eyes and feet could only follow. "One-two-three," he huffed.

I finally realized my feet were to follow his counting, and when they did, I allowed myself to stop fighting him and lean into his embrace as he twirled me around and around.

"What dance is this?" I panted with every word.

"The waltz."

"Is it proper?"

"I certainly hope not." He increased the length of his steps. My toes barely touched the floor, as if he were flying me like a kite.

"Wherever did you learn it?"

"Vienna. As a young man, I was eager to visit the homeland of our former Queen."

Colors swirled by, but if I kept my eyes on him, I didn't feel dizzy. His face was relaxed, devilish, so handsome. Had he been this handsome long ago? "Do you miss being a courtier and living at Versailles?"

His face grew serious. "Not in the least. The man I am today cannot imagine being the imbécile I was."

I wanted to agree with him but didn't wish to spoil the dance.

His white silk jabot was tied in an elegant bow, his hair perfectly coiffed, his scent of a spring hayfield, fresh, seductive. "I joked earlier, but I meant every word I uttered. You are the most beautiful lady in the land, Geneviève."

I smiled and hated that I knew it was a fetching smile. I was being a coquette! What was I doing? I'd embarrassed myself enough for a lifetime with Henri.

"You must dress as a woman more often."

I yanked my hands from his. His arms empty, he cocked his head, questioning me.

I gripped my skirts and fled through the crowd and into the night. Why couldn't anyone appreciate me for who I was? Henri needed me to be a man for a man's job, now LaGarde wanted me to be a woman. Why was it anyone's business who or what I was? Why was I never enough for anybody?

The cold air hit me like a slap. I'd lost my shawl. I wrapped my arms around myself and stood looking up at the château. I wished I'd eaten. I wished I'd drunk more wine. I wished I'd stayed and danced till dawn. Why hadn't I? Why was I so angry all the time? Louisa would be disappointed I had left. So would Tante. And I hadn't even greeted Magali. All the care they'd taken in preparing me and here I was alone in the night, freezing. Alone. LaGarde was right. I could save everyone but myself. I was a calamité.

A crunching on gravel made me jump.

Backlit, I couldn't see the face of a large shadow moving toward me, but my breath caught with the hope it was LaGarde.

He stopped, his arms at his sides, his palms toward me. "I apologize for whatever blunder I have made. Please, return.

Louisa is crying for you." He dropped his head, as if in contrition. How his daughter had changed him.

I sighed. "I'm the one who should apologize." What was I saying? I wanted to leave, but I couldn't. I couldn't leave Louisa, or Tante, or Magali, or Simon. I didn't want to leave LaGarde! Christ, my gown was so tight, I wanted to scream.

"Please, do not let me hinder your apology." He grinned.

His wit really was annoying. I sighed. "It's my fault no one can accept me for a woman or a man since I dress as both. I'm sorry."

The lanterns' light flickered across his wide smile. "May I have the next dance? You may lead if you feel like being the man."

I laughed so hard I bent over my legs. His hands were gentle on my fingers as he pulled me to him and began to waltz me across the meadow. A chill breeze stirred the air around us, yet I was warm. Warm in his arms. Warm in being a woman. Warm for this moment. I didn't want it to end.

"Papa!" Louisa stood, wind whipping her skirts about her.

LaGarde ran to her and scooped her up. "Let us all dance!"

We returned to the cave. LaGarde, holding Louisa against his chest, waltzed us both about the room until Louisa and I were dizzy, and the musicians stopped. We sat at a table with Tante Nicole, Magali, and the other Sisters. LaGarde brought a jug of wine and glasses. Women brought over plates of food, insisting LaGarde taste their specialties, and he did, complimenting each with a unique appreciation.

LaGarde brought his attention to every person and listened as if that person were the most important one right that instant.

Holding Charles's hand, Madame Detré joined us. Louisa quickly sat next to the boy and stared at his curly hair. She pulled a lock and when she let it go and it sprang back, she giggled. Charles laughed and pulled her curl, which also sprang back. The game delighted them.

Tante patted my hand. "Are you not glad you stayed?"

"You always know what is best, Tante."

She tilted her head. "Is that you speaking, Geneviève?"

I laughed, and the tightness in my chest loosened.

Madame Detré leaned toward LaGarde. "Before you leave, tomorrow, Monsieur LaGarde, Henri wishes to speak with you."

I froze. LaGarde was leaving? A thrumming filled my ears, my head, my chest. Had he asked me to let Louisa love me only to take her away? Henri's contrite face glimmered in my mind, so real I smelled the damp forest of Nantes.

"Certainement, Madame." LaGarde smiled warmly.

A tingling shot down my legs, making me want to flee. I stood. "Will you be taking Louisa with you?"

Golden specks in LaGarde's eyes reflected the flickering candlelight. "I am…I hope we—you and I—are taking her to visit the orphanage."

Tante Nicole pressed her hand onto mine. "It is just a visit. You'll be returning soon, Louis?"

"Bien sûr."

"You'll come too, won't you Tante Gen?" Louisa cried. "The orphanage is named for my maman."

LaGarde wasn't leaving me. LaGarde wasn't Henri. Louisa was asking me to join them. Yet, the tingling surged up my back. I bent my knees, trying to stop the sensation. I had to stop running away, but I didn't know how. I didn't want to flee, but my feet, my legs tensed.

LaGarde stood. "I had not the opportunity to ask you earlier, Geneviève. I hope you will join us? You could also visit Auguste."

Tante's hand tightened around mine. Had madame Detré not mentioned it, I'd have awakened with Louisa gone. I had lost everyone I had ever loved and now he was about to take Louisa from me, too. He knew I longed for Auguste, so he added a visit to him to make me do what he wanted. The cave darkened around me. But that was my fear. Fear of Maman dying and Papa leaving me at the Abbey and Henri not loving me and losing Auguste. Not what was really happening. LaGarde wasn't taking Louisa away, and he wanted to take me to my brother. What was wrong with me?

I pulled my hand from Tante's and straightened my back. "Henri has asked me to start training as Châtelain in the morning. I don't believe I will have the time."

I had to find a place to be alone. "I must rise early." I nodded to everyone at the table. "Bonne nuit."

My feet walked of their own accord; I couldn't stop them. What was I doing? I was the one leaving. Did I leave before anyone could leave me? I stopped and inhaled the cool night air. A hand touched my elbow and turned me.

LaGarde wrapped his arms around me so tightly I couldn't move. His breath was hot against my neck and a tingling charged down to my toes.

"I will not leave without you. Even if it means disappointing Louisa. I want her to know about her maman, and you are the only one able to tell Louisa about her birth. Please, Geneviève, come with us."

I struggled to look at him, and he loosened his hold on me.

His eyes, so full of kindness. His mouth so wanting. His scent so seductive. "Now that Henri is back, he should be protecting this estate, not you. Please come with us."

A shiver, warmth, then another shiver moved through me. LaGarde was right. I had done enough for Henri; he should be taking care of things. What did I want? I loved Magdeleine, and I'd not yet told Louisa about her dear sweet maman.

I dropped my forehead against LaGarde's chest. The quivering that raced through me, making me feel as though I had no control over my own body, had stopped. Did that mean I trusted LaGarde?

He swept a curl from my neck and tucked it up into the ribbon. A new sensation moved through me—a thrill of desire I'd never felt, not even with Henri.

"Silver becomes you," LaGarde said softly, his breath warm on my neck. "Like you, it shines in the moonlight."

I wanted him to keep talking, for I had nothing to say. And it struck me, that that was the first time in my life.

"Come with us, Geneviève." He tightened his arms about me. "Louisa and I need you."

I looked up at him.

"And I want you." A corner of his mouth lifted.

He was so handsome when he teased me. My legs went limp, but I forced myself to stand tall. New feelings rushed through me so fast, I couldn't identify them. Nor could I trust myself.

I needed to think. To see things clearly, without the disappointment Henri had caused shadowing everything I heard and saw and felt.

The lines surrounding LaGarde's eyes deepened. "Please."

I needed to see LaGarde clearly, for who he was. I had been getting to know him by constantly comparing him to Henri. How unfair of me. How stupid of me. I needed time to understand and see myself before I could truly see LaGarde.

I smiled, but I knew it was a sad smile. "I'd like to join you, but I…I'll let you know in the morning."

"We will wait." He released me, bowed, and kissed my fingertips. "À demain. Bonne nuit."

And then I was alone. Again. And I didn't want to be.

58

Château de Verzat
November 1796

Pale pink and violet light streaked the gray cloudbank scudding across the sky. Fog rose from the Loire and wound around poplar trees lining the riverbank. It would rain within the hour. Maybe LaGarde would postpone his trip. I laughed at myself. He was a man of decisions and actions, not delays.

I washed, donned a clean shift, and opened the armoire. The blue and gray striped gown shimmered in the pale light. My heartbeat quickened as I inhaled the lingering fresh scent of LaGarde. He'd held me so tightly...and I'd liked it.

Did I like him? Tante was right. Louisa had changed the bully into a man...I...liked. Could I...love him? I had to forgive him once and for all.

In my mind, I saw him in the dining room. Feeling his arms about me as I had sobbed into his chest, crying over the

Chouans. *You care with all your heart, Geneviève. It is one of the qualities I admire most about you.* I sat on the bed, his voice echoing. *You are the most selfless person I have ever known. After you left me, I promised God that if I got out of that hellhole, I would try to be more like you.*

Perhaps it wasn't only Louisa who had changed him. He said I should dress as a woman more often, and I'd fled. What was wrong with me? I fell back upon the bed.

Why had I remained loyal to Henri despite his lack of attention? Why did I seek love where it didn't exist? LaGarde had said I was worthy of love, but just because I was worthy didn't make a man fall in love with me.

I plucked up the blue-flowered print gown LaGarde had left in my chamber at his château. I hadn't worn a corset with it, and I wasn't going to now. I slipped the gown over my head and tied the sash behind me as best I could. Standing before the mirror, I wondered if I was like Maman. Magali had said I looked like her, but did I have Maman's heart? Her gentle touch? Sadness seeped through me again like the mist rolling over the river. I clasped Maman's locket around my neck and sat at the dressing table, brushing my hair like I was trying to sweep away the sorrow, confusion, anxiety that raged like a river current through me.

Louisa's silver ribbon flowed and curled around the pins. Ribbons would always remind me of my mother, and now, Louisa, too.

I stopped brushing, remembering Maman's hands as she threaded the ribbons around my curls. The ache in my heart spread through my chest. I would never stop missing Maman because I would never stop loving her. The pain was still there, but it had dulled, tarnished, frayed, like a long-used ribbon. The pain had become a part of my love for my mother.

LaGarde was right. I couldn't let people love me. Now I understood I feared they would die, just like Maman did. And Magdeleine.

I'd been terrified LaGarde was taking Louisa away from me, and I'd wanted to flee. But he had no intention of taking her away. It was my fear that made me react so…dramatically. I winced at the memory of my trembling. He reassured me. *Louisa and I need you. I need you.*

I ran my fingers along the silky ribbon. *Silver becomes you. Like you, it shines in the moonlight.*

I stared at myself, my small bosom, my dark unruly hair that looked better when I pulled it back and wore it like a man. I lifted a lock up to the crown of my head and pinned it, then another, and another. I wound the ribbon through the curls. *Never sell your hair. It is at its most beautiful upon your head… and about your shoulders.*

A shiver of excitement ran through me. I did look more like Maman when I dressed like a woman. Why did I fear dressing as one? I rubbed my arms. I wore men's clothing so I could guard the woman who needed protection. Yet LaGarde had told me, *You deserve a man who loves you and will not leave you.*

All these years I'd pined for a man whom I didn't think would leave me, but who already had.

I picked up one of the gray slippers, rumpled, scuffed, stained, and closed my eyes. All that waltzing…I stood and danced as the music filled me, the wind chilling my face,

LaGarde's arm gripping my waist. I stopped, opened my eyes, and stared at my reflection. All this time I'd been falling in love with LaGarde.

Memories flashed like lightning through my mind.

At the inn with Madame Lochot, I had accused him of being selfish, but he'd been protective. *I would not leave without you.*

In the cave, when I worried that he would tell me what to do about the Chouans, he left it up to me. *I will support whatever your decision.*

In the stables, when I'd told him to mind his own business, he'd begged me: *At least allow my daughter to love you.*

And the night before, when I feared being a woman, he'd told me what he saw. *…lovely, delicate like a flower…lips glisten like nectar…shines from within to make the stars jealous.*

And he'd shown me he loved me. *And I want you.*

"All this time, he knew I was falling in love with him because he wanted me to fall in love with him!" I threw the slipper. "Bastard."

A laugh burst from my belly. What a fool I'd been. My laughter uncoiled, pitching me onto the bed. He had known all this time; he was just waiting for me to figure it out. I rolled onto my back, howling laughs. How had he been so patient? *You may lead if you feel like being the man.*

My laughter brought tears. I wiped them away and lay there, seeing his face, his gold-flecked eyes, the little depression in the middle of his chin, the way he made his lips pouf when he dismissed something. His roguish smile when he'd said, *Now we are even.*

I stilled. LaGarde loved me for who I was—whoever that was—man or woman—and he knew me better than I did.

And I loved him. I heaved a breath. Shook my head. I was crazy. I loved LaGarde?

I jumped up, whipped my shawl about my shoulders, and jammed my feet into my muddy boots.

I only hoped it wasn't too late to tell him.

59

Château de Verzat
November 1796

"**D**ID YOU DECIDE to join Louis and Louisa?" Tante Nicole's question stopped me as I arrived in the kitchen.

"Yes. I hope they haven't left yet." I expected the Sisters and orphans to be at table. "Where is everyone?" I reached for my cloak hanging by the door.

"They sleep. The party lasted most of the night." Her eyes sparkled. "Would you retrieve my walking stick? Less than an hour ago, Henri and Simon walked me back. I didn't need it, with those two strong gentlemen assisting me."

"I'm happy to."

"Thank you." She motioned for me to turn. "I am glad you are accepting Louis's invitation." Removing my shawl, she retied my sash and turned me toward her. "You are as beautiful as you were last night, my dear, even with muddy boots."

I laughed. "Where is your stick?"

"I left it in the tasting room."

"I'll be right back."

"Your cloak!"

"I can run faster without it." I closed the door behind me and, pretending to be in LaGarde's arms, waltzed down the path to the cave.

A few torches hanging on the walls flicked and sputtered. Plates and glasses covered the soiled tablecloths. Benches sat helter-skelter along the edges of the dance floor. I circled about, my arms around an imaginary LaGarde and spotted Tante's stick in the corner. I dropped my arms, still feeling his heat from the night before, and made my way past the tables and reached.

Footsteps clacked over the stone, sending a prickling across the back of my neck. Anyone from the estate would have shouted a greeting.

"Magnifique!"

Cold slid down my back like sleet. How did Martin find me? I bent to retrieve my dagger but straightened. In my hurry to dress, I'd forgotten to slip the knife into my boot. I gripped Tante's stick, hid it amongst the folds of my skirts, and turned.

Martin wore the Republican Army uniform of a sergeant: smudged white breeches, muddied black boots, and red frock coat with tarnished brass buttons, giving him more significance than he deserved. He rested his wrist on the pommel of the sword hanging at his side. A jagged red scar arced from his ear to his chin, for which he would exact revenge.

"It's been more than a year, and you look lovelier than ever,

Mademoiselle." His smile was too broad, like a cat with a cornered mouse.

LaGarde had warned me Martin would expect me to act as I did the last time. I resisted trying to smile—that charm worked only once. "And you are uglier than ever." I kept the stick behind my skirts and side-stepped toward the tables and benches.

He stopped and crowed a laugh. He abruptly stilled his face. "Thanks to you, Mademoiselle."

His words slid into each other, making me realize that I had cut through the corner of his mouth and, as he spoke, he chewed at the scar. The puckered skin pulled, making his lower lip and the corner of his eye droop. His face, never handsome, was now a macabre mask.

He advanced, his eyes roving over me. "I never understood why you dressed as a man when you are such a lovely lady." From inside his frock coat, he withdrew a small sword—LaGarde had warned—the most lethal weapon because it was easy to wield and pierce deep wounds.

I could not let Martin get close enough to use it. But how could I keep him at a distance? The silver swan's head at the top of Tante's stick was slippery with my sweat. The image of a soldier holding the tip of his dagger at Tante's throat flashed in my mind. As the soldier threatened Tante, Simon picked up her stick, released the hidden blade from its tip, lunged, and skewered the soldier through his belly. I had to do the same to Martin. Or he would kill me.

"Cat got your tongue?" Martin huffed a laugh. "Maybe that's what I'll slice off first."

"I made you sound like a drunkard." I forced my fear into a challenging, mocking tone. I wanted to unnerve him.

He whipped the blade through the air and laughed harder.

He laughed like an unpredictable madman. Pressing my palm against Maman's locket, I silently prayed, *Maman, help me.* I slid behind a table—I would use it as a shield. I hoped he would not trade his small sword for the sword hanging at his side.

Sneering, Martin sauntered toward me, his wrist flicking the blade in a circle.

He would expect me to run, but I dared not turn my back. My legs trembled. I bent my knees and strengthened my stance, keeping Tante's stick hidden in the folds of my skirts.

Martin jumped up on the bench, perching like a vulture.

My pounding heart deafened me.

Quick as a snake, he sliced the short sword's blade close to my face.

I jumped to the side but immediately positioned my feet, gripping the stick, ready to lunge.

He followed me, his face glowing with satisfaction. "I've got you right where I want you." He thrust the blade, and I ducked.

I wanted to seduce him from his murderous intent, but if I did, I'd fall into his trap. I had to take the advantage.

"And you're right where I want you," I bluffed. I drew Tante's stick from behind my skirts and held each end before me.

"You going to hit me with your little stick?" He stomped one foot on the table and towered above me.

If I tilted my head, I'd expose my neck. I stared up at him, terror crawling up my back.

He whisked the blade side to side, advancing closer and closer.

I forced myself to stay still, watching for a weakness.

A flick of his wrist turned into a jab, pricking my cheek. His hot stink whooshed over me.

I jerked my head to the side, but I could not stifle a gasp. My face stung.

He licked my blood from the tip of his blade.

"You killed Pierre, you bastard."

His guffaws shook him, jerking his body about as if his laughter possessed him. "And I'm going to kill you, too!"

Keeping both hands on the stick before me, I planted my back foot, bent my knees, kept my elbows close to my sides, and twisted the stick's handle, silently ejecting the blade from its tip. If I only injured him, he would become enraged, and I wouldn't survive his retaliation. I had to kill.

Flicking the short sword in menacing circles, he brought his other foot upon the table, and leered. He squatted on his haunches, enjoying his perceived power over me, taunting me, terrifying me. Yet presenting an irresistible target—his groin.

I lunged and thrust the blade between his legs. Blood spread over the crotch of his dirty breeches. Crimson drops sprayed over the white tablecloth.

He huffed a little laugh, like he was merely surprised. He thrust the small sword but winced.

His shock would wear off. I had to kill him. My arms burned as I gripped the stick and twisted the blade.

He screamed.

I pressed the blade further into his flesh.

Growling like a rabid dog, he tried to stab my arm, but he

faltered. The blade stabbed the tabletop. He grasped Tante's stick.

With both hands, I yanked the stick back, the blade slicing his palms and fingers.

He stared at his open bleeding hands, like a child not understanding.

"You're not going to kill me, you bastard." I stomped my feet into my stance and lunged, shoving the blade into his belly and up under his sternum. Blood poured down the stick. My arms burning, I wrenched the stick to the right and then the left, like I was drilling a hole in him.

He toppled over onto his side, his arms flailing, his legs collapsing onto the table. He fell onto his back, writhing, groaning. He reached out, his fingers clawing the air.

In my mind, I saw the tear-stained faces of Pierre's wife and son when I told them Pierre was dead.

I stepped upon the bench and looked down into Martin's pinched black eyes. "This is for Pierre's family." I brought up the stick and plunged the blade into Martin's throat. Black-red blood spurted, blooming across the white cloth as fast as a wine stain.

A gurgling sound, like water falling over stones in a brook, bubbled from Martin's mouth. Just like the sounds made by the soldier Simon had killed.

Martin's eyes dulled, emptied; as soulless as those of a river eel.

Panting, I pushed down the nausea rising in me. I wiped my sleeve over my face. Traces of blood stained my sleeve. I ran my hand over my cheek. The cut was not deep and only the length of my finger. He could have carved my face. I stood shaking.

I wiped my hands on my skirts and pulled the blade from his body, held onto the tabletop, and climbed off the bench. Flecks of light swirled, forcing me to sit. The coppery stink of his blood filled the air, but I inhaled shuddering breaths. The tablecloth dripped blood onto the floor. I had killed a man. Committed a mortal sin. But I was glad I killed him. With every breath I heaved, I was glad.

I jolted. Other soldiers, guards, gendarmes must be after me…and Simon. I had to hide the body.

Cold air from the fermenting room flowed over me. I could take the main tunnel that led to the underground tunnel connecting to the château kitchen. But it was dark. Only one torch flickered. If soldiers saw the blood on my gown, they'd know I killed Martin.

I wiped Tante's stick on a tablecloth, ran to the wall, grabbed the one torch that still flamed, and, keeping my hand against the wall, I entered the darkness, counting my steps in case I had to retrace them.

The torch flickered out. I stood still, holding my breath, listening for soldiers' footsteps.

"Is he dead?"

A scream burned, caught in my throat. Had I imagined the whisper?

As if a rope wound tightly around my chest, I could not take air in. Light trickled around me.

"Did you kill him?" a woman's voice asked.

My heartbeat throbbed in my throat. There would be no escaping the guillotine now. Slowly, I turned.

The two Chouan women stood, wide-eyed. One held a lantern, the other a mushroom basket.

I slapped my hand over my mouth to cover my cry.

They were beside me in an instant, pulling me up, for I hadn't realized I had fallen to my knees.

Their strong arms held me as I jerked about uncontrollably.

"Anne and I will help you hide him," said the children's Tante Thèrése.

"I can't endanger you." I clutched my skirts.

Anne held my arm firmly. "You have endangered yourself for us. Let us help you."

Thèrése leaned closer. "He killed our sister."

Martin was just as much a monster as my father. "I'm glad I killed him." My voice cracked.

"We are grateful to you. We know these caves." Thèrése rubbed my back. "Go find Simon. He will help us."

The memory of burying the soldier Simon killed skittered in my mind. "But if more soldiers come—"

"We've no time to lose. The soldiers will fear getting lost in the smaller passages. Tell Simon we've taken the body through the mushroom tunnels. He'll know where to find us."

These beautiful women were risking their lives to save mine. I wanted to weep.

Anne pulled off her apron. "Wear this over your gown to hide the blood."

I tied it around my waist. "I will bring Simon and LaGarde." I gripped their hands in mine and kissed them. "Merci."

I followed them out to the tasting room. They ripped cloths from the tables and draped them over Martin's body.

Rosey morning light glowed beyond the doorway. I paused and looked back. I had escaped Martin by running into the dark—I'd not been afraid of it. I had used the darkness for protection. I no longer feared it. A giddiness rose in my chest.

I would burn in hell for killing a man, but did God consider killing in self-defense a sin? It would have been a bigger sin *not* to defend myself. But I was proud and glad I had exacted revenge, most of all for Pierre, but also my father, and myself. The giddiness dissolved into a yawning hole. I should have felt remorse. A better person would. Had my father felt proud and glad when he sent people to the guillotine? Shame washed through me.

My legs were limp as I walked out of the cave. I gulped clean, fresh air. I'd killed a man—who deserved to die. And I killed him as the woman I was. I straightened to my full height. All this time I had been dressing as a man to feel powerful, when all along, I *was* powerful. I was a powerful woman. And I was proud.

I wiped sweat from my face, my neck, my bosom, my mother's locket. *Thank you, Maman.* I shook the trembling from my hands. I had also let two women help me, and I was grateful to them.

If soldiers discovered Martin, they'd kill Simon, the Chouan women, and every single person on the estate. And I didn't kill Martin to endanger anyone else. I ran.

60

Château de Verzat
November 1796

"**S**IMON!" I SHOUTED as I reached his cottage. I bent over and heaved a breath. Imaginary soldiers searching for me taunted me.

The cottage door banged open and Simon, shrugging on his cloak, ran out. "What's wrong?" He neared. "You're bleeding!"

I scanned the estate, searching for the red of soldiers' uniforms. Simon reached me and I pulled him close. "I've killed Martin." Simon began to pull away, but I kept him near and whispered, "The Chouan women are dragging his body through the mushroom tunnels."

He nodded sharply and backed away. His eyes glimmered, perhaps with pride but also worry. "We will bury him with the one I killed." He ran.

"I'll get LaGarde." Watching for soldiers, I ran.

61

"**W**HAT HAS HAPPENED?" LaGarde slammed the door of his cottage behind him and rushed toward me, his face creased with worry.

I flung myself at him, and his arms wrapped around me. My legs gave way.

"Blood stains your face and gown." His breath was hot on my neck. "Are you injured?"

"Just a scratch." I shook my head. "I killed Martin." The words whooshed out of me.

LaGarde's arms tightened. "How did he find you?"

"He must have stolen the letter Simon wrote to me, letting me know Madame Lochot and Little Pierre were safe here. He's been hunting me all this time." I leaned into LaGarde's warmth. "I'm still wanted."

Horses' hooves thundered down the hill. I turned. A soldier. "Martin was a soldier."

"Calm. Show no fear." He turned me toward him and held me close.

I stared up at him. His eyes held warning. Would this be our last embrace?

The soldier brought his mount to within an arm's length of us. He cleared his throat.

LaGarde broke our embrace but held onto me. He looked up. I never thought I'd see it, but LaGarde wore a stupid face, his mouth gaping, his head tilted, his eyes dim. He blinked at the soldier as if wondering how he'd gotten there.

"Bonjour, Citizens."

I twisted my neck to see a lieutenant astride a black stallion. God in heaven help us. "Bonjour." I gave a weak smile.

LaGarde rubbed my back. "What can we do for you, Lieutenant?"

"This is the Verzat estate?"

LaGarde nodded. "All the land you can see on this side of the river."

"Your papers." He put out his hand.

Mine were in my chamber. Sweat made my clinging gown cold and wet. LaGarde dug into his waistcoat, pulled out his papers, and offered them.

The soldier examined them. "Yours, Citizeness?"

"She is my wife. You can see on my papers." LaGarde's voice was subservient. "She just killed her first chicken!" He turned me around to show my gown. "Made quite a mess of it, but it is a start. We have been married for years and, finally, she can kill a chicken." LaGarde's smile beamed with pride.

Wife? My heart pounded. Chicken? I opened my mouth, and LaGarde quickly pecked a kiss upon my cheek.

"Have you seen any soldiers today or yesterday?"

LaGarde pushed out his lower lip, pretending to think while holding me close. "No."

"We search for a dangerous man, impersonating a sergeant. He wears a uniform, but he is no soldier. Have you seen him?"

My heart thumped so loudly I feared the soldier would hear it.

LaGarde shook his head. "We know everyone who lives on the estate. There are more than four hundred families. We have seen no strangers. If anyone else had, we would know."

I bit the inside of my cheek. LaGarde let me turn my head back so I could see the man.

"Be on your guard and protect your wives and daughters. The man, Martin Garat, has killed three women."

My breath left me. I bit down hard to stop a sob threatening to burst out of my chest.

"What does this Garat look like?" Was LaGarde torturing me on purpose or trying to convince the soldier we were good, obedient citizens?

"Slight, of average stature. Charming smile but devious eyes. He has dark hair and a scar running from ear to chin."

"What should we do, should we see him?" LaGarde was acting dumb.

"Shoot him on sight. The cur murdered my daughter. After he'd taken her." He turned in his saddle and spat.

"I am so sorry." Tears sprang, and I blinked furiously.

"Merci. If you do kill him, you will have my eternal gratitude." He clicked his tongue and rode down the valley.

I wrapped my arms around LaGarde, never wanting to let go. His chest rose and fell. His slow, strong, and steady heartbeat was like a lullaby to me. I wanted his calm to spread through me. I lifted my face to him.

His eyes were serious. "Where is the body?"

Everything in me contracted. I dropped my arms and stepped back, trembling. "The Chouan women found me. They're dragging his body through the mushroom tunnels. I sent Simon to hide the body."

He watched the soldier riding in the distance. "It is dark in the caves."

"Yes."

"You are afraid of the dark."

"Not anymore." I straightened.

He looked at me with such pride I wanted to cry. "Are you going to help us hide the body?"

He smiled. "Bien sûr."

62

Château de Verzat
November 1796

BY THE TIME LaGarde and I had reached the caves, Simon and the Chouan women had dragged Martin's body deep into the tunnels. LaGarde sent me and the women outside to keep watch for soldiers. He and Simon hid Martin's body in the secret chamber next to the other soldier.

When LaGarde and Simon emerged from the caves, I realized I had been holding my breath. I bent over and finally exhaled.

They left LaGarde and me. Simon was so tall, walking between the two women into the morning light, illuminating the rising mist. Simon was a man now, a brave and smart man—who could be conscripted into the army in another year.

LaGarde put his arm around my waist.

Wanting him to keep his hand there forever, I placed my

hand over his and looked up at him. "I want to join you and Louisa. Should we leave now?"

He pulled me close. I was limp as an unstrung marionette, and I let him support me. "In a few moments." His mouth covered mine.

A hot tingling flooded me. I leaned into him, wrapped my arms around him, and kissed him with all of me.

Too soon, he let go of me and stood back. Cold rushed in where his warmth had enveloped me. I stood, longing for him.

LaGarde ran his thumb softly across the scratch on my cheek. He crossed his arms, quirked an eyebrow, and stared at me.

What would I say? I hadn't thought about how I would tell him I loved him. But at least I did not feel like running. I cleared my throat. "You were right."

His arms dropped. "Excusé moi? I do not think I heard you correctly."

I pushed back my shoulders. He was not going to make this easy. Why did I think he would? He was LaGarde. I pulled in a steadying breath. "I didn't let people love me. I didn't let Louisa give me her love, and I'm very sorry."

"Truly?" He leaned his head to the left then the right and then straightened his neck. "Whom else?"

Scoundrel. "Sister Magali."

He pushed out his lower lip. "Anyone else?"

I had to get this all out so I could kiss him again. "You. Damn it. I didn't let you love me. You made me fall in love with you. And you knew all along that I was falling in love with you. You were so damned patient with me, and I was so stupid." I slapped my skirts. "You waited all this time until I figured it out!" I flung out my arms. "I hope you're proud of yourself."

He pouted. "I do not think anyone could make you do something you do not want to do."

I dropped my arms. "How do you know me better than I know myself?"

He grinned. "I love you more than you love yourself."

I pushed out a long slow breath. This was not going as I had planned. I was angry with him, and I had wanted to tell him I loved him. What was wrong with me?

He leaned against the stone wall. "Anything else you wish to tell me?"

I stood still, my heartbeat thundering. I wanted to fall into his arms. "I love you." My voice was softer than a breeze.

"Pardon?"

A growl caught in my throat. I looked him in the eye and shouted, "I love you."

Keeping his eyes on mine, he took my fingers into his. "Did you not say a lady likes to be asked?"

The tingling rushed through me, making me tremble. I could only nod.

He knelt before me. "Will you Geneviève be my wife and partner, share my life and daughter, and allow me to love you for eternity?"

I knelt opposite him, entwining my fingers with his. "Yes. And will you, Louis, be my husband and partner, share your life and daughter, and allow me to love you for eternity?"

The gold flecks in his eyes sparked. "You called me Louis!"

THE END

ACKNOWLEDGEMENTS

UN GRAND MERCI À

Dr. Berry Edwards who often resorted to speaking French to drag me back from the eighteenth century. Thank you for making me laugh. You are my chevalier.

Aunt Di for your love, support, laughter, and craziness.

Mireille Belt without whose generous gift of two weeks in her Paris apartment this book would not have been conceived.

Paulette Adams for being an eternal inspiration.

My web designer, Elena Saygo for her brilliance and humor.

Teachers and coaches: Susan Penberthy-Nowak for instilling in me a love for the French language and culture, Priscilla Long, Don Maass, and Lorin Oberweger and Brenda Windberg of Free Expressions.

Attorney Matthew Dresden, Dresden Law PLLC, for his generous time and counsel. And Washington Lawyers for the Arts https://www.thewla.org/.

Librarians everywhere. In particular, the Bibliothèque Nationale de France, and Art at the Lionel Pincus and Princess Firyal Map Division of the New York Public Library.

The gracious and generous Monsieur Thierry Sarmant, conservateur en chef, Cabinet Numismatique, and the very kind and helpful staff at Musée Carnavalet, Paris, France.

The gracious staffs at the Château de Brissac, Château de Chenonceau, Château de Meung, and Château de Versailles.

Critique partners, first readers, and editors who asked the right questions and demonstrated great insight, patience, humor, and honesty: Cynthia Anderson, Allison Basile, Dr. Marty Blalock, Cynthia Blair (Cynthia Baxter), Sandy Bremser, Tiffanny Brooks, Chris Butler, Julie Cooper, Kate Dane, Bill Dickett, Vaughn Entwistle, Ejner Fulsang, Lisa Glasgow, Gabi Herkert, Bharti Kirchner, Joanne Khuns, Susan LeMiles, Marylee MacDonald, Jody McCoy, Jill MacGregor, Jody McCoy, D.R. Ransdell, Ed Ratcliffe, Jane Sutherland, JoAnne Tompkins, Jennifer White, Robin Yak. And the late Richard Askern and John Zobel.

Subject matter experts: Charlotte Rose Basile, William A. Edwards III, and Jane Sutherland.

My gracious and helpful French hosts: Dominique Cale-gari-Jehl (Côte Sud—chambres d'hôtes village troglodyte, Troo, France), and Julie and Jeremy Kolbé (Les Rosiers Loire Valley Gite, Monteaux, France). Concierge, Estelle Hoglund, at Paris Marriott Hotel Champs Elysees.

Cultural events and websites helpful to my research and cultural understanding:

- *Emilie* and *The Revolutionists*, plays by Lauren Gunderson https://www.laurengunderson.com/
- Alliance Française: https://afusa.org/
- Bonjour Paris https://bonjourparis.com/
- Courtney Traub's Paris Unlocked https://www.parisunlocked.com/
- Dani Belau's Girl's Guide to Paris https://girlsguidetoparis.com/
- France Magazine https://francetoday.com/
- France Today https://francetoday.com/
- Gallica, the digital library of the National Library of France and its partners. https://gallica.bnf.fr/
- Irene Levine's More Time to Travel https://www.moretimetotravel.com/
- Janine Marsh's The Good Life France https://thegoodlifefrance.com/
- Kristin Espinasse's French Word-A-Day https://www.french-word-a-day.com/
- Paris American Club https://parisamericanclub.org/

- Christina Consolé's Parisian Niche https://www.
  parisianniche.com/post/top-5-paris-based-books-
  we-can-t-wait-to-read-in-2023

Communities in which I have participated with many generous writers: Community of Writers at Squaw Valley, Free Expression's Inner Circle, Historical Novel Society, Hugo House, Sisters in Crime, The History Quill, Women fiction Writers Association.

If you're looking for a book club that reads and discusses books that take place in France, check out Parisian Page Turners: www.parisianniche.com/parisian-page-turners

UNCLE LOUIS'S LENTIL SOUP

A Soup of Château de Verzat

INGREDIENTS

½ Cup diced parsnips

½ Cup diced carrots

½ Cup diced celery

½ Cup diced red pepper

½ Cup diced yellow pepper

2 Sliced leeks, white part only

1 Small onion, chopped

A few splashes of extra-virgin olive oil

1 Pound turkey or chicken sausage, sliced into bite-size pieces (optional)

1 ½–2 Quarts chicken or vegetable stock

2 Cups lentils, rinsed and picked over

½ Cup dry white wine

4 Cups chopped kale or baby spinach

Sea salt & pepper

Dash cayenne pepper

DIRECTIONS

1. Wash, peel, and dice the first 6 vegetables. Allow them to dry on a towel.
2. In a large stock pot and over low to medium heat, sauté batches of first 5 vegetables in olive oil for about 5 minutes, do not brown. As they begin to soften, remove from pot, and add more vegetables.
3. Add leeks and chopped onion, do not brown.
4. Cook all vegetables until they are soft.
5. If you are using sausage, remove vegetables from pot, add a bit more olive oil and sauté sausage slices until lightly browned.
6. Return all cooked vegetables to pot.
7. Add the stock and cook on low for about 10-15 minutes.
8. Add lentils and cook for 15 minutes, until lentils are soft but not mushy.
9. Add wine. Simmer for 5 minutes.
10. Add kale or spinach and more stock if needed. Cook on low until greens wilt.
11. Add cayenne pepper, salt, and pepper to taste.

© Debra Borchert, Author,

Her Own Revolution

DISCUSSION QUESTIONS

A few questions to fuel book club discussions of
Her Own Revolution

1. Geneviève replaces names on the guillotine list, a traitorous crime
    for which she could be sent to the guillotine. She breaks the law.
    Do you think her actions were wrong? Can you think of circum-
    stances today in which you might break a law?

2. During the French Revolution, impersonating a man is also a
    crime for women. If Geneviève had been caught and brought
    before her father, do you think he would have imprisoned her in
    an asylum and order her head to be shaved?

3. Although Geneviève loves her former lover, Henri, and corre-
    sponds with him, do you think he loved her? Do you think she
    truly loved Henri?

4. Louis LaGarde changed from a self-centered bully into a kind,
    selfless, and caring man. What or whom do you think caused him
    to change the most?

5. Harboring members of the clergy is also a traitorous crime. Was Geneviève right to rescue the Sisters at Pentemont Abbey? Was she right to offer shelter to the Catholic Chouans, even though she was endangering every person on the Verzat estate?

6. Why do you think Geneviève promises herself that she will never reveal Magdeleine's true cause of death? Was it the right thing to do?

7. Geneviève experienced conflicting feelings about her father. Had he been your father, would you have acted as she did?

8. Geneviève dislikes her stepmother, but Etty was a typical woman of the time: wanting her stepdaughter to be safely married. Was there a time in recent history where the roles of women a generation apart were as different?

9. Were you shocked during the trial when you learned of the improper actions taken by Geneviève's father? Why do you suppose he was able to remove a name and replace it with another without being found out? Why did no one stop him from executing the wrong people?

10. Do you think Louis improved the lentil soup for the orphans for more than one reason?

11. Who was your favorite secondary character and why?

12. Do you think Geneviève and Louis are well suited to one another? Why or why not?

ABOUT THE AUTHOR

Debra Borchert has had many careers. She debuted, at the age of five, as a model at a local country club where her crinoline petticoat dropped to her ankles in the middle of the runway.

Since then, she's been a clothing designer, actress (starring in her first television commercial with Jeff Daniels for S.O.S. Soap Pads,) TV show host, spokesperson for high-tech companies, marketing and public relations professional, and technical writer for Fortune 100 companies.

Her work has appeared in *The New York Times*, *San Francisco Chronicle*, *The Christian Science Monitor*, and *The Writer*, among others. Her short stories have been published in anthologies and independently.

A graduate of the Fashion Institute of Technology, she weaves her knowledge of textiles and clothing design throughout her historical French fiction. She brings her passions for

France, wine, and cooking to all her work. The proud owner of ten crockpots, she is renowned for her annual Soup Parties at which she serves soups from different cultures.

Debra's debut novel, *Her Own Legacy*, is the first in a series that follows headstrong and independent women and the four-hundred loyal families who protect a Loire Valley château and vineyard, and its legacy of producing the finest wines in France during the French Revolution. *Her Own Revolution* is the second book in the Château de Verzat series.

She lives in the Pacific Northwest with her family and standard poodle who is named after a fine French Champagne.

SPREADING THE WORD

Word of mouth is the best way to discover books, so if you'd like to help spread the word, please share your review. Your feedback is greatly appreciated.

WWW.AMAZON.COM/AUTHOR/DEBRABORCHERT
WWW.GOODREADS.COM/DEBRA_BORCHERT

If you'd like a complimentary e-story and monthly recipes, visit my website and subscribe to my newsletter: WWW. DEBRABORCHERT.COM

A NOTE ABOUT THE TYPE

The title font of this book was set in the typeface *1786 GLC Founier*, designed by Gilles Le Corre and inspired by numerous documents, books, and hymns printed in Paris during the late 1700s.

The body of this book was set in the typeface *Adobe Caslon Pro*. William Caslon's types were based on seventeenth-century Dutch old-style designs. Because of their practicality, Caslon's types became popular throughout Europe and America. Printer Benjamin Franklin rarely used any other typeface.